Also by Lorie O'Clare

Hot Pursuit

Lorie O'Clare

St. Martin's Paperbacks

This is a work of fiction. All of the characters, organizations, and events portrayed in this novel are either products of the author's imagination or are used fictitiously.

HOT PURSUIT

Copyright © 2013 by Lorie O'Clare.

For information address St. Martin's Press, 175 Fifth Avenue, New York, NY 10010.

ISBN: 978-0-312-53458-5

Printed in the United States of America

St. Martin's Paperbacks edition / April 2013

St. Martin's Paperbacks are published by St. Martin's Press, 175 Fifth Avenue, New York, NY 10010.

10   9   8   7   6   5   4   3   2   1

Hot Pursuit

Chapter One

Ben Mercy pulled into the complex parking lot and stared at his second-floor apartment. Stacy Hunter sat on the flight of cement stairs that led up to his place. She stood when she saw him.

Ben had decided shortly after meeting Stacy that she would have been who the Beach Boys had sung about, if she'd been born fifty years earlier. Stacy's long, straight blonde hair fell to the small of her back. She had thin, long, perfectly tanned legs that she drew attention to by always wearing four-inch heels and incredibly short skirts. Her hips were narrow and her waist so small he could wrap his hands around it. Those double Ds were firm, and he swore her nipples were always hard. She was every man's wet dream, the epitome of a California Girl.

Stacy smoothed her light cotton mini-dress with her thin, long fingers. She watched him tentatively. He wished she weren't there.

Ben pulled into one of the two stalls assigned to his two-bedroom apartment. Stacy's convertible was parked in the other stall. She came down the stairs, brushing those long blonde locks over her shoulder. He watched her moisten her lips. Remaining straddled on his motorcycle wouldn't prevent the inevitable.

Her bright blue eyes made it clear she was ready for round

two. Ben just wanted to go upstairs, pop open a beer, and kick back on his couch with the remote. He hadn't had a bad day. It had been a bad fucking week. Stacy put her hands on her hips and squared back her shoulders. Those double Ds pressed against the thin fabric of her dress. The vine tattoo that started at her shoulder and went down to her elbow also wrapped around one breast. When he'd first met her, he had thought that the hottest thing he'd ever seen. Now, as he glanced at her arm, he wondered how it would look when she got older and gravity did its number on those perfect boobs.

Knowing Stacy, he thought she would pay to keep her breasts perky and tempting for as long as possible.

"Why did you buy this bike?" she asked, putting her weight on one leg and pointing her painted toes upward as she tapped her high heel on the sidewalk. "You wasted all your money on this thing just so you could copycat that boss of yours, didn't you? You know, Ben, in the real world no one cares about him at all. You need to focus on getting your life straightened out."

Ben pulled off his helmet and stuck it under his arm, then got off his bike. "What I need is a shower," he muttered. It was none of her business how much his boss sold this bike to him for. But he'd gotten it for a steal, and with gas prices the way they were, Ben was real glad to have it.

"Although I do admit you look pretty sexy in all that black leather." She tried touching his fingerless glove with one of her long fingernails.

He moved just in time to avoid her touch. Stacy wouldn't help any of his problems right now. He doubted fucking her for hours would take away the grief, pain, and, yes, fear. He hated fear. But if the cops came over to talk to him—Ben gave himself a mental shake. Dwelling on all of it wouldn't make anything better.

Stacy was just over a hundred pounds, and if dieting didn't keep her at that weight, surgery would. Ben wouldn't shove her out of his way but stepped around her as he headed for the stairs. Stacy tried reaching them before he did but didn't succeed. Ben knew her tricks. If she thought her climbing the stairs ahead of him would change his mind about their relationship, she really didn't know him. He was done with her trying to change everything about him. If she wanted some suave, debonair gentleman, she could go find him. That wasn't Ben. God, he was no fucking gentleman. He didn't have a car door to open for a lady, which had been repeatedly pointed out to him. Nor did he feel in the mood for ladies first, in spite of Stacy's efforts to climb the stairs in front of him. He honestly didn't care whether she had panties on right now or not.

Her heels clapped against the cement stairs as she hurried up behind him. "I decided we should talk," she informed him when they reached the top.

Ben slid his key into the lock and turned it. Shit. He really didn't want to let her into his apartment.

"We talked last night."

"You talked last night," she pressed. "And, as always, I was the dutiful girlfriend who listened," she added, and pursed her lips into a pout. They curved into a temptuous smile a moment later. "I know just how to talk to you, too," she whispered.

Keep talking, he thought. It would help him remember why he broke up with her the night before. Ben turned the lock with his key and pushed open his apartment door.

"Goddamn," he blurted out when he looked at her.

Stacy had lowered the thin straps to her dress so they draped over her arms. She revealed a white lace strapless bra that was cut low enough that her round, puckered nipples were in plain sight. His dick didn't seem to care whether she was a meddling bitch or not. He was instantly hard.

Stacy giggled. She leaned into him and stuck one foot up in the air behind her. "Now see, Ben my love," she cooed. "I know exactly how to appease that big, bad temper of yours."

"I really don't need this right now," he snapped. They could be watching him, waiting to see if his co-worker, Micah Jones, showed up at his apartment. Ben had no idea whether Micah would or not.

She started pushing her dress farther down her waist. Ben shot a hurried look up and down the cement walkway in front of all the second-floor apartments, then scanned the parking lot. He didn't see anyone but shoved Stacy into his apartment.

A moment later he realized that was exactly what she'd wanted. Stacy regained her balance easily and turned to face him. She adjusted her dress, but Ben looked away before she covered her breasts. He wasn't interested. Fucking her would be a big mistake.

"You know I don't like that rough stuff," she scolded.

Ben guessed she meant how he had shoved her into his apartment. That was far from what he would consider "rough stuff."

"And I don't want to have to kick some man's ass when he rapes you after catching a glimpse of you half-naked outside my door," he snapped, and closed his front door, managing not to slam it. "Damn it, Stacy, when will you get some sense in your head?"

"Sweetheart, I have plenty of sense in my head," she said coolly, not missing a beat. "I already knew no one was out there." She cupped both of her breasts in her hands which were now once again covered by her dress. "These are for your eyes only, darling," she purred, smiled, and started closer to him, with a slow, sexy walk. "And your mouth, if you want," she whispered, and flicked at her nipples. They puckered and pointed through the thin cotton fabric.

Ben caught himself watching how she was fondling her breasts. He wasn't really listening to her, though. Half of what came out of Stacy's mouth were lies or persuasive manipulation to accomplish some goal she was after. That realization zapped his brain. He raised his attention to those bright blue eyes of hers.

"What do you want, Stacy?" he asked, then walked around her toward his kitchen and that beer. The remote and couch might have to wait, but damn it, he had earned that beer.

"I want us not to be broken up!" she cried out, and stamped her foot on the floor.

Ben didn't know many five-year-olds, but he imagined none of them could throw a tantrum as well as Stacy. He opened his refrigerator and bent over, resting his hand on the door as he stared into the refrigerator for a moment.

"Why? Why are you trying to do this? We don't work well together. I told you this last night. I'm not going to change. I don't *want* to change," he stressed, and reached for the longneck bottle of Budweiser. He screwed off the lid with his hand and tossed the cap into his trash can. "Want one?" he asked, feigning politeness. Stacy believed beer, especially bottled beer, was for the working class and red-necks. Ben was cool with being called either. There were worse names a person could be called.

Stacy wrinkled her nose and made a face. "Eww, you know I hate beer," she complained. "Now a martini might hit the spot right about now. Do you have olives?"

"I have beer!" he roared. "And I was really looking forward to drinking my beer while sitting on my couch and watching my TV."

Stacy took a step to the side and gallantly waved her hand toward the couch. "By all means. Be a bum on the couch."

Ben seethed. He'd been up since 5:00 A.M. chasing idiots around Los Angeles who had jumped bail, not gone to court, and pissed off their bondsmen and the family member who had put up the bail for them. He'd been putting money back for months in order to get the felony that never should have been on his record in the first place expunged. Until he did, Ben would never be the one who actually captured and slapped cuffs on any of the jerks they chased around L.A.

On top of that, Micah Jones, the bounty hunter Ben worked with, had been accused of incredibly heinous crimes and had done an amazing disappearing act. Ben had done time, another issue Stacy had with him, and knew how terrible prison was. The crimes Micah, one kick-ass bounty hunter who had worked at KFA with Ben up until two days ago, had the cops hot on his trail for crimes so numerous he might not know life in prison. If they caught Micah and managed to convict him of even a few of the charges against him, it could be a needle in the arm. Ben knew what it was like to do time for a crime he didn't commit.

Today Ben had finally accepted the truth that Micah had disappeared, taken off and run from the cops. Ben doubted he'd ever see Micah again. Here Ben was, doing his best to live the life of an upstanding citizen and put his life back in order. Then out of the blue Micah might be the notorious assassin who was all over the news right now. Ben hated not being sure whether the charges were legitimate or not. Micah had been that kind of guy. Ben never doubted the man had his back. But there was a darkness inside Micah, something about him that almost made it believable that he could have been a mass assassin.

The cops had shown up at KFA, where Ben worked. They were looking everywhere for Micah. Ben didn't want them here. The last time cops showed up at Ben's home he'd been arrested and done time for a crime he didn't commit. He wished the best for Micah but just wanted to be left alone. None of which he could discuss with Stacy.

"Go home, Stacy. I'm too tired to fight." He tipped his bottle of beer to his mouth and enjoyed the perfectly chilled brew. He considered burping just to egg her on further. "Go find a nice man who will wine and dine you. You deserve that, darling. I'm just not that man."

Stacy adjusted her bra, glancing down to make sure her breasts were perfectly situated. Ben made himself look away and stared down at his kitchen table. A long white bulky envelope was placed in the middle of his table. Ben drank more beer and focused on the envelope with mild interest, his thoughts still on the chaos they'd all endured at work since Micah had disappeared. Ben's first name was printed in block letters on the envelope with a black marker.

"What the hell?" he murmured.

That envelope definitely hadn't been there before he'd left for work. An odd, unsettled feeling sunk into his gut. He knew before he opened the envelope what was inside. But what he didn't know was why.

"Holy fucking crap!" he gasped, and stared at the hundred-dollar bills that fell over one another onto his table when he ripped open the envelope.

"Oh my God!" Stacy squealed, leaping at the money and reaching for it.

Ben stuck his hand out and stopped her. "No!" he said harshly.

"Look at all that money," she gasped. "How do you have money like this after buying that noisy motorcycle?" she accused. "Oh my God, sweetheart. Is this your money to clear your record? Are you going to be an upstanding citizen now?"

Ben growled under his breath. He was already a fucking upstanding citizen.

There was half a piece of typing paper folded so it was the size of the money. Ben grabbed it and unfolded it, staring in disbelief at so much cash before reading the note.

Some call this blood money, but at least now it can be put to good use. Take care of your lawyer fees and do what you have to do to become a great bounty hunter. You'll be one of the best. I don't have to tell you to burn this note. Take care and listen to King. He has a lot to teach you.

"Micah," Ben whispered. He would definitely burn the note. Micah had more or less just confessed to being what everyone already suspected him of being, the Mulligan Stew assassin. Ben went cold as the reality sunk in and his fingers grew damp.

Still holding the letter, he grabbed Stacy's arm and pushed her toward his front door. "Leave now," he snarled.

"But, but all that money," she complained.

Ben pushed her out the door and closed it. He turned the lock and leaned his head against it.

Goddamn! All that money! *Some call this blood money.*

Micah Jones had worked with Ben at KFA for four months

but now was gone. Greg and Haley King were pretty convinced Micah was the Mulligan Stew assassin, as the news had been calling him since the gun used on one of the men KFA was chasing matched the one that had shot and killed a CIA agent in Washington, D.C. Both bullets came from the same gun.

The assassin was a ghost. No one had ever seen him. But he was allegedly responsible for the deaths of over fifty men and women. Each time the Mulligan Stew assassin struck it was a shot straight to the heart. And each person killed had done terrible things. They were drug lords, Mafia members, rapists, and pedophiles. If there was a terrible person in town and someone had the cash to dish out, they could have that person eliminated, without having to wait for the cops to catch them and the judicial system to find them guilty. The news had been vague on how the assassin was contacted. But apparently once the Mulligan Stew assassin was paid all he needed was whatever information a person had on a bad person in their city. The assassin did the rest, found the person and killed them. Then the assassin disappeared without a trace.

"Which it appears you've done again," Ben mused, and slid into the chair at his table. He slowly began gathering the bills that had poured onto his kitchen table. "Good Lord, man, there's ten thousand dollars here."

Ben shivered with fear and excitement. His heart was beating so hard he couldn't breathe. Ben dropped the money on the table and stared at it. For a year now Ben had been trying to save up the money to pay the lawyer to have the felony on his record expunged. He was pretty sure he hadn't bitched about how much it cost to pay to have his innocence back. Although there were times when he'd wanted to actually commit a felony or at least pound something until all of his frustrations went away. In a country where a man was innocent until proven guilty, coming up with cold, hard cash to prove his innocence had been almost too hard to pull off.

For three years they'd locked him up. Ben would never forget the nightmare of being arrested for stealing cars in his hometown of Duarte, California. They'd pulled him out of his parents' home, dragged him to the street, where police car lights had flashed off all the neighbors' homes and lit up the night. People his parents had known for years came out of their homes, watched while Ben had been handcuffed, searched, and stuffed into the backseat of the cops' car.

"I can't believe you did this," Ben muttered. He stacked the bills neatly and counted them once again. Focusing on the task helped put memories of his past out of his head. "This is a hell of a lot more than I need to get that damned felony expunged from my records."

And to pay his lawyer fees. Once Ben's record was clear he could get licensed in the state of California. Then he would be a bounty hunter, instead of the errand boy and driver he'd been so far for KFA, which stood for "King Fugitive Apprehension." He would soon be apprehending those fugitives who had blown off court dates, disregarded the bond paid on them, and thought they could get away with it. Maybe KFA would get a case where they had to hunt down a criminal wanted for something more serious than fleeing from the courts. Either way, Ben looked forward to the day he would be the one tackling them to the ground, slapping on the cuffs, and informing them they couldn't run from crimes they'd committed.

Maybe then his mother would once again be proud of him.

That thought doused the happy thoughts he was having and left a sour taste in his mouth. His parents had never believed him innocent. His mother had begged him to admit he stole those cars. Ben would never forget the day she looked at him with tears welling in her eyes and told him she couldn't believe she had a son who was a car thief. His father had held Ben's mother close and told him if he would tell them how he did it possibly the judge would go easier on him. His parents had thought Ben was lying to them and to the judge.

To this day, Arnold Shots, the asshole from hell, had never been arrested for stealing those cars. The prick had framed Ben, and all over a fucking girl. Ben had slept with Arnold's girlfriend; make that "ex-girlfriend," since they'd been broken up at the time. Arnold had never been right in the head, but he had been a thief and a manipulator. He could make his own mother believe he was a pure saint, then turn around and sell drugs out of her house.

Ben still didn't know how Arnold had convinced the cops he had nothing to do with three brand-new cars being stolen off a car lot in Duarte. That was, if the cops ever talked to Arnold. Ben had never found out. Arnold had stolen two cars before from the same car lot and had driven them out of town, then sold them. He would have done the same with these three, but when he found out about Ben, after getting back together with Sally something or other—he didn't even remember her last name—Arnold had driven all three cars behind the restaurant where Ben worked. Arnold had shown them to Ben, which was how Ben's fingerprints got on them, and had told him they would be there overnight and gone before the restaurant opened the following morning. Ben had insisted Arnold not leave them there. Ben had told him it was stupid and Arnold was looking at life in prison if he didn't get rid of the cars. Arnold never went to prison. The cops showed up at Ben's house that same night, having received a tip that the cars were there. Ben believed to this day that Arnold had called the police and turned in an anonymous tip that three cars were behind the restaurant and that Ben Mercy had been seen with the cars.

"Ten thousand dollars." A slow smile spread across his face. "I'm going to hire the best lawyer out there and put you behind bars, Arnold Shots. You're going to rot in hell before you die."

Ben wouldn't have accepted this much money, or any amount, if Micah had tried giving it to him. If Micah had left it for him and had still been in town, Ben would have given it back. Micah was gone, though. The money was Ben's, and he would put it to really good use.

He looked up from the cash. It suddenly hit him. "How the fuck did you get in here?"

There wasn't a back door to Ben's apartment. He could tell there was no damage to his front door. It was pointless to check the windows, although he would do it out of curiosity. Micah had skills that were out of this world. Ben would probably never know how the man got into Ben's apartment, left that cash, then took off. More than likely no one saw him do it, either.

Ben picked up the stack of bills. Interesting how one-hundred-dollar bills had a different feel to them than other bills. Crisper, with a strong smell of money. It was as if these bills knew they were more important than an average twenty or ten. They were smooth, not crinkled, the way money was when it came out of an ATM. Ben doubted any of these bills had seen a bank or been in circulation recently.

Whatever crimes Micah had committed, or allegedly, he hadn't done anything recently. Ben had worked long hours with the guy, day and night, and could account for his whereabouts up until a couple days ago. Quite possibly Micah had been sitting on this cash for a while. Which was impressive and smart. Micah had lived in a dump of a house in one of the low-income parts of the city. He never had much cash on him. To all appearances, he had seemed to have struggled financially just as Ben did.

It was still damn hard to wrap his brain around Micah being a cold-blooded killer. Quite possibly, at least the way the papers were telling it, the best assassin in the world.

The law would hunt Micah. Ben prayed they never caught him and hoped Micah was as good at hiding as he was at sitting on so much cash. As for the other crimes, as far as Ben was concerned, Micah was the most respectable murderer he'd ever met. And he'd met a couple while in prison.

He stood, walked over to his sink, opened the drawer to his left, and pulled out a book of matches. Then striking a match, he stared at the flame as it came to life, growing and shifting in color as it began to move down the stick toward Ben's fingers. Then he burned the note that had come with the cash. He held the paper as it burned, watching it curl and turn black. When it got too small he dropped it into his sink. It curled into itself one last time and was nothing but ashes. Ben turned on the water and rinsed the ashes down the drain.

"Be careful, Micah, and be safe. Don't let them catch you."

Chapter Two

One year later

Wolf Marley pulled into a convenience store and parked. Fresh caffeine and a bit of walking and stretching, and he would be good as new. Or at least somewhere close to it. It had been one hell of a long drive. All the road construction and detours had been a bitch. His map was up-to-date. And although his new SUV came equipped with a GPS program, if Wolf wanted some lady telling him where to drive, she'd be sitting in the seat next to him. And at that, he could think of much better things she might do than tell him what road to take. He hadn't gotten lost, but nothing sucked worse than seeing the interstate you needed to be on and driving underneath it while on the wrong road.

Los Angeles was an endless maze of neighborhood after neighborhood. He'd driven into L.A. this morning and with the afternoon ready to peak was, he hoped he was close to his destination. This was the third time he'd exited, believing he had the right neighborhood. If he was wrong a third time, he might get pissed.

Patience was the name of the game, though. That and not getting so aggravated he couldn't think straight.

He shut off the engine on his silver Escalade. It beeped when he locked it. Wolf looked over his shoulder at his SUV as he headed to the store's entrance. Dark-tinted windows made it impossible to see inside. The sticker price had been almost sixty grand. Wolf had paid fifty grand in cash with his last bounty check and owned his sweet ride free and clear. That Escalade had made driving across the country a hell of a lot nicer than previous road trips. He was still sore and stiff.

Not getting any younger, yet the bounties just kept getting bigger. The hell with patience. Perseverance was the name of the damned game.

He'd earned every damn penny it had taken to buy the Escalade. Just as he would earn his bounty now. The road trip had been hell, grueling, but already he felt that nip of excitement tighten in his gut. He was close. He could feel it.

Fifteen minutes later Wolf came out of the convenience store grumpier than he had been when he had entered. It would always be a mystery why these damn places were called convenience stores when there wasn't a damn thing convenient about them. He climbed back into his Escalade and breathed in the new-car smell. When he had time he would figure out how to get rid of that smell. He didn't want his car smelling like anything. Wolf hunted men and women below the radar, and he lived a life with nothing about him giving away any noticeable characteristics for someone to remember. As expensive as his Escalade had been, it was a silver SUV with no markings on the outside. The whole point was for it not to stand out in a crowd any more than he did.

Wolf didn't fuck with Karma. He was very good at capturing men and women no one else could find. He did this by living the way they did. Buying the Escalade might have been an indulgence, but the SUV didn't stand out. At thirty-five, he'd been doing this a while. That didn't make the job any less demanding. The more years under the belt, the more captures he credited himself with, the more he expected himself to be able to do. He'd earned a comfortable ride while doing it. And Wolf needed a vehicle that would get him everywhere he needed to go, which was often all over the goddamned country.

He started the engine and cranked on the air when it started getting tight inside the car. Los Angeles's summer heat was starting to get to him, although it was nothing compared to the summer mugginess back in Oklahoma. Wolf adjusted the AC and opened the folder on his passenger seat.

"There's the address," he said, staring at his own handwriting and the notes he'd made while in his hotel room that morning. "King Fugitive Apprehension, KFA . . . catchy name. Do I go in looking for work, or maybe advice? Advice might do the trick. Looks like the owner of KFA used to be a cop. He'll be a cocky son of a bitch." Wolf shook his head. "I bet he banged his head against the wall for months after the Mulligan Stew assassin left when he realized one of *America's Most Wanted* actually worked for him. That would seriously sting the pride."

Wolf had read everything he could find on the great Greg King, who had repeatedly been referred to as the best bounty hunter in the state of California, as well as nationwide. He and his wife owned KFA. They had their office right in their home and had started the business with their two sons working for them. Apparently, their kids were no longer in the picture. Greg and Haley had one bounty hunter on staff, working on commission. From what Wolf had learned, Haley King ran the office and helped in the field when needed. KFA had been in business eight years. Prior to owning KFA, Greg King had been a cop for the LAPD. Haley King, his wife, worked for the school district as a substitute teacher and was a homemaker. Now the two of them would have to live down their business being the last known place of employment for the Mulligan Stew assassin, although that was alleged.

"Alleged my ass," Wolf mumbled, flipping through the papers in his file. He knew men like King. The man had clout, was established in his community, had an incredible reputation in his field. If all that power couldn't keep his name from being associated with the Mulligan Stew assassin in the papers, it meant King hadn't been able to deny it. Responding to reporters with "no comment" got your name in the paper. Adamantly denying something, insisting there was no way it could be true, and threatening lawsuits for slander was a much better way to stay out of the papers. Wolf glanced at one of the articles he'd clipped. King hadn't adamantly denied crap, just refused interviews.

All the information Wolf had so far still had him at the cutting ground. He needed to know personalities, their insights, what made the people he would be contacting happy and what pissed them off. Wolf had to gain all of that information based off his facts. He'd gotten better at building a character profile over the years. One thing he'd learned so far, the almighty bounty hunter Greg King hadn't gone after the Mulligan Stew assassin. That tidy bit of information spoke volumes.

After his last case Wolf had given himself some much-needed downtime, but once he'd started researching the Mulligan Stew assassin he knew he had to have him. There was a million-dollar bounty on the assassin's head. Research was as important as footwork. Wolf had spent three months researching the Kings and learning what made them tick. There had to be a solid reason why Greg King didn't chase down the assassin. King would have known the man better than anyone else. And King had to believe the man he'd employed as a bounty hunter was the assassin and guilty of many murders. Yet King had let the man run.

There were articles about KFA, quite a few of them. The only one that had interested Wolf was the article that talked about the bullet that shot and wounded a fugitive KFA had apprehended. That bullet came from the same gun that had shot and killed a CIA agent in Washington, D.C., six months prior. Police had scoured the area where the fugitive went down and hadn't found the weapon or the man who shot him. A Harley-Davidson motorcycle had been spotted leaving the scene. That same bike was later found parked outside a church. The police searched the church and questioned the priests. They still hadn't found their shooter.

None of this surprised Wolf. The man who shot the fugitive KFA had been tracking and who shot and killed the CIA agent in Washington, D.C., was the Mulligan Stew assassin. All investigators were sure of it. The men who had contacted the Mulligan Stew assassin and hired him to kill the CIA agent had been apprehended, had confessed, and were doing time. For killing the CIA agent the Mulligan Stew assassin was wanted by the FBI, the CIA, and probably every other agency in D.C. as well as multiple law enforcement agencies around the country.

What did surprise Wolf was that the assassin had used the same gun, which created a personal signature on each bullet it shot, on the CIA agent and the fugitive KFA picked up. The fugitive had been a nobody. He had written bad checks around L.A. and had simply ignored a bondsman and not shown up for court dates. He didn't fit the profile at all of the kind of terrible scumbags the Mulligan Stew assassin usually killed. Wolf found it interesting that in all the newscasts and articles he'd compiled over the past months no one had mentioned this obvious aberration. In his opinion, the shot fired at the fugitive running from KFA bounty hunters was personal.

Of course, within a week of the Mulligan Stew assassin disappearing tornadoes tore across the Midwest, destroying homes and taking more lives than tornadoes had in recorded history. Hurricanes ripped through the Atlantic and hit the South, doing horrific damage. Almost at the same time, tsunamis terrorized the Pacific, damn near wiping out entire cities. News on the Mulligan Stew assassin took a back burner.

Wolf preferred criminals he chased not being the main spotlight in the news. He didn't need a bunch of amateurs out there trying to catch the guys. There was a million-dollar bounty on the Mulligan Stew assassin's head, and Wolf was going to find the motherfucker and make himself a very rich man. Not to mention secure his reputation so he'd no longer have to take every case that came his way. He would be able to pick and choose who he hunted.

"Not too shabby for someone whose mother threw him away," Wolf muttered, looking over the file he'd created on the assassin.

Wolf waited for the busy parking lot around the convenience store to open up so he could reach the end of his road

trip and the beginning of his hunt for the assassin. He was in
the Mulligan Stew assassin's old stomping grounds now.
Hell, maybe the guy had frequented this convenience store.
Wolf didn't have a picture of the guy, nor did anyone else, so
he couldn't hold it up to the clerk and ask if she'd seen the
guy. He was cool with that, though. It made the hunt all the
more challenging. He had absolutely no problem earning his
living.

Wolf drove by the KFA office, impressed with the spread
where the Kings lived. He would live that way someday. He
was getting there, slowly.

Next he drove by the church where the motorcycle had
been found.

"Interesting," he mused, glancing over his shoulder as he
drove by. There hadn't been any mention in any of the articles he'd read that a grade school and what looked like a
high school as well were attached to the church.

That told him something right there. Wolf wondered how
much other information was not mentioned in the news clips
he'd gathered. This wouldn't be the first case he'd worked
where he'd learned so much more simply by casing out
where his man or woman had last been known to spend their
time. Freedom of press simply meant reporters wrote what
they thought would get them headlines. Although if they'd
mentioned an assassin spent time inside a church while children were playing at recess yards away, that would get headlines. Wolf was going to find out why that rather notable bit
of information was left out.

The next stop was the family home of the woman who
had allegedly disappeared with the Mulligan Stew assassin.
Wolf stopped at the house once he got there. It looked homey,
like there were happy times here. Shutting off his SUV,
Wolf then headed up to the house. It was time to get to know
the people who had known the assassin.

Chapter Three

"You've got it?" Haley King asked, her face bright with a large smile.

"Read it and weep." Ben couldn't help grinning as well. He held out a single piece of paper that meant so much. His future was printed out on that one piece of paper. "I'm now licensed in the state of California."

Greg King patted Ben on the back. "Congratulations, son. Would you like a job?"

All of them laughed, and Ben crashed on the couch against the wall in the KFA office. He stared at his certificate that showed he was a licensed private investigator in the state of California. This was the best day of his life. No one knew about the money that had shown up on his kitchen table the day after Micah had disappeared. No one talked about him anymore. Some things were better off not mentioned. Wherever the guy was, Ben silently gave him thanks.

"Are you hiring?" Ben asked, staring over the piece of paper at his boss. A drained blue sky shown through the blinds in the window behind Greg.

Greg sat at the unused desk opposite the couch where Ben was. Haley leaned against the office manager's desk, a role she was currently filling since they were in between office managers again.

"We might be if we found the right man." There was a glint of humor in Haley's eyes. She was a beautiful woman, actually sexy. And she had to be around fifty. It was her casual yet feisty manner that had any man who walked through that door almost always drooling in her direction. Haley only had eyes for her husband, though, and she looked at him now. "What do you think, Greg? Think Ben here would make a good bounty hunter?"

"Nope," Greg said without hesitating. "I only train men to be outstanding bounty hunters."

Ben knew he was grinning like an idiot and tried to rein in some of his happiness and appear cool. It dawned on him he'd come running to these two when he'd received his certificate authenticating him as a private investigator, which entitled him to be a bounty hunter. He hadn't told his parents yet. Greg and Haley had been there for him, all the way through dealing with the courts and getting his record expunged. There was money left, secure in a bank account, and he still considered trying to take down Arnold Shots. The anger and hatred Ben had for the prick were still there, but getting his life back had allowed some of his determination for revenge to recede.

"I still have a lot to learn," Ben admitted.

Greg lazily lifted his arm and gestured at Ben while looking at his wife, his expression one of pretentious innocence. "I also train humility into them."

Haley's laughter was melodic when she pushed herself from the desk where she was perched and walked over to peck a kiss on her husband's forehead. Greg grabbed her, pulling her onto his lap, and made a show of molesting her. The alarm system wired throughout their home beeped, announcing someone had just opened the office door from the street. Greg just as easily released her, and Haley straightened, although a contented smile was plastered on her face.

Ben took in the stocky man who entered KFA. The man was shorter than him, definitely under six feet. He had brown thick wavy hair that looked windblown, except there was no wind outside. Ben would be the last to describe eye color, but this man's dark green eyes were intense enough to draw attention as he took in the office.

"Something I can do for you?" Ben took the initiative.

"Maybe," the man said, but shifted his attention to Greg. "I bet you're Greg King, though, aren't you?"

"Guilty as charged," Greg said in a relaxed tone. He and Haley had busted through four cases in the past two days. Greg was content amusing someone off the street for a minute, and it showed on his face.

"I'm not charging you with anything." The man didn't smile, which made his words seem more as if they were meant seriously than as a joke.

"Good to know." Greg cocked an eyebrow. "Who are you? What do you need?" he demanded.

"I'm Wolf Marley, and I'm a bounty hunter."

Ben straightened on the couch. He'd put over a year in with KFA doing everything from filing paperwork at the courthouse to helping Haley haul her old freezer out of the garage and putting her new one in its place. He'd emptied trash, even washed fucking windows. There were many times when he rode with the Kings as they went after whoever it was they'd agreed to apprehend. Ben went over the files; he learned the stats on their guy or woman and even put his input in on what to do to catch them. He would be damned if some asshole would walk off the street and try applying for the position that was rightfully his.

"We aren't hiring," Greg informed the guy.

Ben hoped he didn't noticeably relax. Haley looked over at him and grinned, though. Ben leaned back, rested his arms on the back of the couch, and listened to the two men talk.

"I don't need a job."

Wolf wasn't stocky as first thought. He was muscular, with very broad shoulders and a slim, narrow stomach. There was probably a defined six-pack under that T-shirt. He would be one of those guys who spent hours lifting weights instead of getting muscular through sheer hard work. And what kind of name was Wolf anyway?

"I'm here because you used to have an assassin on your payroll," Wolf said.

Greg King was six and a half feet tall. Sitting down, he looked intimidating. Greg didn't stand, but he definitely appeared to grow in size.

"I did not have an assassin on my payroll," he said sharply.

"I believe you did." Wolf might be short, but the asshole had balls. He looked Greg straight in the eye. "I need to ask you a few questions about him."

"I did not have an assassin on my payroll," Greg snarled, barely moving his mouth.

Wolf cocked a thick brown eyebrow. "So that was your gun that killed the CIA agent and shot the fugitive you were apprehending a year ago?"

Greg stood and towered over Wolf Marley. "Get out of my office," he snarled.

Either Wolf had more nerves than was good for him or he was an idiot. Possibly both.

"Withholding evidence during an investigation for one of America's most wanted criminals is a serious crime, Mr. King," Wolf said quietly, not budging. "I'd appreciate it if you answered just a few questions."

"Get out before I throw you out!" Greg roared.

"Suit yourself." Marley seriously did not appear intimidated. He shrugged and turned to the door. "I'll be back," he informed them over his shoulder, opened the door, and closed it again.

"Son of a bitch!" Greg roared, and hit the middle desk with his fist.

"You're going to send your blood pressure sky-high," Haley warned, and rubbed his arm with her hand. "I thought we were done with people coming in and out of here looking for Micah."

"Apparently not." Greg put his arm around Haley and turned them toward the door leading into their house. He glanced at Ben. "Congrats again on your certification. We're both really proud of you."

"Yes, we are." Haley smiled at him. "Come on inside and have a beer."

"I'll take a rain check." Ben had learned that turning down a chance to hang out with the Kings out of the work environment didn't mean there wouldn't be other chances. The Kings were laid-back and more than willing to socialize when they weren't working.

"Sounds good. Next case that comes up, you're running point throughout."

Ben knew he was grinning like an idiot again. He picked up the certificate that he'd laid on the couch next to him and stood. "I'm ready. More than ready."

He laughed along with them and headed out. When he left the office and turned off the private road that ran along the beach and the exquisite homes that lined it, a silver Escalade pulled away from the curb and followed him. Ben went home, showered, then headed back out. He was going to celebrate, and he might even pick up some willing lady and bring her back to his place that night.

Three hours later Ben had given up on finding a lady but was doing a pretty good job at winning at pool. His phone vibrated, one short, one long, one short—meaning KFA was calling. He missed his shot.

"Damn it!" he cried out, and stepped away from the pool table. "Hey, man," he said, turning to one of the regulars at the pool hall. "Stand in for me, will you? Work is calling."

"Go catch the bad guys," one of the girls who had been watching called out when she overheard him talking.

The rest of the crowd echoed her sentiments when Ben headed for the door. He waved over his shoulder and stepped out into the warm, dark night. Pulling his phone from his waist, he returned the missed call from the office.

"What's up?" Ben asked, and sauntered toward his bike and away from the loud music bellowing from the bar.

"Sorry to interrupt your night." Greg's deep voice spoke crisply through the phone. "We have a situation."

"What's wrong?" Ben reached his bike and pulled his helmet free.

"Haley found a bug attached to the office door."

It took Ben a moment to realize what Greg was talking about. Something hardened inside him. "Was it that Marley guy?"

"That's what we're thinking."

"I can head over." He was already straddling his bike. He'd text his buddies inside, but it wouldn't be the first time he'd disappeared on them for work. Fortunately, they understood. "I can be there in ten minutes."

"I ran a check on this Wolf Marley," Greg went on, not commenting on what Ben had just said. By Greg's tone he was in serious work mode. "He's legitimate, a bounty hunter. He's out of Oklahoma."

"Oklahoma?" Ben asked incredulously. "What the hell is he doing here?"

"I think he's doing exactly what he said he's doing."

There was silence between the two of them for a moment; then Ben said, "We didn't give him any information, so he decided to try and get it on his own."

"Yup," Greg agreed. "According to my research on him, he drives a silver brand-new Escalade."

Ben let out a low whistle. "He's doing all right for himself."

"Marley has an impeccable track record. He goes after the really huge bounties, something I've never had an interest in doing."

"What do you mean by 'really huge bounties'?"

"As in fugitives wanted by the United States government," Greg said coldly. "And to date, he's always got his man."

The hardening in Ben's gut twisted into an unpleasant knot, and bile rose to his throat. Something akin to panic built inside him. "He's going after the Mulligan Stew assassin," Ben whispered, and glanced around him at the dark, quiet parking lot. The only noise was the distant sound of music inside the bar.

"This guy is going to go to whatever extremes to gather any information he can. He bugged the office. Hard saying what else he might do. I don't need you to come in," Greg said finally. "But keep a close eye around your place."

"My place?" Ben asked. "What would he want at my place?"

Suddenly he was sick. Marley wouldn't know whether Ben had any contact with Micah or not.

"Where are you right now?" Greg asked.

"I went out for a few hours. I've been shooting some pool, celebrating a little."

"So you haven't been at your place?"

Ben understood without Greg saying anything. "I'm heading there now."

Ben was home in record time and bounded up the stairs to his apartment. Lights from the parking lot shone on to the second-floor walkway and at the front of Ben's apartment. His door didn't appear tampered with, and he slid his key in the lock and unlocked it. Before he entered he spotted the edge of the screen to his living-room window. The side of it was bent outward slightly.

"Son of a bitch," Ben hissed.

He rushed into his apartment, hitting the light switch and walking clear through to his kitchen, turning on all lights as he went. But he didn't need every light to see the damage. His home had been ransacked. Ben picked the file and note-book off his floor that he'd been using to keep notes in preparation for getting his private investigator's license.

"Goddamn it!" he roared, throwing the file and notebook at his wall.

Papers flew everywhere. He glared at his living room. Then, stalking into his bedroom, he glared at his open dresser drawers, the clothes strewn from his closet, and his mattress that had been slid sideways from the box spring.

"I'll kill you, you son of a bitch," he snarled, and his hands became fists at his sides.

He felt all of his muscles hardening. He'd been violated, his personal space ransacked. It was fucked up, and the ass-hole would pay.

Ben called Greg, and he and Haley were at Ben's apartment in the next fifteen minutes.

"Have you touched anything?" Greg asked the moment he entered Ben's apartment. Greg walked through the living room, taking in the damage as he glanced over everything.

"No, just stared at it and got more and more pissed." Ben tried to sound civil, but the more he looked at his apartment the more he wanted to put a fist through the wall.

"Listen to me," Greg said calmly, almost too calmly. He came around and stood in front of Ben, facing him.

"What?" Ben should be cool with his boss, but this was too much. Somehow he'd find that Marley bastard and put his head through a wall.

"When someone does this," Greg said, and gestured at the damage in the living room with his hand. "Obviously they are looking for something."

"Obviously," Ben muttered.

Greg sighed and tilted his head. He stood several inches taller than Ben but had never come across as intimidating. "I know you're pissed," he said under his breath. "I was livid when I realized he'd bugged the office. He might have bugged your place, too."

Ben noticed for the first time that Haley was setting up some equipment she and Greg had brought with them. "If he did," Ben grumbled.

Greg put his hand on Ben's shoulder. "Chill for a moment. We'll sweep the place and see what we find."

Haley began running what looked like a small metal detector through Ben's living room. She walked through every room in his apartment, stepping over anything that the asshole had tossed on the floor.

"Nothing," she said after sweeping floors, walls, and everything in between.

"Here's the deal," Greg said immediately, his hand once again on Ben's shoulder as he leaned into him. "When someone breaks in to look for something there are certain methods every perp follows, unless he's exceptionally good. Our guy is a bounty hunter, not a burglar. We're going to start under the presumption that he's going to act like a million other people when they enter someone's house to find something."

"Okay," Ben said slowly.

"First," Greg began, gesturing with his hand. "We don't touch the condition of the property—"

"I didn't," Ben interrupted.

"We take a look at it as is," Greg continued, and straightened next to Ben. He continued looking around as he walked through the apartment. "Is there a room that appears more disturbed than other areas?"

"You're joking, right?" Ben also glanced around his trashed bedroom, then looked at Greg incredulously.

Greg faced Ben. "No. I'm serious. Look at your room again. Don't see the intrusion, the personal violation, and let go of your anger. Take a look at this room again and this time remember how it was when you left and try to find any area where he spent more time."

"Meaning something there appealed to him." Ben got it. He looked away from Greg again and focused on his bedroom.

Haley managed her way around Ben through the limited space at the end of his bed and his dresser. Ben stared at the bed. Marley had lifted the mattress to look underneath it, didn't find anything, and dropped it. He didn't bother straightening it. He was in too much of a hurry. Ben pictured the guy going to Ben's closet next. Marley opened the door, stared at the few hanging clothes, didn't see anything there, and went to the floor of the closet. He pulled out the few pieces of clothing there, which were actually Ben's dirty clothes, and didn't find anything. Once again, Marley didn't bother putting anything back. He wanted to be in and out of the apartment as quickly as possible. He wouldn't know for sure when Ben would return. Marley pulled out Ben's dresser drawers, found most of them were damn near empty, and turned his attention to the top of the dresser. Everything that had once been on the top of the dresser was now on the floor.

The top of the dresser.

Ben bent down and started to pick up the items on the floor.

"Remember to not touch anything," Greg said. "If we have to call this in, I won't have an earful of how we compromised the crime scene."

There were good and bad aspects of Greg being an ex-cop. The good obviously was he had pointed out how to look at a trashed room. The bad was how the hell was Ben going to confirm his fears if he couldn't touch anything?

"Then I need gloves or something," Ben complained.

Haley laughed. "It's your apartment. What do you have here?"

Ben muttered under his breath, stood, found a pen that was still on top of his dresser, then squatted and pushed things out of the way to look at the items on the floor. He was overly aware of both Greg and Haley bending over to see exactly what he was doing.

There was no getting out of telling them. His behavior had alerted them, and if he told them he wasn't looking for anything, they wouldn't believe him. Ben had never lied to either one of them yet.

"There was a postcard," he began, speaking under his breath.

"A postcard," Haley repeated.

"From whom?" Greg demanded.

Ben sighed and stood. "There was nothing written on it."

Both Greg and Haley looked at him.

Ben gestured to the living room. "I'll show you."

They returned to the living room, and Ben remembered he'd hurled his notes and file against the wall when he'd first gotten home. Turning in a slow circle to see all the papers that had flown out of the file on the floor, Ben ignored Greg and Haley when they sidestepped to get out of his way.

"What are you showing us?" Greg asked.

"The other postcard," Ben began. When he straightened and fought the anger that built inside him once again, faster and harder than it had the first time, he added through gritted teeth, "That isn't here, either. That lousy motherfucker took the postcards. I'm going to catch him and kill him."

"Okay, calm down." Haley was probably the only person on the planet who didn't mind putting her hand on the chest of a seething man without blinking an eye. Possibly being married to a man who was six and a half feet tall and having given birth to two boys who had turned into men both at least that tall had made her immune. "When you find him, you can get pissed. Right now tell us what you're talking about with these postcards."

Ben stared at her a moment and saw understanding in her eyes. Before he had even finished the thought of chasing down the asshole, Haley already voiced that she knew he was leaving to go after Marley.

"What are you talking about?" she whispered, and dropped her hand to her side.

"I've received two postcards since he left." Ben stared at Haley.

She stared back at him and a second passed before she mouthed the word, *Oh*.

"They went through the mail?" Greg asked.

"Got them in my mailbox." Ben nodded. "They were postmarked so I could tell what town they were mailed from, but nothing was written on either one. One of them was buried under a few things on my dresser. I got it a while back. The second one showed up about a month ago. On the day it showed up I was getting paperwork ready for my PI license so I stuck it in the folder along with those papers. I never took it back out. Both are gone."

"He was touching base," Greg muttered, and stared across the living room.

Ben didn't say anything but agreed. Micah had made contact with him, and Ben had a general idea where he was, or at least where he had been when the postcards were mailed.

"And now Marley has those postcards," Haley grumbled.

"I'm going after him."

Both Haley and Greg looked at Ben.

He raised his hands in the air in surrender. "I know. You already guessed as much," he said. "I've worked my ass off and jumped over more hurdles than most trying to get my license so I could be a full-fledged bounty hunter. And now I can be one." There was no way he could explain how indebted he was to Micah. Without the money Micah had left for Ben his life wouldn't be the way it was right now. "I can't let that asshole find Micah and turn him in," Ben whispered. "I know I'd be leaving you two with no one—"

"Don't worry about that. In this line of work we don't always get to choose when we stay home and when we're off on a hunt." Greg put his arm around Haley and hugged her against his side. "We've been talking about slowing down a bit. We just hadn't decided when to do it. Looks like we don't get to choose when that happens, either, but now is as good a time as any."

Haley looked up at her husband, then at Ben. "We had talked about doing some traveling. Go see our son out in Colorado, and our niece up in Northern California. I've always wanted to go to Alaska."

"Her California blood won't be able to handle that for a minute," Greg muttered. "Go find Micah."

"We know you can find him," Haley reassured, that motherly look she got sometimes appearing on her face. "And don't think for a minute you have to play it tough all the time. We're a phone call away."

"A smart man knows when it's time to brainstorm and bounce ideas or thoughts off someone else," Greg said.

Ben nodded. "I'll definitely let you know when I find him." He looked around his apartment. "I'll straighten up here a bit, then head out."

"You leaving tonight?" Greg asked.

"Yea. The first postcard came from Santa Clarita. It's less than an hour's drive north of here."

"Why the hell would he run and then stop once he was only an hour away?" Greg asked, frowning.

"I figured they stopped at a gas station somewhere and

decided to buy the card and mail it to me to let me know they were gone, then they probably hit the road again."

"Maybe," Greg said, rubbing his chin the way he did when he was trying to think something through.

"Where is the second postcard from?"

"It was postmarked out of a town called Zounds. I had to look on Google Maps to find out where it was. It's a good ten-hour drive north of here and on the ocean."

"How long ago did you get the second postcard?" Haley asked.

"A month or so ago," Ben told her, glancing from one of them to the other as he shifted his weight. Already he was anxious to get on the road and warn Micah.

"Head on out then," Greg said, and slapped Ben on the arm. "Be safe, and remember that cocky bastard aims and never misses. If they are hiding out in some small town up north, Micah will always be alert."

"Don't worry," Ben said, holding his hand up and smiling. He was looking forward to finding his old friend, no matter if he was a notorious assassin. "I know Micah. And although I'd love the challenge of sneaking up on him and pulling it off, I do like living."

Haley rolled her eyes, then gave him a big hug. "You call us and check in, young man. Do you hear me?"

"Yes, Mom," he muttered, rolled his eyes dramatically, then endured the punch she gave to his arm before hugging her again. He would really miss these two and knew in his heart he wouldn't be seeing them again anytime soon.

Chapter Four

Wolf sat on the edge of his bed in his motel room in Santa Clarita. He was too wired to go to bed yet. He pondered over the two postcards he'd found in Ben Mercy's apartment. The guy had done little to personalize his apartment, which meant he was never there. Wolf hadn't found any mail lying around, which told him Mercy took care of his business the moment he had something to take care of. Yet there had been these two postcards. A girlfriend or family member or even a mild acquaintance would have written something on the postcard. Yet both of these postcards were blank.

Ben and Micah, the Mulligan Stew assassin, had worked side by side for four months. Ben Mercy probably didn't suspect a thing about his co-worker until the day the assassin made his very first mistake. It was the mistake that sent him running—and running fast. Micah probably pulled out of town that very same day.

Wolf mused over why the assassin would have made this mistake. He had at least fifty kills under his belt that authorities thought they might be able to pin to him. He'd never made a single mistake, not once. Yet he shot a man who was trying to get out of going to court over bounced checks. And that had been the assassin's fatal error. The guy the assassin shot was a nobody. He sure as hell didn't fit the profile of absolutely every other man and woman the assassin had allegedly shot and killed.

So why would the assassin, who had a perfect track record up to that point, make such a fatal mistake, shooting a man with the same gun he had used to kill the CIA agent?

"Because of a girl," Wolf muttered, and pulled up the picture of Maggie O'Malley that he'd printed off his computer. "They are the only poison that makes a man stupid."

He could certainly relate to that poison. Now wasn't the time to dwell on Rebecca, though.

"Pretty lady," Wolf said to himself as he stared at Maggie O'Malley instead of thinking about Rebecca Cleary, the only woman he'd been stupid enough to fall in love with. "Can't get much more Irish than a name like O'Malley."

"You know, sweetheart, your brother seemed really concerned about you." He stared at Maggie's picture and shoved Rebecca, whom he'd forbidden himself to ever think about again, out of his head. "When I talked to him at the door, he was quite anxious about you. And by the way, you had an incredible home. Your parents don't live there anymore. They're in a retirement community. Are they failing because you disappeared on them? Your brother really wants to hear from you, sweetheart," he whispered, and ran his thumb down the length of her chin in the picture. "I sure hope Micah is worth what you've done to your family."

Wolf didn't know a lot about family. Once he had turned eighteen and freed himself of the system, he'd tried looking up his birth mother. He wasn't sure why he had. She had obviously hated him, since she'd named him Waldorf, then given him away as soon as he was out of her.

It hadn't been hard to track her down. He had been born in Grove, Oklahoma. It was just over a thirty-minute drive from Vinita. Wolf liked to think of the experience as his first investigation. At the age of eighteen, Wolf had stared down at the grave site where his mother was buried. She had died from a drug overdose when Wolf had been three. He would have been an orphan even if she hadn't given him up. One of the ironies in his world.

"Okay, Maggie, talk to me," he said, focusing on her picture. "Why is such a pretty lady like you with the Mulligan Stew assassin? Your priest is worried about you, too, you know. Although he did imply you are with Micah by choice."

There was a clammy flush that spread over his skin when he thought about the fabricated story he'd told the priest at Holy Name church. Wolf needed something—a bite, a lead—something to give him a jump-start in the right direction. Father Charles had been politely close-lipped. He'd mentioned Maggie always had a family with her church. It was the only thing the priest had said that led Wolf to believe Father Charles knew Maggie was with Micah.

Wolf sighed, ran his hand through his hair, and stood. He put Maggie's picture down next to his duffel bag then he stared at the mirror on the wall as he stretched. The longer his brown hair got, the more curls there were. He didn't have time for a haircut right now and really didn't care how he looked. More than one person had told him it was time to settle down and quit running around the country. The way he looked right now no woman would look at him twice.

Running around the country was how he made his money. There weren't any criminals in Vinita who would bring in the bounties he'd collected over the years. When he was twenty-five, he made a thousand dollars capturing a convict wanted in Oklahoma. That got Wolf hooked, and he'd never looked back. At thirty-five he was now going after the largest bounty of his life. He would capture the Mulligan Stew assassin or die trying. Wolf didn't care where he had to go. Traveling light made it easy to move from location to location. And location led to another question that was bugging him.

"Why Santa Clarita?" Wolf walked over to the window in his motel and pulled back the curtain. There were cars and a few trucks parked throughout the parking lot. Across the street, lights from businesses and fast-food restaurants glowed in the clear, black night. "Pretty town. Clean and quiet," he mused.

But Santa Clarita wasn't that far from L.A. If Micah was getting the hell out of Dodge, why did he stop here? Why wouldn't he and Maggie have driven as far away as they could get?

"Was it because he believed everyone would think he would go as far away as possible?" Hiding under everyone's noses had worked for criminals in the past. "Or, was there someone here you wanted to see?"

Wolf dropped the curtain and returned to his duffel. He pulled out the file he had placed at the bottom of the bag and opened it. All of the information he had gathered on the Mulligan Stew assassin was in there.

"Assassin, or may I call you Micah?" he added wryly.

Those little bugs were damned expensive if you wanted one where you could actually hear what was being said without it being all muffled and staticky. He'd hit the jackpot with this one, though. It hadn't surprised Wolf that the information gained by planting the bug in the KFA office would come within minutes of planting it there. It's what was said in those first moments of outrage over Wolf sauntering in and out of their office. Nor had it surprised him when the Kings found the bug and destroyed it.

Wolf had taken everything he'd known about Greg and Haley King and had decided lying or pretending to be someone he wasn't wouldn't get him far with those two. Wolf respected King as a bounty hunter, and one who had paid his dues in the business. Therefore, Wolf had taken the direct approach. In order to learn anything, though, because he'd known before entering their office the Kings wouldn't tell him a thing about the Mulligan Stew assassin regardless of what they might have known, Wolf had decided to put a bit of a punch in it.

The Kings hadn't gone after the assassin. They hadn't been interviewed. They'd refused comment when asked if he'd been their employee, which had been the only reason speculation rose that he had worked for KFA. That told Wolf that the Kings had liked the Mulligan Stew assassin, maybe had even respected him. The guy might be the nicest person anyone would ever meet. With a million-dollar bounty on his head Wolf didn't care if he were the son of God.

It had taken about as long as Wolf had figured it would. He hadn't been inside the KFA office more than five minutes.

And he'd run to his car, barely able to get the earpiece in his ear, when he'd heard that precious first name.

"Micah," he whispered.

First and last name would have been better. He wasn't complaining, though. "What's in Santa Clarita, Micah? Why run and stop an hour later?"

After arriving in Santa Clarita, Wolf had driven around the city. It was nice, clean, with lots of new additions. He'd walked through a mall and their downtown, enjoying the drop in temperature after dark. He hadn't expected to learn anything, but he enjoyed seeing different cities. Now, holed up in his motel room and not ready for bed, he paced and brainstormed.

He had a running theory with no way to back it, but possibly there had been someone here in Santa Clarita. With Micah hiding out in L.A., which Wolf was sure he'd been doing, possibly anyone working with him might have been hiding nearby. A CIA agent was a much bigger kill than anything else the Mulligan Stew assassin had ever done. It was a shot straight through the heart, which fit his MO. But it made sense he would lay low afterward. So, Micah was in L.A., but who was in Santa Clarita? Did the Mulligan Stew assassin work alone? Or was there someone in the background taking his calls, doing his research?

Wolf had no doubt Micah spent time learning about each man or woman he killed. None of them had nationwide attention at the time of their death. But all of them had been scum.

Someone knocked on the door. Wolf glared at it.

"Wrong door, buddy!" he called out, although not too loudly. He wasn't at the cheapest place in town, but it was far from a four star hotel. Wolf didn't waste his money. All he asked for were clean sheets and a pillow.

Whoever it was knocked again, this time firmer and with more determination.

Wolf sighed and put the file back together. He slid Maggie's picture on top, then tucked the file underneath his clothes in his duffel. There were several more knocks, much louder.

"Someone needs to teach you some manners," he mumbled, zipping the bag, doing a quick glance around the motel room, then walking over to the door.

He looked through the peephole but saw no one. There was nothing but darkness outside. Opening the door, Wolf had less than a second to react before Ben Mercy's fist headed straight for his face.

"Son of a bitch," he hissed, ducking but taking a few knuckles across his cheekbone. "It was nothing personal, Mercy," he informed the kid, and returned the greeting in kind.

"My home is personal!" Mercy yelled, and did a pretty good job of dodging Wolf's fist, although it sent him back a few paces.

Wolf had his key card on him so let his motel room door close and lunged into Mercy. He didn't take lightly to being followed or being hit. Nor did he ever back out of a good fight.

"Get over it!" he snarled, and tried again to lay a good one on the young brute's pretty face.

This time Wolf connected, but Mercy knew how to fight. His fist made contact with Wolf's stomach, knocking the wind out of him.

Wolf doubled over, and Mercy was on him, shoving him into the brick wall in between the motel room doors. Mercy was good sized, six feet if not taller. Wolf might not have been blessed with height, but he had muscle and knew how to use it. In his line of work not knowing how to hold his own in a good brawl was a death sentence.

Wolf growled as he shoved the kid off him, then charged when Mercy stumbled backward. The kid lost his balance at the end of the sidewalk and stepped sideways off the curb into the parking lot. Wolf came at him, returning the gut punch and doing his best to angle it so Mercy didn't fall against his Escalade.

There was a motorcycle next to it. Mercy howled from Wolf's punch hitting his stomach and bent over the bike.

"Give back what you took or I'll beat your face into the ground!" Mercy roared, and came at him like a mad bull.

The two men fell onto the sidewalk, throwing punch after

punch. Wolf didn't try getting up until he heard yelling. He'd be damned if he'd spend the night in jail when he was on a hunt. Apparently, Mercy was thinking the same thing. The kid scrambled to his feet and away from Wolf when two women and a man were running toward them yelling in Spanish.

"It's cool," Mercy told all of them, holding his hands up in the air. "No need to call the police. We're done."

Wolf cursed under his breath, and Mercy glared at him. Apparently, the kid could cool his temper pretty easily, but Wolf still seethed. Mercy had a six-pack that was as solid as a brick wall, and Wolf's knuckles stung worse than if he had scraped flesh to the bone. The two women held back, but the man, who had been at the front desk when Wolf checked in, puffed his chest out and stuck his hands at his waist.

"You both get out of here, now," he said in perfect English. "There is no fighting at my motel."

Wolf didn't see need for conversation. He stormed around the desk clerk and pulled his key card out of his pocket. So much for a good night's sleep. There were advantages to traveling light, and this was one of them. He entered the motel room with the desk clerk at his door, yelling at him to get out. Wolf grabbed the small bag that held his toiletries, unzipped his duffel and shoved it inside, then zipped the duffel up and headed out the door.

"Thanks for the fine service," he grumbled, slapping the key card into the desk clerk's hand, and headed to his SUV.

Apparently, the motorcycle belonged to Mercy, because he was on it and had already backed out of the stall. Wolf hid a smirk when he looked at the punk's red face. There was a damn nice-looking bruise trailing down the right side of it. Mercy's eyes looked a bit puffy. Either that or he was crying.

"Have a fun time riding that thing," Wolf muttered, but took a moment to admire the fine machine Mercy was sitting on.

Wolf had a Harley at home, too. Now wasn't time for nostalgia, though. He started his large SUV and rolled down the window. The motel had his name and tag number. He'd paid with cash, his preferred method of travel, but nonetheless there were shoddy motel owners out there and he didn't want trumped-up charges or any attention drawn to him.

Wolf rested his arm on his door and nodded to the man, who still stood there. "There were no damages done to your motel."

"You scared families in other rooms," he pointed out, once again puffing himself to his full height of five-ten or so.

Wolf learned a lot from observing people. Standing at five feet, ten and a half inches, he'd spent his youth obsessing about his height. Which was probably how he'd noticed that men who weren't as tall as other men looked a hell of a lot more impressive when they didn't try puffing out like a peacock. Very few tall men did that. This desk clerk was doing his best to look as scary as possible and failing.

There was worry on the man's face, though. Wolf saw that the man was trying to protect his motel single-handedly. The two women had already left.

Wolf nodded toward Mercy. "The kid is hot-wired. He thinks I wronged his mother."

The desk clerk narrowed his eyes on Wolf, obviously not approving of men who abused women. Wolf didn't, either. "He's wrong, though. He threw a punch before he realized I'm alone and not with another woman. I would never do that to his mother. I love both of them. I'll take the kid and calm him down. I do apologize if anyone was upset, or scared by the outburst."

"Outburst" was putting it mildly, but the desk clerk calmed down a bit, his puffed-out chest relaxing. "Have a good night, señor."

"You, too," Wolf told him, then rolled up his window and glanced over at Mercy.

The kid was leaning on his handlebars. The parking-lot lights cast shadows over his face, but Mercy was going to have one hell of a shiner.

By the time Wolf hit the interstate heading north it was also apparent Mercy planned on following him. His Escalade could easily cruise over a hundred miles an hour if he wanted to push getting a ticket. Mercy, on that bike, could pace him without any problem. That one lone headlight in the middle of his rearview mirror became a thorn in his side as the evening wore on.

A few hours later Ben was eternally grateful when Marley took an exit off the interstate into a quiet, sleepy town. The tall, bright sign advertising the several motels along a strip off the road had never looked better. Wolf chose the closest one and pulled his Escalade in under the awning outside their main door. Instead of going inside, he came around his SUV and walked up to Ben.

"Do you plan on following me wherever I go?" Wolf demanded, his voice harsh but his face gray and slightly bruised. It would probably be colorful by morning.

"You broke into my home and took two postcards from me. I'll do whatever I damn well please."

"Suit yourself." He pointed a thumb toward the motel entrance. "I'm going to get a room—*another* room," he stressed, "and get some sleep."

A pillow and blanket sounded so good. Ben considered his options. It was still a good six-hour drive to Zounds, if he didn't hit any heavy traffic. It was seriously late, and his eyes were burning with exhaustion. The night wind slapping at him as he rode the motorcycle had the rest of him aching for a hot shower. Ben climbed off the bike and opted for a room, too.

He allowed himself only two hours of sleep. It was a high price for a short nap, but there was no way he could let Micah down, not after all he'd done for Ben. He would beat that damn bounty hunter to Zounds if it killed him. Then, the best thing that could happen was Micah wouldn't be there. Marley wouldn't have a clue where to go from there to find Micah any more than Ben would.

Ben was heading to his bike, seriously needing coffee, when Wolf Marley came trudging out to the parking lot. Ben cursed under his breath as he stared at the wild brown mop of hair covering the muscular, shorter man's head. He couldn't see Marley's face, but it looked as if the man was walking stiffly.

Good, Ben thought. At least he wasn't the only one hurting. Marley pulled into the twenty-four-hour gas station across the street when Ben did. Neither acted as if he knew the other when they got coffee.

"I know what you're doing." Marley stood outside his Escalade and stared at Ben through the steam of his coffee.

Ben gulped down half his cup. He would love to go buy another cup but wouldn't risk having to stop for bathroom breaks. "What's that?" he asked dryly.

"You're headed up there to warn him."

Ben had given a lot of thought to what Marley might accuse him of doing while following him. Driving after him up the state of California because the guy trashed Ben's apartment seemed a bit extreme. More so, Ben had devised a plan so he'd know what to say when confronted.

"To warn him?" Ben cleared the distance between him and Marley.

The man stood a few inches shorter than Ben, and Ben probably had a good forty pounds more in muscle weight. Not to mention the guy was probably a good ten years older. To his credit, Marley didn't shy down.

"What exactly do you think you found in those postcards?" Ben asked.

"I think Micah was letting you know where he was."

Ben shook his head, refusing even to acknowledge the name Marley threw in his face. "If that is what you think, I'll be collecting this bounty without any problems," he said, laughed, and walked back to his bike.

"Collecting what bounty?" Marley called after him.

Ben turned around. "We knew the Mulligan Stew assassin was in L.A.," he began, then shook his head, trying to make it appear the memory was a bad one. "I knew we were close to nabbing him, although now it's even sweeter with a million-dollar bounty." Ben waved his free hand as if this should all be common knowledge. "Then, we're out apprehending a client. It was no big deal, a routine case. We're a few yards away from capturing the son of a bitch and some asshole shoots him. Less than an hour later police are swarming our office and it's all over that the Mulligan Stew assassin shot our guy."

Ben shook his head, drank more of his coffee, and stood with his back to his bike facing Marley. The guy was staring back at him, digesting what he'd just been told.

"If what you're saying is true," he said slowly, "it explains why he shot someone that didn't fit the profile compared to everyone else he killed."

Ben nodded, getting into his act, and pointed a finger at Marley. "And that he shot him with the same gun used to kill that CIA agent. It was how he let us know it was him. Otherwise we would have believed we had a random shooting. The son of a bitch was taunting us."

"That doesn't explain the postcards."

Ben hardened his expression. He knew Marley was probably snickering over the shiner Ben had. And it did hurt. Nothing that wouldn't go away in a day or so, but when he frowned he felt the bruised skin tighten on his face.

"You broke into my home and stole those. By all rights I should be kicking your ass again instead of discussing anything about the assassin with you."

"Kicking whose ass?" Marley laughed.

The man was hard as nails. It had felt as if he'd been hitting a wall the few times Ben got in a good punch the night before.

"Seems to me you've got some mighty dark bruises there, son."

Marley wasn't that much older than Ben that he rated calling him son. But fighting with the guy would just make him even more determined to beat Ben to their destination.

"I guess we both look alike more than we would otherwise," he said coolly.

"These postcards came from the assassin, from Micah." Marley's voice was insistent. He was so sure he was right and wanted confirmation.

Ben wouldn't give that to him in a million years. "You're wrong," he said softly, shaking his head. "I don't know the assassin. But I will. I'll get to know him real well when I haul him in."

Marley narrowed his eyes. "Don't think for a second you're going to claim any bounty." His tone and expression grew mean. The man didn't change his stance, though. He remained relaxed and blew on his coffee before taking a drink. "Why do you have two blank postcards?" he finally demanded.

Ben's answer was so rehearsed in his head he couldn't wait to spill it out. "A friend of mine helped me track him after that man we were chasing down a year ago got shot. I didn't have my PI license yet and wasn't going to do anything to allow the feds to back out of paying me my due once I turned him in. When he thought he'd spotted him in Santa Clarita, we tore that city apart trying to find him. My buddy headed north on the chance the Mulligan Stew assassin would go that way instead of west or south. I stayed in L.A. finishing up what I needed to do to get licensed so I could officially be a bounty hunter and go after him, too."

Ben knew Marley had seen all his paperwork to get licensed as a private investigator. It made sense, he had decided, to throw that bit in to make it more believable. Greg King had taught Ben many things, and one of them was about visuals. Let a man see something and it made it a lot easier to convince him it was true.

"When the second postcard showed up, I dropped everything and drove up there. Zounds, California, isn't a big town and we thought we had him. The bastard slipped through our fingers once again."

"Then why are you following me up there if you've already searched and didn't find him?"

"Is that where you're headed?" Ben shrugged. "You owe whatever you know about him for trashing my place. If I have to find it out by following you, then that's what I'm going to do. I've put a lot of hours in on this, and you aren't going to find him before I do."

Wolf studied Ben, weighing the odds on the punk feeding him lies or whether he was telling him the truth. It didn't take much to conclude whatever the truth was, Ben would hold out on any true valuable information he might have.

"That's a good story," Wolf finally said. "There's no doubt in my mind you'll lie about what you know or don't know about the Mulligan Stew assassin. You'll accuse me of withholding information by tempting me with information you may or may not have."

To his credit, Ben didn't bat an eye at the insinuation. "Are you going to tell me what you know?"

"Not on your life."

"I think it would be best if we worked together." Ben grinned as if he knew his suggestion would twist unpleasantly in Wolf's gut.

Wolf didn't work with anyone. Stepping on someone's toes took up time. He preferred doing his own analyzing and research. He also preferred claiming any bounty all to himself.

"Works for me." Wolf opened his SUV door. "I guess I'll see you in Zounds."

Chapter Five

Angelina Matisse, although she preferred Angel, despite the fact that the name didn't suit her, lugged the heavy box across her storeroom floor just as the bell tinkled in the other room. She straightened, feeling the strain in her back, and rubbed her hand over her tailbone. No time to dwell on aches and pains. She had a customer.

"Hi, Angel," Maggie Mall said and strolled into Angel's bookstore wearing a broad smile on her face. "The book was great."

"I knew you'd like it," Angel said, matching the grin as she walked behind her counter. She glanced at the clock. Four P.M., which meant another three hours to go before closing time.

The bell over her door tinkled again, and Mrs. Pointer hurried in with her four kids, who immediately raced over to the children's books, except for the oldest Pointer boy, who made his way to the magazines.

"Mrs. Pointer," Angel said, nodding and holding on to her "never a care in the world" smile.

When the Pointers entered, Maggie spun around as if she were expecting someone to come into the store behind her, but then visibly sighed. She was usually quiet, except when she and Angel were alone. Then Maggie opened up and glowed with a personality impossible not to love. Angel knew the signs of a beaten woman. Maggie lived with her husband outside of town. Angel had never seen the man. Some town folk thought Maggie made him up. Angel believed Maggie had a husband and that he was a hermit like Maggie told everyone. She also thought he must be a rough, possessive man by Maggie's actions. She never spoke of him but always dutifully hurried back out of town as soon as she got what she came in to get.

"So which book are you getting today?" Angel asked Maggie when she turned back around.

"The next book in the series. Also, do you have any books on expanding your home?"

"Expanding your home?" Angel looked pointedly down at Maggie's belly.

"Oh no! No." Maggie laughed, getting Angel's drift. "I'm not pregnant." She said the last sentence with a wistful sigh. "We're thinking about expanding, and with such a sporadic Internet connection where we live I thought books might help us get a grasp on what we're taking on."

"You can get all your answers in books," Angel said, and cringed. "I sound like my dad. You never want to be like them but then have to laugh when you sound just like them."

"I know exactly what you mean." Maggie laughed. "I look in the mirror and say hello to my mother every day," she added, and followed Angel to the part of the bookstore where self-help books were shelved.

Angel didn't hate her father. She'd grown up knowing she would take on the family business after all. Bob's Bobbins and Books had become Angelina's Bookstore six years ago when she'd turned twenty-five. By that time, she had worked in the store for ten years and had considered it her own for at least as long. Her mother and father had owned the store together, having been Zounds natives, which made Angel second generation. When Angel took over, the seamstress part of the store, where her mother had sat in her corner and mended, altered, or created whatever needed to be done, had been closed down. Angel could barely thread a needle. As her mother used to complain, Angel spent too much of her time buried in books to know one end of the needle from the other.

"Isn't this room gorgeous?" Maggie asked. She had the brightest, prettiest eyes, which were the only part of Maggie that belied Angel's suspicion that Maggie was abused. Her eyes and face always glowed of happiness.

Angel looked at the glossy page in the book Maggie held up. "Yes, it is." She envied Maggie. Angel's friend had been coming into the bookstore almost daily since she and her husband had moved here, and although Maggie was chatty, this was the most she'd spoken about her home life, and it wasn't much. Angel lived over the store, and there would never be any remodeling. Especially with Emilio Cortez owning the building Angelina's Bookstore was in. His rent was so exorbitant it was all she could do to get it paid each month, let alone think about remodeling.

The bell over the door tinkled again, and Angel peered around the bookshelves. "Over here!" she called out.

When Zoey walked around the corner into their aisle, Angel shoved thoughts of Cortez out of her head. As evil as the asshole was, his daughter, Zoey, was the epitome of perfection. She neared both women in a cloud of wonderful-smelling perfume, and her incredibly straight—not a wave anywhere— black hair was pulled away from her face in a blue headband. Angel's hair was also pulled back in a headband, but her plain short brown hair was an uncontrollable mass of waves and curls that not even her pristine mother had ever been able to control.

"Hi, Angel," Zoey said in her soft voice. She shot a wary look at Maggie. "Hi there," she said, and smiled.

Angel didn't get these two. Both of them seemed like broken souls to her, but for different reasons. Zoey lived under the rule of her tyrant of a father, although she had sworn multiple times that he'd never hit her. And Maggie lived the life of a recluse yet had this look in her eyes at times that made Angel think she wasn't as concerned about being around people as she let on.

Although neither would probably ever confide in her,

Angel suspected both were battered women. Some men thought a black eye on a woman marked her as his property and kept other men from looking at her. Other equally sadistic bastards kept the pain more personal, making sure bruises were left where no one would see. Zoey and Maggie both needed mending. Maybe Angel couldn't replace a broken zipper, but she ached to fix these two women. As her mom would say when someone brought in a piece of clothing for alteration, *Oh, there is a lot of life still left in them.*

There was so much life inside Maggie and Zoey, which was why Angel liked both of them.

"Hi there, Zoey," Maggie greeted with a smile, and flipped the page of the large hardback book she had in her hands. "Oh my, look at this room. Isn't this gorgeous? Angel, I'm buying this book. And this one," she added.

Angel hurried over to the romance section and grabbed the next book in the series that Maggie had originally asked about and brought it to the counter. The Pointers met her, each one of them shoving books at her. After checking them out and watching all of them traipse out her door, Angel turned and smiled at Zoey, who had come to the counter. Maggie was right behind her. Angel rang both of them up.

"Busy day?" Zoey asked. She looked after the Pointers and continued staring out the large windows facing the street and courtyard outside the store.

"It's been steady. I'm getting some work done." Angel nodded toward her back room.

Zoey snapped her attention back to Angel. "You got more books in? Any of them biographies?"

"I haven't unloaded that far," Angel told her.

Zoey bit her lip. Angel knew damn good and well what she'd ordered. She'd learned a long time ago to make her customers wait until she was able to shelve new stock.

"Oh, I almost forgot." Zoey reached into her purse and pulled out a thick envelope. "I'm supposed to give this to you," she mumbled, and held the envelope for Angel to take as she glanced back toward the street, not making eye contact. Her fingers trembled when she dropped it on the counter.

Angel looked at the envelope as if it might reach out and bite her. Even Maggie paused before leaving and stared at the thick envelope. Zoey looked as if she wanted to fade into the woodwork.

"I'm sorry," she whispered. "I don't know what it is. My father asked me to give it to you when I told him where I was going."

"Next time don't tell him where you're going," Maggie said, and smiled when Zoey looked at her, terrified. "It was a joke," Maggie said, her pretty blue eyes glowing with laughter.

"No use prolonging the pain," Angel said, and ripped open the envelope.

"Wow, would you look out there? He's gorgeous," Zoey whispered, apparently aching to change the subject off her tyrant of a father and whatever was in the envelope.

Angel didn't blame her. One glance at the legal-looking form in the envelope and she knew it wasn't good news. She looked outside just as a silver Escalade with black windows circled the courtyard slowly. The driver's side window was rolled down. Dark curls and well-defined arm muscles grabbed her attention before she took in the barrel chest and profile of the face of the man driving the SUV.

"I'll say," Angel humphed. "New blood in town."

"I saw him first," Zoey teased, but then shrugged her shoulders. It wasn't as if she'd ever pursue a man, no matter how gorgeous. Her father would never allow it.

"Darling, I think he's a bit too old for you." Angel tried patting her curls into place.

"With those perfect curls," Zoey said, and dragged her delicate-looking fingers down a long strand of straight hair, "you would probably snag him the moment he came in to buy a book."

"Sweetheart, these curls are a nightmare." Angel laughed. "I am just the right age for a man driving a Cadillac Escalade. Anyone who can afford that has paid his dues, and I certainly don't want a pup."

"A what?" Zoey searched outside the windows that faced

the circular-drive courtyard on the edge of downtown Zounds.
"I was talking about the guy on the motorcycle."

"It's a Harley-Davidson," Maggie informed her. "I've got
to go, ladies. Talk to you soon."

"Bye, Maggie!" Angel called out. She then frowned at
Zoey. "I didn't even see a guy on a bike. I was too busy drooling over the man driving that Escalade. Did you see how
muscular his arm was as it rested on his open window?"

"I didn't notice." Zoey turned to leave, then remembered
the book she'd just bought and grabbed it from the counter.
"See you soon. And Angel," she added, her large dark eyes
sincerely forlorn, "I'm so sorry about the envelope. My father
is such an asshole," she said, whispering her final comment.

Zoey was glad to leave the bookstore before Angel read
whatever was in the envelope from her father. It wouldn't be
good news. With her father it never was. He was an evil,
vindictive man, who got pure pleasure out of making others
suffer, her in particular. If he mentioned Hector Isley to her
one more time, Zoey would scream. Her father had ranted
all of her life about how she would marry in the church,
which was his way of saying she'd marry a Catholic Mexi-
can. He and Hector's father had both decided that their
children's marrying each other would create an invincible
financial dynasty. Hector had agreed to the marriage. Her
father didn't care if Zoey wanted to marry Hector, or not.

Zoey got sick every time her father brought it up. Not to
mention, he hadn't stepped foot inside a church her entire
life. Well, he might have once they moved to Zounds, but only
to inform the poor priests that he now owned their church
and all tithings would go to him. Which was fitting. Her father did think he was God.

She walked down the street with her head held high,
knowing anyone who noticed her hated her for being Cortez's daughter. She wanted to scream to everyone who looked
away when they saw her that she hated him even more than
they did.

Especially now. Her father would not shut up about how

once she married Hector they would all be incredibly rich and unbelievably powerful. He would then pat her on the shoulder and remind her she would be secure for life. As if she cared a bit for any of his bloodstained money or abusive power.

Zoey knew what her father did. She knew he was sucking this town dry. And that was simply because it entertained him. Emilio Cortez had moved to Zounds ten years ago because it was directly in between San Francisco and Seattle, two cities he held onto by the balls, as he would put it. Zounds was the perfect place for him to hide from all of the criminal activity he oversaw in both of the large cities.

When she reached the other end of downtown, Zoey turned toward the library, where she'd parked her car. Zounds wasn't big enough for her to entertain herself for long. But since her father ruled over her as cruelly as he did everything and everyone else, Zoey wasn't allowed to leave town. She seriously jonesed for a large shopping mall or a movie theater that showed more than two movies at any given time. Or a classy restaurant with a classy man at her side.

Images of the man on the motorcycle, the Harley-Davidson, popped into her mind. He had looked tall, which meant he probably wouldn't look twice at someone as short as her. She'd reached five feet, two inches by the eighth grade and had never grown another inch. Even in her three-inch heels that clicked against the paved sidewalk, Zoey only hit five feet, five inches.

The man on the Harley had to be at least six feet tall. He'd rode around the courtyard in front of the bookstore long enough for Zoey to get a pretty good look at him. His helmet had covered his face, but she had almost hyperventilated over all of that packed muscle under his T-shirt. He might have been riding for a while, because his shirt clung to him, as did his faded jeans.

She slowed when she reached the library, which was on the opposite side of the street. Zoey didn't cross the street, though, but stared straight ahead. The bed-and-breakfast was on the corner in one of the town's historical Victorian homes. A blond man relaxed on the front steps that led up to the wide, long front porch. Zoey came to a complete stop when she was sure he was looking right at her.

The man was too far away to see the color of his eyes, but they were light. And they pierced right through her. Zoey wasn't sure she could have moved if she'd tried. At the moment, though, she wasn't thinking about walking. She was trying to remember how to breathe.

He was gorgeous, absolutely sinfully perfect. Her mouth went dry staring at him. Her heart began pounding too hard in her chest. She felt her breasts swell and her nipples harden. They pressed against her low-cut silk bra and itched painfully. It was all she could do not to twist or fidget, anything to relieve the sudden pressure that built inside her until it sunk deep between her legs.

The man stood. It was a lazy movement, and Zoey caught herself tilting her head and admiring his lethal body as he pushed away from the steps and straightened. He tugged on his T-shirt, making it stretch over too many rippling muscles. Then he was walking toward her.

Zoey suddenly came to her senses. She couldn't be talking to some stranger passing through town. There were eyes everywhere. She knew this to be true. If she even had a polite conversation with this man her father, would hear about it. If not tonight, soon. He would chastise her, lock her in her room, or force one of his thugs to escort her around town until she remembered how to behave as a Cortez should.

"How's it going?" the man asked before he reached her.

Why did he have to speak to her? Her pride and self-esteem had been thrashed by this town as long as she'd lived here. Damn her father! She wouldn't be rude.

"Fine," she said, glancing at him, and caught herself staring at a rippling six-pack as it pressed against his shirt.

Polite or not, she wouldn't stand and gawk and pray he continued to speak to her. She turned to cross the street. He held out his hand, and for a moment it looked like he would grab her arm.

"Don't walk away now." He didn't touch her but simply raised his hand to detain her, then dropped it to his side. "You noticed me staring at you, and I couldn't help see that you were staring back at me."

"Of course I was," she said curtly, and didn't look up so he wouldn't see her burning cheeks. "You were looking right at me, and I thought maybe I knew you."

She again tried crossing the street. This time Zoey walked into a rock-hard muscular arm. She looked at the taut, well-formed muscles in his forearm and bicep as she took a step backward and licked her suddenly dry lips. Zoey bet every inch of him was packed as hard as steel. Every inch of him.

"My name is Ben," he said hurriedly. "Don't run off. I don't know anyone here."

A thought hit her, and she almost choked from the truth that might be in it.

"Why are you here?" she demanded, facing him and this time looking up at his face. "Why do you want to talk to me?"

If he even indirectly mentioned her father, she was bolting across the street. It would be just her luck for the sexiest man alive to be talking to her because she was Emilio Cortez's daughter.

"Looking for work." His light blue eyes were clear and alert as he stared down at her.

"What kind of work?" Zoey asked, not convinced yet that he wasn't here because her father had brought him here. Or, worse yet, because he was after her father.

"I can do anything, pretty much. But hunting, trapping," he told her, his eyes lowering and taking in her body as he spoke. They were back on her face when he finished. "I'm at home doing those sorts of things. But like I said, any kind of work as long as it pays a fair wage."

"Good luck with your job hunting," she said, smiling. Zoey didn't want to tell him that finding a job in Zounds would be hard as hell to do, unless the job was with her father.

"I was sitting on those porch steps thinking about wandering around, getting a feel of the town. It would be perfect if someone who lived here gave me a tour."

"It's just about dark," she pointed out. "You wouldn't get a good view of the town."

Ben was by far the best-looking man she'd ever laid eyes on. There wasn't a man in Zounds, single or otherwise, who compared to him. Zoey hastily pointed out to herself that he probably would have asked anyone who came along to give him advice on the town. If they talked to him as she had, he might have asked for a tour. He was a man, just like her father's thugs, his accountants, his business partners, and gave her an appraising once-over like all the rest. None of the men on her dad's payroll looked like this, though.

"You're right, of course," Ben said.

For a moment she thought he had responded to her thoughts, which was ridiculous.

"How about a ride?" he asked.

"A ride?" Zoey looked up at him, and a slow, lazy smile appeared on his lips. She wasn't convinced yet that Ben wasn't on her father's payroll or trying to be. But wouldn't it be scandalously wonderful to spend time with someone who had absolutely no ties, voluntary or otherwise, to her dad?

"Stay right here," Ben ordered, pointing at her before turning and jogging back toward the bed-and-breakfast.

Every inch of her demanded she march across the street to the library and get in her car. She might have actually done that, but she was mesmerized staring after Ben as he jogged away from her. He didn't look like any jogger she'd ever seen. His legs were thick with muscles that pressed against his blue jeans. And his ass, holy crap! "Buns of steel" was just too cliché—an overused expression. There wasn't anything clichéd about his ass.

For the most part asses had never been her favorite part of the male anatomy. Zoey would have to say a hard cock was her favorite part of a man's body. However, if asked, Zoey would say the chest appealed to her the most. If a guy had a broad, muscular chest, it caught her eye every time.

She continued staring, lost in the perfect formation of his body. Ben didn't really jog, she decided. He ran slowly, like a dangerous beast, content with his surroundings already and satisfied that anything in his way would move so he could reach his destination. That level of raw, carnal confidence appealed to her as much as his perfect body did.

"Shit!" she hissed.

When he disappeared from sight, the trance he had her under broke. Zoey scowled at the sidewalk, trying to shake sense back into her head. No way would she be lured by a man she didn't know. And in spite of physical perfection and an incredible show of self-confidence, she didn't know anything about him. Her attention shot to the bed-and-breakfast when the sound of a motorcycle starting up grabbed her attention. She couldn't go riding with Ben on a motorcycle. Why hadn't she been thinking? When he said "a ride," of course he had meant on a bike. He had been the man she had seen on the bike earlier.

The thought of being on that large, rumbling motorcycle immediately had her trembling with need. Not just wet between her legs. And not just feeling her breasts swell as lust created a feverish desire inside her. But a full-blown tsunami-strength wave of passion that pressed under every inch of her skin.

Ben revved his bike, and she swore she felt the vibration in the sidewalk as it seared up her body. There was no way she could do this. Even if she wanted to, and God, she wanted to, taking off with a strange man on his motorcycle was absolutely insane. Beyond the obvious, her father would have her head if she was seen in the company of another man when she was supposedly engaged.

Zoey darted across the street. Her car was one of only a few left in the library parking lot. She slowed when she neared it, but her timing was off. Ben entered the parking lot and slowed his bike, then came to a stop in front of Zoey.

"Get on," he instructed.

"I don't think so." She shook her head. "I don't think this is a good idea."

"I do." He did sound sure of himself. "I only have one problem."

"What's that?"

"I don't know your name."

"Zoey Cortez." Zoey watched for his reaction.

"Well, Miss Cortez," Ben began, and pushed down the kickstand to the large, rumbling bike and climbed off it.

Zoey was entranced by his long, powerful-looking legs. There were roped muscles pressing against his blue jeans, and they flexed in his thighs and just above his knees as he agilely slipped off the bike and faced her. She bet if he weren't wearing his jeans, his legs would be covered with a thin spread of hair. A man as rough and tough looking as Ben probably would have a scar or two. Her gaze rose slightly when she tried picturing his flat stomach. But she didn't look that high up his body. Her view got locked on the slight bulge in his pants.

Before she let her mind wander down dangerous territory, Ben grabbed her by the waist and lifted her into the air.

"Oh God!" Zoey cried out, immediately clutching his tan arms.

"Spread your legs," Ben instructed, his voice soft and so calm sounding.

"What?" she gasped. It was more like a yelp—a very unladylike yelp.

"Wait! Oh my God!" Zoey would have screamed. It was right there in her throat ready to come out. But instead she clipped out an, "Oh!" when he placed her on the back half of the long, wide leather seat on his motorcycle.

Instantly she felt the vibration of the motor between her legs. Then Ben raised his leg and straddled his bike once again. He situated himself in front of her, which basically meant her crotch was pressed against his ass and her inner thighs rubbed against his outer thighs.

"Put this on," he instructed, handing her a black helmet.

Zoey took the helmet. She slipped it over her head just as he pulled the bike around and left the parking lot.

"This is kidnapping!" she yelled over the loud motor.

"Oh?" Ben slowed instantly and began crawling down Summer Street, the main street running downtown. "Want me to go back?"

Zoey wanted to bury her head in his back. It wouldn't do any good. Most shoppers had headed home for the evening. But the slower he drove, the easier it was for anyone to glance up, check out the new guy in town, and wonder what the hell Zoey Cortez was doing on the back of his bike. Her father might very well already be getting a call.

There was a mixed blessing in that. He would be pissed, beyond livid. And there wouldn't be a damn thing he could do about it. He wouldn't control her. If, somehow, Zoey could tarnish her reputation by riding on this motorcycle with some drifter and it resulted in Hector Isley never wanting to see her again, she'd do it. At the same time, her father's temper was nothing to take lightly. Zoey had spent her life learning how to keep her father from hitting her, and on how to convince the few people she called friends to believe he didn't. Not because she cared about her father's reputation but because she cared about her own. It was exhausting work being her own bodyguard. Zoey wasn't a tyrant like her father. Bodyguards deserved vacations from time to time.

"No!" she yelled over Ben's shoulder, which she was able to do only because her part of the seat was noticeably higher than his. "Just keep in mind everyone knows me in this town and you just paraded us through downtown. So don't even think—"

His laughter cut her off. "You're in the most trustworthy hands in the state of California."

She prayed he was right. For once, she would take a walk on the wild side, or make that a ride on the wild side. She was doing something because she wanted to do it. It was daring, spontaneous, and dangerous. And she prayed she wasn't making the worst decision of her life.

Zoey was terrified, stimulated, turned on, and entranced

all at the same time. Her heart beat too hard in her chest, and her tummy was doing flip-flops. Gorgeous men simply didn't come along and sweep her off her feet, literally.

She adjusted the helmet on her head so she could see better around her. If anyone did step out from any of the shops downtown to get a better look, Zoey wanted to know who was doing the staring. Or if early-evening strollers stopped in their tracks to check her and Ben out, Zoey would know who. So far no one had, not that Zoey could see inside shop windows. But if her father informed her he'd received a phone call, before going on to berate her for humiliating him and the Cortez name—not that he didn't do that every day—she would at least have a good idea who made the phone call. So far, Zoey had seen no one staring at her and Ben.

Daring to relax just a bit, she dropped her hand on her leg. Already one of her hands rested on his waist. If she wrapped her arms around him, leaned into his hot, muscular backside, she might very well forget about the potentially dangerous situation she was getting herself into. Instead she allowed herself to enjoy the muffled rumble of the motor from inside her helmet. It gave her the odd sensation that she was suddenly in her own world where nothing else she'd just left mattered anymore.

"Hold on, sweetheart," Ben said over his shoulder, and straightened his arms in front of his handlebars.

His legs moved, and she was forced to adjust hers. Then they were moving. Really moving. Instinctively Zoey wrapped both arms around his waist, clinging to him at first. After they'd ridden a few blocks and were no longer downtown, her grip relaxed. Zoey realized she'd had her head pressed against his back and raised it to look around.

"So give me the tour," Ben said, looking over his shoulder at her.

"It seems more as if you were giving me the tour."

Ben had an ornery smile. Dimples appeared on either side of his mouth as he smirked at her. It was harder to see his eyes, but focusing on his profile she also noticed his eyelashes were long and thick. His blond hair bordering the strong features on his face helped give him a charming look. Zoey imagined Ben to either be an incredible troublemaker or the type of man who would always save the day and make sure no one was ever harmed. She couldn't imagine him being both but also couldn't decide which way his nature went.

"Are there factories in Zounds, or maybe any contractors who might need a painter or a carpenter?" he asked. "I'm pretty good with my hands."

She just bet he was. "Rod Greene hires temporary help from time to time when he's working on a home," she offered.

"Greene?" Ben asked, again turning his head slightly when he spoke to her. His hands rested on his handlebars, and he leaned forward slightly but then straightened his arms once again when they reached the end of the street. "Left or right?"

"Umm, right," she decided. Not that it mattered. It was dark now, and there wasn't anywhere she could take him at night that would help him find work. Nor could she think of any part of town worth showing off in the dark. "And yes, Rod Greene. I don't know how he hires his help, but whenever he's working on a home he always has men with him that I've never seen before. And I know they aren't always the same guys."

"How do you know that?"

"Because if Rod always had the same crew I would know his men."

Her heart fluttered when he did that little smirk thing with his mouth. "Drive me by where he lives," Ben instructed.

"You can't stop by his place tonight."

"Nope. Wasn't planning on it. But if I know where he lives, I can hopefully be in the right place at the right time in the morning to find work."

Ben had no intention of looking for work. He honestly hadn't planned on trying to pick up on one of the locals, either. That was until he'd spotted Zoey and his entire body had responded to the regal way she'd walked down the sidewalk. He was incredibly aware of the short skirt she was wearing and how, at the moment, it had to be scrunched up around her hips. He knew it was wishful thinking, but Ben swore he felt the heat from her pussy soaking through the back of his jeans.

Her arms loosened around his waist, and her hands began slipping from where they were to his thighs. Before she could relax her grip too much, Ben took both her hands in his and held them against his waist. It forced her to lean into his back. She was wearing two tank tops, one white and one pink. Their thin straps draped over her slender shoulders, and the material from the shirts swooped low over her breasts. He had guessed she wore a strapless bra, which he hadn't seen. It might be made with lace instead of a lot of padding, because when her fairly large breasts pressed against the middle of his back, there was no mistaking her nipples hardening and poking into his shirt.

It was a cool evening, but he guessed Zoey was a lot more used to this climate than he was. He wasn't driving fast. Not to mention his big body was likely blocking the chilly breeze from her petite, perfectly shaped, hot, little body.

Instantly Ben was hard. Feeling her against him, imagining how tight she might be if they had sex, had his dick stretching against his jeans, which made it uncomfortable as hell to turn corners or shift his body weight in any direction as he rode down the dark, sleepy roads in this quaint little town.

There hadn't been that welcoming curiosity on any of Zounds's town folk's faces when he and Marley had driven into town. They'd both gassed up, refurbished the caffeine, and asked about the best place to stay the night. The middle-aged man working at the gas station had stared at the two of them for a moment, his masked expression either aghast that they would want to stay the night in his town or wary of why they were here in the first place.

Ben had noticed that same masked expression on many faces as he and Marley had gone from the gas station, to the bed-and-breakfast, then to a small grocery store, and finally back to the bed-and-breakfast. He'd finally broken free of Marley when he'd perched his ass on the front-porch steps and tried to understand what vibes he was getting off this town. If Micah was still hiding out here, Ben seriously doubted anyone in Zounds would know who he was or that he was even here. That's when Ben had spotted Zoey.

She had strolled down that sidewalk with her long black hair swaying slightly just above her ass. He could tell, even from the distance when he first spotted her, that she wasn't wearing stockings. Her dark, perfectly shaped legs were bare and her pretty little feet shown off in her high-heeled black sandals. The tight black skirt she wore could have been seen at a high-class function in L.A. With the loose-fitting tank tops hanging off her slender figure, she had that casual look about her. But when she got close enough for Ben to see how incredibly beautiful she was, he also noticed that same masked expression on her face that was on the face of every other citizen of Zounds he'd seen so far. Her good looks turned him on, but her composed features intrigued him even further. It wasn't until he lifted her on his bike, mainly because she was too short to straddle it easily on her own but also to see if he could rattle that all-too-composed expression that he'd seen true fear appear in her large, doe-like eyes.

"Left or right?" he asked again at the next intersection.

"Right, then left in two blocks. Rod lives on Autumn Street."

Ben drove by the contractor's house, feigning interest, then turned at the next corner without asking which way to go. He caught a whiff of the ocean and continued in that direction until they reached the calm bay where tons of boats rocked silently against the waves. He didn't get a lot of chances to go to the beach back home. Something told him if he suggested they do something, Zoey would want to be taken back. So instead of voicing his plans, Ben rode until the road T'd off and narrowed into a one-lane road running parallel to the sandy and rocky beach.

"We can't park or anything," Zoey complained when he stopped his bike. "I mean it. You have to take me back to my car now."

He left the bike in neutral and straightened his legs so that his boots were on the road. "You're safe with me, Zoey, always. I want you to know that."

"And I should just take your word on this? I don't know you," she snapped, her tone rising as her uneasiness flourished. "I shouldn't have ridden with you at all. Now just take me back to my car right now."

"You aren't enjoying yourself?"

"That's not the point."

"That's the entire point," he cut in. "Unless experiencing pleasure is somehow forbidden in this town."

"Huh?"

Ben shifted on his bike but couldn't see Zoey's face to his satisfaction. Her thin, smooth legs almost seemed to clamp down against him when he decided to get off the bike. It was as if she seriously thought pinning her legs against his would prevent him from doing anything. He stood, stretched, pulled off his helmet, and took in the black blanket embedded with millions of stars over his head. When he straightened, Zoey had taken her helmet off, too, and was combing her hair with her fingers. He caught her staring at his belly where his shirt had risen up inches from his belt.

"What is it I'm sensing in this town?" Ben asked, and took Zoey's helmet from her without asking.

Her long, incredibly straight black hair was breathtaking when it tumbled over her shoulders, over her breasts, and down her back. Zoey grabbed it with both hands, pulled it to her nape, then continued meticulously combing tangles out with her fingers. Ben ached to take over the task and watched with fascination.

"I'm not sure," she said offhandedly. "I don't sense anything."

Zoey wasn't giving him wary looks any longer. Her tone had gone noticeably flat, and that masked expression he swore every citizen in this damned town had to practice in their mirrors was back on her face. As she tugged her fingers through tangles and slowly had her hair falling in glossy black tumbles down her sides, Zoey slipped off his bike and stared at the ground in front of her. Not only did he sense that his question bothered her, but he also got the feeling she knew exactly why everyone in this town acted the way they did.

Which bugged him. At the same time his curiosity was piqued. Not only did he want to know the answer, he also wanted to know the woman sitting on his bike a lot better. Zoey was one of the most sensually distracting ladies he'd ever laid eyes on. Most women seemed at least mildly interested in him after meeting him. There had to be at least one woman who simply saw nothing in him at all that appealed to her. Maybe Zoey was that woman. If that was the case, though, wouldn't she have been more adamant about not going on a ride with him?

He decided it was better not to care. Ben was here to protect Micah, to return the huge favor that had been done for him. Micah had helped turn Ben's life around by leaving all that money. There was no way Ben would ever be able to pay it all back, but Micah would have known that. If it was at all possible, though, Ben would help save Micah's freedom.

Ben knew Micah was trying to turn his life around. He had retired and was no longer an assassin—alleged assassin. Unfortunately, the statute of limitations would never run out on the crimes Micah was accused of committing. Ben could make sure Micah wasn't hauled in. At least not this time around.

"Are you sensing something weird right now?" Zoey asked.

Ben blinked. He didn't realize he'd been staring into space until he snapped out of his thoughts and focused on Zoey's face. A small, amused smile lit up her face. That masked expression he knew he hadn't misread a moment ago was no longer there.

And goddamn! Zoey was so far beyond beautiful it stirred more than his groin to life. Her caramel-colored skin glowed in the moonlight, with the help of a nearby streetlight. Her dark eyes were large and looking up at him. For once, he had all of her attention. Her lips, which were full and appeared moistened, were just a few shades darker than her skin.

"Actually, yes," he murmured, and dared a step closer.

Zoey couldn't be much more than five feet or so. She wore heels, which helped bring the top of her head possibly to his chin. She wasn't petite but thin. Zoey didn't strike him as fragile, in spite of how small she was. There had been something wary in her eyes, possibly because she'd agreed to do what women were taught never to do. Ben would have thrown a fit if any lady he knew took off with a man she didn't know. He wasn't sure what had compelled him to force Zoey into the ride, but since he had, he needed her to know she was safe.

"And what might that be?" Zoey didn't look wary now.

Ben reached out and stroked her shiny black hair. "It has me curious."

"My hair has you curious?" Zoey had to lean her head back to look at his face. "I've never heard that line before."

He shook his head slowly. "I'm not giving you a line. Honestly, that really isn't my style."

"And what is your style?"

He'd just convinced himself leaving her alone was his best bet. Making a move on her wouldn't help convince her he was a trustworthy man passing through her town. Ben didn't want Zoey talking about him or in any way drawing unwanted attention to his being in Zounds.

The last thing he needed was some hot cutey with large brown eyes that seemed to stare up at him with wonder interfering with him helping out Micah. Ben needed to be discreet. He needed to remain focused. He also needed to leave soon and spend his evening trying to find Micah. It wasn't as if the guy would have a cell phone or address that Ben could look up.

Ben couldn't argue with any of his thoughts as he finished stroking Zoey's hair and cupped her chin. It took a bit more reminding of why he was here to get himself to let go of her.

Zoey grabbed his wrist. Her hand was noticeably smaller than his. Her fingers didn't wrap all the way around his wrist. She held on to him with a cool touch. Her hand was soft and her fingers smooth. Not that he wouldn't have guessed it about her, but whatever she did for a living, it wasn't physical labor. He needed to leave her as a stranger and quit being curious about the different layers he was already noticing in her in the short time they'd been together.

"This isn't my style," she began, her voice sultry as she spoke just above a whisper. "Zounds makes me nuts. I go stir-crazy. There's nothing to stimulate me and I'm—" She cut herself off, breathed in slowly as if to regroup, and quit staring at his chest. She raised those big dark eyes to his. Zoey blinked, flashing thick black lashes that were more distracting than such a small body part should be. "I'm trying to say that this isn't how I usually behave."

"Do you mean taking rides on motorcycles with men you don't know?"

"That's exactly what I mean," she said with a quiet laugh.

He got an odd impression that she didn't laugh enough. Ben knew from enough experience not to judge a person too soon.

"This was a bad move, stupid, incredibly dangerous, and I'm going to ask you in a minute to return me to my car. I'd appreciate it if you did just that and not keep me out longer."

"In a minute?"

"Yes," she said. "Since I've made this bad, stupid, incredibly dangerous move, once I go home I'd rather not berate myself over it all evening. I would prefer to go home and think about other things."

"What do you want to think about?"

"Kiss me," she said. It wasn't quite a sentence and not completely a question.

The two words hung between them only for a moment.

Ben pulled his wrist free from her grip, then wrapped his hand around her arm. He pulled her closer when he lowered his head and kissed her.

All thoughts against Zoey dissipated from Ben's brain. His curiosity about the town and the impression he'd received so far from everyone living there vanished. There simply was no room in his mind for anything else other than that kiss.

Ben let go of her arm and slid his hand behind her neck. Her skin was so soft. Her lips were full, wet, and a feast he could spend hours enjoying. As his fingers stretched around the slight curve at her nape, Zoey let her head fall back and opened for him.

God! She tasted of everything that was perfect in the world. This was nothing like kissing Stacy, who by now would have one of her long legs wrapped around him while her hands frantically tried to undress him. The thick blanket of lust enclosing his brain thinned to a veil, allowing him to see through it.

Zoey's hands weren't on him at all. Her head was tilted back. In fact, he supported it with his fingertips pressing against the base of her skull. Her mouth had opened for him without him pressing for her to do so. Her tongue had ventured into his mouth but now swirled around his in her own mouth. She had relaxed, almost gone limp, and her breathing was so calm he barely felt her lungs fill with air when he pressed his hand against her back. When he slowed the kiss down and simply moved his lips over hers, she remained relaxed. Zoey didn't straighten, touch him, try to end the kiss, or keep it going.

Had he ever had a one-sided kiss before? Ben was fairly certain he hadn't. Women had dumped him in every way humanly possible. But he was pretty sure he'd never been snubbed with the first kiss.

Ben moved his hand from Zoey's back and found her hand. It was damp, and for a moment he thought she trembled. He intertwined their fingers together and ended the kiss.

"You're amazing," he whispered, straightening and studying her face for her immediate reaction.

Zoey hummed instead of answering. Her eyes were still closed, her lips parted, and the prettiest shade of pink he'd ever seen was splashed across her cheeks. Ben stared down at her, speechless. He'd fought not to get hard kissing her, since already she'd taken a leap of faith in riding with him and she'd said as much to him. But now as he gazed down at the result of kissing her, there was no fighting it. Ben was hard as stone so fast it made him light-headed.

Maybe it hadn't been a one-sided kiss. Had he only been with aggressive women in the past?

"It was amazing," Zoey purred. There was no other way to describe how her words sounded.

Ben hadn't detected any type of accent in her voice when they first met. And he wasn't sure he could dub this a Hispanic accent now, but there was a thickness in her words. It was absolutely erotic. Even more blood drained to his cock.

Her long, thick black lashes fluttered as she opened her eyes. She stared up at him with her milk-chocolate orbs. As she licked her lips, he imagined her tasting their kiss and without giving it thought touched her full lips. They were the color of wine, he decided, and damn if they weren't as intoxicating.

But when she looked at him, more than his cock got hard. Never had a woman drawn forth such a primal desire inside him to hold her, caress her, and guide her through every step of earth-shattering sex. Zoey's expression almost looked grateful, as if he'd just given her some incredible gift and she wanted more.

She made no demands, offered no propositions. Zoey didn't say a word. Ben waited until she looked away to try to put his brain back in the proper gear before he proposed they find a better location to continue. Already he was picturing her naked. A small smile remained on her face, and color stayed in her cheeks. That made it even more challenging to draw the blood back into the head on his shoulders

and remind himself what he needed to be doing tonight—
and without Zoey.

"I'll take you back to your car before I kiss you again."
Ben didn't add that if he did, it definitely wouldn't stop with
just a kiss.

Chapter Six

Wolf was up at six. He could have slept longer. The bed in his room at the bed-and-breakfast was comfortable as hell. Nonetheless, he tossed the sheet and thick blanket back and walked barefoot over the oval carpet to the cool wooden floor at the edge of his room. Parting the curtains, he stared down at the small parking lot behind the large old Victorian-style house. Ben's motorcycle was there. It hadn't been at two in the morning when Wolf had woken up last.

After showering and dressing, Wolf left his room, taking care to close his door quietly. He'd heard someone enter one of the rooms around eleven the night before, which told him the walls were fairly thin. It hadn't been Ben, who'd rumbled out of the parking lot around seven the night before and still had been gone at two.

Wolf was dying to know what the man had been up to. Whatever it was, if Ben had been trying to find the assassin, he'd either had no luck, or decided not to cut Wolf in on his action.

Wolf didn't trust Ben. In spite of their truce and agreement to hunt the man together, a million bucks was a million bucks.

Ben had been out late. Wolf would let him sleep in. Fair was fair. Wolf would do his own sniffing around this morning.

"Good morning, Mr. Marley." Betsy Watson held up a

pot of coffee from the doorway at the other end of the spacious dining room. "Take it black?"

"I do, and thank you."

Betsy Watson reminded Wolf of Aunt Bee from *The Andy Griffith Show,* which he used to watch when he was a kid. She even sounded like her.

"Have a seat anywhere," she said, waving her plump hand in the air and holding the coffeepot with the other.

Wolf chose a seat by the front window. There were five round tables in the dining area, each covered with a checkered tablecloth. As he sat, Betsy paused next to him and up-righted the white cup from its saucer in front of him, then poured rich-smelling coffee into his cup.

"You're the early bird. Any plans today?" she asked.

"Figured I'd get a feel of the town and ask around to see who is hiring." He and Ben had decided their covers would be that they were searching for work, having been unlucky in previous towns. They agreed to tell anyone who asked that they'd been working their way up the coast in hopes of finding jobs.

It was a cover that wouldn't last for long, especially if anyone decided to try to prove their story true. They weren't planning on using their cover any more than necessary, because if Ben and Wolf snooped around properly, they would find the Mulligan Stew assassin. It was a believable cover, though. And since few places were hiring these days, people would shy away from them once they mentioned "unemployed" and job searching. It was the perfect way to get away from people they didn't need to waste their time with and allow time to focus on questioning people who might give them information they needed.

"I can get you started with a good homemade breakfast," Betsy promised.

Wolf didn't doubt for a moment that "good" would be an understatement. "Whatever I smell coming from your kitchen has got to run circles around 'good,' Ms. Watson."

The older woman laughed, and her thick fingers fluttered

over her ample bosom. "Now you call me Betsy. Everyone does. And you probably smell my cinnamon buns. They'll be out of the oven in just a few minutes. I'll bring one out to you as soon as they're ready."

"Sounds perfect." Wolf leaned back and enjoyed his coffee after Betsy hurried to her kitchen.

His window in his room offered a great view of the back of the house and parking lot. He knew how many people were at the bed-and-breakfast, give or take one or two if groups traveled in one car. There were two cars parked in the parking lot other than his car and Ben's bike. Now, seated where Wolf was, he had a nice view out the front of the old house.

Wolf took in the dining area. He'd always loved shiny hardwood floors, the kind that were so glossy they reminded him of gym floors from grade school. The thick door frames were natural wood as well. There was one modest-looking chandelier hanging in the middle of the ceiling. It had probably hung over a dining-room table that might have been in this room for years before the house was turned into a place of business.

He stood and walked to the large, clean glass window. The circular drive was thick with large white gravel, and the neat lawn around it was still green in spite of it being late in the year. There wasn't a car or person in sight. He wondered if that was normal. Since Betsy didn't strike him as the kind of woman who would stay calm and collected if something bad was happening, he decided it must be how this town was at this time of day. Wolf wasn't sure he could stand a town so quiet and serene. He preferred a bit more activity, chaos even, action as it were. Something for him to observe. Zounds was a bit too orderly for his tastes.

Leaving the window, he glanced at the doorway where Betsy had disappeared. Those cinnamon buns were making his stomach growl. When had he last had home cooking? Or, for that matter, eaten anything that hadn't been wrapped and handed to him through a drive-through window?

He walked over to a far table where a newspaper was.

"Damn," he muttered. It was actually four newspapers, all this morning's paper and each one embarrassingly thin. Zounds didn't have a lot to talk about. The paper was four pages thick. Definitely not enough action.

It was almost chilly out when he left not too much later. Wolf had enjoyed the best damn cinnamon roll he'd ever had in his life. The coffee rated right up there, too. Betsy had been willing to talk and had shared some information about her town, which she'd apparently lived in for the past forty years, since marrying her Herb, God rest his soul. Most businesses were family run, and with times being hard, most were struggling. She'd shared with Wolf how a man named Cortez was making the hard times even harder on those unfortunate enough not to own the buildings their businesses were in. Betsy had owned her home free and clear before her grandsons spent three months converting it into the bed-and-breakfast. Now, with Betsy having a loan to pay off to the bank, Cortez had made a few threats that she didn't like.

Wolf nodded to a man gardening just up the block. The man nodded back and paused, watching Wolf walk by with mild interest. He was new in town, in a small town that possibly didn't see a lot of newcomers. Keeping a low profile might be next to impossible to do. He'd worked under worse circumstances. Using his and Ben's guise as unemployed men searching hard for a paycheck might help keep them under the radar of the assassin—if he was here.

Wolf really hoped he was here. There was nothing more exciting than narrowing in on the hunt.

He turned at the end of the block and was taken aback by the sunrise. It was beautiful yet blinding. Just like a woman, he thought morosely, so beautiful you couldn't look away, but then when you didn't she'd make you regret it to your dying day. In this case, his eyes would suffer if he didn't get sunglasses. It sucked that he'd left his pair in his Escalade.

"Damn good excuse to enter some of these stores," he muttered, squinting as he approached downtown Zounds. Looked like he was going to buy a second pair of sunglasses and get an opportunity to chat with a few more of the town folk.

Maybe he'd find a cute salesclerk who might know who had moved to Zounds in the past year. Goddamn he was a glutton for punishment. No one burned Wolf Marley twice! Although, he mused to himself, there was a big difference between flirting or even enjoying a one-night stand or two and entering into a long-term relationship. He would never do that again.

Downtown Zounds was only a couple blocks long. What a ridiculous name for a town. Wolf wasn't sure he wanted to hear the story behind the naming of this town. After he passed a few shops his mood dropped. It appeared no one around here opened before eleven. Was there even a twenty-four-hour grocery store or drugstore in this damned town?

At the end of the two blocks of shops, the road ran a circle around a grassy garden courtyard with a large statue in the center of it. Wolf stared at the statue of a man, or sailor it appeared, with his hand above his eyes, as if warding off the sun, except he was facing the wrong direction. The man stared off toward the sea.

Wolf searched for a plaque, didn't see one, and decided he didn't care. He wasn't in Zounds to learn about its history or to care if some guy named Cortez was giving the town people grief. The only reason Wolf would care was if it would draw the Mulligan Stew assassin out of his hiding place. Even at that, Wolf almost preferred the assassin remained hidden.

"I'll find you," Wolf whispered to himself, and looked away from the statue.

Something caught his eye, and he started across the street, glancing both ways then shaking his head in disgust. There probably wasn't a running vehicle in a two-block radius, if not farther. What time did people get up and go to work around here?

Wolf tilted his head and looked alongside the edge of the building in front of him, down an alley. Not a dark alley. He doubted Zounds had any dark alleys. The town was too quaint, and so far its citizens appeared just as quaint, if not gullible. The last store on the street was next to the alley, the side of the building painted white. A field stretched out on the other side. It was probably the brightest alley he'd ever seen.

He glanced at the sign attached to the building over its front doors. ANGELINA'S BOOKSTORE. He saw rows of books through the tall glass windows on either side of the entrance. Books weren't exactly his thing. If he needed information he couldn't get by using his wit and keen observation, he looked online.

Wolf's thoughts shifted to the Cortez guy Betsy had mentioned. If Cortez was persecuting and bullying the town, people who lived here might be existing in denial because they didn't know how to stop him. They didn't leave their homes unless necessary. The stores were only open six, or so, hours a day, then shopkeepers hid from this Cortez monster. Wolf shook his head, pulling his attention from the bookstore back to the alley. What a sad way for people to live their lives.

A woman was in the alley doing something with boxes. If that was Angelina in the alley, stomping on boxes or doing some bizarre type of alley dance, she was one hot mama. With a body like that he hoped she was anything but an angel.

The woman looked up from her task when Wolf started in her direction. Brown curls framed a thin, long face. Her nose was just as long and narrow, but turned up just a bit at the end. That nose defied an otherwise regal, almost aloof natural expression. With the sun behind her he couldn't tell the color of her eyes. But he saw her gaze tighten and sensed her cautious nature when she straightened from her task and tugged at her T-shirt.

As he approached he saw it was a Redwood National Park T-shirt, and the picture of the trees on her shirt stretched over perfectly shaped full, round breasts. She was slender, not tall, with thin legs. Her skinny jeans showed off just how nice those legs probably were. In fact, the entire package would rate right up there as mouthwatering.

Wolf could interrogate anyone through the guise of light conversation, but taking a minute to chat with a beautiful woman made the job all that more enjoyable. As he neared the woman he saw dark blue eyes studying him. They were so dark blue they were almost lavender.

God, a man could lose himself in those eyes. She moistened her lips, and they parted, full, naturally red lips on a small, round mouth. A man would give up more than his heart to this woman; he would lose his soul, then thank her for taking it.

At least another man might. Not Wolf. Not ever again. Four years of happiness didn't compensate for the pain that had ripped out his heart. In one night, one hour, his world had been destroyed. Wolf had rushed home, because that was all the time he had to spare, just for a romantic weekend, only to be given the dump. He should have driven on to his next job. Although, as he'd been informed when he'd mentioned that during the heat of an argument, he would have received it all in a letter.

Four years ended in a fucking letter. The twit!

Rebecca had told him the hours he'd spent on the phone with her every night while out on a hunt, the flowers he would have had sent to her when he ended up being on the road longer than originally thought, or even boxes of Godiva chocolate, her favorite, he would special-order online and have delivered to her office weren't enough. Rebecca didn't want a ghost for a boyfriend. She'd dumped him five minutes after he'd arrived home on that treacherous night over a year ago, her suitcases in hand. The next day she'd sent movers to his home and damn near emptied it out, claiming all furniture they'd bought together during their time together. Since he'd hit the road again early that next morning, wanting to be anywhere but in his house with no Rebecca, he hadn't found out about the furniture until seeing the charge for the movers when he'd looked at his account online. She had used his credit card to clean his house out of all of the furniture bought with his money during the years they were together.

"Are you lost?" the woman in the alley asked, her tone

brittle with sarcasm. Those dark blue eyes were radiant from the sun light. And so large, almost catlike. She was short, but something about her suggested she had no problem with her height or taking on the world or anyone else who might challenge her alley.

"In this town? Hardly," Wolf retorted, and noticed an adorable spray of freckles over her nose. Spitfire, he decided, and thought fueling that fire might help bridge him into conversation. There was a lot to learn in a little bantering. "You, on the other hand, either seem confused on how to use a box or are taking out your anger on an inanimate object when you should just punch the asshole in the face."

The woman straightened, ran her hands down the sides of her T-shirt and jeans. She stared at him. For a long moment, she didn't smile, blush, or tell him to go to hell. Finally, she moved a tight little brown curl away from her forehead.

"I think I'll punch the asshole in the face." She still didn't smile. "You aren't by any chance a lawyer, are you?"

"No, I'm afraid not. Why? Need a divorce?"

When she shook her head, the curl plopped right back into the middle of her forehead. She didn't seem to notice. "No, but I'd love to know how many laws the asshole is breaking in doing this to me."

It was Wolf's turn to shake his head. "I'm not sure making a pretty lady dance on boxes in an alley is against the law," he said dryly. "Unless there is a city ordinance against it."

"I'm not dancing on them; I'm trying to crush them," she snapped. "But books are sent in really sturdy boxes and they aren't crushing easily."

Wolf walked up to her. "Now crushing I can do. It was that dance I was a bit leery of."

"By all means." She made a flourish with her hand and moved to the side, giving him room. "I just can't believe I'm now required to break down all boxes from my store before putting them in the city Dumpster, or risk a fine. And he wants an inspection, too."

"Trashmen can't be overworked, you know."

She made a humphing sound as if she might disagree.

Wolf would have to agree with her when she said the boxes were sturdy. It took a bit of muscle to collapse all of them. When they were in a flat stack at his feet, Wolf turned to find the woman leaning next to a door watching him.

She pointed to the Dumpster on the other side of the alley.

"You ask a lot of a stranger." Wolf lifted the stack of collapsed boxes and took them to the trash.

"A stranger in my town." Her tone was soft, alluring.

She was possibly five feet and two or three inches. Wolf would wager few people thought of her as short. This woman saw herself as larger than life. Her arms were crossed just under nice-looking breasts. She stood straight and tall, as tall as her small physique would allow, and stared at him head-on. He saw no fear, no hostility toward him, not even mild curiosity. What he did see as she continued watching was confidence, a comfortability in her world.

She was angry. She'd already admitted it. But not at him and she wasn't the type of woman to lash out at someone because she was angry with someone else. He saw that in her nature as well. This woman was too focused for any misdirected energy.

Wolf managed not to stare at the cleavage swelling from the top of her T-shirt. Instead he focused on a smear of dirt next to her cute, narrow nose. That was another character trait he guessed she possessed. There was no way to know for certain without putting it to the test, and he saw no reason to do that. But this woman wouldn't tolerate any man treating her as a sexual object. With this lady, it would be mind and body or nothing at all.

Wolf didn't consider himself an expert on noses. He was rather indifferent to the type of noses women had. Decent boobs, nice ass, and, if he was lucky enough to find out, a tight pussy, and the rest of her might impress upon him if he hung around long enough to find out. Or at least that was how he had been prior to making the mistake of being snared into a relationship. The lady staring at him definitely would go out of her way to show a lack of interest in a man like Wolf.

If she knew him. Which she wouldn't. It wouldn't be

difficult at all to initiate a conversation with this disgruntled
bookstore owner, which he'd concluded because an employee wouldn't be concerned about receiving a fine. Wolf
would sift through any information gained from her and, if
he was lucky, walk away with something that might indicate
whether the assassin was in Zounds or not.

"M'lady's task is complete," he said after tossing the collapsed boxes in the Dumpster. "Oh wait, did the collapsed
boxes need to be placed inside the Dumpster in any particular way?"

Her smile was genuine and made her eyes light up once
again. Wolf wasn't much into the poetic beauty of a woman.
She was hot, or she wasn't. This lady, however, held herself
in such a way she would be able to make a man beg to change
his ways simply to be blessed with her sincere and glowing
smile. Wolf instantly wondered what other attributes she
might have to make a man beg for more.

"Now if you'll excuse me, I'll be on my way before your
husband decides to squash me like I did those boxes."

"Oh my God! Did you really just say that?" Her laughter
was damn near contagious.

Even when it was very clear she was laughing at him.
Wolf feigned a look of uncertainty, willing to make her state
her accusation.

"Your husband doesn't squash strange men like boxes?"
he asked, keeping his expression somber.

"I have enough hot coffee to share if you collapse the rest
of the boxes for me." She was shaking her head at him as she
spoke. "Your question and your assumed accusation don't
merit a response on the grounds that they were a feeble attempt to gain information." She turned on him and headed
to the door that likely led into her shop. "Come on," she said
with a wave of her hand indicating he should follow.

"I've had some really good coffee this morning." He followed her through the open door and into the back room of
the bookstore. There were stacks of books everywhere and a
lot more boxes. He would be put to work before getting any
information out of this woman.

She closed the door to the alley. "I make really good coffee."

"Better than Betsy's over at the bed-and-breakfast?"

"Ouch," she moaned, then fisted her hands on her hips. "A gentleman never plays his best card this early in the morning."

"I'm not a gentleman."

Her blue eyes darkened until he swore a torrential storm was about to erupt inside her. She put the meaning he'd intended into his words, and it seemed to leave her breathless. For the first time, her assessment of him changed. It was barely noticeable, but Wolf was watching her every move. When she gave him a quick once-over, there was definitely a spark of interest.

"I have a cappuccino machine," she purred softly.

He had one back home and loved it. Already he was sold. "How many boxes?" he countered.

"All of these," she said, waving her hand at the stack between them. "I'll go make cappuccinos. And thank you so much." She reached out, touched his arm with cool fingers, then hurried out of the storage room, leaving the door to her store open after her.

Wolf peeked after her before taking on the boxes. The bookstore looked a lot larger from this angle than it had looked from the street. He turned his head in time to see her walking quickly toward the counter. Her jeans hugged a nicely shaped ass. He liked a nicely shaped ass on a woman. Something to hold on to when he entered from behind. Wolf didn't necessarily consider himself an ass man. The whole package had to turn him on. And damn, Miss Bookstore Owner, and he was pretty sure that was who she was, had a mighty fine package.

He respected a woman's mind, too. Intelligence had its appeal because then gaining her submission was just about as hot as it could get. Something told him this little lady had quite a bit of intelligence. He wouldn't need her submission, just her compliance in telling him all she knew about who lived in Zounds. It seemed to him he was off to a good start.

Already she'd allowed him into her store and was making cappuccinos for them. Turning, he began whistling as he stacked the boxes and hauled them to the alley.

Angel was shaking as she started the machine, then stared at it as it began making the cappuccinos. She would be too wired to think straight if she had a cup after the coffee she'd already downed this morning. Either that or she'd burn out by noon and have a hell of a time keeping the store open during the afternoon. It would serve Cortez right if she closed the store early today. Just thinking about that damned letter Zoey had brought in yesterday got her pissed off all over again. She didn't want to think about Cortez, his informing her that all trash had to be properly broken down so it wouldn't fill the Dumpster too quickly, or that an inspector would be stopping by sometime later that day to inspect her store.

Inspect, her ass! Cortez was sending over one of his spies to learn whatever it was he wanted to know about her or her store and was too much of a coward to come out and ask. Not that her store was any of Cortez's goddamn business. The asshole made her so fuming mad!

The man in her storage room was whistling. He pulled her out of her hateful thoughts, and she glanced over her shoulder. Angel was tempted to go back outside just so she could watch his arms bulge as he broke down the boxes and flattened them. He had stomped on a couple of them, and leg muscles had stretched and flexed pressing against his jeans. She imagined he was strong enough to lift her over his shoulder and toss her body onto her bed.

"Oh crap," she breathed, and gripped her counter to steady herself.

She was certifiably insane. Not only had she never seen this man before in her life, she also didn't know his name or anything else about him. Well, she knew he was staying at the bed-and-breakfast and that Betsy Watson made an incredible cup of coffee. And she was pretty sure he was the same man she'd seen in the Escalade the day before. She wondered why he'd been walking today. Maybe it wasn't his

SUV. Maybe he was some worker brought in on a crew for construction and had been driving a boss's car.

Angel could always call Betsy. The old woman loved to talk, and gossip about someone new in town would be right up her alley.

Angel could hear it now. *Hello, Betsy. . . . What? . . . Oh no, I don't have any more Agatha Christies in. I'm pretty sure you've read all of them. . . . And no, I don't think they are releasing anymore anytime soon. But I was wondering. That incredibly sexy hunk staying at your place. . . . That's right. The one with so many muscles bulging it's a damn distraction. Well, yes, could you give me his name, please? I just want to know what to cry out when I fuck him senseless.*

Oh yeah. That would go over real well. Poor Betsy Watson would finally join her husband, Herb, in heaven. God rest both their souls. Angel was definitely insane.

She tried focusing on her task of making cappuccinos as she stared at the rich-smelling brew filling the two cups. The machine had been a gift from Zoey last Christmas. Angel, Zoey, and Maggie had met at Angel's store on Christmas Eve, trudged through the snow to the Catholic church in town, then back to her store to exchange presents. Maggie and Zoey were both Catholic. Angel had no preference or any religion at all. But she'd had fun watching the children perform the birth of baby Jesus during Christmas Eve mass. Then the women had walked in the cold back to Angel's store. The three of them had talked during the entire walk and barely noticed the cold. When they'd snuggled together in a small circle, all of them sitting cross-legged on the floor with Angel's space heater glowing brightly next to them, they had exchanged gifts. Angel had been shocked over the cappuccino maker. Zoey had cheated. They had all agreed not to spend over twenty dollars a gift and give no more than two gifts to each of them. Zoey had insisted she hadn't gone over the price limit but had purchased wholesale through one of her father's vendors. She'd given Maggie a five-piece set of china and matching pots and pans, which Angel knew Maggie needed since she'd complained numerous times about her and her husband eating off of paper plates. When Maggie made the same accusations, Zoey had shrugged, blushed, and murmured there was no harm in taking advantage of what her father had. Angel and Maggie had both shut up. If Zoey had ripped her father off to give her and Maggie such nice gifts, Angel really didn't have a problem with that.

Angel carried two cappuccinos around the corner a minute later, careful not to spill the foam. She entered her back storage room, which was in desperate need of some serious organization, and didn't see the stranger. All of the empty boxes were gone. Then pushing the door to the alley open with her foot, she squinted against the bright morning sunlight and glanced up and down the alley. He was nowhere in sight.

"What the—," she started to complain. "If he didn't want cappuccinos, he should have said so," she muttered.

Maybe he'd walked back to the bed-and-breakfast. The guy didn't strike Angel as the kind of man too shy to accept gratitude after finishing a job. She looked up and down the alley, her immediate anger shifting into dismay. At least the gorgeous hunk of a man wasn't after handouts, if he'd left so fast. Holding the two cups in her hands, Angel started feeling foolish. She headed toward the door to her back storage room. He hadn't been dressed like a bum, she mused. If anything, his jeans had appeared new and his T-shirt—the one that stretched so nicely over all of that brawn—looked clean and pressed.

She wished she had been more attentive to details. Hadn't she read enough novels to know the telltale items to look for to learn something about a person? Were there calluses on his hands, indicating he'd worked with his hands a lot? Was there a suntan line at the ends of the short sleeves of his T-shirt or at the back of his neck, indicating he might work outside for a living? Angel hadn't bothered to check.

"I was looking—"

"Oh my God!" she wailed, and almost tripped in the doorway to her shop.

The stranger appeared out of the shadows alongside the end of her building. Had he been there the entire time?

"I was looking at the wiring back here," the man informed her, his baritone relaxed and serious. "The light doesn't come on in your storage room. I found lightbulbs," he added, picking up the four-pack of 75-watt bulbs she'd had back there on one of the shelves forever. "And I tried putting a new bulb in for you."

"Just because I don't care to smash down boxes with reinforced siding doesn't mean I haven't already tried putting in a new bulb. The light doesn't work in my storage room, and it's not because it needs a new bulb," she said, immediately defensive.

The man turned into the dark shadows behind her door to the alley. "Your problem is back here."

"Please, take this." Angel held out his cup of cappuccino and did her best not to bite her lip from her burned hand where some of it had spilled when he'd startled her.

"Thank you," the man told her, appearing once again from the shadows.

Angel would definitely have a blister from the amount of pain she was experiencing. The man took his cup, and she left him, not caring about the light at the moment. It was one of many things that didn't work properly in her shop. She got by.

Angel hurried inside to the small half bath in the corner of the storage room. She cranked on the cold water and stuffed her hand into the flow.

"Damn," she muttered, staring at the small red spot on the back of her hand as cold water rushed over it. This was all she needed today.

"If you have wire cutters, I could probably splice and fix it." The man filled the doorway of the small bathroom; then suddenly he was next to her. "You burned yourself."

Angel gave him a look. "You're quick."

He returned the same look, which darkened his features. "Actually, I am," he said in a low growl.

Staring at him turned her insides into electrified need.

She looked away and watched water run over the red spot on her hand. No man would control her, not even sexually. There was a raw, rather primal nature about him. That wasn't her style of man. She wouldn't ever be some Neanderthal's little woman. Angel ran her own life, made her own decisions, and had no plans of ever submitting to anyone. Which, of course, was why Cortez made her so damned mad. And proof as to why she was the wrong type of lady for a guy who thought he could turn her into putty in his hands with a look and a low-baritone, rough edge to his voice.

That look on her sexy stranger's face definitely did something to her insides. Ignore it, she ordered herself, getting grouchy from the pain in her hand and uncontrollable reaction to this man. She started when he put his hand on her wrist.

"What?" she demanded, suddenly pissed.

Why was he standing so close? Why didn't she get a grip and take control of this situation, give him an order, remind him this was her shop and she was the boss?

He slipped her mug from her hand and set it on the edge of her sink.

"Let me see," he whispered. "This is my fault. I scared you outside and should have realized I'd do so. I get a bit too focused when I'm working on something."

"You startled me," Angelina insisted. "You didn't scare me."

The stranger lifted her hand in his. When he brought her hand to his lips and kissed her right next to skin that would soon blister, Angel shot her gaze to his.

"My fault again. You don't strike me as the kind of woman who scares easy."

Where was the rough-and-ready, dark seducer who had entered her bathroom just a moment ago? Although just as sexy, this side of the stranger, suddenly polite and considerate, was doing the same wicked number to her insides. She caught herself staring into his eyes a moment longer than she should and looked down, sliding her hand from his.

"You're right. Nor am I an idiot," she added for good measure just in case he was up to something. Which of course he probably was. Gorgeous men didn't just appear out of nowhere, ready to do her grunt work, without a reason.

"What's your name?" His breath scorched her not-already-burnt flesh.

She studied his face, wishing she knew what deception looked like. "Angel."

"Are you the Angelina whose name is on the bookstore?"

"Everyone calls me Angel."

"Are you one?"

She smiled in spite of herself. "No."

"Me, neither. My name is Wolf. And now is when you should be scared."

"Wolf?" But she didn't have time to question him about his name.

He placed his cappuccino next to hers. Those muscular arms she'd been drooling over wrapped around her. That powerful chest packed hard as steel pressed up against her body. Wolf tilted his head as he lowered it, his dark green eyes attentive until his face blurred before her.

Did he think she would balk? Was he intentionally cornering her in the confines of the bathroom to try to scare her? Or was he the kind of man who liked forcing his women to submit?

Regardless of what type of man he was, Angel had every intention of showing him what kind of woman she was. And she was definitely the type of woman who wanted her man to be a certain way.

It was amazing how well their bodies molded together. She wasn't a tall woman, and when she'd gone out with men six feet or taller it had been awkward, if not uncomfortable, kissing each other. Wolf was the perfect height.

Angel leaned her head back, opening for him, and the kiss turned from enticing to savage in seconds. She ran her hands against warm skin stretched taut over tight muscle. Her dry hand slid over smooth flesh, and her wet hand sizzled as heat between them dried it instantly.

Her hands pressed against his solid body, pushing into

his shoulders. Angel pressed her body flat against his, and instantly her nipples were hard, aching, and she was torturously aware of the swelling in her breasts. He was turning her body into a throbbing mess. Angel needed to know she was putting him in the same miserable state of unbearable need.

He slipped his hands under her shirt and up her bare back and pressed her closer against him. There wasn't enough air in the bathroom, and she grew light-headed.

"How far are we taking this?" Wolf asked, moving his lips over hers.

"If you have to ask, then you probably aren't the right kind of guy for me," she answered, not bothering to open her eyes.

His response was a growl that set her insides on fire. It was too much. The pressure inside her was damn near so intense she would come right here in the storage room bathroom. No way would he control her body like that. She didn't know this man. He knew nothing about her. And if he did know her, he would understand that she called the shots, in every aspect of her life.

Angel pressed her hands against his chest and pushed, then pushed harder when he only grunted. Wolf lifted her against his body until her feet dangled between his legs as he stepped backward into her storage room.

"The door," she murmured, pointing out that it was still open.

Wolf lowered her, and the ride as her body slid down his damn near turned her legs into wet noodles.

"In a few I'll fix this light for you."

"Good thing." Angel grabbed him by the shirt when he finished locking her door and dragged him into the store.

Thankfully there weren't any fine citizens of Zounds outside her store on the street when she continued dragging Wolf along the far wall to the door that opened to a flight of stairs. If she was going to have sex with a complete stranger, it wouldn't be among boxes or in a small bathroom. She would have him in her bed.

By the time she reached the top of the stairs, Angel was so turned on she turned around and wrapped her arms around Wolf's neck while he was still on the top stair.

She was eye level to him and searched his face for a moment before narrowing her eyes. "You don't have a wife or girlfriend stashed away anywhere, do you?"

"I was about to ask the same of you." He looked away first and stared around them. The flight of stairs opened into the middle of her living room. "Quaint," he mumbled.

"Quaint?" she snarled. "Mister, I promise you nothing about me is *quaint*." She spit out the word as if it were something terrible, and it was to her. Her old aunt Harriet was quaint. Nana Matisse had been quaint. A word Angel's father had used when trying to find a nice way to describe the old, unmarried women in their family. She would never be quaint. "And I promise I have no wives or girlfriends stashed away anywhere."

Wolf snapped his attention back to her, and his dark green eyes smoldered. His hair was the same color as hers but fell in soft waves that were so damn sexy she ached to tangle her fingers in them. Angel wondered what he'd do if she grabbed his hair and pulled. He might go by "Wolf," but something told her he would be more like a bear. She grew even more soaked thinking about it.

"I have no wives or girlfriends stashed away, either," he growled, and grabbed her around her ribs.

Wolf lifted her in the air and took the last step into her home. The staircase opened into the middle of the living room with half a wall built around it so there wouldn't be a gaping hole in the middle of the room. That addition had been made when Angel was a toddler and she and her parents had lived above the store. Otherwise, very little had changed in the home she grew up in, other than her parents were no longer here.

Some might call her short, but she wasn't skinny. Wolf lifted her as if she were a child, holding her before him as he walked at will into her home. A small voice issued a tight warning that this man was not only a complete stranger but also an incredibly strong and capable man. It was all of those attributes that made him so appealing. But even in her fog of lust, she saw it made him equally as dangerous.

Without waiting for his next move, she reached up and grabbed both sides of his face. She held him as he continued walking and kissed him. To hell with all the precautions. Angel was thirty-one years old, a business owner, and successful in her small town. Her life might not be perfect, but she was in charge of her own actions. And at the moment, rough sex with this stranger sounded so good she could barely wait to have him buried deep inside her.

She deserved this. With Cortez trying to suck the life out of her when otherwise she might be making a decent profit off her store, life could be better. A diversion like this was exactly what she needed.

Wolf turned his head to the side, leaving her breathless.

"Bedroom." His voice was rough, tormented.

"Couch," she managed, and struggled to be free.

"You sleep on your couch?"

When he lowered her to the floor, she felt how hard his cock was in his jeans. She daringly pressed her palm against the swell in his pants. A rumble rose from his throat, and his expression bordered on dangerous. Angel's heart raced as she stared up at him. Her palm turned damp, but she didn't move her hand. Had she taken on more than she dared with this man? With this stranger?

"No. But it's closer," she said bravely. He wouldn't see her as anything other than wanting this without any hesitation. And she did. More than her next breath. She looped her fingers inside the top of his jeans and tried pulling him forward.

"Why me?" Wolf didn't budge. He raised his hand lazily and dragged his finger around the swell of her breast, then tapped her hard nipple through her shirt. "Do you make a habit of dragging strange men up to your lair, Miss Angelina?" he asked darkly.

Her breath caught in her throat as she lost herself in his smoldering gaze. She didn't remember when anyone had last used her given name. Angel might not be the best name in the world, but it was a lot better than Angelina. For some reason, the way he let her given name roll off his tongue with a seductive growl fueled her fire.

She should consider it a good quality in him that he wanted to know more about her before fucking her. She would die if he was backing out and changing the direction they were headed.

"You're the first," she admitted.

He continued running his finger over her breast as he studied her with eyes so dark the core of danger might have lain deep within them. "Then again, why me?"

"I don't want to talk," she decided. "Ask what you want after. You want this as much as I do. We're single consenting adults. So shut up and fuck me, or leave."

Wolf studied her for a moment. He let his head tilt to the side. It was an action he appeared to do so absently it almost seemed he grew tired of holding his head upright and it simply fell off balance without him realizing.

Angel barely had time to register the determined look that crossed over his face before he grabbed her and flipped her around. His hands were on her, forcing her to bend over. She reached in front of her, desperately trying to grab ahold of anything in order to maintain her balance. Her palms slapped against her coffee table at the same time that her knees gave out.

His knuckles pressed into her flesh, and he found her button and zipper on her jeans, undid them, and forced her jeans down her legs. They tangled at her ankles as leaned into her, his thick, muscular body covering hers. She was suddenly kneeling on her coffee table, and her hands were forced forward. Angel clung to the edge of her couch. Then his fingers were inside her. His body was over hers, preventing her movement. All she could do was hold on.

It was all she could do not to fall between her coffee table and couch. At the same time, sensations tore through her that she'd craved for too long.

"Is this what you want?" he whispered over her, and shoved his fingers deep inside her.

"It's what we both want."

"How would you know what I want?" There was a sneer in his voice she didn't like.

Angel tried twisting but he held her captive. His hold on her waist was relentless. His fingers twisted inside her, and his knuckles brushed over the sensitive folds at the edge of her entrance. When fingers brushed over her clit, she cried out and managed to push both of them backward.

There wasn't time to step out of her jeans. He held on to her so her back pressed against his steel chest. Her mind was too clouded with need to worry about their positioning. Maybe she should have agreed to the bed. Wolf had her in a hold so submissive, leaving her with absolutely no control or ability to touch him. Maybe her brain was such complete mush at the moment she didn't mind him running the show, but it would be nice to have made that decision on her own.

It was by sheer willpower, even as he continued tormenting her and leading her to the edge of her climax, that she managed to speak.

"If you didn't want this, too, you would have left," she hissed through clenched teeth.

Wolf chuckled over her. He thrust one more time, this one fierce, driving, thrusting deep inside, and her world toppled.

Angel exploded. Her orgasm tore through her igniting shades of lavender and mahogany that faded into each other before finally everything threatened to go all black. Not once had she passed out from an orgasm, nor had she ever soaked herself or anyone else to the extent she did now. She was flying, the eruptions continuing inside her. It took a minute, maybe more, to register that he was still fucking her deep and hard with his fingers.

Then she was floating backward. Strong, capable hands lifted her. Her jeans slipped free from her ankles. Without asking or confirming she wanted to take things further at this point, Wolf cradled her in his arms, nestling her close to the strong beat of his heart, and walked into her bedroom as if he'd known where it was all along.

Angel's heart pounded with a lot more velocity than Wolf's. When she stretched out on her bed, her orgasm ebbing but her body extremely sensitive and ready for the next round, she thought it was time to sit up and take control of the next round. She would in a minute. Lying in the middle of her bed was so damn comfortable.

Someone pounded on her door downstairs, and Angel flew to a sitting position.

Years of working the family business allowed her to clear her head instantly. She'd been interrupted from almost everything imaginable to take care of the shop, although stopping in the middle of what would have been for sure mind-blowing sex was a first.

"What the hell?" she whispered, glancing at the clock next to her bed.

Wolf appeared equally alert. Angel saw the protector in him come through strong as his entire body tensed. "Are you expecting someone?" he asked.

She scooted to the end of the bed. Wolf didn't try to stop her.

"Of course not. The store doesn't open for another two hours."

"Delivery perhaps?"

She shook her head. "Nothing before the store opens. It's always been that way."

"Didn't you mention an inspection?"

Angel turned and looked at Wolf. The dark clouds of dominating lust were gone. His clear dark green eyes were focused on her bedroom door. She imagined him capable of springing forth and removing any threat that might exist around her without breaking a sweat.

Whoever it was knocked again, this time hard enough Angel heard glass rattling as they hit it with their fist.

"Good God," she groaned, sliding off the end of her bed and returning to the living room.

She knew when she bent over to grab her jeans she gave Wolf one hell of a view. For some reason she liked the idea of keeping him tormented. It served him right after the way he controlled her body and kept her pinned over her coffee table and couch. He'd made her come so hard she was still weak from it. She stepped into her jeans, pulled them up, and fastened them. Then turning to face him, she tugged on her T-shirt.

"Rain check?" she asked.

Wolf's hand shot out when she turned to the stairs. "Maybe you should put something else on before going downstairs."

The pounding sounded again. "Angelina Matisse, unlock these doors," a male voice ordered from outside her store.

Angel glared at the stairs leading down to her bookstore. Wolf had guessed accurately. She didn't doubt it for a moment. It was whoever Cortez had sent to do the inspection. Her anger rose faster than her orgasm had hit her. How dare that man assume he would be granted entrance when the store wasn't even open. His bullying tone pissed her off to the point she clenched her fists at her sides.

"I'll be damned if I'm putting on something nice for that motherfucker's henchman," she snarled.

Wolf's touch was unexpectedly gentle. "Don't dress up," he said calmly. "But don't give the slime bag an eyeful, either. He definitely doesn't deserve it."

She stared at Wolf. Angel couldn't decide if he was being protective or simply kind. If he was trying to lay some claim on her, he would be seriously disappointed. She wasn't single because she couldn't find a man, far from it. Or maybe he was being logical. Wolf saw how much she hated Cortez. Maybe Betsy had complained about him, too. God knows if a guest was willing to linger at the bed-and-breakfast long enough, they would learn all there was about Zounds that was worth complaining about.

"Fine," Angel decided, and marched past Wolf back into her bedroom.

She pulled off the clothes she'd put on this morning before heading down to clean out and organize her storage room. Now, other than a light, it was cleaner than she probably could have found time to make it herself. Although she doubted this inspection would have anything to do with how clean her store was.

Angel tossed her T-shirt and jeans, which now she noticed were a bit smeared with dirt from the work she'd done before Wolf had shown up, into her clothes basket and walked naked across her bedroom. Wolf had moved and lingered in her doorway, watching her. Angel didn't look at him. The man outside on the sidewalk yelled for her again to unlock her store and let him in. Angel decided on a thong and matching lace bra. She then donned a pair of her comfortable jeans and a sleeveless V-neck sweater. Then facing Wolf, she marched toward him, and he moved to let her out. She wasn't sure whether she was grateful that he didn't touch her or not.

Angel's knees were weak when she reached the bottom of the stairs and realized it was Brutus. She'd been pissed when she had thought Cortez would send one of his bulldogs to do an inspection. He hadn't sent his bulldogs. Brutus was Cortez's pit bull. If she made him wait much longer, Brutus would rip off the front door to her store. He was pure-bred asshole.

She rushed to the front of the store and around the counter. Then, grabbing the keys to the store, she raced back around the counter to the front door. She was vaguely aware of Wolf, standing quietly in the middle of the store with his arms crossed against his muscular chest.

"Don't you ever make me wait that long again before letting me in," Brutus snarled as he stormed into her store. "Do you understand me, Miss Matisse?"

"I was upstairs," she began, fighting her rage.

Brutus curled his lip as he glared at Wolf. The man's bald head glowed red with anger when he gave Wolf a disapproving snarl.

"Who the fuck is this?" Brutus glowered at Wolf, but the question was addressed to Angel.

She opened her mouth to answer.

"Who are you?" Wolf asked, his voice so relaxed it was insulting.

Brutus ignored the question and turned on Angelina. "Tell him to leave."

"I'm staying," Wolf told him.

Brutus spun around. "You aren't from around here, are you?"

"Even if I were, your method of intimidation wouldn't work on me."

Angel stared at the two men. Brutus was all muscle and, yes, the master of intimidation. She understood he wasn't the backbone of the threat, though. Cortez was the only man who could seriously make her life hell. Wolf, on the other hand, didn't know anything about her history with the monster who had laid prey to Zounds ten years ago. Within a year of living here, Cortez had bought almost every commercial building in the town. He practically owned the entire community, and his demands had grown more and more unreasonable with every passing year.

"I received the letter informing me there would be an inspection." Angel gave Wolf a hard look when Brutus slowly turned his twisted expression in her direction. "Exactly what is it that you want to inspect?"

"Everything," Brutus snapped. "The boss needs to know each business under contract with him is withstanding. If not, we'll put in a business that will be."

Angel put her hands on her hips and stared Brutus down. She gathered her inner strength that she possessed regardless of Wolf standing just behind Brutus.

"I am not under contract with Mr. Cortez. I'd appreciate you reminding him of that for me."

"Yes, you are," Brutus snarled. He started toward the counter. "I need to see all receipts for the past week, or the past month, which would be better. Where are they?"

When Angel remained planted where she was and didn't move, Brutus shoved her out of the way and continued to the counter. She stumbled into the bookshelf nearest the counter. She and all of her self-help books damn near tumbled to the ground.

Wolf grabbed her by the arm, steadying her, but then let her go and moved with silent ferocity after Brutus.

"Stay away from my register," Angel ordered, outraged that this prick had just shoved her.

She was grateful that Wolf prevented her from falling along with a bunch of books and possibly hurting herself and damaging merchandise. But this was her store. She was in charge here. Except one man was bullying her and another man was dominating her.

"If your bookstore isn't making the cut, Miss Matisse," Brutus warned, "when your lease is up another store will move in here."

"Like hell!" Angel rushed around Wolf to Brutus. "You have no right to do this. It's illegal. I pay my rent every month on time and have as long as this bookstore has been here. How much the store makes is none of your goddamn business. Leave, Brutus. This inspection is over."

Brutus turned his beady glare on her. His gray eyes had always reminded her of a dead soul. She instinctively took a step backward when Brutus stalked toward her.

"The boss is aware of your continual insubordination," he hissed between clenched teeth. "Refusing this inspection will be the death of your precious bookstore." He pointed behind him. "Where is the key to that register?"

"There isn't any money in it," she informed him, straightening to her full height.

Brutus could crush her with half his weight. Angel would never let him see her fear, though. The prick was a bully and a criminal. Somehow she'd figure out a way to shut Cortez down, if it was the last thing she ever did.

"Open the register."

"What kind of inspection is this?" Wolf demanded, his tone still so relaxed it sounded odd considering the amount of tension already built in the air since Brutus entered.

"You'd be smart to do as you're told," Brutus warned, lowering his voice and his head as he stared hard at Angel. "People who challenge Mr. Cortez don't stay in business very long. If you aren't making enough money, you have until your lease ends to vacate the premises. If you don't do as I ask, you'll be out of here by the end of the week."

"I stay in business because I run an honest, legal store," Angel said. She prayed neither man noticed her trembling and at the same time was grateful her parents never had to endure this Mafia madman who'd seized Zounds and was slowly squeezing the life out of it. "Those who don't run a straight-up business are the ones who won't last long."

Angel saw Brutus charge, but she wasn't out of his way in time. He grabbed her arm, pinching her skin with his fingers as he held it up between them, and tried giving her a firm shake.

"Are you threatening Emilio Cortez?" Brutus roared.

Angel went limp in Brutus's hold when she stared at the gun Wolf held pointed at Brutus's head. Where the hell had that come from? She barely managed to not start panicking and wouldn't dwell on where Wolf had the gun stashed when he'd been pressed up against her.

"Let go of her and leave," he said in that eerie calm tone of his. "And if you ever step back in this store again, you or your boss, you'll regret that you did."

Chapter Seven

Betsy had told Ben that Wolf had his breakfast almost two hours earlier, then had left for a nice walk. Ben hadn't wanted to talk to Wolf but had knocked on his door. When there was no answer, Ben accepted that the man wasn't there. His Escalade was parked in the parking lot behind the bed-and-breakfast. Wolf didn't seem like the walking type, but maybe the bed-and-breakfast owner had been right and the guy did go walking around the town.

Ben didn't have any desire to walk around town searching for him. He would make other plans for the day.

After dropping Zoey at her car the night before, then following her on his bike to a beautiful old Victorian home, he'd driven around for several hours searching for any sign of Micah. He'd found none.

Initially, picking up Zoey had been the perfect ruse to leave the bed-and-breakfast without suspicion. Ben didn't want Wolf suspecting him of doing anything other than what they'd decided together that they would do. If Wolf thought Ben was driving through Zounds searching for something, he would quickly jump to the conclusion that Ben knew where Micah was. Right now, Ben had Wolf convinced he was after the bounty on Micah's head just as Wolf was.

Ben walked across the parking lot, aware of how much colder it was than it had been the night before. His blood wasn't used to the chill in the air, and he wondered if the light leather jacket he wore would be enough on his bike. He reached his Harley and straddled it, then stared at his side mirror. Leaning closer, he squinted and read the message that looked as if it had been written in lipstick.

> *Redwood National Park at noon. 1.4 miles after main entrance, turn right, go one-half a mile, turn left, and park at the third tree.*

His heart skipped a beat, then began pattering against his chest. Ben patted himself down, searching for something to write with, and finally gave up and put the message to memory. He used his palm to smear the message off his side mirror and gunned his Harley to life.

It was a hell of a lot colder in the mornings in Zounds than it was in L.A. He sat on the bike for a moment, letting it warm up. If he'd learned anything from Greg King while working for him, it was to never race into a situation without analyzing every angle of it.

The first angle Ben explored and accepted was that he would freeze his balls off riding on his Harley without a heavier coat. Turning the bike off, he recited in his head the directions that he'd just smeared off his rearview mirror as he hurried back into the bed-and-breakfast.

"Sorry," he apologized to a startled Betsy when he bounded up the stairs to the second floor.

"You're in a hurry." She laughed after regaining her wits about her.

"I forgot my heavier coat!" he called over his shoulder.

Back on his bike, he was a lot warmer with his heavy leather jacket. He'd also taken time to jot down the directions he'd been given. He needed to buy a GPS to have on his bike. Ben had made it so far getting around without one, but then he'd never driven in unfamiliar territory.

The directions didn't tell him how to get out of Zounds or which highway to take to get to Redwood National Park. He knew the redwoods were north of Zounds only because he and Wolf hadn't run into them on their drive up here from L.A. So Ben would head north. He left the bed-and-breakfast and kept to the twenty-mile-an-hour speed limit until he reached one of the main roads of Zounds.

Then turning north, he found himself heading into the small downtown area. He didn't care if it was a guy thing, Ben wasn't much into asking for directions. It wasn't that he was opposed to someone explaining how he should get somewhere. But too often another person might give bad directions or worse yet, wrong directions.

Pulling his cell phone from his inner coat pocket, he glanced at the time. It was ten. He would stop somewhere and grab an atlas. Then he could confirm where he was going. It didn't bother him arriving early. Ben preferred casing out the area, especially for a meeting like this. Micah was in deep hiding, but it was imperative Ben speak with him.

That is, if the message was from Micah; lipstick on a rearview mirror didn't quite seem his style. Although his new wife, Maggie, might have left the message.

Ben pulled into the first place that would carry atlases, which happened to be a small grocery store. The parking lot was a fraction of the size of his grocery stores back home. Ben hadn't decided how he felt about such a small town. Having grown up in the L.A. area he only knew the big-city life. He watched two women pass each other at the one set of automatic doors leading into the store. They stopped to talk to each other, ignoring the few people who came and went around them.

Ben parked his bike in the first available stall and started toward the store. A woman left the store with a paper bag of groceries in her arms. She moved around the two women as Ben walked up to the store. When the woman with the groceries in her hands looked up and met Ben's gaze, she froze.

"Maggie," Ben said, although not loud enough for anyone to hear him.

As quickly as she froze, Maggie sprung to life and hurried away from Ben with her head down.

"Maggie," Ben said louder.

When he realized the two women talking had looked his way, Ben diverted his attention from them by looking down and taking long strides across the parking lot. Maggie neared the corner of the grocery store, dropped her bag of groceries, and took off running.

"Damn it!" Ben broke into a sprint after her. "Maggie!" he shouted once he was around the building.

Instead of a neighborhood, there was a hill leading down to a two-lane road behind the store. Ben damn near slid down the hill toward the road. There was no way Maggie could have escaped him that easily. Ben looked both ways when he reached the road.

"Goddamn it, why are you running?" he grumbled under his breath when he didn't see her.

Then he spotted her ahead of him, on the other side of the road, working her way down another hill, this one covered with large rocks. The ocean was beyond that.

Ben hauled ass, jumping over rocks and clearing the distance between them.

"What the fuck, Maggie?" he shouted. "Do you really want me yelling where everyone can hear me? Why are you running from me?"

He leapt over three large rocks, hitting each one with his boots before going to the next one. Halfway down the rugged hill, Ben paused, caught his breath, and gulped in the fresh morning sea air. Whether it be big city or small town, Ben never grew tired of staring at the ocean. Something about its picturesque magnificence always seemed to calm him. At the moment, he only had time for a glance, but the ocean did its magic. Somewhere deep inside, he felt a sense of regrouping, of suddenly being grounded at the core of his soul.

Ben had just gained a valuable piece of information. Micah was still in Zounds. If he worked this right, he'd learn where he was.

"Fine, Maggie!" he shouted. "If this is how you want it, fine. I don't understand why you would run from me. But if suddenly I'm the bad guy, then what the fuck ever. I'll just stand here and shout because I know you can hear me. I have a message, and if you want me screaming it over the waves on the beach, well, I guess I can do that."

He waited, watching, then once again spotted her.

Maggie slowly stood. She was actually just a few large rocks away from him. She'd found one large enough to squat behind, and truth be told, if he'd kept running he would have gone right past her.

"Goddamn, woman," he snarled, willing to complain for a minute. "Why the fuck did you run?"

"Why did you chase after me?" Her expression was pinched, possibly because she was squinting into the sun facing him.

He shook his head. "Because you ran from me," he pointed out.

A lump of fear sunk in Ben's gut when Maggie raised a gun and pointed it straight at him. He hadn't noticed it in her hand when she'd stood. She pointed it straight at his head, holding it with both hands.

"It's cool, Maggie," he cried out, stretching his arms out on either side of him. He really hated having a gun pointed at him.

Goddamn if she didn't have the advantage. Maggie was surrounded by rocks large enough they might be boulders. He honestly didn't know the difference other than size and didn't care at the moment. All of his attention was riveted on the small gun, what most would call a lady's gun, aimed to kill.

"Why are you here?" she demanded.

"Because you ran!" he yelled at her hard enough he felt the veins pop out in his forehead.

Waves crashed against the rocky beach below, and it dawned on him if she fired that gun there was a good chance no one would hear it.

"Why are you here in Zounds?" she asked again, this time through gritted teeth.

Ben wasn't too comfortable looking around him, not with that damn gun pointed at him. Once again all the training

Greg King had given him over the past couple years kicked in. He couldn't yell at her that he needed to see Micah.

"I'm up here with a friend," he answered, speaking softer this time.

"A friend," she repeated. "I see."

When she gestured with the gun, Ben could see how she was shaking. He didn't know Maggie that well. Micah was incredibly private about his life, current and past. But Ben guessed she wasn't overly used to firing a gun. Micah probably gave her lessons out of necessity. But firing at a bull's-eye, or whatever item was created for target practice, wasn't the same as shooting a person.

"Take your shoes off," she told him.

"What?" he asked, surprised.

She straightened her arms and braced herself. "Take your damn shoes off!" she yelled.

"Christ, Maggie," he complained, confused as hell. The last thing he'd expected when he'd rode up here with Wolf was to not receive a warm welcome.

"Do it," she insisted.

"Fine!" he shouted, no longer scared. He was pissed. "This is insane," he complained, and kicked off one boot, then bent over, giving Maggie a wary look, before balancing on the uneven ground as he slipped out of the other boot.

"Toss them to me."

"I'm not tossing over my boots," he informed her. "What the fuck is this?" he demanded. "Do you not realize who I am?"

Maybe that was it. They didn't really know each other, and she'd probably lived a life of fear and terror, unlike anything she'd ever known, after leaving with Micah. Maybe she even regretted being with him now. Who knew what fucked-up reasons she might be thinking to hold that gun at him?

"I know who you are. I don't know why you're here." She straightened her arms again. "Toss over your boots," she said coldly.

Ben reached down. "Take it easy, Maggie," he said softly.

"I'm on your side, always have been and am now, too." He grabbed the sides of both boots in one hand and held his other hand out at his side. His gun was inside his jacket and felt heavier than normal, like a lump of steel against his chest.

"Good to know. Toss over the boots."

"Jesus Christ, Maggie." Ben tossed the boots at Maggie.

She didn't try to catch them but moved from one rock to the next and adjusted her aim. "Next time I promise I will shoot."

Then with incredible agility, Maggie hopped over the rocks and back up to the road.

"I don't get why you did this when he sent a message for me to meet him!" Ben howled in frustration.

He could have pulled his gun at this point. Possibly he could have even shot her gun out of her hand. Ben had no intention of pulling his gun on Maggie, though. Not to mention, if he'd missed and even scraped one finger, Ben didn't want to imagine how Micah might react.

Ignoring Maggie and letting her go, Ben gingerly worked his way over the rocks and rough ground to his boots. This was a visit he could have lived without it happening, but he had learned something from it. Now to figure out where Micah was.

Now, beyond a doubt, Maggie and Micah knew he was in Zounds. And, apparently, he wasn't a welcomed visitor. It had never crossed his mind that Micah wouldn't want to see him. Or that Micah might try killing him on sight, even if he did recognize him. That turned the lump in his gut to an almost unbearable level of terror.

He had told Maggie he'd come to Zounds with a friend. That was a lie. It was the best he'd been able to come up with at the moment and at gunpoint. Ben now worried that comment might result in a death sentence. What if Micah and Maggie had already known he and Wolf were in town? Now that Ben thought about it, of course Micah would know. Which meant the two of them probably already knew who Wolf Marley was.

And Ben had called him a friend. There weren't many men on this planet Ben was even mildly afraid of—except Micah. If the man wanted you dead, you were history.

After gathering his boots. Ben sat on the rock where Maggie had been. He slid them back on while facing the ocean and pondered his next move. One thing he knew, he wasn't going to chance riding out to Redwood National Park. Maggie had been surprised to see him but maybe not as shocked as she might have been. Micah knew Ben was here, had told his wife to leave the lipstick message. There was a good chance she'd left the message, then stopped at the grocery store before returning home. Damn it! Ben shouldn't have chased her. He should have followed her home.

It was time to regroup and give exceptionally careful thought to his next move. If Maggie had pulled a gun on him, Ben didn't want to think about what Micah might do.

Zoey adjusted the pillows on her bed and flipped the page of her book. She was reading about Catherine the Great, a Russian empress. Biographies were Zoey's absolute favorite genre. She'd read mysteries and romances, women's fiction and thrillers. She'd even picked up a Western or two when the cover caught her eye. Zoey liked to think she would read anything if it was good, but it was hard not to have a favorite genre. She guessed everyone did.

Biographies helped her escape. And at the moment she was willing to be anywhere other than where she was. Getting comfortable on her thick pale gold, not quite tan, comforter, she stretched out the length of her bed. It was queen size, although Zoey's toes didn't reach the brass bed frame. Her comforter matched the long curtains hanging on her windows. The shade her father had selected was ugly. The color reminded her of spicy mustard. She hated spicy mustard.

She forced herself to pay attention to the book and not her father yelling downstairs. Catherine the Great had a terrible husband. He reigned over Russia with a cruel hand; in a similar way Zoey's father reigned over Zounds.

Catherine was beautiful and had lovers who adored and

supported her, before and after she took over and killed her husband. Zoey glanced across her room at her full-length mirror. She wasn't too sure about the "beautiful" part. As for lovers, what if she made Ben a lover? Wouldn't that make her father blow a gasket? As for killing her father and taking over in his place, she had no desire to do either. She had no desire to commit a crime, especially murder. No one could pay her enough to want any part of her father's business.

Zoey returned to the book. Imagining how others lived their lives was so much better than trying to figure out her own life. Catherine hated her husband and rebelled against him, then eventually took the throne. She did so much for Russia and was so loved by everyone that she became Catherine the Great.

Maybe Zoey would never rule a country. She sure as hell wouldn't run her father's criminal activities or have a thing to do with them. But she would get away from him, somehow, someday.

Emilio Cortez was a prick with no soul. He was evil to the core. Zoey was grateful to the mother she'd never known, for she obviously took after her and not Zoey's father. She'd heard too many times how she looked just like her mother, who was some poor woman who made the mistake of falling for Zoey's father. Zoey knew the story surrounding her mother all too well. Emilio had dated Zoey's mother for a while. She had lived with Zoey's father in his home in San Francisco. But they had split up after about six months. Less than a year later, Zoey's mother showed up at Emilio Cortez's home with an infant, claiming the baby was Cortez's. Zoey's mother had threatened to take everything she knew about Cortez to the police if Cortez didn't give her a sizeable monthly allowance as child support.

Emilio Cortez didn't handle threats or blackmail too well. According to what he'd told Zoey, he took her from her mother and decided to he would raise Zoey. As he put it, no mother should ever use her baby for profit. Her mother's name had been Zoey. Her father had given Zoey the same name to help remind him never to make that mistake again.

Zoey never had found out what her name had been the first six months of her life.

Cortez made using a baby for profit look like child's play. Among crimes so insurmountable Zoey couldn't even begin to count them, he would force his daughter into a marriage she wanted nothing to do with. A marriage that would unite two dynasties and make both families even wealthier than they already were.

The yelling downstairs got louder, and Zoey pulled her knees to her chest. As a child she had crouched here in terror, afraid to even breathe for fear her father would remember about her and come stalking into her bedroom. Emilio Cortez seldom had anything nice to say to his daughter. When she was growing up, it had been a good day when her father didn't say anything to her at all. Today she detested him. Her fear of him had been replaced with disgust and anger. Anger for the way he abused everyone in Zounds and disgust with how he treated his own blood.

The door opened and Zoey jumped. Her book slipped off her legs and almost fell to the floor. She grabbed it as Melba, one of their housekeepers, the upstairs maid, stuck her head in the door. Zoey's father insisted on titles for all servants. She hated thinking of anyone who worked in her home as lower in rank than herself. At least they had jobs.

"Sorry to startle you," Melba apologized. "Your father wants you to talk to him in his den."

"Why?" Zoey whispered. When she was alone with the staff, they were very informal with each other. There were those loyal to her father, and Zoey knew who they were. Some of the staff, like Melba, let their guard down when they were alone with her.

"I don't know. He didn't say." Melba entered Zoey's room and opened her closet doors. "He told me to bring you downstairs. You're also to be presentable."

"Presentable?" Zoey rolled her eyes. "I should go downstairs in cutoff shorts and a T-shirt."

Melba looked over her shoulder, her hands already in Zoey's closet on her clothes. "And cost me my job," she said dryly. She turned her back to Zoey and slid a few outfits along the bar hanging on thick wooden hangers in the walk-in closet. "This one would be lovely on you."

Melba was probably the same age as Zoey but had been a house servant since she was nineteen. The Cortez home was her second place of employment, and she'd been here almost a year, which was a record for a Cortez servant.

"All right," Zoey said, closing her book. She was sick of being an ornament her father would parade around when the mood hit him. It was seriously becoming time to plot her escape. If only she could figure out a way without risking her life at the hands of his henchmen.

"I don't suppose you would go downstairs and tell Dad I'm soaking in a hot bath and will be a while."

Melba shot her a look that might have been wary or possibly daring. It was hard to say with Melba. She'd never let her guard down completely. There was that servant/master line that was impermeable, and Melba had never crossed it. Zoey was far from a master, but Melba was the perfect house servant.

"Why don't you slip into this and I'll help you with your hair?"

"Slave driver," Zoey mumbled, and grabbed the outfit that was still on its hanger from Melba.

Zoey seldom undressed or changed clothes without a helpful audience. The few times she'd protested, it had gotten back to her father, who had insisted she live as the extremely wealthy did and not like a common whore who would grab her clothes, then strip without caring how she looked. Apparently, the extremely wealthy could be undressed and dressed, but they couldn't undress and dress themselves.

Ever since that berating by her father, Zoey had absolutely refused to let any of the servants so much as undo one of her buttons. Melba stood behind Zoey as she stripped out of the sweats she'd been in all day. Zoey took the knee-length skirt and sleeveless blouse from her and put them on while Melba took the crumpled sweats to Zoey's hamper.

"Let me ask you something," Zoey began, and stared in

her full-length mirror as she grabbed her hair and tried piling it on top of her head with her hands.

"What, miss?" Melba asked, then put her hands over Zoey's and lowered them to Zoey's sides so she could start brushing her hair.

"There's this guy," she began again, and shot a furtive look at the mirror to see Melba.

Melba stood behind Zoey with the brush to Zoey's head. "Yes?" she prompted.

Zoey smiled, anxious to talk to someone about Ben. "I met him purely by accident. I was walking to my car and he was sitting on the steps at the bed-and-breakfast."

"Nothing happens by accident," Melba said softly, and lifted a portion of Zoey's hair to focus on the ends.

"He actually got up and met me on the sidewalk." Zoey remembered every minute of her time with Ben. It had all been so incredibly perfect. "He's new in town and looking for work."

There was no way to share the rest of the story without making herself sound cheap. Zoey knew that. She also knew she'd never spent time with a man where it had felt more right.

"Where's he from?" Melba asked.

Zoey couldn't really shake her head with Melba brushing her hair and holding sections of it at the roots. But Zoey smiled and waved her hand at Melba's reflection instead.

"I don't know," she admitted. "But Melba, it was such a wonderful evening. It's like the whole thing was some incredible dream. Nothing like this has ever happened to me before." And probably would never happen to her again. She loved her fantasies, but Zoey was a realist.

"You didn't do anything—"

"No. No," Zoey interrupted, then turned around, pulling her hair free from Melba's hold. "He wanted me to show him around, you know, because he just got into town. And yes, I told him I was going home. But he was so persistent."

"And so good-looking," Melba added, mimicking Zoey's tone.

Zoey stared at her, her stomach clenching. "I went on a ride with him on his motorcycle, and I kissed him." There, she'd told someone. Unfortunately, it didn't make her feel any better. She wished she could go to the bookstore, but she had just been there yesterday. Already her father suspected Zoey and Angel were friends, which would only mean he would make Angel's life hell. A Cortez didn't mingle with a common merchant.

Zoey walked purposefully to her closet and selected a pair of open-toe brown heels that would match the dark tan outfit she had on. When she turned around, Melba stood in the middle of Zoey's bedroom with her hands clasped in front of her. Zoey had only seen Melba in her uniform, a plain black dress, with her light brown hair pulled tightly in a bun behind her head. She imagined Melba was very pretty with her hair down and in something more complimentary.

"I needed to tell someone," Zoey whispered. "If you saw him, you would understand. He was so tall and muscular, with blond hair, and he rode a Harley-Davidson motorcycle. I doubt there's ever been a man in Zounds who could come close to how incredibly sexy Ben is."

A small smile played at Melba's lips, and her expression relaxed. Was that pity in Melba's eyes? Zoey's father's opinion of how his daughter should live her life was no secret to the household. He was quite fond of screaming at the top of his lungs, and he had an uncanny knack of making his voice bellow off the walls when it came to correcting his insolent daughter. Melba looked at Zoey for a moment as if she might say something but instead nodded once toward the door.

"Best not to keep your father waiting," she whispered.

Zoey slipped into her shoes. "Right, of course," she said dryly, but then exhaled. Melba's position in this house was based on how well she impressed Zoey's father, not Zoey. If Zoey didn't appear in a timely manner downstairs, it would go badly for Melba as well as Zoey.

"Thanks for listening," she added, and hoped her smile showed her sincerity.

"Of course, miss," Melba said, not moving. More than

likely the moment Zoey left, Melba would fluff Zoey's pillows and make sure her bedroom was in immaculate condition before leaving. "And miss, I hope you get to see him again."

Zoey grinned until her cheeks hurt. "Me, too."

Once downstairs, Zoey wished she were back in her bedroom. Or better yet, she just wanted to leave. Her house could kill the soul of a saint.

Leon, their butler, was at the side of the foyer near the dining-room doors talking to two maids when he noticed Zoey descending the main stairs. He looked just the same as he had when Zoey had been a child. He used to bounce her on his knee and give her hugs when she cried from a scraped knee. Today the most she got from him was a warm smile like the one he gave to her now.

"Mistress Zoey," he announced in his deep baritone. At the same time, with the slightest wave of his hand, he dismissed the two maids. "As always, you are absolutely stunning."

"Thank you, Leon." Once Zoey would have laughed at Leon's comment or waved it off with a snide comment. Her father had reprimanded her enough, which more than once had meant humiliating her in front of the staff, on how young ladies didn't treat the household servants as if they were drinking buddies. "Where is my father?"

"He's in his den, miss."

Zoey reached the bottom of the stairs and walked across the large foyer. Her father had purchased the most extravagant Victorian home in Zounds when they had first moved there ten years ago. At the time Zoey had been confused, then angry, that her dad had taken her from the excitement and thrills of the big city to a quiet, uneventful life in a small town. She had been thirteen at the time. Today she begrudgingly accepted her boredom but dreamed of escape and once again living in the city.

The parlor off the foyer was large, with long, narrow windows making up two of the four walls. Zoey used to love this room most when it rained. She would sit on the cushioned chairs by the windows and imagine buggies and trotting horses outside her home. That was when she still believed her imagination could rescue her. It would take imagination but also a lot of shrewd planning to get out of the clutches of Emilio Cortez.

She glanced at one of two matching chairs on opposite sides of the windows. They weren't gold but more like a light burnt brown. She spotted the flecks of gold. This wasn't new furniture, but the servants cleaned the chairs as regularly as they shampooed the thick Persian carpet that ended a foot from the walls. Glossy wooden floors were waxed on a regular basis. She lived in the most pretentious house in Zounds. None of this made it a home. Glancing around, she would admit that if someone was to enter her house who had never been here they would think it beautiful. But hang around for ten minutes and the ugliness would seep toward them. The place disgusted her. She looked away from the chair, not interested in sitting and waiting patiently to be yelled at.

A long hallway came after the parlor. Zoey stopped when she entered it, spotting Julius standing with his back to her father's closed door. She found it rather pretentious that her father believed one of his henchmen needed to stand guard outside his den when he was inside.

"If you wish to sit in the parlor, I'll have JoAnne bring you some hot tea." Leon was right behind Zoey when he spoke.

Zoey pictured herself marching up to Julius and informing him that her father had pulled her out of her reading to come downstairs and see him. If he wanted to speak with her, he could do it now. She stared at Julius's scowling expression. His hands were clasped together in front of him just as Melba's had been upstairs in Zoey's room. Julius looked a lot more dangerous. And it wasn't just appearances. Zoey knew Julius had killed for her father.

She imagined Catherine the Great marching down the hallway and demanding that Julius move. Ben probably liked women who were aggressive and didn't allow anyone to tell them what to do. If he knew Zoey lived in a home full of servants who all told her what to do instead of the other way around, he would be disgusted. Hell, it disgusted her.

"I'm not thirsty, Leon," she mumbled, half-turning when she answered him.

"I'm sure your father won't be long," he said, as if he knew her thoughts.

"It doesn't matter."

It did matter, and she wanted to scream it loud enough to make her father come running to her for a change. Leon moved to the side, allowing her to leave the hallway and go where she wished, as long as it wasn't far from her father's office.

She returned to the parlor, knowing if she were insubordinate it would be even harder to get out of this house. Zoey would wait until the moment was right to make her escape. She heard her father's den door open when she paused in front of the parlor windows.

"I want insurance the first one is taken care of," her father barked, and didn't glance in her direction when Zoey reappeared at the end of the hallway. "You say he never showed up?" Emilio Cortez pulled a pocket watch out of his smoking-jacket pocket and frowned at it. "That was two hours ago," he mumbled. "And he's not at the bed-and-breakfast?"

"No, sir." Brutus moved around Julius and faced her father.

Zoey tuned in at the mention of the bed-and-breakfast but kept her expression from revealing how she suddenly felt inside. Her father was a criminal, a thief, a murderer, and the destroyer of people's lives. If he didn't kill them, he abused them. He took money from the rich and the poor. Her father was the lowest of all forms of life.

Brutus and Julius did a lot of his dirty work. Zoey hated both of them as much as she did her father. She swore the two large men seemed to thrive on carrying out her father's instructions to ruin people's lives, or worse.

Her insides twisted painfully when she guessed why her dad wanted to see her. Be presentable, her ass. Her father was a prick, and now he would scold her as if she were still a child. It shouldn't surprise her that he knew she'd been with Ben. But having his henchmen go after Ben simply because he gave her a ride on his motorcycle and kissed her pissed her off so much it was all she could do not to fist her hands at her sides. Or, worse yet, march down the hall and inform Brutus and Julius that they would ignore her father's orders and leave Ben alone.

"Where would he be for two hours?" her father mused, his voice contemplative.

When he looked up, finally piercing her with his soulless black eyes, Zoey didn't think he really saw her. He looked away from her after a brief moment and focused on his men. "Find him. It can't be that goddamn hard with him riding that fucking noisy motorcycle. Do whatever it takes. And that other one!" he bellowed, the full energy of the demonic man that he was coming to life. "No one pulls a gun in my town and lives to see the end of the day!" he yelled.

His voice bounced off the wide hallway walls. Zoey didn't hear Brutus or Julius acknowledge her father, but both men left by a side door halfway down the hallway, which took them through rooms that would take them outside, behind the house. Her father once again glared at her, which was her cue that it was her turn to be under his scrutiny. Her stomach no longer twisted with nerves when her father wanted to see her in his den. She'd grown numb to his insults and ridicule years ago. Thinking of Ben, she wanted to race out of there and warn him to watch his ass.

Pedro, a short, slimy-looking man, closed her father's den door behind Zoey. She was pretty sure Pedro took notes on everything said in this room so her father could mull over it later. It better allowed him to twist what was said and use it against whoever was misfortunate enough to have been in her father's company.

Emilio walked around his massive desk and took his time pouring a drink for himself from his personal bar before sitting. He sipped, stared at the thick cut glass in admiration, then slowly placed it next to him on his desk. Pedro promptly appeared and moved the glass so it was on a coaster.

"Zoey," her father began, and leaned back in his chair. He

clasped his hands behind his head and studied her with those cold black eyes of his.

Zoey was pretty sure her father hated her more than he did most of his adversaries. He looked up and down her as if she were no more than a piece of furniture that he couldn't decide whether to keep or get rid of.

"We're flying to San Diego in an hour," her father announced, and picked up his whiskey.

"San Diego?" Zoey asked, confused. "Why?"

Her father grinned as if he'd just done something that he knew would please her. That was so far from the truth.

"We're meeting the Isleys, sweetheart." He leaned back in his chair, still holding his drink and tapping one finger on the edge of the glass as he stared at his daughter. "I know you're anxious to see Hector. The two of you had fun last year at Christmas, then you spent quite a bit of time together this spring when we were in Hawaii."

He and Joseph Isley had all but drooled over Hector and Zoey spending time together. But only because Hector's father was as big of a crime lord as her father. They looked at Hector and Zoey, and instead of seeing their two children possibly falling in love and being happy, the men saw dollar signs.

"I remember him," she said, guessing her father was waiting for a response.

"I believe tonight might be a very special night for you, my dear. I'm told Hector can't wait to see you again." Without waiting for her response or saying anything else, like possibly asking if she wanted to see Hector, Emilio turned to Pedro. "Zoey needs to wear something provocative. I want her appearance to reflect willingness, a guaranteed good time, yet also class and a lot of money."

"Exactly, sir," Pedro said, nodding and smiling.

"She's got the body; make sure her maid knows to select something that shows all of it off. Oh," her father said, snapping his finger as he turned his office chair so he faced Pedro. "A bikini . . . make it one of those string things, one that pretty much gives it all away. Zoey must come across as a sure thing. Tell her maid to pack lingerie."

"Possibly one evening gown," Pedro added. He was the only servant her father had on staff who didn't flinch when Emilio Cortez gave him his full attention. Instead, Pedro smiled. His thin lips peeled back over uneven teeth. It was eerie how Pedro's grin was as soulless and demonic as her father's. "When the happy couple join you and Joe Isley at Isley's club in San Diego, they're quite likely to make an announcement?" Pedro finished, his smile widening with his last presumption. "It would be appropriate at that time for Miss Zoey to be in an evening gown. I don't know if we should do tea length or floor length." The slimy little bastard tapped his pen against his lips.

Emilio waved his hand in the air. "Arrange for her to have both and check out the club. Everything must be in order ahead of time. Do we have confirmation yet on Hector?"

Zoey's jaw almost dropped when Pedro tsked at her father. No one she'd ever known had ever relaxed that much around Emilio Cortez.

"He's a boy, just over twenty. The lad will play confused, but you know as well as I do, sir," Pedro said, and waved his pen in the air as if he were conducting an orchestra. "If Master Hector Isley wishes to enjoy his father's fortune, he'll do as he's told."

"Then we're set," Emilio said, held his glass up in the air in a silent toast to their well-conceived plan, and downed the rest of his whiskey.

"Excuse me." Zoey wasn't sure she'd ever been so completely ignored, and as well treated as if she were nothing more than an inanimate object. "There is just one thing."

The pleasant look on her father's face changed in the time it took for him to look away from Pedro and switch his attention to her.

"Go prepare yourself to leave," her father instructed. His black eyes gleamed with hatred. "Remember, we leave in an hour, and I won't have you delaying my pilot."

Zoey held her hands together in front of her to keep them from trembling. She didn't fear her father. She definitely loathed him, which tore at her only because it seemed wrong to hate her only parent. This man glowering at her with eyes so cold they gave her chills might have aided in giving her life, but he was hardly a parent in any other sense of the word.

"I'm not going with you to San Diego." She held her ground when Emilio gripped the sides of his leather chair and a fiery glow burned in his eyes. Zoey wondered if he saw the same loathing burning in her eyes when she looked at him. "Hector doesn't appeal to me, and I have no intentions of trying to seduce him."

"Did I ask if he appealed to you, or if you wanted to seduce him?" Emilio Cortez spit out, his words laced with venom. He stood then, pushing his chair back, then started coming around his desk like a cruel predator. "The truth is, *sweetheart*," he snarled making the term of endearment sound more as if he'd just insulted her, "you can't think. You don't know what you want. I tell you what to think and I'll tell you what you want. Am I making myself perfectly clear?"

"Your opinion of me has been clear all my life!" she yelled, taking a step backward when he continued toward her. "But you seem to forget that I'm a person. I have feelings. My future matters to me and it doesn't involve marrying some crime lord's son so the two of you can combine your millions."

Zoey didn't have time to react before her father slapped her across the face. His hard hand connected directly with the side of her face. Zoey went flying to the side of his office, losing her balance and twisting her ankle as she stumbled to the floor. Pain radiated from her head and her foot at the same time and met in the middle of her body. She wanted to fly at him, attack with the same fierceness. And at the same time she simply wanted to crawl away, have a good cry, and nurse her wounds. As much as the latter had its appeal, doing so would convince her father even more that she was simply a tool at his disposal.

Emilio Cortez turned and calmly returned to the other side of his desk. "Just think about it: Hector," he said jovially, as if he hadn't just smacked her senseless. "In twenty years I'll have a grandchild. We can go after one of those midwestern families. I doubt I'll be around for great-grandchildren, but I'll definitely still be at the helm to see our dynasty grow even larger," he mused, chuckling.

Zoey fought for her bearings. She didn't know how people on TV could be hit in the face, knocked to the ground, and leap back to their feet. Yes, she did know. That was fiction and, unfortunately, this was her life. She tugged on her skirt before struggling to stand.

"Zoey, since I do think for you, let's be very clear. I'm very aware that you're a person," he said flatly. He wasn't looking at her but staring straight ahead.

Her father steepled his fingers and appeared to choose his words carefully. Was he not looking at her because he couldn't stomach the fact that he'd hit her so hard? She doubted that. She also doubted he considered his words. Cortez didn't care if he hurt his daughter.

"For twenty-three years my money has housed and clothed and educated you. Don't you dare imply you're too good or righteous to appreciate the sources of my income. That money allows you to have your nice wardrobe. You drive a nice car, buy those precious books of yours whenever you please, and have a staff of servants who wait on you hand and foot. I've never once heard you complain about any of that. Now you're grown and all of the money I've put out on you will be paid back. You will do as you are told. What you think or how you feel has no bearing on you and Hector. You will dress as you are told and impress him to the degree that you are instructed. Is that clear enough for you, *Daughter*? Would you like me to be more specific?"

Her father's hateful words pounded around in her head. Zoey pushed herself to her feet. Her knees burned. Her hip felt bruised. The entire left side of her face pulsated with a piercing pain that affected her jaw, her cheekbone, and her temple. Was her father's hand that big? Zoey was pretty sure she was the same size she'd been the last time he'd hit her. At the moment she couldn't remember how long ago that was.

In spite of her brain telling her to stay and fight, Zoey was pretty sure her body wouldn't withstand his next level of abuse. In the past that had been anything from him physically grabbing her and throwing her at the closest hard object he could find, the wall, his desk, across the room. Emilio Cortez wasn't overly original when it came to abusing his daughter, but he was consistent.

Zoey made it to her feet and took her time brushing strands of hair from her face. Her eyes burned badly enough that tears had streamed down her face and her hair stuck to the moisture.

"Be careful, Father dear," she said softly. Her voice was more venomous than she'd expected, but the words fell out nonetheless. "Hector might be turned off making love to a bruised body."

She turned and limped out of his den, closing the door behind her. She didn't want to hear anything else her father might have to say.

Zoey started toward the stairs, wishing she could hide in her room. But there wasn't a safe place for her anywhere in this house. Her father intended to fly them out on his private jet, then whore his daughter out to Isley's son in return for the merging of the two crime lords' businesses. Her father didn't care if he had to beat her senseless to do it. The truly sad and depraved part of this entire ordeal was that Hector probably wouldn't care how battered she was. On the two different times she'd met him, Hector had seemed shallow, cold-hearted, and eager to do anything to remain incredibly wealthy.

Instead of taking the stairs, Zoey slipped down the hallway alongside them. JoAnne was in the kitchen talking cheerfully with another servant. Zoey couldn't imagine what they were doing and didn't care. She kept walking until she reached the back door. It was the door for deliveries but one she used on occasion since it was a faster way to reach the garage and her car. Leon used two young boys as the Cortezes' valet service, but Zoey didn't take advantage as much as her father wanted her to.

The side of her face throbbed. Already she had a headache so severe it was hard to think. Her eyes watered to the point Zoey doubted she could drive. She reached the garage but kept walking. There were always servants everywhere, and someone would spot her and be confused. If she didn't respond, they would tell Leon, or Pedro, or even her father.

She kept walking and reached for her cell phone. It was hard to bring the screen into focus, but she did a search, found the phone number for Betsy's bed-and-breakfast, and placed the call.

"Betsy, hi, this is Zoey Cortez." Her voice rang in her ears and sounded strange to her.

"Hi, Zoey, how are you doing, dear?" the cheerful old woman asked.

Already tears streamed down Zoey's face. It was impossible not to keep her voice from cracking.

"Betsy, please," Zoey said. "I need to speak with Ben." She prayed the old woman wouldn't ask her what his last name was.

"Of course, dear."

There was silence; then the phone rang twice in her ear before a solemn male voice answered.

"Ben?"

"Who is this?" he demanded.

"This is Zoey Cortez. You gave me a ride on your motorcycle last night." She didn't want empty small talk right now. "Ben, I'm hurt. Will you come get me, please?"

Chapter Eight

Ben was acutely aware of how unstable Zoey was on the back of his bike. He had yet to meet this Emilio Cortez but couldn't wait to give the bastard a taste of his own medicine. He had to be a monster to do this to his own daughter. Fortunately, Zounds was a small town and it didn't take long to return to the bed-and-breakfast. Zoey made no attempt to climb off Ben's bike once he'd dismounted.

"This might not be a good idea." Zoey's face was puffy, her eyes swollen, and the imprint of her father's hand on the side of her face was starting to bruise.

"I'm going to clean you up and put ice on your face. Argue with me later."

Her pretty, dark eyes were glazed over when she raised her attention to his face. "My father controls the bed-and-breakfast. Betsy is an old woman. He'll make her life hell if he learns I ran here after he hit me."

Ben's insides swelled with an overwhelming urge to wrap his arms around her and protect her from any and all evil. He also wanted to hop back on his bike and go after Zoey's father. The only thing worse than a bully was a bully who hit women. Zoey looked almost disoriented when she glanced around her furtively.

All that mattered right now was making sure Zoey was all right and getting her comfortable. "Betsy was making bread when I left. She'll still be in the kitchen." He looked around the small parking lot behind the bed-and-breakfast. "I know what the other guests are driving and no one else is here right now. If we enter through the side door over there, Betsy won't see us. No one will. I can get you upstairs. You'll be safe and no one will know you're there. You have my word."

Zoey didn't fight him when he lifted her off and into his arms. Within minutes they were upstairs and in his room. She deflated against him, her entire body snuggled against his chest and in his arms.

He wondered at how easily she trusted him. With the life it appeared she led, trust probably didn't come easily. Maybe he was witnessing desperation from her and not trust. Either way, Ben would gain her trust. Zoey needed him. Ben believed in fate. He didn't question why he'd been placed in her life at this moment; it was very clear. Zoey didn't know it yet, but he was her best bet for protection right now.

He sat her down on his bed where he'd been lying and watching TV when she called. In a way, he needed her right now, too. Zoey was the perfect distraction. Ben hadn't been able to wrap his brain around Maggie's reaction to him earlier that day. He couldn't accept that Micah would think of him as a danger or suggest to his wife that Ben would try hunting Micah down. Well, Ben was trying to hunt Micah down, but not for the same reason Wolf was.

"I can't stay here." Zoey stood slowly, running her hands down her straight-cut skirt.

"Yes, you can."

He took a moment to take in her perfect petite body. Ben always went for the tall, willowy ladies. Tall, tan, built, and blonde. Not that he'd had a lot of luck with that particular breed of ladies, but they were the ones who always ended up latched at his arm, sprawled out next to him in bed, or complaining how he spent his money. Stacy barely entered his thoughts and she was gone. Ben took in Zoey's incredible figure. Her breasts were a good size, more than a handful, and on a lady her size they looked mouthwateringly good.

She had hips and a well-rounded rear, both features he loved on a lady. To notch her up to perfection, her waist was so narrow Ben bet he could wrap his hands around it easily.

Her black hair was long, straight, tapered, and ended right above her ass. Ben loved long hair, loved gathering it in his hand and pulling until a lady arched her back, let her head fall back . . .

Zoey gathered her hair at her nape, pulling it from her face. In the light, shades of green and purple swelled down the side of her face. Jesus Christ! He was a total ass! What kind of man drooled over a woman who had just been knocked around as badly as Zoey had?

She turned to take in his room and lost her balance. Instead of stretching her arms out to brace her fall, Zoey's hands seemed to reach for her face in slow motion. Fortunately, Ben was close.

He grabbed her, pulling her next to him and back on to the bed. He sat, easing her so she sat next to him. His arm was around her so that his hand stretched over the voluptuous curve of her hip. This time he focused on her face and the almost blank look in her eyes. Ben might be incredibly attracted to her, but he wasn't a beast. She already had enough of those in her life.

"Stay here. Don't move and I'll be right back," he said, keeping his voice just above a whisper, soft and gentle. "I'm just going into the bathroom to get a cool cloth."

"I'll sit here for a couple minutes," she conceded.

"That's fine."

Ben brought a damp washcloth and held it up to her face. Zoey looked up at him, what makeup she'd been wearing now smeared and stained down her face. She was still so incredibly beautiful, a severe distraction.

"Here," he whispered when she made feeble efforts to dab the washcloth at her face.

Ben took the washcloth and Zoey leaned her head back against his hand so he could wash her face. He was careful to avoid the bruised parts but managed to clean her up. When she blinked and those radiant pure black eyes looked up at him, something broke inside him. Ben would do anything for this woman. Never before, when first meeting a lady, had he known with such clarity that she would mean this much to him. With Zoey he had absolutely no doubt.

"I can't stay here," she repeated with more urgency.

"I know. You're worried about Betsy."

"You don't understand. My father rules this town. He owns all the bank loans on all the buildings and if business owners don't do as he says he puts them out of business. Betsy has lived here since she was first married."

"Betsy isn't going anywhere." He looked around the room, then grinned down at Zoey. "I like this place."

The corner of Zoey's mouth was slightly bruised. Her lips were already full, though, and when she attempted a small smile every inch of him hardened. Which made him feel like a jackass.

"I'll go find you some ice." He stood and tried gently pressing her against the many pillows he'd tossed to the floor the night before. Betsy had diligently stacked them against the headboard of his bed while he'd been gone this morning. "I'll only be gone a minute."

"No!" she shrieked, leaning forward, then grabbing her head. "Oh," she moaned, but then persisted, "You can't leave."

"It's okay, Zoey. The ice machine is between here and the door to the house. No one will get to you, I promise."

"You don't understand, Ben." Zoey seemed to become more coherent than she'd been since he'd picked her up. She stood, walking away from him and to the mirror over the dresser in his room. "You're not from Zounds. You don't know the power my father holds over everyone who lives here. I'm not safe here, or anywhere. I'm sure he's already sent Brutus and Julius looking for me. This is probably one of the first places they will look."

She leaned forward, moving her hair behind her shoulder, and examined the damage to her face. "I can't let him find me," she whispered. "He'll blame me for this, and I'll probably get hit again. He's such a goddamn idiot."

"He's not going to touch you again," Ben said with conviction.

"You don't get it," Zoey hissed, spinning around and facing him. Her hand hovered over her bruised face, but she didn't sway this time. "I told you any business owner who has a loan out with the bank answers to my father, because the bank was the first thing he took over in this town ten years ago when we first moved here. Now, business owners, such as Betsy," Zoey said, and waved her hand dramatically through the air as if Betsy were everywhere in this room, "because she took out a fifty-thousand-dollar loan after her husband died to create her dream and make this place into the incredible bed-and-breakfast that it is today, once a month she also pays my father. Then, because making business owners pay him in order to have a business loan is illegal, once a month he sends over his henchmen and they do inspections. If the business owner refuses to cooperate, their utilities are shut off." Zoey began pacing as she explained the level of criminal activity Emilio Cortez had wrapped around this poor town. "Not because he owns the utility companies, but because he owns all wiring and utility poles leading up to each business and he owns the plumbers, the electricians, and the city officials in Zounds."

Zoey stopped pacing with her back to the door of Ben's room. She looked over her shoulder at it as if it might come alive, then scurried to put him between the door and her. Zoey was a mixture of a confident woman and a doormat. She was strong yet had succumbed to the cruelest type of bullying there was. She had a beautiful personality that glowed. She cared about the town her father was slowly destroying. She was obviously intelligent and understood how her father's business ran, crooked as it might be. Zoey was also drop-dead gorgeous. Even with the side of her face glowing with shades of green, purple, and light streaks of yellow that outlined the imprint of her father's hand, it was hard to fault her physically—make that damn impossible. Ben hadn't noticed until now that her heels, which probably brought her to just under five and a half feet, were open toed. Her painted toenails and one incredibly adorable toe ring topped off a perfect sexual package.

In spite of her seductive appearance, there was something oddly innocent about her. Ben guessed she led a sheltered life trapped under the shadow of a monster. Right before she spoke again, another thought occurred to Ben and turned his stomach.

Zoey had run from her home, then called him. He doubted she lounged around her house dressed to the nines as she was now. If her getting hurt had something to do with how she was dressed and possibly Zoey refusing to do whatever her father wanted her to do while dressed like this enticing seductress facing him, then Cortez wouldn't be safe in Ben's presence. His blood boiled as several possibilities ran through his mind as to what Zoey might have refused to do to earn the stamp of Cortez's hand on the side of her face. Ben kept his expression placid for Zoey's sake as he stared at her, but his anger flared inside and hatred brewed for a man he hadn't had the pleasure of meeting yet. He couldn't wait to kick the monster's ass.

"It's even worse than what I've described so far, Ben," Zoey continued, and swallowed before straightening as if building some inner strength to discuss the evil she described to him. "When they show up here looking for me, Betsy will let them in. Not because she wants to but because if she doesn't my father will destroy this place. If you don't answer the door, they will tell her to unlock it, and she will. If you try and protect me, they will tell her you aren't good business for her to have under her roof. They will tell Betsy not to let you have a room here, and she will listen and ask you to leave."

"Why would your father think that you might be here?" Ben asked, listening to every sound in the house. The walls were solid, but he was pretty sure he'd hear someone coming down the hallway, especially if there was more than one of them. "Have you mentioned me to your father?"

"No," she said adamantly. "If I ever mentioned a man to my father, he would kill him. And I don't mean that figuratively. My father has already decided who I am going to marry."

She sucked in a staggered breath and this time looked Ben square in the face. Her nipples created perfectly centered little beacons against the sleeveless blouse she wore. He didn't let his gaze falter from hers, though.

"My father planned for him and me to fly to San Diego. We were to leave in an hour and meet the Isleys. Hector Isley is the son of another businessman in the same line of work as my father, and whom I'm supposed to marry just so the Cortezes and Isleys can gain power and wealth." She hesitantly touched her fingertips to the bruising on her face. "It's been maybe thirty minutes since I left my father. He believed I was freshening up to leave but I'm sure knows by now that I'm no longer there. He'll have his men scouring Zounds for me. We might have as little as ten minutes before someone shows up demanding to search the bed-and-breakfast."

Ben understood Zoey's worry for Betsy. The old woman wouldn't handle being bullied by some asshole's thugs. He took quick inventory of what was in his room. There was nothing that would reveal who he was or what he did for a living. "You haven't explained why you're so sure he's going to come looking for you here first. Do you and Betsy have a special connection?"

"I barely know her." Zoey shook her head. "Earlier, I was in my bedroom when one of our servants told me my father wanted to see me. I was told to dress nicely and go to him immediately. When I came downstairs, I had to wait because my father was in his den with Brutus. It wasn't until the two of them walked out of his den that I overheard."

"They were talking about me?" Ben didn't panic. Micah was in this town somewhere, successfully for a year now keeping a very low profile, especially with Zounds being owned by Cortez. If Cortez, or anyone else in this town, learned the truth of why he was here, it would turn Zounds into a bloodbath. Ben had to keep his priorities straight. First and foremost he had to protect Micah's anonymity.

"Not by name. All I heard when they came out of my father's den was him complaining about someone not showing up for something at noon. Then my father asked if whoever they were looking for was at the bed-and-breakfast. He then started yelling about how it couldn't be that hard to track down a noisy motorcycle." She looked at Ben and her eyes grew wide. "Did you pull a gun on Brutus?"

"Pull a gun? Who is Brutus?"

"Okay. They were probably talking about other people, too." Zoey sighed and shook her head. "I only try to keep up with what my father is doing in order to protect everyone in Zounds, if I can." She sighed. "Anyway, that's why I'm willing to bet this place will be on the top of his list of places to search. It's probably because you're new in town, but you're already on the deadly Cortez watch list."

Ben understood. He couldn't change the way things were in Zounds, but he could see to Zoey's protection.

"We need to find something a little less conspicuous for you to wear."

Less than fifteen minutes later, Zoey was out of her high heels and her ass-hugging skirt and the cute sleeveless blouse that showed off her nice boobs. Fortunately, Ben wasn't acclimated to the colder climate in Northern California and had packed sweatpants and sweatshirts. Zoey looked ridiculous in his clothes, which they'd had to roll up considerably in the arms and at the ankles. The two of them had worked methodically until his clothes weren't falling off of her. Then to complete the picture, Ben also put on a pair of his sweatpants and a sweatshirt.

"Now then," Ben said, coming out of his bathroom after changing and walking to his large window that overlooked the parking lot outside. "We need to leave without anyone knowing we've left."

He had thought about pulling Wolf in to assist in helping Zoey, but one look out the window and he saw that the man still hadn't returned. If Wolf had somehow learned where

Micah was before Ben had, it would make things a lot tougher for Ben, especially after his comment to Maggie about coming with a friend. Ben would simply have to rely on his friendship with Micah still being intact and the man still having incredible foresight. Micah had to know Ben would never turn against him.

Right now Ben needed to protect Zoey. He had tried making Maggie understand earlier that he was on their side, and she'd held a gun on him. If something had happened to Micah, Maggie would have said something. Ben had to believe that. So for now, he'd accept that Micah was alive and well. Ben would learn where he was once he had Zoey safe.

"Think you can climb out the window to the ground below?" Ben asked, whispering.

Zoey leaned out the open window just as Ben was doing. "Are you serious?" she asked incredulously.

There wasn't time to convince her that it was easier than it looked. "Come here," Ben said, and pulled her into his arms.

"What?" Zoey gasped.

Ben was already easing both of them out of the window. "Hold on really tight and don't say a word or make a sound," he instructed.

Zoey did just that. Ben had his arm around her, but Zoey wrapped both of her arms tightly around his waist and buried her face in his chest. She held on so tight that Ben really didn't need to hold her against him. He did anyway, just for his own peace of mind.

Once they were outside, Ben reached inside and did his best to pull the window closed. He made it within a few inches. But that was enough. At least now it wouldn't be obvious he'd crawled out the oversized window. For all anyone might know, he had opened it a bit for the fresh air. Betsy hadn't seen him return with Zoey so would be able to cooperate fully without incriminating herself or her business.

"Hold on, sweetheart. I won't let you get hurt." Ben tightened his grip around Zoey's waist and leapt from the wide brick windowsill to the flat roof of the back porch.

From there he didn't dawdle. If there was a noise, Betsy would come investigate. He'd learned long ago never to underestimate the power of an old woman with a thick broom handle. He didn't warn Zoey when he scurried to the edge of the roof. The ground wasn't much more than seven feet below. Nonetheless, he couldn't risk either of them twisting, spraining, or, worse yet, breaking an ankle or any bone.

"I'm going to let you go now."

"No," Zoey hissed into his chest.

God, she was trembling. More than anything Ben wanted to console her. Both of their asses were on the line now. He didn't have time to assure Zoey he'd been in a lot more dangerous situations. That didn't mean he wouldn't do everything in his power to protect both of them. Ben happened to like his ass.

"You can cry later. Hell, I might cry with you." Ben pried her loose and gripped her jaw.

When he realized he could be hurting her, he let go of her immediately and ran his hand down the side of her hair. That long, perfectly black shiny hair would be a dead giveaway.

"You're going to sit right here and stuff all of your hair inside your sweatshirt. Do it now, darling," he ordered in a hushed yet urgent whisper.

She let go of him and sat down on the edge of the roof. Zoey gathered all of her hair at her nape just as headlights appeared in the driveway.

"Quick! Lie flat!" Ben all but shoved Zoey down on the roof. He then lay down flat right next to her.

The car didn't drive around to the back of the bed-and-breakfast and park in the parking lot. Instead it parked at the entrance to the driveway, and a moment later the headlights went off. Zoey lifted her head, but Ben shook his head and put his finger to his lips. He didn't dare say a word. Any good hunter would have their senses finely tuned the moment they arrived at a possible dangerous location. Until Ben knew otherwise, he would assume these were the men looking for Zoey—and him. He wouldn't tell Zoey, but if her father was looking for him, Ben doubted it was simply because Ben was new in town.

Ben wasn't so cocky as to believe that working for Greg King would put him at the top of any crime lord's radar. But possibly someone had seen Ben riding with Zoey last night. Or, worse yet, Ben hightailing around the grocery store earlier that day chasing a madwoman whom the locals in town probably didn't know that well.

Two car doors opened and closed. There was the sound of boots crackling on the drive, then ascending the front porch steps. A loud knock sounded on the front door, and Zoey jumped and squealed. She slapped her hand over her mouth and stared at Ben wide-eyed. Consoling her would have to wait. Ben needed all his attention trained on any sound that might help him understand why Zoey's father was the one who had sent him the message to meet at Redwood National Park at noon. Because if what Zoey said was accurate, it had been Emilio Cortez who had wanted Ben to drive north of town, not Micah.

Crap! That meant Micah might not have known Ben was in Zounds. Well, he did now. Ben would worry about that as soon as he and Zoey were away from the bed-and-breakfast.

The front door opened and low baritones mixed with Betsy's higher, excited voice. Then the front door shut.

"Let's go, now!" Ben hissed, springing into action. "I'm jumping; then you are. Don't hesitate. There's no time."

He didn't elaborate but scooted to the edge of the roof until his legs hung over as far as they could. He just touched a chain-link fence that went along the edge of the screened-in back porch, then extended around the yard. Ben used it as a brace, lowered himself so he stood on it momentarily, then leapt to the ground.

He spun around instantly, not bothering to assess any damage. Thankfully, Zoey didn't hesitate, either. She jumped, landing on top of him. Ben grabbed her in his arms and staggered backward before going down to his knees.

A moment later they were running from the bed-and-breakfast. Ben banked on the fact that Betsy would take the men up to his and Wolf's rooms. More than likely she wouldn't have her keys on her and would have to go to the kitchen, grab them, then return to the impatient growling men.

There was always an off chance that the men in the car weren't Cortez's men but simply travelers looking for a room. If that was the case, Betsy would be occupied with them and wouldn't be able to answer any questions about Ben's or Wolf's whereabouts if, and when, Cortez's men did show up.

Ben and Zoey reached the sidewalk right where they had stood and spoken the previous night before he'd hurried to get his motorcycle. At the time, he'd thought of Zoey as the perfect diversion for him to leave the bed-and-breakfast and be able to explain to Wolf later where he'd gone. Ben hadn't expected to be so incredibly attracted to the petite black-haired beauty. Nor had he guessed in a million years he'd be on the run with her the very next night.

"They're not going to catch me." Zoey pulled him out of his thoughts with her sudden declaration. Her voice was soft but gave hint to determination she possessed to change her life.

"You're right," he said, looking down at her profile and her bruised face. If anyone thought this woman tiny, they didn't know her. After one day Ben saw a world of courage packaged in damn near perfection.

"Everyone thinks I'm this broken, fragile flower," she said bitterly.

Ben didn't know what others thought of her. That wouldn't be how he would describe her. She was an erotic flower. She did appear fragile at first, but he was starting to see the woman under all her sensuality, and she was driven. Zoey kept pace with him on the sidewalk, he noticed. In fact, it seemed that she knew where she was going and was leading the way.

"All right, my sturdy flower, where we headed?"

Zoey looked up at him, and her white teeth appeared to glow in the darkness against her caramel skin when she smiled. "My friend, Angel, owns the bookstore. We can't stay there, or I'd get her in trouble, too. My father is already after her business simply because he doesn't like me spending so much time there. But she'll probably be able to drive me out of town, where my father doesn't have the same jurisdiction that he has in Zounds."

Ben wasn't sure why it bothered him that he would no longer be her escort. But it was for the best, he quickly pointed out to himself. He sucked at relationships and sure as hell didn't need to be tangled in her life right now when his good friend's life was on the line. Ben had a debt to pay to Micah, and all his attention needed to be on that.

"You're positive she will do this for you?"

Zoey nodded. "I'll call her."

"Use my phone."

"She won't answer a number she doesn't recognize."

"Then you keep calling until she does."

They'd turned the corner and were now walking along shops downtown. All the shops were closed, and it was quiet. Long shadows stretched past glowing streetlights. For all purposes, it seemed like a peaceful, quaint, sleepy downtown with hints of salt in the air every time the breeze shifted from the ocean. Nonetheless, Ben grew anxious and wanted to pick up their pace when he spotted a large sign on a building at the end of the street. ANGELINA'S BOOKSTORE. He wanted to grab Zoey's hand and hurry them to the store.

He could hear the phone ringing as Zoey held it to her ear. It went to voice mail, and a woman began speaking. Zoey hung up and sighed.

"Call her again."

Zoey nodded to the bookstore. "She lives upstairs. Her lights are on, so I know she's there. Why can't I call her with my phone?"

"Most cell plans allow a person to see what calls or texts were made after fifteen or thirty minutes," Ben explained. "There is also the possibility that your father keeps your phone tapped. As well—crap," he groaned. "Turn your phone off."

"Turn it off?" She looked up at him questioningly as she redialed Angel's number.

"Yes. Now," he ordered. "There is probably a GPS in it. Your father can track where you are with your phone."

"Is that so?" Zoey pulled her phone out of her oversized, baggy sweatpants.

Something crossed over her face Ben hadn't seen before. Her dark eyes narrowed and her mouth straightened into a determined line. Then before he could react, Zoey hurled her phone into the delivery road between two buildings. They heard the sound of shattering plastic, then silence.

"I guess I threw it too hard," she said, and surprised him when she giggled. "I wanted him to search for the GPS and find my phone in a trash Dumpster."

"You're such an evil woman," Ben muttered, and ran his hand up and down her back without thinking of how his action might appear to anyone who might be watching. Although with continual side-glances he didn't see anyone around them.

He dropped his hand to his side when they reached the bookstore. Zoey beckoned him to follow when she walked around the corner of the building. They were on a similar delivery road, except there wasn't another building on the other side of the bookstore. He listened as Zoey held his phone to her ear until the same woman's voice began speaking the voice-mail message. Zoey hung up and redialed.

It rang once, twice, then stopped ringing. Someone had picked up.

"Why the hell do you keep calling Angel's personal line?" a man bellowed loud enough Ben heard him easily.

Zoey shrieked and let go of his phone as if it had burned her. Ben somehow grabbed his phone and Zoey before either crashed. He held Zoey close, aware of her trembling again. She bent her arms so they were between her and Ben and rested her cheek to his heart.

"Hello?" Ben demanded, casting an eye around them at the dark gray shadows looming everywhere against the still and quiet downtown. It was almost too quiet. His radar was up. Zounds had seemed friendly enough when he'd first arrived, but the town was veiled with an evil that was trying to close in around him.

"What do you want?" a raspy baritone demanded.

"Where is Angel?" Ben glanced up and down the narrow road. He saw no one, not even a car.

"Right next to me."

The voice sounded familiar, but that didn't make sense. Wolf wouldn't be answering the bookstore owner's personal phone line.

"Tell her to open her back door." Ben stared at an unmarked door that appeared to open into the back of the store.

"Why should I tell her to do that?"

"Someone here wants to talk to her," Ben said, almost positive he was speaking with Wolf. Ben would save questions as to why the man was in the bookstore at this hour and answering the owner's phone. At the moment, Ben focused on Zoey. "And she's hurt."

The line went dead and seconds later someone turned the dead bolt on the other side of the door in front of them. It flew outward and at the same time Zoey pushed herself out of Ben's arms and into the arms of a woman, who had opened the door.

"What have you done to her?" the woman demanded as she held Zoey in a tight embrace. "Here, let's get some lights turned on and we'll get you all fixed up."

"No, no lights," Ben announced, holding out his arms to silence everyone. "Use whatever lights were already on."

"I wondered if you could drive me out of town," Zoey asked the woman.

"Drive you out of town?" the woman asked.

"What are you doing here?" Ben asked Wolf.

"What's going on?" Wolf asked at the same time.

"I'm in trouble," Zoey whimpered.

In spite of her being barely audible, everyone stopped asking questions and looked at Zoey. Ben glanced over the women between them and met Wolf's curious look. Then the bookstore owner shifted her attention to Ben. He met the woman's cold glare.

"Not because of me," he said hurriedly, shaking his head. "Zoey came to me for help."

"What happened?" the woman asked Zoey gently, and when she stroked Zoey's hair away from her face, the dim light coming from inside her home shone on Zoey's face. "Oh my God! Zoey!"

"I know!" Zoey cried out, but then lowered her voice again. "Is it okay to come inside? It's not a good idea to talk out here. And Angel, you really don't want me here. I'll bring you trouble. I won't stay. I promise."

"You aren't trouble," the woman murmured, and pulled Zoey into her arms.

"Her father is Emilio Cortez," Ben told Wolf. He was really curious what Wolf was doing here, but that explanation would have to wait. "Have you heard his name mentioned yet?"

"Yup." Wolf studied Ben. "Had the privilege of meeting one of his associates earlier today."

"Brutus and Julius were at the bed-and-breakfast." Zoey suddenly came to life. "I heard their voices. I know they're looking for me."

Angel took Zoey's arm and backed up inside, pulling Zoey and causing Wolf to back up as well. Ben followed and closed the door behind him. The four of them stood in a storage room. Wolf reached up and tugged a string, causing a light to flood over all of them.

Zoey squinted. "I thought that didn't work."

"Wolf fixed it." Angel shrugged it off as if Zoey might already know Wolf and him fixing things in this bookstore might be an everyday occurrence.

Ben studied Wolf for a moment. The man's attention was on the women, and he didn't return the look. If this was how the man learned if someone was in town, by getting seriously close to citizens in the town, Ben might have underestimated Wolf's methods. Not to mention skills. Angel was a good-looking woman. She was older than Ben, with wild brown curly hair that was cut short. Angel wasn't much taller than Zoey. She was cute and a business owner and apparently single. More than likely men would hit on her on a regular basis. Angel probably had enough street smarts running this store to not be taken by just any hustler. Ben gave Wolf another appraising once-over before focusing on the ladies.

"What the hell happened?" the woman demanded harshly, taking a step back from Zoey and studying her. "We aren't going anywhere, or worrying about who might be coming here, until you fill me in."

"My father had called me into his den. And, as always, he spent more time talking to Pedro than to me. Father did take the time to inform me that he and I were flying out soon and going down to San Diego. We were going to meet Mr. Isley and his son Hector. He talked as if I were his personal whore instead of his daughter, and as if this wedding he's conjured up is a done deal!" Zoey wailed, throwing her arms up in the air.

"Then without another word to me he turned to Pedro. He didn't ask if I wanted to go, not that he ever asks my opinion about anything. He starts talking to Pedro about how my dress should be sexy and revealing when we go to dinner with Hector and his father."

"The ass," Angel seethed. She then held her hand out as if to touch Zoey's face but dropped it.

Instead Zoey touched Angel's face. "It's okay. I wholeheartedly agree. My father is an ass and so much more." She sighed, collected her thoughts, and continued until she'd explained the entire sordid conversation between Cortez and Pedro. "I'm done with him, Angel. I can't take this any longer . . . ," she trailed off.

"Who could blame you?" the woman consoled gently, and ran her hand down the side of Zoey's head, stroking her hair.

Ben ached to do the same thing. Instead he stuffed his hands in his pockets and scowled at the ground. He didn't like what happened next. Even as Zoey related how her father hit her, knocking her to the floor, then demanding she do as she was told or else, hatred closed around Ben's heart in a way he'd never experienced before. It was a cold, unnerving chill. His hands clenched into fists in his pockets. Ben had to exert an effort to relax if just for Zoey's sake.

"I'm sure many blame me." Zoey was slowly regaining the confidence and determination she'd shown Ben on the way to the bookstore.

"Then they're idiots," Angel said sternly. But then her expression relaxed and she gently touched the side of Zoey's face with her fingertips. "You need to see a doctor."

"I can't stay here." Zoey pulled back and against Ben. "Angel, do you think you could give me a ride? Remember that cabin outside of Zounds that is for rent?"

"You don't know it's still for rent." Angel glanced at Ben when he placed his hands on Zoey's arms to steady her. "Maybe we should all go inside and discuss this further." She gestured to a door that appeared to lead to the dark interior of the bookstore.

Since Zoey had mentioned Angel lived above the bookstore, Ben guessed the stairs leading to her home were through the store. With the lights off and the glow of the store sign on the front of the building, at least it would be hard for anyone outside to see movement inside unless they were standing in front of the store, or had really good night binoculars, he mused.

Zoey was shaking her head before answering. "Ben and I barely escaped the bed-and-breakfast. You know they'll come here next looking for me."

"Your father's guard dogs?" Wolf grinned and rubbed his hands together before looking at Angel. "Round two. I can't wait."

"You are not pulling a gun on Cortez's men again," Angel snapped.

"What?" Zoey and Ben demanded at the same time.

Chapter Nine

Wolf didn't like the idea of Angel being without a car. Otherwise, the plan was solid, with only a few minor loose ends. Zoey Cortez wasn't his chief concern, though. If Ben Mercy wanted to chase after the hot, little dark-skinned beauty, that was his choice. Wolf thought she came with way too much baggage. But she'd distract Ben, which would assure Wolf that anything he uncovered leading to the Mulligan Stew assassin would be a fresh lead.

Wolf much preferred Ben taking Angel's car and leaving with Zoey. Wolf would stay here. He'd already confirmed Angel had the only bookstore in Zounds. If he stayed the night, hung around some tomorrow, he might get a good feel for the citizens of this town. Who knew what one of them might say? It sure as hell beat driving aimlessly around the town and surrounding area, wasting his gas, when he didn't know what the assassin even looked like.

They'd barely made it to the top of the stairs, with Wolf following Angel and getting one hell of a nice view of her swaying ass, when someone pounded on the front door of the shop downstairs.

"Oh crap," Angel swore, spinning around and almost sliding into him as the front windows rattled when whoever it was put some force into knocking on the bookstore doors.

"Don't hurry to answer." Every muscle had stiffened in

Wolf's body. He braced himself on the narrow flight of stairs, grabbing Angel when she slid down a step toward him.

"We know who it is," she pointed out. "Why postpone the inevitable?"

Because it was so much more fun to toy with the enemy. "So we can discuss how we'll handle this," he told her, lifting her up backward and climbing the remaining few stairs until they were in her living room. "There will be questions. Our answers need to be solid, exact, and not conflicting."

"You're right. They'll want to know what you're doing here."

"That answer should be obvious." He grinned when she narrowed her eyes on him.

Her eyes grew wide when the pounding repeated. A moment later the phone rang downstairs and simultaneously Angel's cell rang, which Wolf had forgotten he'd slid in his shirt pocket. He pulled it out, handed it to her as it rang a second time.

"Answer. Sound sleepy," he told her, plotting as he spoke. "Sound agreeable and tell them you'll be down in a second. Then hang up on them even if they keep talking."

Angel stared at him, her nervousness apparent, when she answered and did as he said. Her swallow was forced when she hung up and dropped her hand to her side with her phone still in it.

"Now what?" She glanced around her home, lit by a few lamps. "They are going to look everywhere." Without waiting for him to keep plotting and decide their best plan of attack, she walked to her bed, pulled down the blankets, and scattered the pillows. "Take off your shirt. Make it look as if you just threw clothes on."

Wolf had no problem letting the assholes outside think he'd been getting it on with the hot bookstore owner. He tossed his shirt to the floor and kicked off his boots and socks for good measure.

"Where is your car?" he asked, ready to prep her with answers to questions that she would inevitably be asked. But when he looked up after pulling off his socks, his jaw dropped.

Angel was stark naked, bent over, and grabbing Wolf's shirt. She pulled it over her head and let his 2XL T-shirt fall over her slender figure and past her thighs. Her grin was wicked when she turned and tousled her curls.

With a shrug that made him proud she said simply, "it was the closest thing I could find." Then sobering, she pondered his question for only a moment. "Zoey called earlier, asked if she could borrow it to go to Seattle to see some friends. Since I was a bit preoccupied," she said, smiling again and tugging at his T-shirt, "I left the keys under the floor mat for her to get and take the car so we wouldn't be disturbed."

"I like how you think, lady."

Wolf didn't like how Brutus and Julius thought, however, and had no problem delaying their search and possible destruction of Angel's property by refusing to relinquish his gun to the men.

"Unless you're officers of the law, your demands are pointless. I'm not committing a crime," he said, stressing the last sentence with a hard, pointed stare at each of the ugly bastards. "What the fuck do the two of you want, anyway?"

"Zoey Cortez," Brutus sneered. He tried stepping around Wolf toward Angel. "Where is she?"

Wolf moved and blocked his path. A vein popped out on Brutus's bald head as he growled, sounding as fierce as an abused guard dog.

"It's okay, Wolf," Angel said, putting her hand on Wolf's arm. "She isn't here, Brutus," she added, with too much civility.

"Put your dog on a leash," Julius snarled, a man with no neck and a face so puffy it was impossible to see his eye color through two narrow slits.

"I will when Cortez does," Angel said sweetly.

This time both men growled and Wolf grinned with satisfaction, then decided to be amiable. "Zoey called Angel earlier."

"Wolf," Angel said, looking at him as if she didn't want this information revealed.

She was good at this. Wolf looked down at her and patted her hand, which was still on her arm. "They'll tear your place apart if you don't tell them the truth."

"Where is she?" Brutus demanded.

"Probably headed to Seattle," Angel said, sighing. She didn't look at either man but at the floor between the four of them as she spoke. "She did call me. I'm not sure, maybe less than an hour ago. My phone died or I'd check for you." She waved toward the stairs leading to her apartment.

Wolf was brimming with pride at her skills but kept his focus on her instead of looking at the two men to see if they were buying it.

"She asked if she could borrow my car and said she was going to visit friends in Seattle. I was busy." She glanced at Wolf, then at Brutus and Julius.

"I put the key under the floor mat." Wolf pointed to the storeroom door. "The car was parked outside. It might still be out there. She didn't say when she was getting it. Go look for yourself. Don't let the door hit you in the ass on your way out."

Brutus curled his lip at Wolf and gestured to Julius. "Go see if the car is out there," he rumbled under his breath. He turned to Wolf. "What are you doing here?"

Wolf doubted pulling a gun on the man would work twice. He'd seen men like this before. They would kill without hesitation. Wolf knew Brutus had shared what happened when he'd come to the bookstore earlier with his employer. Wolf was probably on the Most Expendable list right now. He'd been on lists like that before.

Smiling, he stepped into the man's space. "Once again, that would be my question for you. Pretty sad that a man of your stature is playing babysitter."

Brutus rumbled and his chest puffed out as the sound vibrated through him. "Answer the question, asshole."

"It's none of your goddamn business what I'm doing here," Wolf growled, his smile fading.

"What are you doing in Zounds?"

Wolf turned, reached for Angel when Julius returned from

the back room. She looked panicked. She was hugging herself, her eyes wide as she shifted her attention from one man to the other. Wolf wondered how she'd managed her store over the years with men like these around to terrorize her.

"Car's not back there," Julius grunted, and shrugged.

Brutus pointed a finger at Wolf. "Don't move. I'll deal with you in a second." He stepped around Wolf toward Angel. "You're going to tell me exactly where Zoey went and—"

Wolf wasn't about to follow orders from these thugs. He put his hand on Angel's arm, gently moving her out of reach of Brutus. Wolf wouldn't shove or manhandle her. That would make him no better than these thugs.

"She doesn't know. It's late. Leave now."

Brutus assessed Wolf. It wasn't hard to see in the man's hardened, cruel gaze that he'd made a career out of being a bully. There were always areas to strike. Wolf searched for them. He hoped the jerk saw few opportunities when he studied him.

"Why are you in Zounds?" Brutus asked, almost whispering. "What would such a successful bounty hunter want in our small little community, I wonder?" His tone turned sweet, with just enough malicious undertones to make it clear he knew how to fight with words, as well as his fists. "I can't imagine you came to Zounds to look for work. Although I'm sure I've heard on the streets that is why you and your friend on the motorcycle are here. There isn't much need for bounty hunters to work in Zounds. We don't have a very high crime rate, and, I promise you, not one criminal has ever escaped our grasps."

Brutus looked pointedly at Angel. "Why is your bounty hunter friend here, Angelina?" he asked.

Angel's mouth moved. Her confusion was clear. "I don't know," she said honestly.

When she looked up at Wolf, searching his face for confirmation that what Brutus was telling her about Wolf's profession was true, Wolf knew Brutus had succeeded.

"Ah, he hasn't told you he's a bounty hunter. I see. Miss Matisse, your friend here, Wolf Marley, has a very solid reputation for collecting some of the largest bounties out there. He doesn't go after small-time, but the big fish in the water," he finished, his voice a sneering whisper. "Do you think you'll catch a whale in Zounds?" Brutus laughed. "Don't think getting snuggly with our town folk, or tapping our pretty bookstore owner, will help you catch a whale. Miss Matisse, call us if you need protection from this man who makes his living collecting hard cash trying to catch men and women before the law can."

Brutus nodded toward the door, and Julius fell in line as they started to leave. He turned, his hand on the glass door, and looked pointedly at Angel.

"If you think he's one of the good guys, you're mistaken. There is a reason why bounty hunting is illegal in over half the states in this country. Your kind isn't welcome here," he snarled at Wolf, then left with his grunt man behind him.

Angel let out an audible sigh and reached behind her to grip one of her bookshelves. "Well, that was fun," she said with a nervous laugh.

"Do they bully you often?" Wolf asked, aware of his protector's instincts flying off the chart at the moment.

"Not usually in person." She ran her hands through her curls, looking beyond adorable in his shirt with her bare legs and feet. "Usually I get nasty letters, like the one that told me I had to collapse all of my boxes in the Dumpster."

Wolf stared out the windows at the dark, sleepy town outside. Brutus's threat had been clear. It didn't bother Wolf so much that Angel knew what he did for a living. Normally he kept information like that to himself and, admittedly, quite often lied to anyone who asked, especially on a hunt. It didn't seem as important at the moment why he didn't care if Angel knew. What mattered more was how these thugs and their crime lord boss might make Angel's life even more miserable with Wolf there. He was torn between leaving her, which would make her an open and very unprotected target, and staying. He wanted to stay.

"They didn't search the place for Zoey," he mused, searching the outside. He and Angel stood in the dark bookstore. At the moment he was glad she didn't have security lights in the store at night. It didn't make it any easier to see where the two thugs had gone, though. "As much as that asshole enjoyed trying to make me out as some kind of threat, I know their instructions were to find their boss's daughter."

"So you and Ben know each other?" Angel asked.

He pulled his attention from the darkness outside and looked at Angel. She walked over to her counter, next to her register, leaned against it and watched him. Her arms rested underneath her breasts. His T-shirt gaped loosely showing off her long, slender neck.

"Yes," he told her. "We met driving up the state and came here together."

"Why are you here?"

It was a question he expected but hadn't had a lot of time to formulate the best answer to give her. Angel was an incredible woman. She had held her own just now in the presence of two men who could scare the crap out of most people. Wolf wasn't most people. He had experienced men and women a lot more dangerous and less sane than Brutus and Julius. But Angel didn't waver or fall apart. He had a feeling even if he hadn't been here, she would have remained strong and protected her store at all costs.

"You can't tell me, can you," she concluded on her own, letting out a regretful sigh.

He hadn't thought of giving her that answer, but her reluctant acceptance of a truth she'd deduced worked for the moment.

Wolf returned his attention to the darkness outside. Headlights beamed across the circular patch of grass with the fisherman statue in the middle of it pointing toward the sea.

"They're sitting out there," he said, content to change the subject. The less Angel knew about why he was here would protect her and make his job a hell of a lot easier.

"Oh, are they?" Angel came around the counter, her bare feet making soft sounds against her tiled floor.

"They are probably waiting to see if you'll kick me out, or not," Wolf said dryly.

"At least they don't know why you're in Zounds, either," she pouted.

Wolf glanced down at the adorable curls that framed her face. His shirt looked better on her than it ever had on him. When she looked up at him, her blue eyes so full of emotions they were almost lavender, he couldn't help smiling at the blatant way she showed her frustration about not knowing something about him.

"Just tell me this much," she said, searching his face as she moved to stand in front of him. "Is it Cortez? I promise I won't tell anyone."

"That promise I'll hold you to, in spite of not being able to enlighten you. The fewer people who know why I'm here, the easier it will be to do my job. I'll tell you this much, though," he said, hating her pouting expression when she accepted what he said but obviously didn't like it. "Zounds will be a much safer place once my work here is done."

Angel smiled and her entire face lit up. She glanced outside her shop where the headlights still glowed like two soulless eyes staring at them in the night. "Why are they just sitting there? Do they think you'll leave and will follow you? Or come back in here and try harassing me?"

Although he liked how she said "try," Wolf worried they could and would make Angel's life hell for knowledge they wondered if she might have.

"They are more scared than we are," Wolf told her. He took one of the curls alongside her face and let it twist itself around his finger. "Cortez has found out I'm a bounty hunter. He has guessed Ben and I are partners, and he doesn't know where Ben is. I'm sure he believes I've closed in on him and am sitting here gathering any final evidence. Since his men didn't tear your place apart tonight searching for Zoey, I'm pretty sure I'm right. They don't like me in your bookstore and haven't decided if there is anything they can do about it yet."

"I think you've just made me the happiest woman in town," she whispered, and wrapped her arms around Wolf's neck as she leaned in against him.

Wolf grabbed her rear end, quickly pushing his shirt out of the way so he could stretch his fingers across her smooth, cool flesh. "Why is that?"

"Zounds is my home. I grew up in this store and now it's mine. My life is almost perfect except for Cortez. And if his goons are going to sit outside my store and wonder if you're leaving or staying, I must insist you stay."

Angel had already decided she wanted Wolf to stay the night, if he was willing. It had been a long time since she'd been this attracted to a man. His shrewd nature and incredible good looks were wrapped up in a perfect package. It had stung a bit hearing from someone other than him what he did for a living. Angel wasn't stupid, and she wasn't spoiled. Why he hadn't told her made sense.

She tightened her grip behind his neck and arched into him for a kiss. His hands were on her instantly, caressing and fondling. In spite of the fact that she knew it was hard for people to see inside her store at night, even in a car with headlights trained on the front windows, Angel wasn't into the idea of putting on a show for anyone.

"Let's go back upstairs," she suggested.

"Are you asking me to stay to piss off Cortez?" Wolf whispered against her lips.

"Just that you'd ask me that makes me want you to stay even more."

When she studied him a moment, she thought she saw a hint of emotion swirling in his dark eyes. They were what she'd call hazel. She saw streaks of green and brown surrounding his attentive black pupils. His wide cheekbones and strong, sharply chiseled facial features made it easy for him to look hardened, wise, and a bit calloused toward the world. Angel had a feeling she wasn't the first person who had entered Wolf's life and tried good and hard to find the real emotions and feelings floating around deep inside this man.

"I don't want to hurt you." Wolf's voice was raspy.

Angel blinked. And here she'd been thinking that he might be hurt thinking she only wanted him to stay to take a stab at Cortez. It had been on the tip of her tongue to tell

Wolf she wouldn't have sex because of Cortez, whether he willed it or forbade it.

She laughed, let go of Wolf, then wrapped her fingers around his thick wrist and started pulling him to her stairs. "I'm a big girl, Wolf," she told him. "Unless you toss me too hard onto my bed, you aren't going to hurt me."

The thought of him doing just that almost made her trip over her own feet when they reached the stairs. Wolf wrapped his hands around her waist when she began climbing, leading them up to her apartment.

"You like the idea of being tossed on your bed," he whispered into her hair as he held her waist firmly and moved up the stairs behind her.

She glanced over her shoulder, enjoying how the tension in the air had shifted to something light between them. This was what she wanted, what she needed, a relaxed, mature relationship with a gorgeous man who understood where both of them were coming from.

"Only because I'm not strong enough to toss you onto the bed," she said, grinning.

God, she loved how he growled. Would he do that when he came? Angel sure planned on finding out.

The second they reached the top of the stairs, suddenly her bed seemed so far away. Wolf's hands were all over her, and his shirt was quickly a crumpled pile somewhere on her living-room floor. His strength turned her on as much as his skilled hands and incredible moves. Not once did she feel that unbearable awkwardness sometimes experienced when two people didn't know each other that well and both were eager to get off.

Angel didn't remember him pushing her backward, but he must have when she suddenly felt her living room wall pressed against her backside. Her wall wasn't all that uncomfortable. Wolf's kisses were off the chart in the hot index, though. Their mouths molded together, their lips scorching hot and their tongues performing a lovers' dance that had her soaked and swollen.

Reaching between them, Angel tugged at the button on

his jeans, then unsuccessfully tried unzipping them. He was making it incredibly hard to accomplish the task when his mouth left hers and he began kissing her neck.

"I want these off," she demanded, tugging at the top of his jeans. "Unzip them now."

"I never thought I'd like bossy in a woman."

"I'm not bossy." There was a smile on her lips, though, when Wolf reached between them and unzipped his jeans, then shoved them down his legs. "That's far enough."

Angel pushed against his bare chest, loving all those tight, coarse hairs that were rough against her palms. His expression was pinched, his eyes wild with lust when she caused him to take a step backward.

"I want to do it," she informed him, hearing how raw her voice sounded.

His brown hair was tousled around his face. Had she messed it up like that? And his mouth was open, his lips moist and dark from their kisses. She imagined she might look exactly the same way. When she put her hands on the top of his jeans, he helped her, stepping out of them without wasting any time.

"Whoa! What?" she cried out when Wolf lifted her into his arms. "I was joking about you throwing me around."

"No, you weren't," he told her, carrying her easily to her bedroom in spite of her trying to twist against him in his arms. "That isn't why I'm carrying you, though."

Before she could ask why he was, Angel was airborne. Wolf threw her on to her bed, but with such grace and just enough force that she sailed from his arms, experienced air whooshing against her scorching flesh, before she bounced on to the middle of her bed. She landed on her back, her arms and legs stretched out to brace herself.

"You're driving me wild, Angel." Wolf stood at the end of her bed. He was fully exposed for her mouthwatering scrutiny. "If we had stood out there much longer, I would have fucked you in a matter of minutes. I want to watch you come before I do," he finished.

Men only really said that in books, right? She stared up at

him, not feeling as fully naked, with every inch of her revealed for his viewing pleasure, when Wolf not only stood there so she could enjoy the eye candy but also revealed a bit of his compassion. The man had many hard edges, but Angel bet there was a soft, loving heart buried deep inside his warrior-like exterior.

"If you think I'm going to play with myself while you watch, you can think again."

His grin sent shivers rushing across her flesh. Fortunately, with her large window that faced the street front offering minimal light into her bedroom, Angel was pretty sure he didn't notice.

"You never masturbate?" His tone made the question sound so innocent.

She sighed and rolled her eyes, not caring if he saw her do that. Then propping herself up on her elbows, she took her time focusing on the many amazing parts of his body.

"I masturbate all the time," she admitted easily. "Which is why I'm not going to do it tonight. The real thing is right in front of me. Toys are for times when there isn't a man present."

"Toys?" He sounded eager.

She couldn't help laughing. Some characteristics in men were all the same. Their love of toys, no matter what kinds of toys they were, never varied regardless of the man. Although the few times in the past when a man had asked her about her personal use of sex toys, she'd dubbed him an unstable pervert and banned him from her store. She hadn't noticed anything unstable about Wolf and had no intention of banning him.

"Don't even go there," she teased.

Wolf's deep, sultry laugh created a swelling that spread painfully between her legs. Moisture pooled in her pussy. Her inner thighs grew damp, and in spite of her refusal to play with herself while he watched, she ached to touch herself there. She wanted everything possible that a man and woman could do together, and possibly some of those acts more than once.

"What do you want me to do to you?" Wolf asked, and knelt on the edge of her bed. He began crawling over her.

"I want you to show me what you're best at doing." Angel didn't want it scripted, but telling him so would be doing just that.

"You'll have to let me know what I'm best at doing and I'll be sure and do it twice next time."

Next time. She liked the sound of that.

"I'll make notes and remember." She was reaching for him, digging her fingers into all that muscle on his shoulders, and drawing him to her. Her actions weren't premeditated. And although her mind seemed clear in noting what he said and did, Angel moved on instinct. The painful swelling inside her spread. It throbbed. It intensified. All she was able to focus on was that Wolf was the only man who could appease this craving inside her that now ignited like wild fire. Angel pulled his mouth down to hers before acknowledging she wanted him kissing her again.

He wet his lips just before their mouths became one again. Already she knew he would be kissing her everywhere with those lips. He would use the tongue that warred with hers now to taste her entire body. Wolf was a damn good kisser. If his skills were as finely tuned elsewhere, she was in for one hell of a ride. Wolf deepened the kiss. He impaled her mouth with his tongue. His lips were moist and soft against hers. He seared their mouths together. That wild fire inside her escalated. She wanted—needed—more before every inch of her burned out of control.

Angel lost track of time. He kissed her for either seconds or minutes.

It wasn't until after experiencing erotic torture for what seemed like forever that he adhered to her wishes and began moving down her body. Angel didn't notice she was pushing her hands against his shoulders once again until solid muscle twitched against her fingertips. Maybe Wolf was so much man that focusing on everything he was doing to her made it impossible for her brain to also register what she was doing to him.

Which wasn't fair, she decided immediately.

"Wolf," she began, intending to find out what would give him the most pleasure. Angel wasn't a selfish lover. If a man was good to her, she wanted to be just as good in return. Since already, possibly at some sub-conscious level to start, but now foremost in her brain, Angel understood this wouldn't be a man she would take long walks with or sit lazily after a meal and learn all there was to know about each other, all she could do was come out and ask, "What do you want?"

"Hush, darling," Wolf purred in his raspy baritone. His mouth was just over her belly. He placed a wet kiss there before looking at her. Light from her storefront shone through her window and cast long shadows across his masculine face. "Let me make you come."

"Oh, I will." She smiled and reached for the side of his head. His brown hair was thick and soft. Already one of her favorite things to do was drag her fingers through it. For such a rough and tough man, his hair almost had a baby-soft downy feel to it. "But I doubt I'll hush."

His grin was a mixture of masculine satisfaction and something bordering on wicked. "I'd possibly like it less if you did."

"What does it take to make the great Wolf howl?"

She swore his eyes turned raven black. "Once I know the lady, then I'll know the answer," he informed her, and began kissing her again.

His eyes remained locked with hers as his mouth surged a path down her body until he'd reached the mound at her pelvic bone. Wolf was layered with more characteristics than most men possessed. She'd never known a guy who wouldn't profess if he was an ass man or a breast man. There were men who swore it wasn't good sex if they didn't get a blow job out of the deal. Other men were more passive and spent all their time getting their lady off, leaving only a few minutes for sexual intercourse before they exploded. Still others were into darker, kinkier sex and wanted it anally or even possibly to spank or inflict nipple torture.

Angel hadn't known men who had displayed all those

different sexual preferences. She'd had a few lovers, most of them normal, although normal wasn't what she read about in *Cosmo* or in paperbacks. Her customers had told her plenty of stories about their husbands and boyfriends over the years.

Wolf ran his hands down her legs then up her inner thighs. He spread her legs apart until she felt the strain of her inner-thigh muscles. Angel didn't know when she'd closed her eyes. She blinked them open, focusing on him. Wolf slipped his hands under her rear, cupping her ass, then dipped his tongue inside her pussy.

"Oh God, yes," she rejoiced unable to restrain her excitement.

The burning pressure would soon be appeased. All that sweet torturous pain he'd ignited inside her would soon reach its boiling point. All he had to do was keep doing what he was doing. Angel knew how her body worked. She was equally excited that he'd figured out her body without instruction.

When he flicked her already oversensitized nub with his tongue, her entire body jerked in reaction and her head flung up to look at him.

"Christ!" she gasped.

"Relax," he instructed.

"Do that and I won't."

"I told you I'm going to make you come. Fight me and we'll do it my way."

So he did have a way he liked it. It was on her tongue to press and find out what that was when meaning seeped into his words. Fight him? But she hadn't fought him. He'd hit a spot too sensitive, and she'd responded, letting him know with a look to ease off in certain places. That wasn't fighting him.

"I have no intention of fighting you," she murmured, relaxing and stretching her arms over her head like a cat as she enjoyed the sheer pleasure he offered. "Possibly not ever," she added with a chuckle.

When he laughed and his lips moved over her entrance, she wiggled her rear end to show her appreciation. Wolf's tongue dipped deep inside her, twisting and performing what had to be some kind of magical act. Angel always had thought herself sensitive to all sensations inside her. She prided herself on that making her a good lover. She could feel when a man tightened, jerked, or swelled while having sex, which enabled her to speed up or slow down their lovemaking depending on how close both of them were to coming. Wolf wanted to make her come. Angel never planned on having sex where both she and her partner didn't experience orgasms.

"Many women think they're coming. They experience pleasure, but they're holding back," Wolf whispered just over her clit. "A strong woman often prefers controlling her release, which makes it harder to really experience a true orgasm."

Her brain was a cloud of lust, but she wouldn't let him know that. "And a smart woman might think you're issuing a challenge." She noticed when he'd quit impaling her with his tongue and moved his lips over her clit.

"Simply an observation." Wolf's lips latched down on that sensitive piece of flesh again. This time when she lashed out, her arms flying off the bed and her body jerking as if electricity had just raced through her, Wolf grabbed her.

Angel didn't have the strength. Not when Wolf managed to grab both her wrists with one fluid movement and pin them against her belly. He held both her hands with one hand, spread her legs farther apart with his other, and performed more of that magic with his mouth. Sparks zapped over her flesh. Her swollen pussy seemed to explode. Waves and waves of fiery hot pleasure swarmed from inside her as a pool of excitement, of raw unleashed pleasure, released again and again.

"Oh my God! Wolf!" she cried out, grateful that no one would hear them, unless possibly they stood outside on the sidewalk and strained. If they did, let them hear. She honestly didn't care. "Crap, crap," she gasped. "It's too much. No, it's enough," she amended instantly.

The moment the peak of her orgasm passed, Wolf let go of her wrists and moved over her. He crawled up the bed on his knees, lifting her limp legs and opening them so he could press the full, round tip of his dick against her throbbing entrance.

"Look at me, Angel."

She did her best to focus. Her brain didn't clear as quickly as her vision. Before she could say anything, Wolf thrust deep inside her. At that moment, she was glad she was watching.

Wolf tilted his head back to her ceiling, his lips pressing together and his expression tightening as he filled her completely. Hard bulges in his chest tapered to lean ripples in his abdomen. Dark curls were tight just above his cock, which repeatedly plunged deep inside her. His thighs were taut with muscle that stretched long and lean from hip to knee.

Power emanated from this man. Angel couldn't remember a life that knew no boundaries. Wolf went after what was right. He didn't hesitate with her, with Cortez's men, or with whatever direction he might be heading. In a matter of twenty-four hours Wolf had shown her that his world would always consist of unchartered territory, which he clearly embraced. Her world was full of restrictions and barriers reluctantly accepted.

Angel was strong and intelligent. She was attractive enough that she could grab the attention of someone like Wolf. But she had known repression, penalties when she tried to reach too far, and punishment when she tried claiming too much. Wolf was giving her a glimpse of how freedom might work. Angel wouldn't accept freedom through the actions of another. She would have to figure out how to make it work for herself.

But was it real? Maybe what Wolf showed her was simply an illusion brought on by a man with capabilities so far beyond her own. Wolf was real. What was happening between them right now, this incredible sex that she didn't doubt would leave her sated for quite a while was very real. His ability to handle incredible situations that Angel wouldn't have fathomed how to manage was real.

Wolf plunged again, and again, into her soaked heat. Angel let go of her thoughts, giving in to the physical pleasure this man offered. She hadn't decided yet if she'd let him know that he had indeed given her an orgasm unlike any she had ever had. As her climax built once again and she soared, more than ready and willing to let go and know that perfect moment when she truly peaked, Angel knew at least one revelation.

First and foremost, if at all possible she would want to fuck Wolf again. But another thought took form, and she immediately grabbed it, unwilling to let go. Angel would learn how to take on Cortez and his deadly henchmen and keep her store. Even if she had to kill them herself. Angel had been so busy showing him that she was a strong, competent woman that she hadn't noticed, until now, how weak and battle-weary she'd become prior to Wolf walking into her life. That would all change now.

Chapter Ten

Wolf whistled as he walked around the corner toward the bed-and-breakfast. Sea air had never been one of his favorite smells. But something about the smell in the air in Zounds, in spite of how persecuted some of the community was, invigorated him and made the morning even better.

Granted, the large to-go cup of cappuccino Angel had sent him out the door with, not to mention that glorious flush in her cheeks that hadn't been there the day before, was enough to make the morning perfect. It had been well over a year since he'd woken with a lady cuddled into him, warm and sleeping peacefully. It had been at least as long since he'd actually felt good about having her there.

Angel had made it clear that this was a "no-strings" relationship. She knew he was here to collect a bounty. She hadn't pried into his personal or professional life. When she'd climbed out of bed shortly after he had, she'd been cheerful, offered him a shower, and had cappuccinos going once he'd joined her downstairs.

Wolf saw immediately that part of Angel's appeal was that her life was as full as his. She didn't need to pry into his business, because she focused on her own. They'd had damn good sex. He definitely wanted more of that. As long as everything remained casual, which he already sensed would be easy to do with Angel—she wanted it that way as much as he did—then this might be the best relationship he'd ever had. Leave it to the Mulligan Stew assassin to help round out Wolf's life and show him exactly what type of relationship worked best for him. Wolf wouldn't tell the assassin, once he caught him, that he'd done something good in his life. The assassin didn't deserve that.

The smell of strong-brewed coffee replaced the smell of the ocean the minute Wolf entered the bed-and-breakfast. He tactfully tossed his almost empty Styrofoam cup into the small trash can by the door. The small tables in the large, airy room were clean, each dressed with a checkered tablecloth. Fresh-cut flowers scented the air in vases on either side of the room. Wolf glanced at his clock. Betsy would be done serving breakfast. He guessed she would be either cleaning the rooms or in the kitchen preparing some delicacy for later that day.

Betsy wasn't in the kitchen. It was as spotless and well scrubbed as the dining area. The large coffeepot bubbled and burped. He walked over to the glass pot on the warmer and reached for a clean mug resting in her dish drainer. That's when he noticed the luggage by the door.

"Mr. Marley," Betsy said behind him. "Good morning. I see you didn't stay here last night."

Wolf recognized his suitcases and his leather jacket neatly folded over the top of them. His other pair of shoes was in front of his luggage. There was a duffel bag that wasn't his on the floor, leaning against the wall, next to his belongings.

He blew on his coffee and gestured to the luggage, grinning over his cup. "You didn't have to empty my room. No offense, Betsy. I'll be sure and be here at a respectful hour this evening."

Betsy focused on the luggage and ran her hands up and down the simple gray dress she wore. "That won't be necessary, Mr. Marley. And I will definitely refund last night, as well as the remaining week, back to your card," she said.

Wolf frowned. He didn't know the old lady, but since he'd

arrived here she'd been all smiles. Not that she wasn't being pleasant now, but she definitely looked worried. He remembered Ben and Zoey telling him that Cortez's men had been at the bed-and-breakfast the night before.

"What happened?" he demanded. "Are you okay?"

Wolf put his mug on the counter behind him and walked up to Betsy. She remained in the doorway but fluttered her hands in front of him, indicating she didn't need or maybe want Wolf entering her space. He remained at a respectful distance, dropping his hands to his sides, and lowered his voice.

Trying to sound as calm and collected as possible, he pressed, "Did anyone try to hurt you last night?"

"Oh my," she gasped, then walked to the large, round table in her kitchen and rested one of her plump hands on the back of a chair. "No. No, no one would hurt me. It's never like that. . . ." Her voice trailed off.

"If anyone has threatened or bullied you, or your business," he said, his anger rising at the thought of Julius and Brutus messing with the old woman, "you just tell me. I will take care of it."

"No!" Betsy snapped, her watery light brown eyes alert when she focused on Wolf. "I've taken the liberty of gathering your things, and your friend's possessions, Ben Mercy's. I can't let you stay here any longer. You are welcome to search your room to make sure nothing has been left behind."

"You won't let us stay here." Wolf let the implication of what she wasn't saying sink in.

Betsy lifted her gaze to his and set her jaw stubbornly. "Absolutely not," she said sternly. "Please confirm all of your belongings are intact. If you don't vacate the premises . . ."

Wolf held his hands out in surrender, and Betsy let her threat hang in the air between them. He imagined she had been a mother and possibly grandmother to be reckoned with. The old lady was always cheerful, gracious, the perfect hostess. Wolf saw now she would hold her own defending her business. Very much in the same way Angel did, except he'd ensured her safety. Had there been anyone here last night to protect Betsy when those two thugs had entered the bed-and-breakfast?

"It's fine," he told her, staying calm. "I'll check both rooms and take the luggage out to my car."

"I appreciate it," Betsy Watson said, tight-lipped.

Wolf let his anger surface once he sat in his Escalade. The engine purred, and warm air cleared the frost from his windshield. He wasn't mad at Betsy Watson. Whether she was scared, had been fed a line of crap, and now believed Wolf and Ben were no-good lowlives, criminals on the run, or whatever else deceitful story Brutus and Julius might have fed her, the old woman's resolve was clear. Honestly, Wolf didn't blame her. Betsy was no match for Cortez and his thugs. She would do what they said, however they said to do it, so she could continue to run her bed-and-breakfast as she pleased.

His rage grew as he became more familiar with a monster he had yet to meet. Cortez had turned the small oceanside community of Zounds into a repressed hell for those who lived here. And like many, the citizens of this town probably didn't have enough money to relocate or maybe loved their town and put up with his crap so he'd go away and they could live in peaceful denial.

Wolf stared out the driver's side window at the back of the restored old home that he already knew Betsy had raised her children and enjoyed a long, happy marriage in. That old lady didn't deserve the bullshit Cortez inflicted, and all because he hadn't managed to keep a leash on his daughter after beating her.

And all of which, overall, was none of Wolf's business or anything he needed to distract him. A slow smile crossed his face as an idea surfaced. More like a notion, but it was a devious one. What if the Mulligan Stew assassin chose Zounds because Cortez was here? Anyone coming into the town would pop up on the crime lord's radar. Inevitably, Cortez would have to be dealt with.

"What a fucking perfect distraction," Wolf mused out loud, then spotted Betsy moving the blinds in her kitchen and peering out at him.

Wolf put his SUV in gear and slowly pulled out of the parking lot. He needed to call Ben and let him know they were officially without lodging. Wolf had Ben's duffel, although when he'd lifted it into the back of his Escalade it had felt suspiciously light. Something told Wolf that Ben had taken anything incriminating or that he might need with him the night before when he'd run with Zoey.

Ben might think he was working an angle with Zoey, trying to get to Cortez. Ben possibly thought this was an avenue toward the assassin. Wolf was confident Cortez didn't know about the Mulligan Stew assassin. The assassin had spent years remaining off all law enforcement's radar while killing scumbags just like Cortez. Cortez wouldn't want the assassin in his town. Not only because it would be highly unlikely, considering the assassin's MO, that he and Cortez would have any kind of alliance, but also because Cortez wouldn't want the law or any outside investigators, such as Wolf, coming into his town. If Cortez knew the Mulligan Stew assassin was anywhere near Zounds, he would have used every resource at his disposal to make him go away.

Wolf held on to the theory that the assassin was either in Zounds or close enough to use the town for his mailing address. He didn't trust Ben any further than he could throw the young kid when it came to fully disclosing what he knew. Wolf now also believed the assassin had either stumbled onto the knowledge of Cortez or known about him all along. It was well documented that the hired gun didn't assassinate without being well paid first. It was doubtful anyone in this town could afford the Mulligan Stew assassin.

So the assassin sat, possibly living quite comfortably, under the radar of the oppressive tyranny of Cortez, without the fucking crime lord knowing he was here. Wolf's mood almost returned to the cheery state it had been after he left the bookstore. No one else had closed in on the assassin yet. Wolf needed to tread carefully. If the Mulligan Stew assassin kept close tabs on Cortez's activity, and of course he would, he probably already knew Ben and Wolf were in

town. Wolf had to find a solid lead before the assassin decided to pull up camp and relocate.

Wolf whistled along to the song on the radio as he main-
tained the speed limit and drove through Zounds. He picked
up his cell phone to call Ben just as it rang. It was a local
number, Zounds area code, but not a number Wolf knew.

"Hello," he grunted, navigating with one hand while holding the phone to his ear with the other. Another thought, don't
break even the smallest of laws. Cortez probably owned the
police department and would look for any excuse to harass
Wolf. His grin didn't fade as he searched for his Bluetooth.

"What are you doing?" a woman asked.

Wolf pulled off the road into a gas station parking lot.
"Checking out some prospects and following up on a few
leads," he said, recognizing Angel's voice.

It was the line he'd given Rebecca during their four-year
relationship. Rebecca had always accepted the answer, and
Angel did, too, with a laugh.

"You sound like some seasoned TV show detective," she
told him, a smile in her voice. "I have a small favor, if you
have time," she continued.

Wolf picked up his Bluetooth, noticed it was dead, and
hooked it to the charger on his dash. "What can I do for
you?" he asked gallantly.

"Well, I don't have my car right now."

Wolf's mood lifted even further. It was the perfect way to
go through Zounds, with Angel at his side. "I just left the
bed-and-breakfast. I'll be there in a minute."

"I don't want you to think I'm taking advantage of you
simply because we had sex last night."

"I could offer a few suggestions on ways you could take
advantage again."

Wolf hung up with her laughter ringing in his ears.

There wasn't any point in telling Angel that he was no
longer staying at the bed-and-breakfast. He didn't want any
weird complications between them if she felt obligated to
offer him a place to stay. Casual was best. There would be
no more Rebeccas.

Dialing again before reaching the bookstore, Wolf informed Ben, who sounded a bit sleepy when he answered, that they were no longer staying at the bed-and-breakfast. Ben didn't say anything about where he was, and Wolf didn't ask any questions. He trusted his phone, but a good scrambler would be smart attached to both their phones. Wolf told Ben he was headed to the bookstore, planned on running some errands with Angel, then would touch base later.

"No rush, man. Talk soon." Ben hung up without another word.

Wolf's radar shot up.

Angel rang up her customer and smiled as he headed out the door. Tourists helped keep her bookstore open, even when they made ridiculous purchases. It wasn't her place to complain if the customer would rather buy a book on the Painted Desert in Arizona instead of their own magnificent red wood trees. Angel carried books on the wonders around the world. She always tried to encourage tourists to enjoy the marvels surrounding Zounds.

"Just here for a reunion," the college kid, who was more boy than man, told her with a wink. "But I'm hitting the road and seeing the sites after I leave here."

She smiled, nodded, wished him a good day.

Then daring to lean on her counter, she exhaled and surveyed her store. When wasn't there a day when the children's section needed to be organized? Angel had learned many things growing up in this store, one of them being when there were no customers in the store, take a break. Putting books back on shelves could be done while customers browsed. She glanced toward her back room, when Wolf entered through the stone room door.

"What are you doing?" She paused in the doorway with her back to the store.

It had been busy since she'd opened, and Angel didn't dare sit for fear the bell over the door would ring again. But leaning in the doorway counted as a break.

Wolf glanced up from where he studied her door leading

to the alley. "You'd be smart to put a better security system in back here."

"I'll put that right on top of the list," she told him, smiling. It wouldn't surprise her if Wolf used spy gadgets in his line of work, but he probably had no idea how expensive installing a top-grade security system would be in this store. "In the meantime, would you mind getting me something to eat?"

Wolf entered the store and smiled. God, that grin, and those eyes. And well, the whole damn package. Angel was deep in trouble with this man. He approached her, his hazel eyes, which she already knew were laced with streaks of green and brown, were currently heavy with a smoldering haze as he closed the distance between them.

The man didn't just walk; he swaggered with so much packed muscle he could have her drooling in just the few paces it took to reach her. Angel had to fight not to suggest something completely different for lunch than she had on her mind a moment ago. She barely managed her relaxed expression when he stopped in front of her.

"What did you have in mind?" he asked with that sexy, raspy baritone of his.

"You tempt the bookstore owner when she can't leave her post," she chided, but grinned up at him.

Wolf tapped her nose, the look on his face pure male satisfaction that his allure was effective. "And I might tempt you again later. I happen to know this place isn't open twenty-four hours."

"Good thing," she muttered, laughing. It would be all too easy to fall for this man. It was reassuring and made time with him all the more fun, she told herself, knowing that once he caught his man Wolf would leave. The last thing she needed was to complicate her life with a relationship. Everything was just fine the way it was. "The Burger Stand down the street makes some awesome burgers. Tell Ernie the sandwich is for me. He knows just how I like it."

"If he does, I might just have to kill the man," Wolf rumbled, and waved off the bills she pulled from her pocket. "Lunch is on me. I'll be back soon."

"Definitely smart not to fall for the man," she whispered under her breath as she watched his backside when he walked into the storeroom to leave through the door which he came in.

The bell tinkled over the door in the store, and Angel turned. "Maggie," she said, delighted to see her friend and get her mind off rippling muscle through a T-shirt hugging way too much man.

"Hi there." Maggie glanced around the bookstore before walking up to the counter.

Angel met her on the other side and resumed her position of leaning against it. "You look tired." She remembered the decorating books she'd sent Maggie off with the other day. "Oh! Are you starting to remodel?"

For a moment it seemed Maggie didn't know what Angel was talking about. "Yeah, the books." She nodded but then frowned and shook her head. "How is Zoey doing? I heard through the Zounds grapevine that her daddy is on the warpath right now."

Angel didn't want to think about Brutus and Julius's recent visits. She didn't like any of her customers thinking their bookstore might be in trouble at the hand of the notorious Cortez. And as much as she liked Maggie and liked thinking of her as a friend, there was another rule Angel had learned over her years working in the store. Really good customers weren't the same as really good friends. People like Maggie and Zoey, who meant the world to her, thought of Angel as the means to an escape from their everyday lives. Zoey's reason for escaping was obvious. Angel had never been able to politely pry anything out of Maggie about her personal life, other than apparently she wanted to remodel rooms in her home. Other than that, Maggie was a pro at turning a conversation away from herself and on to someone else.

As she had done just now. Angel didn't press Maggie about her remodeling.

"I'm sure she wouldn't mind me telling you," Angel began, straightening and heading for her coffeepot. "She showed up here last night. Her father hit her."

"The asshole," Maggie sneered.

"He's the devil," Angel conceded. "Zoey met a guy. She left with him and I'm pretty sure her father doesn't know where she is."

"Do you?"

Angel shook her head and brought two cups of coffee to the counter. Maggie took hers and blew over the brim, her blue eyes bright and a lot more alert than they'd been when she'd entered the store.

"So who is this guy she's met?"

"His name is Ben." Angel decided not to mention Wolf. It was probably wise to keep the conversation off herself as well. She was definitely not the kind of woman who slept around. People talked, just as she was doing now, she mused, but they wouldn't talk about her if she didn't give anyone fodder to do so. "He seems pretty levelheaded, is definitely good-looking, and seemed quite taken with our sweet Zoey. She deserves the best man there is."

"Yes, she does. This Ben doesn't happen to drive a motorcycle and just came into town from L.A.?"

"I'm not sure where he's from," Angel admitted. "But—"

Maggie exhaled as if she'd been holding her breath. "Angel, Ben and the man he is with, Wolf Marley, are not to be trusted. They are here for one reason, and one reason only, to collect a bounty. They are going to use anyone in this town, and all means at their disposal, simply to get a fat check by turning someone over to the authorities. They don't care who gets in their way or whose feelings they might trample." By the time Maggie had finished hissing out her words, she was gripping Angel's wrist.

"They are both bounty hunters?" Angel questioned, and freed her wrist only to pat Maggie's hand. Her skin was damp with perspiration, and once again clouds of worry shrouded her pretty eyes. Angel gave her hand a squeeze. "I'm pretty sure Zoey is safe."

"You've met both of them."

"Well, briefly." One day didn't count as a long time to know a person.

"Stay away from them." Again Maggie let out a breath. She looked at her coffee but then shook her head once as if denying herself the extra jolt.

The way she was worked up, extra caffeine probably wasn't a good idea. "Do you know anything about them?" Angel asked, and hesitated, refusing to let her curiosity best her. "You haven't had a bad experience with bounty hunters, have you?"

Maggie noticeably relaxed, although she glanced around the store, shooting a look over her shoulder. "No, not personally," she said, and looked toward the street. She started toward the door. "They aren't hard to research. Especially that Wolf Marley. He's obsessed with money and, according to what I've read on him, doesn't care who he uses to get a cash reward." She opened the door without looking back. "He doesn't even care about the person he's hunting."

The door closed behind Maggie. Angel stared after her. "Now that was really strange."

Wolf slipped around the side of the building. His heart pounded so hard in his chest he could barely breathe. When had he ever had such good fucking luck?

He'd even thought to back his Escalade into the service alley. Jumping into it, he fired the engine up, loving more than ever its quiet purr when he accelerated, then braked before entering the street. He leaned forward on his steering wheel.

There she was!

Maggie O'Malley, the Mulligan Stew assassin's woman, climbed into a small, newer-model Honda. Silver, just like Wolf's SUV, and as nondescript. It would be hard to pick the car out of congestion on a freeway. The car also stressed humble and definitely did not speak of money, when Wolf was positive the assassin had tons of cash.

He endured the tightness inside his SUV as well as the hard pounding against his chest. Nothing would take his attention off that small car when it pulled from the curb and adhered to the speed limit through town. When Maggie reached the edge of town and accelerated, Wolf ignored the tall pines that grew taller and closed in over head from both sides of the road. The giant trees accentuated his tunnel vision, which at the moment was putting her license plate to memory. Wolf would put down a wager right now that the tag was fake.

Would she take him straight to the Mulligan Stew assassin? Wolf needed to prepare. He'd walked up to dangerous criminals before. A few times he'd ended up face-to-face with the assailant he tracked, surprising them both. To date, not one fugitive he'd hunted down had ever slipped through his fingers.

But this was the big one, as big as it would ever get. Wolf needed a clear head, to be ready for all possible outcomes and be ready with a game plan for each. He would bring in the assassin today if he played his cards right.

"You're just a man," Wolf murmured, using the California license plate on the little Honda in front of him as a focal point. He exhaled and took a moment to loosen his grip on his steering wheel and try relaxing as he drove. "Your skills are exceptional, off the charts even, but that doesn't make you too good to catch."

The road curved to the right. Incredibly tall pines closed them in, making it impossible to see the sky. Wolf wouldn't take time to lean forward and try seeing the tops of the trees. He knew this was one of the most beautiful parts of this state, of the country, and he would miss the spectacular beauty of it because of the hunt.

Wolf had made sacrifices before. He had no idea what information Maggie O'Malley thought she had on him. It shouldn't surprise him that the assassin would know he was close and learn all he could about Wolf. There might have been a time or two when Wolf took advantage of situations to make his hunt easier. He wasn't heartless, though. Not once had he used a woman to further his pursuit of a criminal. He would never put anyone in harm's way, especially with them not knowing harm existed.

Wolf tried not to loiter in the bookstore after being given

the boot at the bed-and-breakfast. He might have eaves-dropped on a conversation or two that morning. Angel had a busy bookstore, and he never knew if idle gossip or relaxed conversation between Zounds's citizens might reveal some useful information. Wolf was not using Angel, though. He'd replaced a couple lightbulbs, reinforced several shelves in her back room, and helped organize supplies she had for her store. He'd considered looking into affordable security systems for her store. A knowledgeable cat burglar, who knew how to pick a lock, could rob Angel while she slept.

That thought made his chest tighten and for a moment it was hard to breathe. No, he was definitely not using Angel. He liked the woman, liked her too much. Right now wasn't the time to think about not ever seeing her again once he took down the assassin.

Wolf needed to focus, prepare possible outcomes that might happen once Maggie stopped driving. She gave no indication that she knew she was being followed. Wolf couldn't imagine the woman of the most notorious assassin of this century and the last not being acutely aware of her surroundings. Maggie never looked over her shoulder or accelerated. She wasn't trying to lose Wolf. She was just driving. And eventually she would stop. Every possible scenario needed to be carefully plotted out. There was no room for error at this point.

It took a minute to comprehend the popping sound he thought he heard. A moment later when his steering wheel jerked hard to the side and a second *pop* sounded, Wolf let out a spew of obscenities.

"No!" he howled, watching the silver Honda continue to drive along the road ahead of him. "Goddamn it! No!" He pounded the steering wheel with his fists after maneuvering his Escalade to the side of the road.

With the amount of strength it took to keep his SUV on the road but pulled off far enough for no one to hit it, Wolf didn't doubt for a moment what had happened. Slamming the Escalade into park, he leapt out of the car and glanced at the two completely flat tires on his driver's side. He quickly turned his attention to the tall, ominous trees stretching beyond his ability to see on both sides of the highway.

"Where are you, motherfucker?" he roared, disturbing the peaceful silence around him.

Wolf squatted by his front tire, which was draping off the rim, a shred of rubber, completely destroyed. If he ran his hand along it, he would find the bullet hole where his tire had been shot. It would be the same with his back tire.

The silver Honda was gone. There wasn't a sign of anyone in the trees.

"I'm going to catch you!" he bellowed, feeling a warped sense of satisfaction when his yelling created a slight echo among the large trees. "You're simply biding your time. You're going down . . . soon. Real fucking soon," he growled, not yelling the last words.

Wolf stared at the two flat tires, reluctantly conceding round one to the Mulligan Stew assassin. He had to admit when hunting the best that there was there would be more than one round. Wolf worked to rein in his fury. That was okay. Maybe his pride got snared a bit by having his tires shot out, but Wolf would have the final laugh, when he slapped handcuffs on the assassin and ensured the man never fired a gun again.

Chapter Eleven

"I would much rather be walking in a mall," Zoey told Ben, and accepted his hand when she followed him over a fallen log.

And not just any log. A small car could park inside the hollowed-out part of the decaying tree.

"A natural garage," she mused, staring inside the remains of the trunk as she stepped over the collapsed part of it. "Don't get me wrong. I love the outdoors." She looked around them. The sun streamed down, working its way past the tall branches of the giant redwoods. It instantly warmed the air and seemed to draw out the aromas from the trees and plants around them. "I'd just rather walk along a board-walk with shops nearby. I guess I really miss the city."

"Haven't you lived in Zounds most of your life?"

"Since I was ten." They were still holding hands, although it might have been because of the rough terrain. Ben's large, rough hand held hers tighter when they reached a part of the forest where the narrow path they'd been walking on seemed to disappear. "I've left Zounds a few times, with my father. Usually to visit friends of his, and the wives of the business-men would take me shopping." She smiled at those rare but fond memories. "They were always really nice to me. I would come home with new dresses and mix and match outfits. I think they liked to play dress up with me," she said, laughing.

Ben squinted against the sun that continued finding its way down to them in spite of the density of the forest. His eyes were exceptionally light today.

"I can see why they would like that," he teased, and intentionally let his gaze travel down her body, then back to her face. "Are you still good friends with any of them?"

"If you mean is there anywhere I could go and stay, no." She looked away when it looked as if he felt sorry for her. She didn't want him pitying her. "They were Mafia wives."

"Meaning loyal to their husbands and simply being nice to you."

"Exactly. That doesn't mean I'm destitute."

"God, Zoey. I didn't think that for a minute. You're a strong woman in a small package." Without warning Ben swooped her into his arms and stepped over a creek bed, his long legs clearing the muddy area to the other side where their path became visible again. "And one who likes shopping," he added, lightening the conversation as easily as he had made it serious.

"I'm not a shopaholic. I wouldn't mind if I were," she admitted, and glanced at his profile. "But it's hard to be when there are all of ten shops in downtown Zounds."

"It looks like there are more than that."

"I'm not really into shopping in a hardware store, and I don't wear eyeglasses." She made a face at him and thought of the few shops in Zounds that she didn't frequent. "So I don't count those."

Ben laughed and she watched his eyes dance with amusement. Something fluttered in her tummy. Ever since Ben pushed his tall, muscular frame off the couch that morning, which was where he'd slept the night before, he'd been brooding over something. Their hike into the woods behind the cabin had been a good idea. It seemed to have brought him out of whatever glum thoughts had been possessing him.

"Of course not," he teased.

"You must like the big city," she said. "How long did you live in Los Angeles?"

"I grew up outside of L.A. It was just easier to find work

in the city after I graduated. Have you ever worked in Zounds?"

She made a snorting sound. "Father wouldn't let me get a job. It wouldn't look good for him to have his only daughter working for some shopkeeper," she muttered bitterly.

"But would you like to work?"

"I'm going to have to," she said, staring ahead at the thick grove of trees. It cooled off instantly and got darker as they followed the narrow path through them. "The cash I have on me isn't going to last that long. I won't be able to work in Zounds, though."

"True," he said, also looking straight ahead. "You could easily find work in L.A."

"Are you thinking about going back there?"

"Maybe," he said slowly. "There still might be work up here, just not in Zounds. There's nothing for either of us in Zounds. Shame, too. It's a beautiful, quaint little town. No offense, but the town isn't big enough for me and your father. And you're definitely not going into Zounds."

She shook her head, loving the protector in him and how so incredibly strong that part of his nature was. Eventually he'd see she could stand on her own two feet. All he'd seen so far was the victim, but Zoey was so much more than that. She wanted him to see the part of her that was strong but wasn't sure how to show him. Especially when she didn't know that part of herself that well yet. That was going to change, though.

"What about your hometown? Is it a beautiful, quaint little town?"

"No." He kept his attention on the path ahead of them, reaching out occasionally to move a limb or reach for her when they were forced to step over fallen branches. "I thought you wanted the big city?"

Ben said, "No," when she mentioned his hometown with so much finality, it made her wonder if there were bad memories there. She wanted to pry and thought of how to get him to talk more about himself. His brooding expression had returned. Zoey only glanced at him for a moment when the path they'd been walking was suddenly eaten up by the thick undergrowth from the dense trees all around them.

"Are your parents still there? I mean, do you still have a place you call home?"

"No. There's nowhere in particular I call home." He took her hand again, keeping a firm grip as they worked their way around the trees. "But home doesn't have to be a physical place. Home is where you're happy."

"Then I don't have a home, either."

"You'll find your home, darling. Already you've taken the steps in finding that happiness."

"Yes, I have."

The ground grew spongy, and Zoey let out a gasp, then laughed, when this time Ben grabbed her at the waist, swooped her off the ground, and made her feel as if she almost flew over the muddy ground. Ben placed her down on more solid earth, which was where the path picked up again.

"You're quite the tracker," she praised him, facing him once her boots were firmly on the ground.

After renting the cabin the night before, she and Ben had taken his bike to a nearby town where there was a Wal-Mart. Although nervous about spending her money too fast, Zoey needed to eat. She'd bought some new clothes and the boots she now wore. Her father had always said buying at stores like Wal-Mart was beneath them. Zoey had enjoyed shopping there, though, and liked her new boots. They were comfortable.

Ben moved his hands and clasped them behind her back, pulling her against him. "Maybe we should go look for work together, possibly find that happiness we're both looking for at the same time."

"We could check out some of the nearby towns. I haven't been to most of them," she admitted, staring up at him and studying his solemn expression. It would be so damn easy to fall for this man. She had to keep reminding herself that she needed to keep her feet on the ground, and not just literally. Although the way Ben looked at her right now, she swore he had every intention of sweeping her right back off them again. "The further from Zounds the better," she muttered, fighting to keep her head clear.

When he leaned down and brushed his lips over hers, it left little doubt in her mind. There went her feet, and the rest of her, floating right off the ground as he kissed her.

"We could take a drive, explore the area, and see what we think," he whispered against her lips. "Do you know anyone living outside of Zounds?"

"No," she whispered, and went up on tiptoe to deepen the kiss.

Instantly her insides swelled. Moisture pooled between her legs. Zoey had never wanted a man like this before. Her insides were instantly molten lava, burning hot and completely out of her control. Even the noticeable chill in the air didn't cool the heat or lessen the urgent need suddenly enveloping her.

Ben had skills that seemed fine-tuned specifically to her body. His mouth moved over hers, kindling that heat and igniting the flames that burned hottest in the throbbing, swelling folds of her pussy. Pools of moisture soaked the sensitive flesh there. Zoey tilted her head back, opening to him and demanding more. Ben was sweeping her off her feet. She was pretty sure, although at the moment wouldn't swear to it, that her boots were still on the ground.

When he ran his hands down her back, his fingers tangled in her hair. The sharp pinches at her scalp had her gasping for breath. His hands trailed down her back. Everywhere he touched her, new sensations created tremors inside her.

Ben cupped her ass and brought her to her tiptoes. He crushed her against him as his kiss grew more desperate, more intense. No man should be able to do what Ben was doing to her with just a kiss.

There were good-looking men in Zounds. She'd seen them watch her when she walked down the sidewalk. Occasionally a guy approached her, but usually a seasonal worker who didn't know who she was. The moment someone who lived in Zounds saw him talking to her, they hurried to inform the poor guy his bad choice in who he'd chosen to flirt with. For the most part, Zoey caught curious stares from guys and that was it. But Ben, he knew who she was, knew the truth about her father, and wasn't intimidated.

That in itself was a turn-on, although Zoey knew it shouldn't be. It wasn't the only reason Ben appealed to her.

For one thing—damn—he was one hell of a good kisser. Ben was obviously shy about talking about himself yet at the same time assertive when it came to making a plan of action. He was a romantic but tough and determined. Maybe he was *just* an unemployed laborer, as her father would have put it, but Ben was honest. He was far from lazy. And something told Zoey that once he found work he would convince any employer to keep him on. There was a charisma about him that would take him far.

"What about your friend at the bookstore. Angel?" Ben asked, once again teasing Zoey's mouth as his lips brushed over hers.

"What about her?" Zoey wanted his mouth back on hers. The pressure growing deep inside, and the pain of it, mixed with an intoxicating pleasure from his body pressed against hers. It made it hard to think about what they'd been talking about.

"Maybe she knows someone who lives outside of Zounds."

"I have no idea," she said.

"Okay." He straightened, letting go of her but then taking her hand again and guiding them along the now visible path.

The cabin came into view, and Zoey stepped over the last bit of underbrush before entering the clearing behind the small, rustic structure.

"What kind of work did you do in L.A.?" Zoey asked, and began rubbing mud off her boots on the damp grass around the cabin. A light sleet, more apparent now that they were out of the forest, moistened the air and ground.

"Whatever work I could find." Ben watched her but didn't make any attempt to clean off his own boots.

"Well, what was your last job?"

He didn't answer right away, and when she looked at him he appeared contemplative. "I guess you could say I did odd, jobs and ran errands for this guy who was self-employed," he finally said; then before she could press him to clarify, he shifted the conversation to her. "What type of work do you want to do?"

"Work in an office, I think. I'm pretty good on a computer."

"Good. Let's go inside and see if we can line up some places to go see."

Zoey liked the idea. She needed a plan of action. Hiding and waiting to be found didn't appeal to her at all. She didn't care where they went to apply for work. She had a taste of freedom, and she loved it. Not once in her life had she been able to simply take off and go. Her world had been continual orders and confinement. She hated thinking her freedom wouldn't last long. Emilio Cortez could reach a long way, far beyond Zounds. He had connections. Until he found her, though, Zoey wanted to make the best of this life.

"I would love to make a day of it," she said, holding Ben's gaze and doing her best not to drown in those clear blue eyes. Good looks and a man with integrity. She definitely needed to keep her feelings under wraps and her heart closely protected.

As if he read her mind and decided to challenge it, Ben swooped down and scraped her lower lip with his teeth. Zoey gasped. He dove in for the full course. Wrapping his arms around her, Ben damn near bent her over backward. His tongue dipped into her mouth, tasting, then devouring.

Swept off her feet? She was floating a mile high! Zoey dug her fingers into his shoulders, holding on for dear life. And not just because he had her off balance. But because he was giving her a taste of perfection. Ben was teasing and torturing her. He was putting thoughts in her head of a life with such a wonderful man to savor, take long walks with, discuss day trips with, and more than likely experience the best orgasms she would ever have in her life.

When Ben let her up for air, the look he gave as he studied her suddenly didn't sit well with her. Then she remembered the bruises down the side of her face. He had almost made her forget about them. Without thinking, her fingers fluttered up and brushed her sensitive cheekbone.

"You're bruised," he murmured. "I'm being a jerk."

"Why are you being a jerk?"

"You're hiding out. You need time to heal. I'm supposed to be this noble man here to take care of you, make sure that bastard of a father keeps his crooked paws off you, and all I want to do is get mine on you."

"I want them on me," she whispered, the words out before she could stop them.

"Are you sure?"

"Very."

Ben didn't hesitate. He moved in with a swiftness that stole her breath right along with any further rational thought. This time the kiss was slow, filled with passion, and intense enough that pressure rose from between her legs and filled her entire body within seconds.

"Ben," she gasped in the brief moment their lips parted.

His answer was to kiss her again.

He adjusted their angle, wrapping his arm around her and turning her so his muscular body braced her when he bent her over and ravished her mouth. And it was a good thing he held on to her.

Dear Lord! The man could kiss. Her world toppled to the side. Everything in her head began swarming. How was she supposed to make sure she didn't fall for him when he could turn her entire body to mush with a kiss? Already her body was screaming for more. Her brain wasn't much help, especially when it was lost in a fog of intense sexual desire.

"Tell me, Zoey," Ben whispered, nipping at her lips before moving to her earlobe. "Tell me," he said again, torturing her ear with his breath.

"What?" Her head fell back. She was a lost cause.

"Tell me to stop."

"What?" she asked again, not comprehending why he would think she would want to stop.

Stop? Hell no, she wanted more. Now! If she would tell him anything it would be that they go inside to the one bed in the cabin. Although she wasn't opposed to the couch, the kitchen table, or damn, at this rate she probably wouldn't stop him if he bent her over his motorcycle.

"You're bruised. You're here to get your life in order. What kind of ass would I be if I muddled up everything by falling for you?"

She jumped when his phone rang. Ben instinctively wrapped his arm tighter around her, pressing her against his virile chest as he dug his phone out of his pocket.

"It's Wolf," he muttered over her head, and answered the call.

Zoey barely heard what he said or the words he spoke when he took the call and spoke to Wolf on the other end of the line. Her brain was stuck on what Ben had said right before the phone call had interrupted them.

Falling for her? Had Ben said he was falling for her?

"Two flat tires?" Ben asked incredulously. "How the hell did you manage two flat tires?"

She slowly emerged out of the thick cloud of lust. Her body still zinged from their foreplay, and she wanted more—no, needed more. But when Ben stiffened, in spite of not being able to hear everything Wolf said on the other end of the line she picked up on one word.

"Gunshot."

Zoey pulled away and looked up at Ben's face. He didn't look down at her but stared over her head, straight ahead. She might not know him that well yet, and in her mind, regardless of everything else going on in her life, something told her it was definitely a *yet*, Zoey knew how a man looked when he was suddenly enraged.

Her heart sunk. It would have been nice to have a few days with Ben before her father managed to destroy their time together. Zoey knew it would happen. Her father wouldn't simply shrug off the fact that she'd left and not come back home. It wouldn't slip his mind that his daughter, the tool he'd planned on using to merge his dynasty with another and increase his millions, had disappeared.

Emilio Cortez wouldn't say, *Oh well,* and move on to plan B.

Damn her father to hell anyway. Why couldn't he let her lead her own life?

"What is it?" she asked, already feeling the trepidation ooze down her spine.

Ben answered by tightening his grip on her. Zoey loved how her body melded with his. The way he had her pressed against his chest, his arm of steel holding her there as if he would never let her go, made her feel more wanted than she had ever felt in her life.

He didn't answer but grunted when Wolf continued talking. Zoey listened, trying to pick up on the words coming from the deep baritone through Ben's cell. Whatever Wolf was telling Ben, he was speaking very fast, and quietly. Even pressed against Ben, with his phone just above her head, Zoey just got pieces. That's when she heard a familiar name.

"Maggie?" she whispered, barely speaking, and looked up at Ben. They weren't talking about her friend, were they?

Zoey shivered in spite of herself. She hadn't considered that her father would go after her friends. Wolf wasn't her friend. She didn't know the man. But he was connected to Ben. If her father couldn't find her, she should have thought it through that he'd go after everyone she knew. Was her freedom worth everyone she knew suffering dearly for it?

Ben hung up his cell and slid it into his pocket. "Looks like you're getting your wish," he said dryly.

He was pissed. Zoey took a step back and hugged herself. Her own anger soared as well.

"What happened?"

Ben ran his hand down her back as he escorted her around the cabin to the front door. "Change into something warmer. I'm going to look online for a place to rent a car."

"Why? What's going on?" She turned to face him the moment they were inside the cabin. "Ben, I need to know," she added, her voice cracking.

He stepped around her and headed to his laptop he already had set up at the small, round kitchen table. Ben had been so excited to learn the cabin had Internet access. Although miserably slow, he had been able to boot up and get online using his laptop. Zoey was surprised that Ben traveled with a computer. He didn't appear to have an ounce of geek blood in him. She hadn't questioned why he had it, but Zoey guessed possibly to look for work.

"My friend has a flat tire on the other side of Zounds," he explained. "We can't go get him in Angel's car. It could be noticed. We're going to take the bike and rent a car, then drive out to meet him. Later, when I know it's safe, we'll return Angel's car to her."

A couple hours later, Zoey pulled up at the cabin behind Ben as he parked his bike. She got out, but only long enough to hand over the keys and climb back in on the passenger side. After their heated kisses behind the cabin, then her being pressed against his backside as they drove down the coast to the next town, just a brush of their fingers as she handed over car keys sent her body perilously close to teetering over the edge.

"Is something else wrong?" she asked, noting his scowl when he ended a phone call before getting in the new dark blue Ford Taurus he'd rented.

Apparently, kissing her hadn't left Ben as frazzled. He was all business when he pulled away from the curb and caused the tires to skid on the highway when he took off.

"Wolf isn't where he was when he got the flats. He had his SUV towed and is now in Hummer Hill."

"But Hummer Hill is the other direction," Zoey said, trying to point, but was slammed back in her seat when he accelerated so quickly.

"We aren't going to Hummer Hill."

"Where are we going? And wait a minute, flats?"

"Huh?" Ben only glanced at her as he tore down the highway, slowing only when he entered Zounds.

Zoey's stomach instantly twisted as she searched both

sides of the street. Her father's goons might be anywhere, exploiting anyone. If they glanced her and Ben's way, her life would once again be over. The moment it dawned on her to slide down in her seat they were already out of Zounds and accelerating on a two-lane highway heading north. Within seconds tall redwoods lined either side of the narrow road.

"Oh, sorry," Ben said when she sighed audibly. "I wasn't thinking."

Zoey shot him a look, confused why he wouldn't be thinking about how terrible it would be for her to enter Zounds right now. "Where are we going?" she stressed.

"To where Wolf was—" He broke off, not finishing his thought. "Where Wolf got his flats."

"He got more than one flat?"

"Yeah."

"Why are we going to where he got flat tires?"

"Because I need to find someone."

Angel stared at the brown paper bag as she breathed in the aroma of the cheeseburger inside.

"Since when did your father start delivering?"

Petey, who was somewhere around twelve if Angel remembered correctly, stared at her from the other side of the counter. He always looked undernourished, dirty, and with freckles too big for his face. Petey was well fed, though, and according to his father simply had an incredibly high metabolism and burned food off the moment he swallowed it. As for "dirty," Angel also knew little Petey was a dirt magnet. On rare occasions she had seen Petey with his younger brother and sister heading off to school. Petey started his days off clean and properly dressed.

"He doesn't." Petey grinned and showed off two gaps on either side of his mouth where baby teeth were gone and adult teeth hadn't quite grown in yet. "He made an exception for you."

Angel reached into her wallet, still confused, although her stomach already greedily growled for the burger. "This is for you." She handed Petey a dollar. "And this is for your father."

"Why does Dad get a five and I get a one?"

"Because your father agreed to have it delivered," she said, giving the young boy her stern look. "Where is the ticket?" she asked, opening the bag and breathing in the wonderful combination of burger, bun, onion, and ketchup. Just the way she liked her burgers.

"It's paid for." Petey shrugged.

"It's paid for?"

Wolf had left over an hour ago, and she had begun to think that he'd forgotten about getting her lunch and decided to do something else. She'd been telling herself that she had no grounds to be mad since she had no claim on the man and didn't intend to lay claim when Petey had entered her store.

"Yeah. My dad probably won't want this five," Petey said, looking down when he shoved both bills into his jeans pocket. When he did, the jeans slid down his slender frame and showed off his boxers. "He wanted me to ask you a question, though."

Angel politely looked away when Petey tugged his pants back up into place. She made a mental note to ask Ernie if his son gave him the five when she next saw the boy's father.

"What's the question?"

"Some man called the restaurant and ordered this for you. He agreed to pay three times the price of the burger and charged it to his credit card, which Dad said went through, so it's good money. The man then said to give you a message when we delivered it."

"He did? What's the message?"

Petey dug deep into his other pocket, once again sending his pants sinking down his hips, and pulled out several items. He placed a very shiny rock, an iPod, and headphones back into the pocket. Then, thrusting out his hand, he held a crumpled note, palm up, as he grinned the most mischievous grin Angel had ever seen on a young boy.

"What's this?" she asked warily as she uncrumpled what appeared to be a form used for taking orders. It had been ripped from a pad, leaving the top part of it slightly torn. Turning it over, she saw a note written in pencil.

"It's the message."

Angel read: *I'm sorry I couldn't bring back your burger. Had to go to work. I'll be back as soon as I can. Enjoy your lunch, but leave room for me.*

Angel blushed, crumpling the piece of paper the moment she finished reading it. Wolf had not left such a suggestive message for the store owner down the street to deliver to her!

"Dad wants to know if you have a new boyfriend and, if so, who is he and when do we get to meet him?"

Apparently, Wolf *had* left such a suggestive message. She was going to kill him.

Angel let out a silent sigh. Petey was young but sharp as a tack and seldom missed anything going on around him. She smiled at the boy as she tossed the note in her trash can.

"Tell your dad that I don't have a boyfriend. Thank him for delivering the burger. The man who ordered it—is" she thought quickly—"doing some work for me."

Angel could tell Petey knew what the note said. The boy grinned but didn't move. Was he seriously only twelve? Twelve-year-old boys didn't know about casual relationships, did they?

"What kind of work?" he asked, rocked up on his heels, and grinned even broader.

"And you and your father need to get your minds out of the gutter," she scolded, wagging a finger at him. Again she thought on her toes, deciding there was no harm in letting the boy take a message back to his father. After all, it was good news for all of the shop owners. She leaned forward on the counter. Petey, undaunted, didn't move an inch. "Tell your father my friend is doing work that will benefit all of us. Now scat, before I tell your mother what kinds of thoughts are on your mind."

Petey sobered instantly. "Do you mean Cortez?" he whispered.

"Scat, Petey," she warned, unwilling to say anything more than she already had. Something told her Wolf wouldn't like it if she started talking about what he was doing. "And deliver my message word for word. If I hear that you didn't, I'll tell your mother that your mind was in the gutter."

Petey laughed. "My mother doesn't even know where the gutter is," he informed Angel, and was out the door.

"Wow," she mumbled under her breath when the boy had gone. What a kid!

Angel pulled her burger out and unwrapped the paper halfway, then took a generous bite. She forgave Wolf for leaving the message as she enjoyed her lunch. She washed down her first few bites with a cup of fresh coffee. There was paperwork to do and probably shelves to straighten, but she stole a few coveted minutes sitting on her stool and simply staring out her front windows, food in one hand and coffee in the other.

She loved her town. Zounds was so beautiful and filled with good people. They were a quiet little fishing community. Tourists trickled in from time to time, some of them discovering the beauty of the town on their way to the redwoods or simply traveling up or down the state. Zounds was far enough off the main interstate not to be where most tourists stopped, but that was okay. They weren't a wealthy community, but most in town got by. Of course that was before Cortez had reared his ugly head and dug his devil's fingers deep into the community before any of them had been able to stop him.

Once Cortez had bought the bank and deposited his people into positions of power, either bribing those who had already worked there or managing to get those fired who had worked in places Cortez wanted to control and bringing in his own people, the damage had been done. That had been ten years ago. Angel had been twenty. Her father had already passed on, and her mother had been dying of cancer. The fatal disease had taken both of Angel's parents from her so fast she'd been too preoccupied taking care of them and fighting to keep the store open to cover their bills.

Once she had buried both of her parents, the store had become her lifeline. Angel had buried herself as well in her work, thriving on the long hours with no employees. She hadn't looked beyond her front door to see what was going on in her town. As well, Cortez had left her bookstore alone the first few years he'd lived in Zounds. When she'd first received the letter informing her that there was a buyer interested in buying the building where her bookstore was and that, if she agreed, her mortgage payments would go away and her rent would be a fraction of the amount, Angel had signed on the line with delighted enthusiasm. She'd barely had a penny to rub against another at the time, since she'd still been paying off medical bills from when her parents had been ill.

After she'd sold the building, her rent payments to Cortez had been half the amount of her mortgage payments. Angel had been able to unbury herself from her debts and started seeing a small profit from her bookstore. She'd made some improvements, bought new bookshelves, and given her store a much-needed face-lift. Angel had even legally changed the name of the store. Bob's Bobbins and Books had been retired, put to rest along with her parents. Angel had been twenty-five when her bookstore had officially been born. She still remembered standing outside with pride and staring up at the shiny new sign attached to the top of her storefront that said: ANGELINA'S BOOKSTORE. The town had come in to see their new bookstore. Angel made new customers. New regulars trailed in on a regular basis. The bookstore made even more of a profit.

Angel had been twenty-seven when she'd taken her first vacation. She had hired two girls, who were good workers, each of them working part-time and coming in on opposite days to allow Angel time to do paperwork, go over inventory, and make sure they always carried the right books that her customers liked to buy.

Taking another bite of her burger, Angel remembered with bittersweet fondness the first time Zoey had entered her store. The shy teenager hadn't said a word to anyone as she'd browsed the shelves and taken a fondness to biographies and romance novels. At first, Angel had thought Zoey the daughter of a new family in town. Angel had been kind to her, as she was to all her customers. She understood now the peculiar look on Zoey's face the first time Angel had asked her if there were any particular books Zoey would like to see in the store. Angel had promised to order them and have them in the next time Zoey came in.

Now Angel understood that Zoey was treated like crap for the crimes of her father by those already under his fierce, bloodsucking control. No one had told Angel what Cortez was slowly doing to their community. She remembered Zoey's surprised and almost confused expression over Angel's kindness, because it had been the next day that Angel had been paid a visit. The owner of her building had wanted a percentage of the store's income. If Angel had refused, her rent would triple, which would have made it a lot more than her old mortgage payments had been.

Angel had tried fighting Cortez. She'd called the only lawyer she knew in Zounds, the one who had made up her parents' wills. He had told Angel that he was retired and couldn't help her. A couple weeks later Angel had found out that was a lie. The lawyer was still practicing law. From that point forward, he wouldn't return her calls. Angel had reached out further, searching for legal help outside of Zounds. One lawyer had taken the time to look over the letters and her lease. He had looked at Angel as if she were an idiot when he'd pointed out several clauses in her ten-page lease that allowed Cortez to do exactly what he was doing. Angel had been sick when she'd left the law office and driven back to Zounds.

Cortez took his cut of her earnings. People began speaking about his pretty daughter who came into their shops, acting like she didn't know her father was sucking them dry. Zoey had known. She never complained when she was forced to pay more for an item than the tag said the price was. Angel remembered when Zoey had first asked how much a book was when the price had clearly been marked on the book.

Finishing her burger, she crumpled the paper it had been wrapped in and tossed it in her trash can. That had been the summer Angel and Zoey had begun a kindred friendship, one out of necessity for both of them. It had also been the summer Angel had indulged and taken her first weekend off since her parents had both passed on. She had rented a cabin and toured Redwood National Park. The park was barely an hour's drive from Zounds, yet Angel had never been there, an embarrassing thing to admit to any of her customers.

It had been a wonderful vacation. She had been in awe of the incredibly large and beautiful trees and had even met a man who worked in the park and had dated him for a while. Angel had finally admitted to herself that she was married to her store and had broken off the relationship when he had wanted more of a commitment than she could give.

That had been four years ago. The past year or so, Cortez had sent more letters, made more demands. Today it was impossible to have part-time employees. Taking time off for herself wasn't even in the picture. She sipped at her coffee, daring to dream how all of that might end soon. Angel wouldn't even allow herself to think where her profit margin might lie if Cortez were completely out of the picture.

She spotted Brutus before he entered her store. Angel's lunch and the coffee she had drunk slowly began churning in her stomach when she realized he was coming into her store. When the small work truck pulled up in front yet no one got out, Angel almost breathed a sigh of relief when Brutus stopped and spoke to the driver. It was terrible of her to be relieved thinking Brutus might be ruining someone else's day instead of hers. There wasn't time to feel guilty when Brutus turned from the truck and entered her store.

"No time for small talk today, Miss Matisse," Brutus said, his usual ugly sneer in place.

"Good thing," she informed him, remaining on her stool. Angel was glad no one else was in the store. She had no intention of being nice to the asshole. "Get out of my store, jerk."

Brutus laughed and walked up to the counter. "I don't think so. I see your guard dog isn't on the premises. Where is he?"

Angel felt a wave of confidence she'd never known around this man before. "You'd love to know, wouldn't you?" she sneered back at him, her stomach relaxing a notch. Wolf had Brutus nervous. Angel swallowed a giddy sensation of excitement. It almost made her light-headed. "Maybe you should start looking for another job, Brutus. Although I doubt there is anyone in Zounds hiring assholes right now."

"What the fuck is that supposed to mean?" Brutus roared.

Angel jumped in spite of herself. She wouldn't pray that Wolf show up soon. She hadn't needed a guard dog before now, and she could hold her ground in her own store against this man.

"I wouldn't try to confuse your small brain by explaining," she said callously.

Brutus slapped a pink form down on her counter. Angel glanced at it with mild interest but wasn't going to stand and move closer. In spite of her wave of confidence that Wolf might possibly be taking Cortez down as she and Brutus spoke, she wasn't going to trust her legs not to wobble if she slid off her stool.

"Where is Zoey?" Brutus demanded, changing the subject.

Angel shrugged. "I don't know."

"Oh yes, you do. She has your car. And I seriously doubt anyone would take your car this long and you not know where she is."

Cortez couldn't find his daughter. Angel's confidence grew even more. Zoey was still safe.

"Pretty sad that even with his thugs sniffing around, Cortez still isn't good enough to find his own daughter." Angel grinned at the snarling man facing her.

"Oh, we'll find her. You're going to tell us where she is right now." Brutus pushed the pink piece of paper over the counter with his thick finger.

"I don't do threats," she whispered, ignoring the paper and staring into his cold eyes.

"Oh, you'll do this one." Brutus turned toward the door and made a beckoning gesture.

Angel didn't understand at first when a man got out of his truck, pulling his ball cap low over his face as he approached her door. Instead of entering, he put a small toolbox at his feet and held a screwdriver in his hand. He began messing with the handle on her front door.

"Hey, what is he doing?" Angel demanded, jumping off her stool without thinking.

She was around the counter and blocked from reaching her door when Brutus shoved the pink piece of paper that had been on her counter in her face. Angel took it dumbly and read it, although the words didn't register.

"Your store is being seized," Brutus said, his words ice when they sliced through her and froze her where she stood. "You're being evicted. Your locks are being changed. From this point forward, Angelina's Bookstore is closed for business. You must leave the premises right now."

"You can't do this!" Angel cried out, shoving the pink piece of paper into Brutus's chest.

"Where is Zoey?" he demanded.

His voice was so low and threatening Angel took a step backward.

"I don't know," she whimpered, looking frantically at the locksmith, who seemed to be working at frightening speed in changing her locks. This couldn't be happening. Cortez was going down, not gaining even more power to destroy her life.

"If you want to grab a few personal belongings, you may, but I'm watching you."

"A few what?" Her head was spinning.

"Tell me where Zoey is and all of this will stop." Brutus had never sounded so gentle, so promising.

"I don't know!" she screamed.

Brutus grabbed her arm and flung her toward the front door. Angel barely managed to brace herself as she startled the locksmith on the other side of the door when her shoulder hit the glass. Brutus moved faster and with more agility than she realized he had. He made it behind her counter, grabbed her purse, and brought it to her. Before she could register the reality of what was happening, he yanked open the door and shoved her and her purse outside of her store.

"Until you tell us where she is, you have no store and no home." He nodded at her purse. "Call the number on the card I stuffed in your bag," he said, sounding disgusted that he had to touch anything that was hers. "I doubt you'll like being homeless for long. It gets cold at night and don't think anyone in Zounds will be giving you a room."

Cortez was taking her store. All she had to do was turn Zoey over and all of this would stop. Angel couldn't hold back the tear that burned her cheek. Her lunch swelled in her gut, and acid burned the back of her throat. Everything she had ever known. All that she had ever loved. How could this be happening? That fucking asshole from hell was supposed to be being stopped, not completely destroying her life.

It was Zoey's life—and Angel didn't doubt for a moment the wrath Zoey would suffer if her father found her—or Angel's bookstore.

"Don't do this to me." All of her confidence was gone. Panic gripped her so hard she could barely breathe. She stared at the baldheaded man with his thick, grotesque body and narrow, beady eyes. He seemed to grow bigger, appear stronger, the longer she looked at him.

Dear God! The lowlife thug thrived on her pathetic, pleading behavior.

Angel smacked at her tears, tucking her purse under her arm, and straightened, facing the mean creature destroying her life. "What you're doing is against the law," she hissed at him.

It was as if he didn't hear her.

"You're doing this to yourself, Miss Matisse." Brutus was cold and terrifying when he crossed his arms and stood next to the locksmith, who already had her door handle and lock off of her door and was replacing it with a new one.

Angel caught a glimpse of the locksmith's face under his ball cap and realized with horror that she had gone to high school with him. Her vision was impaired by more tears threatening to fall as she glimpsed curious onlookers watching the scene take place. Angel turned her head, looking down the street at people she'd known all her life. They quickly diverted their attention and went on their way when she managed to focus on them. Even Petey, farther down the street, darted into his parent's store when he noticed that she'd spotted him.

Her town would turn against her, all of them fearing they might be next if they acknowledged Angel at all. Cortez owned this town. Everyone lived in horror that he might look their way if they did anything to displease him.

The fucking asshole had stolen her bookstore, her home, and her community. Angel was suddenly an outcast, all because she wouldn't tell the devil straight out of hell where his daughter was hiding, hiding for her life. Now Angel was no better off than Zoey. No, Angel was worse. Zoey didn't want her life in Zounds. Angel couldn't imagine a life anywhere else.

At the moment, though, she didn't know which way to turn. Suddenly she did want Wolf. She wanted him to tell her his work was done. She wanted Cortez to return to hell and rot there. The sooner the better.

Chapter Twelve

"What the hell were you doing?" Zoey demanded as they drove back to the cabin.

Ben understood why Wolf had taken care of his Escalade. It was one hell of a nice SUV, pricey, too. But it pissed Ben off that he hadn't known exactly where the shooting had taken place. Wolf had given Ben directions, initially to come get him, but Ben couldn't leave Zoey alone and couldn't go to Wolf on his bike. He was positive that Micah had shot Wolf's tires out. Few men could have aimed so accurately, and Wolf had confirmed only two shots had been fired. Wolf's SUV hadn't been hit, just the tires. There was a slight chance that Cortez's henchmen might have known Wolf's SUV was disabled. People lived back in those woods. And people talked. If Cortez had learned Wolf was stuck on the side of the road, he might have guessed Ben would go to assist. Zoey couldn't be left alone.

So he endured her curiosity and questions. "I was looking for whoever might have done that to Wolf's Escalade."

"You really think that the shooter might be lingering around still? It's been hours since he shot at Wolf."

Ben looked at Zoey when he parked next to the cabin. The side of her face was blending shades of green and blue, but all swelling had subsided. In spite of her bruises, Zoey was captivatingly beautiful. Her straight black hair was down, which he guessed she did to try to hide her face. It streamed over her shoulders and down her back, so shiny black and looking smoother than silk. Her eyes were dark, large, and filled with concern and curiosity.

"No," he said easily, hoping to assure her that he hadn't placed her in danger. He couldn't tell her that he knew the shooter, knew beyond any doubt that Micah would never fire at Ben or at Zoey. "The shooter wasn't out there. But there are things to look for, things that could help identify who he might have been."

"Or she," Zoey prompted. "Men always assume a bad guy is a man. Women can do terrible things, too."

"Or she," Ben agreed easily, getting out of the car and coming around to Zoey when she got out on the passenger side. "The ordeal is over. Wolf is waiting on his SUV to be done. There is nothing more for you or me to worry about."

"How do you know what to look for out in the woods?"

Zoey entered the cabin in front of him. Her jeans were tight around her small ankles, and he could see the spike black heels of her new boots. Ben loved how her jeans hugged her legs and curved so damn perfectly around that delicious, sweet rear end of hers.

He blinked, hearing her question and raising his gaze in time when she turned and looked at him. Ben wanted her. He wanted Zoey so damn bad. It was hard fighting the argument in his head that leaving her alone was best. For Christ sake, he'd just come out of a bad relationship and sure as hell didn't need to be starting another. Not to mention, Zoey wasn't in a place in her life where she would want a man anyway. She had more issues to sort out than most when it came to her father. So in spite of how she was nothing like Stacy, so incredibly sensual, and stared at him continually with lustful curiosity, he should keep his hands to himself.

The moment after he had that thought he stroked the side of her face that wasn't bruised, his hand caressing her soft skin before his brain reminded him of what he'd just told himself.

"It's just things I've learned over the years," he said

offhandedly. "And some I've learned from TV." None of that was a lie. But stopping where he'd thought Wolf's tires had been shot hadn't brought him any closer to Micah.

Zoey nodded, smiling when he touched her as her long black lashes fluttered over her pretty eyes. "I guess you're a good man to have around," she said softly.

"I hope so."

He honestly wasn't sure whether she stepped forward or he moved closer to her. But she was looking up at him, her black hair so straight and smooth down her back. Her sweater was sleeveless and cut with a V down her front. A glimpse of cleavage grabbed his attention, her breasts round swells and revealing just enough to stir his dick to life.

"I think you might be." Zoey touched him. Her small hands rested on his chest long enough to send his heart racing before she reached higher and brushed her fingers against his jawbone. "Can you focus on the side of my face that isn't bruised and pretend I'm not damaged?"

"Damn woman," he growled, his arguments a mere moment ago dissipating as all resolve in his brain suddenly commanded that he take her. "Zoey." His voice was gravelly. "You aren't damaged. It's not your fault what happened to you."

"I'm glad you see it that way." She wasn't tall enough to claim his mouth.

"I see a beautiful woman, intelligent and with a craving for freedom, to see all life can offer her. I see that you want to embrace that freedom and explore it without being held back by anyone."

"You've got good eyesight." Her grin was intoxicating. Perfectly straight white teeth contrasted against her dark, rose lips, which were moist and full against her smooth caramel skin. "I'm ready to explore it."

Both hands were on his shoulders now. Her breasts pressed against his chest. Ben cupped her ass, lifting her as he lowered his face to hers. "I don't want to take any of that from you," he growled, his need for her so great he could barely speak.

"You would take away my freedom?"

"No!" he immediately stressed. "God, no."

"I didn't think so," she purred so deliciously that her voice, her body, her sensual nature and cravings became too much.

Ben tried to be gentle. In spite of Zoey making it quite clear what she wanted, there were facts that couldn't be ignored. Facts he shouldn't ignore.

He tasted her soft, full lips, sensed the moment she opened for him, and was unable to hold back any longer. There had never been anything sweeter, any woman more erotic. Ben wrapped his arms around Zoey, crushing her against him, and devoured her mouth.

Her soft moans fueled his desire. Ben lifted her and headed toward the bedroom. His dick was hard and swollen, making it an effort. Thankfully, it was a short distance in the small cabin from the living room to the only bedroom.

The moment he placed Zoey on the bed she scrambled to pull off her boots and socks. Her long hair tumbled around her, fanning her body when she yanked her sweater off her body with one fluid sweep. She reached for her jeans, unbuttoning and unzipping and pushing them down her thighs.

Ben managed to take off his T-shirt. That was too much. He didn't want to miss any movement Zoey made.

"Slow down," he told her, taking her wrist in his hand, which instantly stopped her other hand.

Zoey looked at him, her eyes wide and glazed with an alluring mist of unadulterated carnal lust unlike any he'd seen in a woman before. Strands of her hair fell over part of her face. The rest of her long, straight hair flowed down her bare shoulders. Hair parted from the swell of her right breast and ended in evenly cut strands, partially hiding her flat, firm stomach. With her jeans undone but not pushed down her legs, he was able to watch the rise and fall of her tummy, proof how quickly her breath came.

Ben ached to run his tongue along the edge of that lace bra. He wanted to press his face between those luscious swells, feel her breasts press against his face with the rise and fall from her breathing. He imagined running his hand between the concave dip between her hipbones. Just thinking about feeling, instead of seeing, how quickly her breath came as she wanted him damn near engorged his cock.

"Our first time," he began, drowning in her stormy gaze. "It should be slower. I want to watch you, adore every inch of you. Zoey, I—" He broke off, not knowing how to put in words why it mattered so much that he remember every minute of their lovemaking. He wasn't sure he knew why, just that it seemed very important.

"Yes. What?" she whispered, raising her free hand and combing his hair from his face. "However you want to do this. I got a bit excited."

"I'm more than a bit excited." He grinned at her and leaned his head against her hand before she could pull it away.

"Me, too." Zoey's blush was a beautiful shimmering rose that spread over her pretty skin, dimming the bruises on the side of her face.

Ben crawled over her, pulling her wrist from her jeans as he did. It was best both of them left their jeans on for at least a bit longer. Saying he was excited was an understatement. Zoey's willingness and her excitement to have sex with him damn near brought him to the breaking point before they'd even reached the bedroom.

They sunk into the middle of the soft mattress he swore must have been stuffed with down. Not that he cared a bit how comfortable the bed might be to sleep in. He loved how Zoey relaxed into it as she stretched out on her back. Ben lowered himself slowly on top of her until their bodies pressed against each other.

"You are so beautiful," he praised, letting go of her hand and leaving it over her head. He pressed his hands into the mattress on either side of her as he kissed her soft lips. "More beautiful than any other lady I've ever known."

"With my bruised face," she began.

He hushed her with a deeper kiss, entering her mouth and teasing her tongue with his. Ben loved how she responded to him. Zoey wrapped her arms around his neck, pulling him down closer. She bent her knees and rubbed her bare feet up his jeans. Ben swore he felt the heat from her pussy through her jeans and absorbing into his. It was a good thing his eyes were closed or she might see how her actions caused his eyes to roll back in his head. He groaned his pleasure. Zoey's purr had to be the strongest aphrodisiac he'd ever experienced.

"This will be the last time there will ever be bruises anywhere on your body," he promised, lowering his mouth to her neck.

"I might be a klutz and fall." She giggled and dug her fingernails across his scalp.

"Then I'll catch you."

Ben heard his words and in the back of his mind understood the meaning he was suggesting. He was speaking about long term, about having a relationship with Zoey. There hadn't been thought behind his words when he uttered them. When he spoke them, though, he meant them. He wanted Zoey in his life. He wanted to know her better.

If that was to happen, very soon he needed to share with her who he was, what he did for a living, although he couldn't share with her why he was really here. Would she accept there were things he couldn't tell her? At least he hadn't lied to her about anything so far. He prayed he could continue evading the complete truth, at least until he found Micah. Then . . . would she consider returning to L.A. with him?

Zoey wasn't sure she'd ever be able to catch her breath again. So this was what it was like to have a man adore her body. Arching her rear end off the bed, she fought not to push Ben's face down her body. The ache between her legs was so strong she wanted to scream.

"God, Ben, please," she urged, wanting more yet loving everything he was doing to her body right now.

His promises to protect her were as wonderful as his skills were. Zoey squirmed when he did a dance with his tongue around her belly button. Her insides were on fire. The swelling between her legs spread like a deadly fever throughout her insides. She was going to explode. No matter what she did, how she moved, or where he kissed and touched her, waves from need and desire continued to swell.

When Ben rose off of her and reached between them for her jeans, Zoey thought the aching would stop. It didn't. A frantic urgency filled her. She reached between them also and began shoving her jeans down her thighs.

"Let me," he grumbled, his voice a deep baritone, raspier than it had ever sounded before.

"Just hurry," she complained, unable to keep her hands from helping push her jeans down her legs.

Ben chuckled and Zoey wondered what was so funny.

"I don't think you understand." She frowned up at him. Then she squealed. The moment her jeans were tossed to the side, Ben yanked her panties off of her and spread her legs far apart. "What are you doing?" she cried out.

Ben's gaze darkened when he nestled his body between her thighs, sliding most of his large frame off the end of the bed so that his mouth was inches from the source of her heat.

"I want to taste you," he said, and his breath against her damp, tight curls was the worst torture he'd administered to her body yet. "Let me make you come."

Zoey might be a virgin, but she knew about sex. She'd read more on the act of oral sex than possibly most people had. Everything from smut and porn to sensual, soft romances. So she knew women always wanted this done to them. She hadn't imagined it would be something she and Ben would do their first time together, though. Whenever she'd read about oral sex it seemed to happen between two people very familiar with each other. Unless it was porn; then there were no holds barred.

This wasn't porn, though. She and Ben were making love, exploring each other's bodies in an effort to know each other better. Zoey still thought there was no way she and Ben would have a chance at a lasting relationship. Her father would find her. No matter where she hid or for how long she managed to hide, eventually he would track her down. It would be bad when he did find her. Which was why Zoey wanted the most out of her freedom. She didn't want to think about the hell where she had come from. She wanted only now.

Zoey wanted Ben naked also. Yet he still wore his jeans. She was spread-eagled, the most sensitive part of her body incredibly vulnerable. This made it very difficult to get his clothes off of him.

Ben's mouth hovered over her clit. She could feel the heat of his breath. He wasn't touching her, though.

Zoey opened her eyes, her muddled thoughts sending all kinds of mixed signals. Everything about how sex should be her first time and their first time together slipped from her mind. She didn't care about any of that when she lifted her head and stared down her body at Ben.

"I feel so swollen—" She didn't finish. How stupid did that sound?

Like she could think to form coherent sentences when Ben stared up at her, his face a mere inch at most from her throbbing pussy. His light blue eyes were wide and alert, watching her. They seemed to start glowing, becoming brighter, when she stared back at him. His bare shoulders were a rippling stretch of bulging muscle. She had a glimpse of his bare chest and a sprinkle of hair darker than his straight blond strands that framed his face.

"Exactly how you're supposed to feel," Ben told her.

The breath from his words tortured her enflamed entrance. Her swollen clit next to his mouth pulsed rhythmically, as if her heart had somehow managed to sink down her body and was now lodged there.

Ben pressed his mouth against her damp skin between her legs. He sucked Zoey's small, swollen flesh into his mouth.

"Oh my God!" Zoey damn near flipped off the bed.

His chuckle flooded toward her on torrential waves that grew larger and larger until Zoey was swimming with them. She rode them hard, fighting to stay afloat and not drown. Ben's tongue flicked over her all too sensitive flesh. He then stroked it, igniting even more pleasure inside her. When it

became too much, when she cried out, it didn't dawn on her
how she'd grabbed and twisted the bedspread until she flew
into a sitting position. She was drowning. But then the mul-
titude of waves flowed over her and she was floating. As she
convulsed, riding out what she knew for a fact was her first
real orgasm, a tingling settled over her flesh. Her skin was
damp from perspiration. Zoey's hair stuck to her back. Ben's
long, strong fingers pressed into her thighs, keeping her legs
spread. So many sensations washed over her but only one
really mattered. That unbearable pressure was gone. Zoey
crashed back onto the bed, sinking deep into the wonderful
down as if she'd died and gone to heaven.

"I didn't know it could be like that." She was almost
breathing too hard to speak and laughed at the panting sound
in her voice. "Amazing."

Something began swelling inside her again and she
blinked and stared at Ben as he moved to kneel between her
legs. His face was glossy with moisture. Her moisture. She
wanted to kiss her cream off of him and pushed up to her
elbows. It was as far as she got before laughing some more
and collapsing again.

"I'll kiss you in a minute," she told him, waving her hand
in the air before letting it drop beside her. Every inch of her
was warm with sated delight.

"One hell of a compliment," Ben growled.

She blinked to focus on him. There had to be the most
stupid grin planted on her face.

"That's something I'll definitely want to do again." This
time when she raised her arm she had the strength to keep it
extended. She reached for him.

Ben stretched out alongside her, staring at her breasts.
After a moment, he lazily dragged his calloused index finger
around her nipple. It puckered, greedy for the attention. The
rest of her body sizzled back to life as well. Zoey purred like
a cat and arched into his touch.

"Zoey," he said, dragging her name out slowly on a breath.

"Mm-hmm," she continued purring.

"Have you ever had sex before?"

She rolled to her side, draping her arm over him, then leaned her head back to smile up at him. "I will have here in a few minutes," she teased. But when she tried pulling him on top of her, Ben remained posed where he was.

The glaze of sensual fervor dissipated before her eyes. Ben's expression suddenly shrouded with a brooding mask, as if he contemplated what she'd just said and somehow found her lacking. Zoey could have kicked herself in the rear. A man like Ben probably had been with dozens of women. She almost blushed thinking she wasn't sure how old he was and was about to have sex with him. It didn't matter. The fact that they didn't know every intimate detail about each other didn't matter. She was a grown woman, and if she wanted to make love to this man, she would damn well do it.

She gripped his shoulder and put some force into tugging him to her. "Come here," she whispered. The purr in her voice was gone.

Zoey tried another tactic. This was her moment of freedom. Wouldn't it be wonderful to throw in her father's face, once he finally found her and had her dragged into his despicable den, that she was no longer a sweet, pure virgin? She would decide who to lose her virginity to, not her goddamned father. She let go of Ben's shoulder and reached down between them. The back of her hand grew wet as her damp curls stuck to her. Now wasn't the time for embarrassment. Zoey gripped his dick inside his jeans.

Pure womanly satisfaction brought back her purr when Ben growled and his eyes rolled back in his head.

"I want you to fuck me," she said brazenly.

She was going all the way, damn it. Come hell or high water.

Zoey swallowed thickly at the realization of how long his penis was. She pressed her fingers into him, running them along the length of his shaft. It ended at the top of his jeans.

So what. Size didn't matter. That was the most overused cliché on the planet. She would put truth to it today. She tugged on his zipper, which wasn't an easy task with a swollen dick pressed against it.

Apparently it wasn't comfortable, either. Ben's moan turned into more of a growl, and he grabbed her wrist—hard. Circulation cut off to her hand.

It wasn't a punishing grip. She knew what that felt like. Zoey raised her gaze to Ben's face and saw the desperation. It appeared in pinched lines that darkened the tormented look she saw there.

"I'll be careful," she assured, wiggling her fingers on the hand he still gripped to reach for his dick.

"No," he choked out.

"Then you—"

"No!"

Ben released her hand at the same time he leapt off the bed. He moved so fast Zoey rolled over onto her tummy. She raised herself, pushing up and looking at him in time to see him zip and refasten his jeans.

"What?" she began.

He cut her off. "You're a virgin," he said, his tone harsh, almost accusing, as if virginity were some type of contagious disease.

She happened to know it was not. "Yeah, so?" she said, bristling.

"You won't use me to take your virginity," he snarled.

"I'm not using you!" How could he think such a thing?

Ben turned and stormed out of the cabin. It sounded as if he said, "Not like this," before the cabin door slammed behind him.

Wolf stared at the pink piece of paper taped to the door at Angelina's Bookstore. *Notice Of Eviction.*

"What the fuck?" he snarled, and glanced down the street, beyond the small grassy area where the road curved in a circle before resuming the few blocks of Zounds's downtown. There were a couple children up the street. A single skinny young man walked against the brisk wind, his face down, and disappeared into the hardware store. A car turned the corner, slowed, and pulled into a diagonal parking stall. A stout middle-aged woman got out and hurried into whatever store it was that she'd parked in front of. But that was it. Downtown was dead.

Wolf returned his attention to the slip as he pulled out his phone. Hitting speed dial, he listened as the phone rang, then went to voice mail. Wolf didn't do voice-mail messages. There was never a reason to record his voice or any thoughts he might be having at that moment. He hung up and shoved his phone in his pocket. Angel would see the missed call. That was enough without leaving a message.

He reached for the pink piece of paper. But before ripping it off the door, he let his hand drop. Wolf wasn't an expert on landlord/tenant law in the state of California, but he'd bet hard, cold cash that the eviction wasn't legal. Sleet blew around him as he stepped back, pulled his phone back out, and took a picture of the eviction notice instead. The people of this town needed to take a stand against Cortez and call him on the stunts he pulled. It wouldn't take too much effort to look up the laws and find a lawyer. One would think a good lawyer might take this case pro bono just for the shot of ending a crime lord's tyranny and boosting their reputation. Wolf imagined the publicity would help any attorney's career.

Wolf reached into his Escalade and grabbed his leather coat. Slipping it on, he then pushed the button on his key to lock the vehicle. The temperatures were dropping. He had to reach Angel. He stalked around to the back door of the store and pulled on the door to the storage room. Locked!

Damn it. Was she upstairs? Maybe she'd fallen asleep. Wolf pounded on the back door with his fist, putting some muscle into it. Angel would hear that upstairs. He hated waking her or her hearing someone pounding on her door after what she had to have been through while he was gone.

A sickening feeling twisted cruelly in his gut. Wolf could see Cortez's men entering the store with that fucking piece of pink paper and shoving it in Angel's face. They probably had waited until Wolf had raced out the back door to his Escalade. He had been so focused on following Maggie and finding the Mulligan Stew assassin, Wolf hadn't bothered checking to see who might be outside Angel's store when he had left. All of his attention had been on that little silver Honda.

"Goddamn it!" he roared, not caring at the moment who heard him. He did glance over his shoulder at the service alley. Sleet blew in circles over the ground, but no one was around him.

Downtown could be dead due to the weather. There was an eerie sense of abandonment in the air, though. Angel was a core part of this community. He'd seen her customers trail in and out all day. A lot of them made purchases, but there had been more than a few who had lingered at her counter, gossiping about the latest news in town. Angel had easily carried on conversations with each of her customers, as if she'd been waiting all day for that particular person to come in. Angel had known everyone who walked into her store. And all her customers loved her. None of what any of them had said had meant a thing to Wolf until Maggie had walked into the store.

She had changed her hairstyle and dyed it several shades lighter. Angel had called her Maggie, and the instant Wolf had seen her face he knew it was Maggie O'Malley, or whatever she was calling herself these days.

Wolf zipped his leather coat and headed back to the front of the store. The wind was getting fierce. He hadn't checked the weather, but by the feel of it he'd say they were in for a serious drop in temperature. Already a thin layer of sleet blew down the sidewalk as Wolf started walking toward the rest of downtown.

He entered the Burger Stand without giving it much thought. Had they delivered Angel's lunch to her? And the message? Did she get it? He'd been gone almost five hours, time in which Angel had disappeared and her store closed. He needed answers. Ignoring the thick smell of frying beef and the sudden warmth that embraced him, Wolf moved past the vacant tables in the small restaurant and stepped up to the counter.

A teenage girl walked around a food station where the cook put items under a heat lamp that were ready to serve.

"What can I get for you?" she asked.

"Where's Ernie?" he asked, not knowing who had prepared Angel's burger and deciding he would go straight to the top. That way he hoped he wouldn't have to ask the same question over again.

"Who wants to know?" The young girl's face hardened as she gave Wolf a once-over.

At the same time the man on the grill in the back poked his head up.

"Wolf," Wolf said, making eye contact with the man.

The young girl simply raised one eyebrow. Wolf ignored her. If she didn't like his name that didn't bother him a bit.

"Did you deliver Angel's lunch to her?" Wolf asked, directing his question to the man at the grill.

"I took it to her," a skinny boy announced as he appeared to pop out of nowhere. "And I gave the part of the tip to Dad just like Angel told me to do."

"Good to know," Wolf told the skinny child, nodding his appreciation of the information.

The skinny boy straightened, his expression becoming as serious as Wolf's, and mimicked Wolf's nod. The man left the grill and put his hand on the boy's head. He mumbled something the boy obviously didn't like. The kid rolled his eyes but disappeared into the back of the store. Wolf couldn't imagine growing up with a dad around all the time. The boy didn't know how lucky he was.

"Where is Angel?" Wolf asked the moment the man faced him on the other side of the counter.

"Who wants to know? You got some ID?" With a glance the man scurried the young girl out of sight, leaving him and Wolf alone at the front of the store.

"ID?" Wolf was surprised, not that he hadn't been asked that questions hundreds of times over the past, but this was the first time in Zounds. "Actually, yes, I do. I take it you're Ernie?"

The man nodded once. "Ernie Stockton. Owner and proprietor, and a very good friend of Angel's. Why are you asking about her?" he demanded, and wiped his hands on the white apron that hung slightly crooked off his shoulders.

It was also tied at his waist. Ernie wasn't fat by any means, but the apron didn't hide the slight pooch in his belly that men his age seemed to obtain. Wolf would put the man in his mid- to upper forties. There was a plain gold band on Ernie's left ring finger, and as dull as it was, Wolf bet it had been on that finger since the man's wedding day.

Ernie had a receding hairline, which was a nice way to say the man was going bald. His hair was light brown, with only a few gray strands along the sides. If this place was being harassed by Cortez's goons as much as Angel's store was, Ernie was doing good not to have more gray. He was an inch or two taller than Wolf. Many men were taller than Wolf. It didn't bother him. He made eye contact with Ernie and saw an honest man, who was plagued with worry over something. Ernie was also wary of Wolf but curious about him as well. It had become easier reading people from years of interrogating suspects and questioning witnesses.

Wolf watched the skinny young boy dart out from behind the counter, grab his father, and tug on his shoulder sleeve. The boy whispered loudly but inaudibly. Ernie turned him in an about-face and gave him a gentle push toward the back of the store.

"The ID?" Ernie asked when his son was once again out of sight.

Wolf would bet the kid was eavesdropping. He pulled out his driver's license and handed it over the counter to Ernie.

Ernie glanced at it. "Any other ID?"

"Other ID?"

Ernie sighed but then moved closer to the counter and lowered his tone to a conspiratorial whisper. "Mr. Marley, if you're the law here to take down Cortez, I will definitely testify and give you all the information you need to lock him up for a thousand lifetimes."

Wolf stared at him. Where would Ernie get such a far-fetched idea? Then it hit him. Oh shit! He'd let Angel believe he was in town after Cortez. Although Wolf had thought she would have figured out a bounty hunter only went after people who already had a bounty on them. Cortez had yet to be charged with a crime. Maybe she hadn't impressed that part upon her neighbors.

"Sounds like everyone in this town has enough on the man to put him away," Wolf said. "Makes me wonder why none of you stand up to him."

Ernie bristled. Then raising his hand, he pointed in the direction of Angelina's Bookstore. "Because if any of us did, that would happen to us, too. I've got a family to feed."

Wolf nodded, not quite getting it, but let it be. Cortez sure had picked the right town to conquer. These people were sheep.

"I don't know where Angel is." Ernie crossed his arms and stared at Wolf.

The conversation was over. Wolf had been in his line of work long enough to know when he wouldn't get any more answers out of a person. He left the Burger Stand, instantly feeling the cold, and did a quick survey of the surroundings. Downtown looked like a ghost town, a very cold ghost town.

Flipping the collar up on his coat, Wolf glanced down the street at the shop names. Angel had one of those hoops that kept material stretched tight. He remembered it looked like she was sewing flowers on a pillowcase. Wolf headed down the street a bit farther to a yarn shop.

Two ladies not much older than Wolf had given him the same stubborn look Ernie had. With the two ladies, their exchange had been even briefer. There was a coffee shop on the next block. With each shop Wolf asked the same questions, got the same answers and the same blank stares that spoke volumes. He was growing more suspicious that each person he spoke to knew exactly where Angel was and simply wasn't telling him.

He wasn't the bad guy. Wolf wanted to scream that at each of them. Angel needed him. By the time he had reached the end of the downtown area, a thought began forming and it left a queasy feeling in his gut. What if Angel had seen him follow Maggie? Or worse yet, what if Maggie had called Angel and had told her Wolf was following her?

He seriously doubted the latter would have happened. Maggie wouldn't do or say anything that might cause suspicion. He nixed the last thought. But what if Angel was pissed at him? If she mentioned to any of her wide span of friends that Wolf had upset her, they would rally around her and Wolf would be blocked out. He wouldn't be able to find out where she was at gunpoint.

A sense of urgency hit him. Wolf needed to find Angel, especially if she was mad. Maybe having her burger delivered to her hadn't made up for him taking off on her. What if they hadn't delivered his message to her? He'd told them when he'd called—and hell, he had paid dearly for that burger and to have it delivered less than a block's distance—to tell her that he'd had to go to work. He had thought adding that she enjoy her lunch but leave room for him had been a nice suggestive addition. And it had let Angel know he was sincerely going to work and couldn't wait to see her when he got back.

Apparently, the note hadn't been good enough. Or maybe it had nothing to do with him leaving or having lunch sent to her or the message he had asked be delivered with her burger. Maybe Angel was angry because her store had been illegally closed; then, making it worse, that ridiculous piece of paper taped to her door stating she'd been evicted added to her humiliation. Wolf could just picture how pissed off Angel would have been if that waste of human flesh piece of shit Brutus had handed her that paper and told her she was being kicked out for nonpayment of rent. Rent that barely left Angel with enough money to keep her business open. She had told Wolf she paid it on time each month just to make sure those assholes left her alone. Angel would have been furious beyond control being told she was evicted.

It should have hit him sooner. Wolf had reached his Escalade while trying to second-guess what had transpired while he'd been dealing with small-town, curious mechanics who were dying to know more about Wolf. Apparently, strangers driving seventy-thousand-dollar SUVs with two tires having bullet holes in them didn't grace that shop with their presence on a regular basis. While he'd been out having so much fun, Angel had been minding the shop until Cortez's goons had shown up. Wolf was almost positive they had shown up for one reason—to find out where Zoey was. When she wouldn't tell them or, knowing her, tried kicking them out of her store, things got ugly.

Wolf looked over the hood of his Escalade at the entrance to the bookstore. Then frowning, he walked up to the glass door and stared at the shiny lock above the door handle.

"Motherfuckers changed her locks." Wolf pressed the side of his hand to the cold glass and put his face close to see inside.

The register was open, and it appeared the till was empty. There were papers, what appeared to be invoices and other receipts from different vendors, scattered across the counter. Angel kept her cappuccino maker on a card table off to the side of her counter. It had been thrown to the floor, apparently while in use. A dark stain spread out under shards of broken glass.

Wolf scanned the length of the store, then, pulling his phone from his pocket, held it up to the glass and began snapping pictures. He really did wish any of Cortez's men, or hell even Cortez himself, were watching and would confront him about what he was doing. He'd keep right on taking pictures while shoving his fist through their faces. His temper soared as he walked the length of the front of the store, pressing his face to the glass along with his phone and taking picture after picture of the destroyed bookstore.

Books were all over the floor. Shelves were knocked over. Wolf was sick to his stomach. Everything Angel had in the world was tied up in this small-town little bookstore. Wolf spotted the door leading up to her apartment, which she always kept closed, standing open. Clothes were on the stairs, tossed and left. Angel wouldn't have done that. She didn't do any of this. Not only had they kicked her out, changed her locks, and destroyed her store, they'd also made a point of leaving the door to her apartment upstairs open with her clothing hanging off the stairs, to make sure if she was to look she would see they had violated every inch of her privacy.

"Goddamn assholes," Wolf swore, stalking back to his driver's side and yanking open the door.

It was a lot warmer inside, even though the engine had been off almost an hour during his search for Angel downtown. Wolf turned on the engine, then flipped open his laptop on his passenger seat. He would find a damn attorney. Wolf happened to know a few good men in this state, detectives who had been on the force for years. He had connections. It might take a few days, but he could have more law sniffing up Cortez's ass than the man had the power to exterminate. And these wouldn't be men who would take bribes or look the other way when the law was being broken. Wolf would show them what happened when they messed with the wrong woman.

"Whoa, boy!" Wolf let out a low whistle and pulled his fingers away from his laptop's keys. What was he doing? "You're here to catch an assassin," he reminded himself, speaking out loud as he scowled at his hands, mid-air above his laptop.

Slapping his laptop closed, Wolf leaned back in his driver's seat and stared out his windshield. He didn't pay attention to downtown Zounds. When had he last gotten distracted on a hunt?

Never, he mouthed.

The Mulligan Stew assassin had picked the perfect community to disappear in. Any bounty hunter, fed, or other law enforcement person would have one hell of a hard time not feeling honor bound to help this community out. It would distract them, take up their time, and give the assassin time to run or learn their MO well enough to successfully remain hidden.

"And I fell right into his trap." Wolf scowled, stewing this over and deciding he didn't like the taste of it one bit. No one got the best of him. His record was impeccable.

Wolf hadn't once fooled himself into thinking this hunt would be easy. Hell, he knew it would be the hunt of a lifetime, one he could retire on if he so chose. But he never would have guessed, regardless how well-laid the traps were, that he would fall into them and find it damn hard to get out.

Hadn't he already acknowledged that Zounds was the perfect hiding place because Cortez was here? Wolf had known what the traps were, how they were disguised, and yet had still crashed right into them. How humiliating was that?

Wolf groaned, leaning his head on his hand and resting his arm on his steering wheel as he contemplated his next move. It crossed his mind to march right up to Cortez's door and demand the keys to the store, and Angel. He would tell the lowlife where his daughter was. How would the assassin like to chew on that? Let the Mulligan Stew assassin know he was a hard-hearted motherfucker. Wolf would make it clear to Cortez and the assassin in one deadly move that he wasn't a man to mess with and that no move on either of their part would daunt him. Wolf would get the assassin. Distractions be damned.

"Hell of a thought," he mused, knowing he wouldn't do it.

Angel would never speak to him again if he turned over Zoey.

"Damn that woman." Why the hell was she under his skin like this?

What he needed to do was put the whole damn town, everyone in it, and all of its fucked-up issues out of his head. What he needed to do was focus on his hunt. Maybe getting out of Zounds, away from Angel, away from all of it, might just help. He would find a place outside the community, then turn into a goddamned bloodhound. All that mattered from this point forward was finding the assassin. Once Wolf's work was done, then he would find out if Angel was still talking to him.

Wolf stopped by the small grocery store, the only one in Zounds. He would pick up some food that he could keep in his car. He would get a cooler to keep it in. Wolf always preferred traveling well on a hunt. The work was hard enough, and at the end of the day, he did like his creature comforts. But when the job called for it, he knew how to rough it.

He entered the store, grabbed a grocery cart, and started looking for nonperishable food. No restaurants, no interacting with anyone, not until the hunt was over.

"Excuse me." An old woman cut him off in the aisle, turning her cart so he couldn't pass. "Would you mind handing those bread-and-butter pickles to me?"

Wolf grunted, not feeling overly friendly at the moment. He wasn't an ass, though. Reaching for the pickles, he started to hand them to the old woman.

"Go to the back of the store. Next to the public bathrooms is an employees' door. Go through it and go downstairs."

"What?" Wolf frowned at the old woman.

She shook her head. "And they say I'm hard of hearing."

"Why would I want to go downstairs?" he asked.

"They say I can't figure things out, either," she mumbled, and pushed her cart around his.

Wolf stood in the aisle alone, still holding the bread-and-butter pickles. Go to the back of the store where the bathrooms were, enter an employees' door, then go downstairs? He glanced over his shoulder, but the old woman was no longer in his aisle. Maybe she was just nuts. She hadn't even taken her pickles.

Curiosity got him into his line of work. That and the willingness to search and go where others wouldn't necessarily go. Leaving his cart in the aisle, there wasn't anything in it yet anyway, Wolf headed to the back of the store. Sure enough, next to the public bathrooms was a door that said EMPLOYEES on it. Wolf noticed it didn't say EMPLOYEES ONLY like so many doors in places of businesses did. Apparently, this store was a bit friendlier about who went into areas of the store designed for their employees.

Wolf pushed against the door without looking around him

to see who might be watching and walked into a dark back room. He noticed a flight of stairs before letting the door close behind him. There were voices coming from downstairs, and he easily heard Angel speaking excitedly. Wolf trotted down the stairs. What the hell was Angel doing in a grocery store basement?

Chapter Thirteen

"And I don't have my phone." Angel followed Wolf's movements as he paced the length of the damp stone basement. When he turned, ignoring the other people with her, his eyes were black with fury. "My guess is Brutus slipped it out of my purse when he brought it to me. I had the service shut off on it and reported it stolen once I got here."

"Brought what to you?" Wolf demanded, stopping in front of her.

Angel stared at his broad chest. His entire body was thick with anger.

"My purse," she clarified, remaining relaxed in the office chair she'd been offered when Bob Williams had "rescued" her after she'd come to the grocery store when Betsy had denied her a room at the bed-and-breakfast.

Angel had hated imposing but didn't know where else to go. She'd decided to go through the motions of being practical and had come to the store for a few groceries. After she informed Bob and his wife, Cecilia, about her store being closed, they had told her their basement had a good signal for the Internet. All of them had agreed it was time to start fighting back. Angel had been empowered by the Williamses' willingness to help her take on Cortez.

"Where is it?" Wolf asked.

His tone made Angel think it wasn't the first time he'd

asked the question. She gave herself a mental shake. She wouldn't be able to take down a monster if her brain remained rattled.

"Where is what?" she asked.

"Your purse."

Angel leaned forward in the office chair and picked her purse up from the floor under the small metal desk where she'd been researching laws on evictions on the old, bulky home PC the Williamses were letting her use. The list she was making on notebook paper next to her of the laws Cortez had broken concerning just her store seemed to be endless.

"Why do you want it?" Angel frowned, setting her purse on the desk.

Wolf grabbed her purse from her and dumped all contents on the desk next to the dusty keyboard. Pictures of the Williamses' four children, now grown, rotated in a slide show as Cecilia's screen saver kicked on. Joanie Williams had been one of Angel's good friends all the way through school. A picture of the two of them hugging and laughing at the camera on the day of their high-school graduation flashed on the screen as the contents of her purse rolled all over the desk. Angel flew out of her chair in time to save two pens and a ChapStick from rolling to the floor.

"What the hell?" she shouted, fisting the items she'd just grabbed and raising her hands in protest.

Wolf fished through the contents of her purse, using his finger to move each item so that more of the contents rolled precariously toward the edge of her desk.

"What do you think you're doing?" she demanded, getting seriously pissed.

What had she been doing drooling over his finely tuned body with all of that muscle and swagger? Now he was being a complete jerk.

She'd been glaring at him and not his fingers as he pried through items from her purse. Wolf used her fingernail clippers to pick something up. He held it at face level between them, and she stared at it. Her focus moved to his face when he held one finger up to his lips. Wolf turned to Bob Williams and his mother-in-law, Melba, still holding up the small, flat disk that looked like one of those tiny batteries so both of them could see it. He continued pressing his finger to his lips, silently telling Bob and Melba to not say a word.

"What?" Angel began.

Wolf flew around, frowning at her, and with a look silenced her. Her anger simmered, and she scowled at him for thinking he could take command of her room. She took a half step back when he moved around the desk and into her space. In front of Bob and Melba, who Angel knew were watching her and Wolf closely, Wolf put his arm around Angel's shoulders and pulled her up against him. In spite of the jerk he'd turned into in the past few minutes, her body instantly reacted. Instead of pushing him to arm's length, which was what she should have done, she arched just enough to enjoy his muscle-packed warm body against every inch of hers.

"This is a very high-tech bug that can pick up any conversation easily, even while buried in the bottom of your purse," he whispered into her ear. "Give me something to smash it."

Apparently, he'd whispered loud enough for Bob to hear. That or her friend had moved closer to the desk when Wolf had wrapped his arm around her. Angel didn't dwell on his reasons but stared in shock at the tiny, flat disk that Wolf continued to hold up with the fingernail clippers. A high-tech what?

A bug. A damned spy tool used to eavesdrop. Angel stared in shock at the small thing, her anger no longer simmering but igniting into full-blown rage. She shifted her attention when Bob moved quickly, hurrying to the dark shadows against the basement wall and returning with a brick in his hand. Wolf placed the flat disk on the desk. Angel leapt against the desk, reached across it, and yanked the brick from Bob's hand.

She smashed the small disk. The things from her purse bounced on the desk. Angel hit the disk again—and again.

This time it was Wolf scrambling to prevent everything from tumbling off the desk before grabbing Angel's wrist.

"Good job," he said softly.

"I'd say she shattered the thing into dust," Bob said, laughing.

"And possibly pierced the eardrum of anyone who might have been listening," Wolf added.

"Good," Angel snapped. How dare Cortez have his henchman bug her purse. He had no right to listen in on a damn word she said—ever! "I'm going outside," she announced to no one in particular, and dropped the brick where the disk had been on the desk.

It felt good exerting a bit more energy when she pushed open the old garage door that the store had once used for deliveries. The Williamses had built onto the store back when Angel had been in school, and a new garage entrance on the other end of the store made it much easier for trucks to pull up to for deliveries.

Angel tugged on her blouse when she walked into the icy chill of the night. She didn't even have her coat. The nightmare her life had become in less than a day continued unraveling before her as she thought about the many items she didn't have access to any longer. Her nightgown, her toiletries, her entire home! She shivered uncontrollably against the night air, and her eyes watered. No way would she cry, though. Cortez wouldn't have the satisfaction of making her cry.

Angel heard cautious footsteps behind her. She crossed her arms against the cold and her unwanted emotions. She couldn't ask to be alone. This wasn't her place.

A warm leather coat, strong with Wolf's rich scent, descended on her shoulders. Capable hands came around her and zipped the coat up her front.

"I just found out this grocery store sells locks," he grumbled next to her ear.

Instant warmth wrapped around her. Angel was intoxicated by Wolf's thick scent that held a primal quality to it and was all male.

"They have a small hardware section, nothing major," she told him, her thoughts still jumbled and now distracted. Wolf being close did something to her that she didn't always appreciate. She couldn't even fuck him if she wanted!

"How would you like to break into a bookstore?"

Angel turned around slowly, her heart making a hard thud against her chest. "What?" she whispered.

"I happen to know how to pick a lock and change a lock. Are you game?"

Wolf shuffled things around in the back of his Escalade. Stacking two supply boxes on top of each other, he was finally able to move the vehicle's panel and open the area where the spare tire was.

"What's that?" Angel asked, completely dwarfed in his leather jacket yet still managing to look sexy as hell.

"A box of tricks," he told her, grinning.

The woman always managed to do more than warm his blood, especially when she stood this close to him. In spite of all the leather wrapped around her, he still managed to pick up on her own personal fragrance. It was the strawberry smell of her hair, the musky, female smell of the soap she used, and something unique to Angel. It was a fragrance he could breathe in and never grow tired of.

Wolf scowled, definitely not liking the direction of his thoughts. "Go sit in the passenger seat."

"I want to help," she said, her gaze trained on the box in his hand. "I want to learn what you're going to do."

"No, you don't. And you aren't."

Angel narrowed her brow when she tilted her head back and looked at him. "It's my store."

Headlights snapped on and lit part of Angel's face. Instinctively Wolf shut the rear hatch on his SUV and shoved Angel behind him and toward the curb. A vehicle had been parked opposite them on the other side of the courtyard and even now was partially concealed by the statue pointing to the ocean between them. Even with the glare, Wolf saw that the car had been parked at the far end of the delivery alley between the shops on the other side of the courtyard.

"What are you doing?" Angel almost tripped over herself jumping back when he pushed her with a bit more force so that his Escalade was between her and the street.

"How often do cars flash headlights at you in this town after midnight?"

Angel squinted to see the car through the Escalade's dark tinted windows. "Not often," she said softly.

Wolf's attention returned to the car when it began driving toward them. He should have made Angel stay at the grocery store. She would have been as stubborn about staying there as she was being now. The car came to the road and turned to come around the circular drive. Wolf put his hand on Angel's arm, intending to toss her inside his SUV if he had to. A sudden piercing zing through the calm dark night had him shoving her at his Escalade. He pressed himself against her. An explosion followed the zing.

At least it sounded like one as it erupted the silence in the dead of the night. A terrifying moment passed where Wolf feared he'd frozen from the sound. Not once during his career had he panicked during an ambush. He'd been shot at before and each time his instincts had kicked in and he'd come out of the situation unscathed.

Angel screamed. Wolf pulled her against him. He'd never been in a crisis situation before with someone he cared for so much standing right next to him, either.

"Get inside my truck," he whispered into her hair, his words dull and raspy like an old knife. He heard the desperate edge to his voice. It was as if all that mattered was keeping her safe and he wasn't sure he was man enough to do it. "Don't argue, sweetheart. Lock the doors and lay down on the seat. Here are the keys." He pulled them from his pocket. He wouldn't add if things got ugly to leave, hoping she would figure that part out for herself.

A car skidded to a stop with its tire blown out. That unmistakable flapping rubber sound of the destroyed tire followed in the wake of the gunshot. The car quit moving when it was half on the grass in the middle of the circle and its rear still on the road. Angel no longer argued. She yanked open the Escalade's door and shut it behind her just as fast, disappearing from his sight behind the dark windows.

Wolf searched the direction from where the shot had come from as a spew of expletives filled the frigid night air. Not that he felt the least bit cold. As the men in the car started yelling, a warped satisfaction warmed his insides. He wasn't the only one to get his tires shot out in this county.

"Who the fuck do you think you are?" Brutus roared, leaving the car where it was as he marched toward Wolf. There were shadows of other men behind him.

Oh crap. Wolf didn't doubt Angel would stay in the Escalade. He wasn't positive she would stay on the floor as he'd told her, though. And he really didn't want her witnessing opening fire on these men. He wanted her even less to see him get shot. He pulled his gun from the holster he'd put on before they'd left the grocery store.

"Angel Matisse, get the fuck out of that crap hole right now or tomorrow that building will be demolished, with everything in it being destroyed!" Brutus bellowed.

Wolf didn't have time to yell for Angel to stay where she was when several more zings whizzed through the air. His attention spun from Brutus and the three men with him, to the area where the shots were fired, then back to Brutus. All four men held their hands up before them. Even without direct light shining on their faces, Wolf could tell all of them were stunned. Hell, Wolf was stunned. For all the research he'd done on how incredible a shot the Mulligan Stew assassin was, it was still impressive as hell witnessing it in person.

"I'm not afraid to shoot to kill," Wolf warned, understanding dawning on him as to why the four men had been unarmed, each of their guns shot out of their hands.

If the Mulligan Stew assassin had killed them, word would travel. Cortez would eventually figure out who had killed his men, especially since Wolf didn't carry that kind of firepower. Cortez would go after the assassin himself.

The people of Zounds wouldn't be able to handle that kind of damage.

"Tell your buddy to get out here where I can see him!" Brutus roared loud enough a few of the businesses nearby upstairs lights popped on. Brutus ignored how he'd just rudely awakened some of the town folk and glared into the darkness beyond the edge of downtown where the shots had been fired.

Wolf took advantage of Brutus ignoring his threat and aimed. He might not have the assassin's skills, but he was a pretty good shot. He found his target and pulled the trigger. In the next instant Brutus howled and fell to the side. Wolf would give it to the asshole, he was to the core mean. Instead of falling to the ground, he captured his weight on the foot Wolf didn't shoot and let out a spew of profanity loud enough to wake the rest of the downtown merchants who lived above their shops.

"I suggest you ruin that rim and drive back to hell where you came from," Wolf informed Brutus, aiming higher this time as he started toward the four unarmed men.

The three behind Brutus took Wolf's advice and hurried to the car. Brutus, in all of his evil glory, remained where he was.

"Should I allow your goons to come back and carry you to the car?" Wolf taunted.

Brutus stared Wolf down, but Wolf wasn't intimidated. If the asshole only knew how many heartless men, just like him, Wolf had put behind bars in the past. He didn't stop walking until he was face-to-face with the prick.

"If you aren't out of town by the morning," Brutus snarled, his soulless eyes black with rage, "the only way you'll leave Zounds is in a coffin."

"Think I heard that in a movie once," Wolf said under his breath. "Or was that a few hundred times? Tell Cortez to say that to my face and I might possibly consider it."

He raised his gun to Brutus's chest. Brutus moved fast for a man with a bullet hole in his foot. He raised his hand with lightning speed, intending to knock the gun out of Wolf's hand. Wolf had a lot more experience fighting with his fists than with a gun. Regardless of how people might think of bounty hunters, most of his experience with a gun came from a shooting range. But hand-to-hand combat was mastered only one way.

Wolf moved faster and sent Brutus flying backward by smashing the side of his gun against Brutus's head. The man fell loudly, howling in pain as he did. Wolf moved over him, once again pointing his gun at the man.

"Get up and get the hell out of here," he snarled.

It shouldn't have been that difficult to make Zoey understand why Ben wouldn't take her virginity during casual sex. Goddamn! They'd only known each other a few days, and not under ideal circumstances. Yes, taking walks with her in the forest was fun. Fixing dinner and playing house was bringing them closer to each other. The physical attraction had been there since he'd first laid eyes on her. That part didn't need any help. But Zoey would put more importance on them having sex, since she was a virgin, than Ben was ready to give. How did he explain that for him it would just be sex?

Maybe because it wouldn't have just been sex.

He'd fought that little voice in his head throughout most of the night as he'd tossed and turned on the couch. Whereas before the large couch had been fairly comfortable, tonight, no matter how he tried lying, he couldn't sleep. Partially it was because he knew if he entered that bedroom, Zoey would forgive him if he asked and take him into her bed. Those luscious curves, those incredible breasts and ripe, oval shaped nipples, her smooth taut, concave tummy, and those small, tight shimmering black curls between her legs could be nestled up against him right now.

And he would plow right through her virginity and deep into her velvety heat before he could stop himself. There was no doubt. He wouldn't be able to endure the torture of stopping twice.

"Damn it!" Ben grumbled grouchily, and flipped to his

side on the couch, punching his pillow. It didn't do a thing for releasing the mounting frustration inside him. He *had* done the right thing.

Maybe he wasn't the most noble man walking the planet, but he had scruples. He cared about people. Zoey had been a sultry cat in heat, wild and alive with passion that would have easily misled any man into thinking she had previous experience in bed. Ben should have thought it through before letting it get as far as it did. Zoey was far more sheltered than any lady he'd ever meet in his life. He imagined her father wouldn't let her date unless it was under strict supervision. And the way she'd described to Ben the marriage her father had arranged for Zoey—damn if just thinking about that didn't piss him off even more—it made perfect sense that she was a virgin.

Ben punched his pillow again. This time he sat up and dragged his hand through his hair. He might as well give up on sleep. Although pacing the small cabin wouldn't work with Zoey sleeping close enough he could smell her sweet, enticing scent. He needed a diversion.

Slipping into his boots and yanking his shirt over his head, Ben stalked out the door. He wouldn't be gone too long, but just in case, he took the key to the cabin and locked the dead bolt once he was outside in the cold night air.

And it was cold. Damn, every breath came out in a cloud before his face. He'd thought of tearing across the countryside on his bike, but it was definitely too fucking cold. He barely could stand riding it in this cold fall weather during the daytime.

As dark as it was, Ben could still see low-hanging, heavy clouds above him. Freezing-cold temperatures and rain—just great. His mood was getting better and better by the moment!

The rental car was new and endured Ben's heavy foot as he pushed the Taurus along back highways. If he would just cheer up, the early-morning fog draping around the huge trunks of the large trees might possibly have appealed to him. As it was, he scowled out the front window through the hole that grew larger as the defrost cleared the windows. His hands lazily rested on the steering wheel as he took each curve without slowing. Who cared how loudly the tires squealed in protest? They didn't squeal loudly enough to chase the demons from his head.

He was losing a battle in his brain, and it soured his mood even further. Ben had refused to fuck her because she was a virgin. And he'd seen the hurt in Zoey's eyes when she looked at him, then quickly diverted her gaze. She'd closed down to him, moving around the small cabin so quietly it was as if she didn't want him to know she was there. The one time he'd tried apologizing—and he'd gotten as far as facing her and sighing—she'd cut him off by talking about dinner. She had spoken too fast. It was like it pained her to speak to him, so she wanted to dump all necessary words out as quickly as possible so she could withdraw back inside her inner shell and ignore him.

He hated the thought that Zoey might speak to her father the same way. Just imagining her feeling Ben was no better than that bastard made him feel worst of all. He hadn't wanted to take her virginity during casual sex. And it was eating him alive that Zoey was starting to mean enough to him that making love to her at any point, if she ever let him touch her again, would be a hell of a lot more than casual sex.

Why did the perfect woman for him come with the devil as a father? Ben didn't want to remain in hiding with Zoey. He wanted to take her out, dress her up, watch her face glow with happiness at loud clubs where they would dance the night away. Or take her to his favorite pool hall. He had no idea if Zoey even played pool, but he could teach her. Let his friends gawk over the perfect woman at his side.

Perfect woman?

Ben took a curve too fast and gripped the steering wheel, coming out of it barely without the car hauling ass off the road.

Crap! What the hell was he thinking?

The perfect woman didn't need to be with him. Once she

got a taste of what he really did for a living, Zoey would wave him off without as much as a glance over her shoulder. Not to mention, he didn't want another relationship right now. It was the last thing he needed.

He slowed the car below the speed limit when he realized where he was. Ben had driven to where Wolf had been shot or, more accurately, where his tires had been shot. If Micah had wanted Wolf dead, the man would have been dead. Ben had already parked and walked as far as he dared down quite a few of the gravel roads off this quiet, secluded highway. He didn't want to trespass. Some people in Northern California didn't take kindly to anyone on their land who wasn't supposed to be there. And Ben wasn't looking for private crops, which he knew were in abundance in this part of the state.

Driving farther down the highway, he slowed again when he came to more one-lane roads off the main highway. It was quite possible Maggie had known Wolf was following her. The woman wasn't stupid, and after a year of living with Micah she probably knew fairly well to keep an eye on all of her mirrors at all times. But it was the only lead Ben had at the moment, regardless of how slim it might be.

He glanced down the roads that turned off from the highway. The fog was growing thicker, and a slight mist forced him to turn on the windshield wipers. It was impossible to see down any of the roads.

Why was it so damn hard to find one man in a community that was so small? Maggie would have told Micah that Ben was in town. Why didn't Micah want to see him?

His irritation turning as gloomy as the weather, Ben turned back toward the cabin. By the time he reached it, a heavy sleet fell around him. It was like rain, but louder, crackling and popping when it hit the ground. Did it snow here in October? Ben admittedly didn't know enough about the climate this far north.

Starting toward the cabin, he sidetracked to his bike. Best to make sure it was securely covered so this sleet wouldn't hurt it. As he walked around the bike, he paused. Bungee cords secured the tarps he'd put over his bike. Underneath one bungee that was stretched tight over his handlebars, a piece of paper grew damp from the weather.

Ben pulled the paper out and managed not to tear it. He saw ink bleeding through the paper and flipped it over. The message was still clear and easy to read.

> *Be at my house at ten this morning. Bring Z. M would love to see her. Don't bring or tell anyone else. Destroy this note.*

Ben stared at the address, which was a highway with a box number. He would confirm online, but he was ready to bet this wasn't anywhere near where Maggie had led Wolf.

Micah had been here at the cabin!

Ben swung around, clasping the damp piece of paper as he searched the ground, looking all around him for any indication that the man had recently been there. He stared at the wet stuff that wasn't quite rain as it did its best to leave tiny indentions when it hit the ground. A mean wind picked up. The sleet swirled over the frozen ground as if somehow it had the capability of wiping away all signs that there had been an intruder. There was no evidence that anyone had been anywhere near his bike. No one else had pulled into the parking area next to the cabin where he'd parked the rental car. He walked all the way to the highway just to be sure.

How the hell did that man do it? He was like a goddamn ghost!

Ben headed to the cabin. He was going to wake his sleeping beauty. Somehow they'd get past their first sexual encounter. But right now, he had an assassin to worry about.

Zoey got out of the Taurus rental car, standing as Ben came around the car to close her door. She studied the well-kept rustic cabin hidden in a grassy clearing.

"You're going to meet a friend of mine." Ben's straight

blond hair was more tousled than usual and his expression tense. But it was his eyes, so focused and blue that held her attention.

Zoey looked up and couldn't look away. "Yes; Micah," she said, her voice soft. Something about Ben's actions and behavior since she'd gotten up was off. Instead of being incredibly nice, which she attributed to him trying to make up for walking out on her right before having sex, Ben was tense, anxious. "I'll be on my best behavior," she teased, and smiled.

His expression seemed to tighten further. "I know you will be, darling. That isn't it. Micah and I worked together just over a year ago."

Zoey was all ears. More than once she'd started conversations that would make Ben talk about himself. He was so close mouthed about his life, and good at it, too. Instead of refusing to tell her where he'd lived before Zounds, other than the L.A. area, or if he'd had a girlfriend, or what he did, or anything about his family, Ben had an incredible knack at turning the conversation so Zoey was talking about herself.

"Doing what?" she couldn't help asking.

Ben sighed. His blue eyes seemed to grow larger and darker. "Bounty hunters," he said on the exhale of his sigh.

"Bounty hunters," she repeated, unable to hide her surprise. It wasn't what she'd expected him to say.

"Hey there, you two!" a man yelled from behind Ben. "If you're out here trying to prepare Zoey, you'll be out here all damn day," the man continued, laughing, as he walked up toward them.

"Zoey!" Maggie called out, also laughing. "Oh my God! This is so wonderful. I'm so glad you're here. Do you know how long I've wanted to have company? No offense," Maggie added, her voice full of happiness and laughter as she put her hand on the arm of the man, who must be Micah.

Zoey wasn't sure what she'd expected out of this Micah, but the man who moved in next to Ben was tall, really tall.

And big. He wore comfortable-fitting faded jeans and work boots, which possibly added to his height. Micah had to be well over six feet tall. Ben looked short next to him, and Ben wasn't short. He was taller than her father. Micah's soft, well-worn-looking T-shirt hugged every inch of his torso. Muscles ripped and bulged everywhere.

But it was something in his face, where Zoey spotted several scars that added to this dangerous aura about him, that damn near robbed her of her breath. She made a conscious effort to inhale as she continued with her quick appraisal. His hair was dark and long. It fell in curls and waves to his shoulders. Sexy, she decided, but in a dangerous, definitely scary kind of way. Some girls would find that appealing, but Zoey much preferred the more honest bad boy in a mischievous way that was all Ben.

When it came down to it, there really was no comparing the two men. Apples and oranges were at least both fruit. And although Ben and Micah were most definitely all man, Ben's sex appeal went deeper than his boyish good looks. It was in his eyes, so full of compassion and integrity.

That didn't exist in Micah's eyes. They weren't exceptional in color, probably hazel or a melting mixture of blue, green, and brown. But when Micah looked at her, making no qualms about scrutinizing the bruises lining the side of her face, Zoey felt . . . scared. She wouldn't go as far as to say they were soulless eyes. Brutus and Julius had soulless eyes. Micah's soul was there but as scarred as his body. So yes, sex appeal, but something told her the devil might think twice about taking on this man.

"Who did that to your face?" Micah asked, his soft baritone relaxed.

"She's Cortez's daughter," Ben said flatly, as if that were explanation enough.

"Goddamn it," Micah growled under his breath.

It was the strangest sensation. Zoey watched Micah, unsure what to say or if anything needed to be said. He turned from her, looking at the ground for a moment. Zoey had seen that look on a man's face before, and it instantly brought fear to her gut. Micah looked as if he were losing a battle to demons rising inside him. Whenever her father got that same look on his face, something bad always happened.

The moment his attention shifted to Maggie, though, that look that caused instant terror to twist in Zoey's gut disappeared. Now there was a man in love. His expression transformed so noticeably when he gazed at his wife.

"Maggie has been making me nuts all morning once she found out you were coming. She's so excited to show off her house," Micah said, and smiled.

"I do believe it's our home," Maggie said playfully, looking more relaxed and happy than she ever did when she came into town. "And it's not a house; it's a cabin," she teased, and tapped her small boot on top of his much larger one. Then shifting her attention to Ben, she continued smiling. Maggie was absolutely glowing. "I'm sorry I held you at gunpoint and made you take your boots off."

"What?" Zoey gasped, but then hated how everyone looked at her.

"Oops," Maggie muttered, her smile fading.

Micah caressed his wife's arm. "Take Zoey inside," he instructed, his tone dropping a notch so that it almost sounded like a growl.

"I'll explain later," Ben promised, pulling Zoey into his arms. "Please don't think bad of me," he whispered into her hair.

Zoey tilted her head back and looked up at him. "Why should I think bad of you?"

"She made me take my boots off so I wouldn't follow her."

"Ben was trying to find me," Micah cut in, and patted Ben on the back. "Maggie gets rather protective, I'm afraid. Just one of the many reasons I love her," he added, and again looked at his wife with a reverence any girl would die to have from a man.

"There better be tons of reasons." Maggie laughed. "Come on, girl. Let me show you our home. You'll love it. I've really gotten into interior decorating."

"I'll say," Micah muttered.

Maggie hooked her arm around Zoey's and guided her away from the men. "I'm so glad you're here. Honestly, you're our first visitors. I didn't think Micah would go for it."

"He's quite a man," Zoey said, not sure how to say something favorable when he gave her the willy-jillies.

"He's the best there is," Maggie said dreamily, and pushed open the door to the rustic redwood cabin, proof in itself that the cabin had been there a while. Not many things were made from redwood these days. "But welcome to our home," she said with a dramatic flair, and waved her hand around a spacious, nicely decorated living room.

As simple as the cabin looked from the outside, it made up for it on the inside with its sophisticated and plush look. If growing up under a crime lord's brutal scrutiny had taught Zoey anything, it was how to identify expensive tastes when she saw them. The couch, with two matching chairs, and a wide, oval dark cherry coffee table with end tables of the same set on either side of the couch were all very nice pieces of furniture. Not the kind of stuff picked up at a department store or out of a wholesale factory outlet.

"Living room, obviously," Maggie said, her smile so broad it was all teeth. She tugged at Zoey. "Let me show you the rest of the place."

Maggie danced through their master bedroom and two full baths, one with a Jacuzzi and very large skylight. She opened doors to two more bedrooms, both simply furnished, then brought the two of them into the kitchen.

"And this is my kitchen," she said, sighing as she glanced around with pleasure. "Isn't it marvelously perfect?"

Zoey had to agree. She walked around an island in the middle of the room with a cutting board as a countertop. Glancing at a fully stocked glass wine cabinet, she shifted her attention to a fat wood-burning stove, then took in the shiny chrome appliances. The room was spacious, the windows large and on opposite sides of the kitchen so morning and evening light would traipse across the solid, nicely glossed wooden floor. A long braided carpet covered half of the room where a breakfast nook and round table with two chairs were surrounded by glass, showing off the thick forest.

"I haven't been able to get Micah to eat there with me yet," Maggie confessed, pouring two cups of rich-smelling coffee, then bringing the mugs to the breakfast table. "He prefers eating in the living room."

"This place is amazing," Zoey said, wondering which one of them had the bucketloads of money it would have taken to decorate and furnish the place the way it was. She wouldn't ask, though. "Why didn't you tell me that you knew Ben? I have so many questions."

"And I'm going to answer every single one of them." Maggie's expression grew serious as she sipped her coffee. "Micah allowed you to come out here with Ben because he said, as a crime lord's daughter, you probably have had a lifetime of learning how to keep secrets. Personally, I always knew I could trust you. But it's Micah who has to have the final say in that department."

"What?" Zoey frowned. She shook her head, ready to deny it. "I don't know anything about my father's many crimes. Other than knowing he's a bastard, I always stay away from his business," she confirmed. "You know that."

Maggie nodded once. "I know. But it's why Micah agreed."

Zoey simply stared, wondering what kind of phobias that tall, dark man outside with Ben had. She didn't have time to figure out how to word her question.

"Micah is a wanted man, Zoey," Maggie said quietly, in fact in such a hushed whisper it wasn't clear what she said or meant at first.

"Wanted? You mean by the law?" Zoey asked.

Maggie nodded once. "I'm going to assume that Ben hasn't told you anything, which Micah said he wouldn't. He said Ben would be loyal to him to death."

Zoey was already tired of hearing what Micah said. "Ben wouldn't tell me what?" she demanded.

"About the two of them being bounty hunters."

Zoey sighed and relaxed into her chair. "Ben told me

that." She didn't add that he'd told her that when they'd arrived outside. For some reason she was suddenly feeling defensive.

"Ben and Wolf Marley drove up here together from Los Angeles to find Micah." Maggie paused as if trying to read from Zoey's face whether she knew this or not. Her gaze lingered a moment on Zoey's bruises, but then Maggie met her gaze and held it as if she knew Zoey needed time to process what she was being told.

Zoey's stomach tensed. Already she started thinking she wasn't going to like this conversation. "He told me they came to Zounds looking for work."

"I know." Maggie started talking fast, not taking any more breaks to learn what Zoey knew or didn't. "I don't know yet how they met. Micah is finding that out outside. But we already know Wolf Marley came to Zounds looking for Micah because of the incredibly large bounty on Micah's head."

"How much?" Zoey asked, feeling sick. She'd left a world of crime, run from it. Was it seriously all around her and she was simply too gullible to realize it?

"Over a million dollars last we checked," Maggie said, her voice tight.

Zoey couldn't breathe. Maybe she didn't know the details of her father's business, but she'd overheard plenty of conversations. Her father never tried skating around any topic because of her. A million-dollar bounty was only issued for incredibly heinous crimes. But Maggie was sweet. She was perfect. What had that man done to rate such an incredible bounty?

"Wait a minute," Zoey said, pieces of conversations from the day suddenly swimming in her brain. "Ben and Micah were bounty hunters together, right?"

"Yes." Maggie looked down at her cup, which she held in front of her mouth with both hands. "Micah was raised by his father and uncle. He learned to hunt large game at a young age. Both his father and uncle were avid hunters. When Micah became a teenager he got bored hunting large game. There wasn't a creature out there he couldn't kill with one shot."

Zoey listened, keeping her expression bland for Maggie's sake. It was clear how much she loved Micah. Zoey couldn't stand killing, though. If that man outside was a killer, a murderer for Christ's sake, she wanted nothing to do with him.

"Micah's father and uncle decided there was a way for Micah to be challenged." Maggie stopped and stared at Zoey for a moment as if she was searching for the right words.

"He's a murderer!" Zoey helped her out and pushed away from the table.

"No!" Maggie almost yelled. "No," she said quieter, reaching for Zoey. "Let me explain. Micah is one of the best men you will ever know, Zoey. I promise."

Zoey relaxed back into her chair but already knew she wouldn't like where this story was going. Worse yet, why was she being told? All her life not knowing meant she was safer. Did she want to know about Maggie's husband?

"Micah's dad and uncle brought Micah into the business. Mulligan Stew," she explained. "When someone had a person they needed taken care of," she continued, faltered, cleared her voice, and went on, "a bad person, the very worst, they would contact Mulligan Stew. Now Micah, who always had final say, only accepted jobs when the person had done terrible things. His father and uncle would screen the calls, or often e-mails, negotiate payment; then Micah went out to take the job."

"Oh my God, he's an assassin," Zoey said, covering her mouth.

Maggie didn't say anything but stared at Zoey over the table. She took a long drink of her coffee, then placed her mug on the table. "Micah has killed over seventy-two people," she whispered.

"Maggie," Zoey complained, putting her cup down before she dropped it. "I don't want to know this."

"I have to tell you." Maggie looked imploring. "You have to understand why Ben couldn't tell you anything. Why he had to lie," she continued.

"Ben lied?"

"Micah became so good at what he did he easily could pick and choose his jobs. He was paid insanely large amounts of money, sometimes by entire towns, although there was never a paper trail and there is no way to prove any of this. He has killed mass murderers, rapists, known serial killers, when the law might not have had enough proof in spite of knowing who had committed the crimes. He's killed robbers, hustlers, and crime lords. He's killed abusive husbands, child molesters, and pedophiles."

"So because he has killed so many terrible people that makes it okay?"

"I think it helps show the kind of person Micah is," Maggie said seriously. "A couple years ago, Micah decided to retire. He moved to L.A. and changed his identity. He took a job as a bounty hunter and that is when I met him, and when Ben met him."

"So Ben didn't know who Micah really was?"

Maggie shook her head. "I didn't, either, at first. He'd had a lifetime of keeping his private life private and he's still very good at it," she told Zoey, looking frustrated. With a limp wave of her hand in the air between them, she dismissed any current problems she might have living with such a man in order to get her story out.

"Ben wasn't a licensed bounty hunter at the time. He was working toward it," Maggie offered, searching Zoey's face and again looking as if she wanted to know how much of this Zoey already knew.

Zoey slumped in her seat. "Go on," she prompted. "Ben has obviously lied about everything about himself before coming to Zounds."

"He was protecting Micah," Maggie insisted, as if that made everything all right. "Micah and Ben went on jobs together. There was a lot Ben couldn't do, and a lot Micah taught him while they were on those jobs," Maggie told her.

"Taught him?" Zoey leaned forward, and her stomach clenched. She endured the pain, needing to know the truth. "What exactly did Micah teach him to do?"

Maggie's smile was sad. "No, it wasn't like that. Micah will take his curse of being the ultimate hunter to his grave, I'm afraid. He's very adamant about that. But Ben was a pup when he started working with Micah. He was eager to learn. Micah showed him how to fine-tune the natural hunter inside Ben, or at least that is how Micah has told it to me."

Maggie leaned back, and the glow of happiness, and what Zoey now saw as a sense of pride, of unadulterated love for her killer husband, made her smile shine.

"I see," Zoey said slowly, trying to digest everything while her stomach began forcing bile to her throat.

"The last job Micah did before he retired had come back to haunt him," Maggie continued, once again focusing on her mug. "The law started coming around and Micah decided it would be best for everyone if he disappeared. He tried protecting me, Ben, and everyone else he worked with by leaving without saying anything." A tear slipped down Maggie's face when she looked at Zoey. "But he couldn't do it. You don't know how big of a heart he has. Micah couldn't just leave without giving some kind of explanation to those he now cared about, and who loved him," she finished on a breath.

Maggie sighed as she began running her finger around the rim of her cup. She didn't seem to realize what she was doing. Maggie was looking back to a time that, if the look on her face was any indication, brought her a lot of pain. Zoey never would have guessed her friend was in love with an assassin. Maggie had given up her freedom. She would be in hiding for the rest of her life, whereas Zoey was just now experiencing freedom. It was a strange thought and one she didn't have a clue how to process.

"He went to where his boss and his boss's wife were hunting a guy who had run instead of going to his court dates. Micah has skills no other human on this planet has. I would swear to it. He was able to get close to where they were without anyone knowing he was there. The guy his boss was hunting had bounced checks. He wasn't a terrible criminal, just a man who had made some really stupid choices in life. And he was about to make one more. He pulled a gun on

Micah's boss's wife. Micah shot the man. The law was on it instantly, especially when the bullet that killed the man matched the bullet that had killed a dirty CIA agent, who had been the last man Micah had killed before retiring. Micah had found people who really cared about him. He hadn't known that level of friendship and he'd never felt that level of protectiveness before. Micah wasn't thinking about protecting himself. Possibly for the first time in his life he was focused more on taking care of someone else. Guns make an imprint on bullets when they're fired, like a fingerprint. That's how the law knew that they'd found the Mulligan Stew assassin."

"Oh God," Zoey gasped, wrapped up in Maggie's story. "What happened?"

"Yeah," Maggie said slowly. "The obvious happened. Depending on how you look at it, it was the only mistake Micah ever made. But if he hadn't made that one mistake, a very good woman would be dead right now. And yes, Micah ran. He had no choice. His freedom was over."

"He ran to you?"

"He ran to a church."

"A church?"

Maggie's cheeks were damp. She blotted at her eyes and offered Zoey a smile. "My church," she said, her voice thick with fresh tears that suddenly streamed down her face. "It's been a year and I still can't think about any of this without crying. Micah went to his father and uncle, who were just outside L.A., and told them he was done. He went to my priest and confessed every kill he'd ever made. That's where I found him. I hadn't seen him in days. He was trying to protect me from himself," Maggie said through a choked sob. She waved her hand in the air, as if emotions and memories could be wiped away that easily. With a heavy sigh, apparently accepting the fact that they couldn't be, Maggie continued, her eyes glassy with tears when she smiled at Zoey. "Before we left, Micah had to do one thing. He knew how much Ben wanted to be a bounty hunter, and that because of personal problems in his previous life he wouldn't ever make it as one until he'd saved up a lot of money. Micah left Ben enough money to clear his record and get his private investigator's license. We don't know how Ben got wind of Wolf Marley, but we do know Ben came to Zounds to warn Micah that Wolf is in Zounds to find Micah. I tried warning Angel, but I couldn't tell her too much." Maggie looked at Zoey. "And you can't say anything, either. These two men are in Zounds only to hunt Micah, although both for very different reasons. Ben doesn't want the bounty. He wants to warn Micah that a very real bounty hunter is very close to sniffing him out, and putting Micah behind bars, or worse, getting himself killed trying."

Chapter Fourteen

"How long have you two been here?" Ben asked.

Micah smiled at him. Ben wasn't sure he'd ever seen his friend look the way he did now. He was tanned and more muscular, and his hair was longer. From the looks of the woodshop Micah had behind the cabin, Ben guessed he'd built himself up hauling his own timber. But there was something else. Micah seemed relaxed, happy.

"Not long enough," Micah told him, grinning.

It dawned on Ben that he'd never really seen Micah smile before.

"I hope you can stay here for many years," Ben said, taking in the serene surroundings. "Sure is peaceful here."

"All a man could ask for," Micah agreed.

"You don't get bored?" So much paradise could also make a man restless.

In Micah's case, getting restless could mean a death sentence. For someone else, or even for Micah.

"With a town like Zounds at our fingertips?" Micah laughed, something else new to the man. "That Marley friend of yours is rather entertaining."

"Wolf Marley?" Ben quit taking in the view of rolling hills packed with thick forest, a postcard view stretching out farther than he could see, and looked at Micah. "He's not a friend."

"I didn't think so," Micah said. Long dark waves of hair curled under before touching his shoulders, which were packed with bulging muscles. In spite of this new lighthearted side of Micah, the dangerous, intimidating killer still hung close to the surface. "He's got an impeccable reputation as a bounty hunter."

"He showed up at KFA the same day I got my private investigator's license. Got in Greg King's face."

Micah humphed. "I would have loved to see that. What made Marley head up this way?"

"He broke into my apartment and destroyed the place. He took the two postcards that you sent, the second one postmarked 'Zounds.'"

Micah let out a sigh. "I'm really sorry he destroyed your place, man." He said it as if the destruction were personally his fault.

Ben saw how Micah would see it that way. He brushed off the apology. It wasn't necessary. "He's serious about finding you, Micah. And like you said, he's got a good track record."

"And he's been in Zounds almost a week and is still looking."

Ben studied Micah. "He's not going to give up."

Micah shrugged. "He doesn't bother me." Micah nodded to the house. "That is what concerns me, Ben."

"Maggie?"

This time when Micah laughed there was no humor in it. "Maggie is a blessing I'll never deserve," he said seriously. "But no, I didn't mean Maggie. I'm worried about Zoey Cortez being with you."

"What?" Ben frowned at Micah. Here Ben was trying to express the danger hovering too close to Micah and the man was worried about him? "I'm not the one to worry about, Micah. Think about it, will you? Wolf Marley has a reputation. You've admitted that yourself. Whether he succeeds or fails—"

"He won't succeed."

"Whether he does, or not, sooner or later others will get

wind that he's here. You've got a million-dollar bounty on
your head. Jesus Christ! That's a hell of a lot of money."

"Money I'm sure our government will balk at paying
whether I'm brought in dead or alive."

"Damn it, Micah!" Ben fought to control his temper. Micah was being way too nonchalant about this. If he didn't
take Ben's warning seriously, Micah would get caught. Ben
didn't want to live to see that happen. He honestly couldn't
say what he might do if Marley actually found Micah. "Pull
your head out of your ass. You're not invincible, regardless
of your history. You get too cocky and you'll get caught. End
of story!"

Ben held his ground when Micah closed in on him. Although a few inches taller and possibly fifty pounds or so
heavier with solid-packed muscle, Ben had never feared Micah. He sure as hell wouldn't now, especially since he was
right.

"I've always taken everything I've done in the past, as
well as everything I've done on a day-to-day basis ever
since, very seriously," he said in a harsh whisper. "Every day
I wake up wondering if this will be the day. Not one minute
goes by when I'm not looking over my shoulder. Our home
here, the layout of the place, the positioning of each piece of
goddamn furniture is done with careful thought in regard to
our safety. Maggie worries every time she goes into town.
Remember how she reacted when you first found her at the
grocery store," Micah hissed. "I wouldn't wish this life on
anyone, and definitely not on you. I'm not the one who needs
to pull my head out of my ass."

"I've never told a soul about you," Ben insisted, staring
hard at Micah's face. "It's been a year. No one follows me.
No one questions me. That is, until Marley showed up."

"Others will come sniffing around. It's a lifetime sentence, my friend. This isn't the way you want to live."

"I never said I did," Ben countered. "But I will go to any
length to help make sure you're always safe. That's just the
way of it," Ben stated, slicing his hand through the air. "Hav-

ing lawmen sniff around from time to time isn't shit in form of payment for what you've done for me."

"I don't expect to be paid back for helping friends."

"You helped me out. I'll always have your back even if it means getting in your face when you aren't seeing things straight."

Micah took a slow, deep breath, and his body noticeably relaxed. Bulging muscle smoothed under tanned skin. Ben hadn't noticed until then how tightly wound he had been as well. He, too, breathed in, then blew out the breath and a bit of his frustration.

"I'm seeing things straight," Micah said, his voice drained of emotion.

Ben turned from him. "Have you taught me so much that you can't hear when I'm trying to tell you what's right under your nose?" he muttered, and put some space between them.

Walking toward the small shed, he glanced inside the open door at the magnitude of tools neatly organized inside. He didn't dwell on how much money would have been spent in order to have everything Micah had. None of that mattered to him. Instead he fought to find the right words.

Convincing someone with words had never been his strong point. If someone didn't get what was clearly in front of his nose, a good right clip usually took care of matters. Ben had never scrapped with Micah before. He would, to make a point, if need be. Ben had gone through a lot to find Micah. And Ben would drive his point home one way or another. Micah wasn't safe.

"You're a good friend to trail Marley up here," Micah said behind Ben's back.

"I didn't trail him." Ben ran his finger against a table that supported a jigsaw. It looked homemade and of superior design. Micah was apparently a man of many talents. "That would be like trailing Greg King."

Micah snorted. "You trying to tell me Wolf Marley is as good a bounty hunter as King?" Micah didn't sound worried. His tone was more curious.

Ben turned around. Once again his temper was getting the better of him. "I guess we'll find out, won't we?" he snapped. "It's going to play out that you either run again, or kill a man. Is that how you see it, Micah? Is that how you want it to be? Just kill the man and come home to dinner set nicely on the table?"

Micah shrugged and Ben saw red. So Micah had been the Mulligan Stew assassin. "Had been" being the key words. Micah had retired. He had lived in L.A. and worked alongside Ben as a law-abiding citizen. Ben knew what it took to get a private investigator's license in California. Micah had gone through the same process just so he could get a job working at KFA.

Or wait a minute. "Am I the goddamned fool here?" Ben sneered. "Wolf Marley being in Zounds doesn't bother you a bit. Cortez terrorizing Zounds doesn't matter to you." Ben waved his hand at the perfect and rather pricey-looking spread Micah had created for himself and Maggie. "Have you really retired? Did you pull the wool over my eyes? Over Greg and Haley King's eyes? Is there anything real about you other than you are the perfect murderer?"

Micah stiffened. His dark features were suddenly darker. Ben saw the killer in Micah surface with a vengeance. It was a demon living inside Micah like a parasite. Ben welcomed taking on the murderer inside his friend. The quiet man who had always kept to himself, the man who had been honorable and had fought to uphold the law alongside the best law enforcer in the state of California, was the real Micah Jones, or Micah Mulligan, or whatever the man's name was.

"I'd like to think there is," Micah said, his mouth barely moving when he spoke.

"Who the fuck is that guy then?" Ben challenged. "I come up here to warn you a bounty hunter with bloodlust on the brain is hot on your trail and you tell me you aren't worried. Why is that, Micah? Is it because you're tired of running and simply ready to turn yourself in?"

Micah studied Ben. Maybe he was wrong, but it seemed as if Micah might actually be hearing him. Ben didn't regret pissing his friend off or using words to hit where it counted and make Micah open his motherfucking eyes.

"If I turn myself in, the deaths of all the men and women who were killed would have been in vain."

"All the men and women you killed."

"Yes." There wasn't any regret. Micah agreed to the charges without an ounce of guilt or remorse on his face.

"Forgive me, man," Ben said, swiping his hand through his hair and looking away from those dark eyes that seemed a bit too focused on him at the moment. "I have a hard time seeing you without a soul."

"I have a soul, Ben. And I have a conscience." Micah didn't make a sound when he moved to stand by Ben at the worktable in front of the shed. He pressed his hands flat on the table and leaned on it. There were puckered scars on both his hands. Old puckered scar tissue, and some newer, more recent scars were white against his tanned arms. It was impossible to imagine the life this man had led. "Many can't justify killing monsters. There are those who don't see the justice in wiping out a man, or a woman, who has brought too much harm to those around them. That bloodlust you mentioned this bounty hunter has in him can't possibly hold a flame to what burns in my veins on a daily basis. I found an outlet for mine, and yes, it was lucrative. But, my friend, I am retired. I will never accept money for another kill as long as I live. That part of my life is over, whether you believe it, or not."

Maybe he had an impeccable record as a mass murderer. Maybe he had been smart enough, to this point, not to get caught. But whatever it took, Ben would drive it into Micah's thick skull that Wolf Marley meant business. Though he hadn't found Micah yet, Marley wasn't going to give up until he did.

"Good to hear," Ben muttered. "But whether you justify all the blood on your hands, and I'm not judging you, the government doesn't."

"I'm aware of that," Micah said tightly.

Ben ignored him. "The charges against you aren't ever going to go away."

"Know that, too."

"So does Wolf Marley. To him, you are the ultimate bounty, the cut on his belt he can't wait to carve. He is going to sniff through every blade of grass in this county until he finds you."

"Ben," Micah said with a sigh, turning and facing him. "You've got to let me worry about Marley. You've got to trust me and know I'm going to take care of me and Maggie."

Ben glanced at his friend. "I'm not sure what I would do if he found you," he confessed.

The smile on Micah's face didn't reach his eyes. "You would do whatever you believe is right at that moment," he said, pushing away from the worktable, and walking around it. For a moment he stared out at the incredible view of tree-covered hills that rolled into a faded blue sky. "As much as you worry about me, I worry about you, too," he said, his back to Ben.

"I'm fine, Micah. I've got my job to return to when I go back. I'm up here with Greg and Haley's blessing."

Micah nodded once and turned his attention to the rustic cabin. He stared at it with a fondness, with something that for Micah might almost have been affection. "They are good people. You'll be one of the best before long. I have no doubt." He shot a side-glance at Ben as he raised his hand and pointed to the cabin. "But that is what I'm worried about."

Ben looked at the cabin. The women were in there. Ben could only imagine what Zoey and Maggie might be talking about. Zoey had been so excited to see her friend. It was rather ironic that Ben had run into Zoey the first night he'd arrived in Zounds and it turned out she was best friends with the wife of the man Ben had come here to find.

"Maggie obviously has learned to protect herself. And she protected you, too," Ben told him, grimacing at the memory of Maggie stopping him and making him toss his boots that day behind the grocery store.

"I'm not worried about Maggie. Although yes, she loves me more than I deserve to be loved."

Ben might have argued what Micah deserved, but instead

he frowned, not seeing what Micah was trying to say. "You're worried about Zoey?" Was Micah actually considering taking out Cortez? Ben put the thought out of his head immediately. Micah had just said he was retired. As much as his killing Cortez might solve Ben and Zoey's problem, it would only make matters worse for Micah.

"What I'm trying to say, Ben, is that I'm concerned about you being with Zoey," Micah said, and scowled when he faced Ben. "You're condemning yourself to a life just like mine."

"Zoey isn't wanted for any crime," Ben began.

"You already care about her," Micah deduced, cutting Ben off. "I can see it. The longer you're with her, the deeper those feelings will run."

"That's my business," Ben said, not seeing what his relationship with Zoey had to do with anything. He'd barely known her a week, and although he wanted to continue seeing her, at the same time there was still a strong part of him that believed jumping into another relationship would be a big mistake. None of that, however, was anything he wanted to discuss with Micah. "I didn't come here to talk about me."

This time Micah's grin was genuine. Humor lit up his face. It took Ben back a minute. This wasn't an expression or emotion he'd seen in the man before. It would take getting accustomed to. Knowing Micah was happy made Ben want to ensure Wolf never found him.

"Easier to dish out advice than take it?" Micah taunted, although his tone remained light. "You went to the effort to make your reason for coming up here to see me quite clear. Now it's time for you to listen to why I asked you to come here."

"What?" Ben asked. In the past he'd always taken to heart anything Micah offered. The man was so well trained Ben had watched closely and learned as much as he could about bounty hunting. Of course, at the time, he hadn't known how good Micah actually was at hunting. Or that he hunted to kill and not turn people over to the law. "I'm listening."

"Let her go, Ben," Micah whispered.

Ben stared at him a moment. "Walk away from Zoey?" he asked. He shook his head. "I do that and her father will scoop her back up in a second."

"Can you protect her without falling in love with her?"

"What the fuck business is that of yours?" Ben yelled. "Are you worried she'll learn too much about you, or Maggie?"

"It's my business because you're my friend." Micah stared at the ground and walked to the other side of his shed. He grabbed a rake that had been leaning against it and began idly dragging it over the ground. "As long as she is with you, her father will hunt the two of you. He'll learn that Zoey is with you, if he doesn't already know. Don't underestimate Cortez."

"Trust me, I'm not," Ben growled.

Micah didn't look up but continued dragging the rake over the ground. He bent down, picked up a hand-sized rock, and hurled it into the beautiful backdrop behind his home. Ben watched him do it, noting the ground had been raked before. Micah had been working the land around his work space, making it smooth and flat and free of rocks.

"I think you aren't seeing the big picture. Cortez won't ever give up searching for the two of you. Even if he doesn't want his daughter, letting her go to you, or letting his daughter have say as to when she is free of her father, will mean defeat in Cortez's eyes. His kind of man doesn't do defeat. For as long as she is with you, you will be hunted just as I am. It's not the life you want. You've got everything right now, Ben. Don't fuck that up."

He hadn't thought about being with Zoey in that light. Ben considered Micah's words for a moment. "I get it, man," he said, still mulling over the picture Micah had just drawn for him. At least he was open-minded enough to see the downside to possible actions or choosing not to act. "You're jumping the gun a bit, though. Zoey and I don't have any kind of commitment whatsoever."

Micah looked up from his task. "Have you slept with her?"

It was on the tip of Ben's tongue to tell Micah to fuck off. "Not that who I have sex with or, even more so, who Zoey has sex with is any of your business," he began, straining again for control. Micah was succeeding in pissing him off with damn near everything out of his mouth. "But no, I haven't."

He sure as hell wasn't going to tell Micah that Zoey was a virgin and that Ben had enough scruples to not take that from her. At least not until they were in a committed relationship. Ben blinked, looking away and toward the cabin. His thoughts didn't need to drift toward being with Zoey long term.

"I wonder what they're talking about in there," he muttered, changing the subject.

"Maggie is telling Zoey about me," Micah said.

Ben jerked his head toward his friend. "Telling her what?"

"Maggie thinks it will help Zoey if she knows she's not alone. You see, I do trust Zoey. So does Maggie. Zoey is young, *real* young," Micah stressed, looking hard at Ben. "Maggie knows Zoey's pain. The two of them have known each other almost as long as we've lived here. Maggie adores Zoey and has wished many times that Zoey could undo the shackles her father has put her in. Maggie was so ecstatic when she found out Zoey had finally become strong enough to take that first step. It took a lot to walk out her father's door. I couldn't deny Maggie having her friend out here." Micah's tone dropped a bit when he added, "Even when I knew that by her walking, Zoey would be hunted down like a wild animal whose hunter only covets the head over his mantel."

Ben cringed at the awful analogy. Then another thought hit him. Maybe Micah already knew Zoey was a virgin. Zoey might have told Maggie. Ladies talked about things like that. It hadn't occurred to Ben until now, but it was a strong possibility. Micah and Maggie probably talked to each other about everything. In an isolated life like this, all they had were each other. Maggie wouldn't have thought it a violation of her friendship with Zoey to tell Micah, especially when they probably didn't have any secrets from each other.

Suddenly Ben envied Micah for that. A relationship could be a lifeline. Ben had always viewed it as something to tread through lightly, if he had to endure it at all. He'd never thought of embracing a relationship and doing everything in his power to make sure what he had with another person was always strong. Up until now, anytime things got sticky with a lady Ben knew it was time to walk. Although the women Ben had known weren't anyone he could imagine spending his life with.

But Zoey—she was perfect in so many ways. Zoey was definitely a lady meant for a lifelong relationship. But was he meant for one as well?

"There are few people on this planet I trust that well."

Ben realized Micah had been talking and looked up from where he'd been scowling at the ground. "I appreciate the trust."

"My concern with you and Zoey doesn't have anything to do with not trusting her, or Maggie wouldn't be explaining our history," Micah continued, apparently having not noticed that Ben had drifted off on his own speculative journey for a moment.

"Wait a minute, whose history?" Ben's mouth went dry as he shot a worried look at the only cabin window in view. "Is Maggie telling Zoey about me? About you and me working together?"

Micah shook his head slowly. "Only what Maggie knows."

"Damn it," Ben cursed under his breath, and started toward the cabin before thinking through what he would do.

Maybe it wasn't as bad as he feared it might be. If Maggie mentioned Ben was a bounty hunter, maybe she wouldn't add that Ben was also currently employed and up here simply to give a message to Micah. There would be time to explain everything to Zoey. Possibly once Maggie told her about Micah, it would be clear why Ben hadn't been up-front with her.

Without waiting for Micah, Ben pushed open the heavy wooden front door he'd seen the ladies go through. Ben instantly noticed the security panel on the wall just inside the cabin. It wasn't the type of security system that fed out to a service that monitored the home. Instinctively he glanced around and looked up. One of the first things he'd learned as a bounty hunter, professional criminals always rigged their homes.

Ben spotted the barely noticeable camera almost above his head. Looking farther, he was sure he spotted something shiny in a vent on the wall. Micah's rustic, cozy little cabin was wired to the hilt. Ben would bet good money there was an extensive camera system in this home with monitors, possibly in Micah and Maggie's bedroom, allowing them to see and record every inch of every room. There were probably remote weapons built into his home. That was more than likely what Ben had seen in the vent at the front door. If anyone entered who wasn't welcome, they would be shot.

"I don't believe it!" Zoey exclaimed, and the scraping of a chair across the floor gave away her location.

Ben stepped farther into the home. He was only a few steps into a very comfortable-looking living room when he quit scouring the place for more traps and twisted his head in Zoey's direction.

"Zoey," he breathed, hurrying to her when he saw how puffy her eyes were from crying.

"Don't."

Her one word froze him in his tracks.

Zoey pointed at him. "Maggie has already said I could stay here. I'm done with men using me. I'll never have another man lie to me, or believe me too gullible or stupid to handle a secret if need be. I want you to leave, Ben. I don't ever want to see you again!" she shouted, her shrill cry with her words slicing through his heart like a very sharp knife.

"Zoey, wait a minute," Ben managed, his throat almost closing and making it really hard to talk.

"No!" Zoey spun around and ignored him. "Leave, Ben," she choked, apparently crying again.

Maggie looked over Zoey's shoulders as she took Zoey in her arms and gave him a scornful look. "You should leave," she said quietly.

Ben realized Micah stood right behind him and glanced at him before turning to the door and walking back outside. He didn't want to just walk away.

"Give her some time," Micah said, patting Ben's shoulder once they were outside.

Ben stared at the Taurus, parked as the trees ended and Micah and Maggie's yard began. "She can't stay here with you."

"Why not? Don't think I can protect her?"

Ben shook his head. "That's not what I meant. What if she wants to go into town?" What if she wanted to come to him? He didn't say the last question out loud but felt it hang in the air between them. "Wolf has already seen your car," he indicated, nodding at the car parked next to the Taurus. "If Zoey drives it, or either of you take her anywhere in it, that could be suicide for all of you."

Micah thought about it a moment. "You've got your Harley," he said. "I'll take you to the cabin where you two were staying in the Taurus. Then Zoey will have it if she needs to go anywhere."

As much as the two of them had argued while Ben was at Micah's, the ride was that quiet on the way back to the cabin. Ben was sick inside. At the same time, a growing, warring argument started in his head and wouldn't stop.

Ben had come to Zounds to warn Micah about Wolf Marley. He had found Micah, had told him about Wolf, and Ben's reason for being here was done. Micah was right. He could protect Zoey. In fact, there probably wasn't a safer place for Zoey anywhere than with Maggie and Micah. Ben should take Micah's advice to heart. Maybe in time, once Zoey had completely severed herself from Cortez, she and Ben might have a chance. And maybe after she'd lost her virginity to someone else.

Ben's stomach twisted brutally at that last thought. He didn't want to think about another man ever touching her.

"You've got company," Micah said, slowing when they reached the cabin.

"Crap, it's Wolf!" Ben hissed, a sense of fear just as unpleasant as his previous thoughts tearing into his insides. There was no way this little Taurus would be able to outrun Wolf's Escalade.

"Good to know." Micah continued staring out his driver's side window as he pulled off the highway, blocked the entrance to the cabin, and stopped directly in front of Wolf's SUV.

"What the fuck are you doing?" Ben demanded, but kept his voice low as he watched Wolf roll down his driver's side window. "He's sitting in his Escalade. Are you insane?"

When Micah looked away from Wolf and focused on Ben, the pleasant look on his face was unnerving. But not as unnerving as the realization that Micah not only loved the hunt but also embraced the thought of out-thinking another hunter. Ben stared at Micah, unable to figure out what his next move would be.

"You and Zoey went to one of her friends. Use any name but Maggie. You got in a fight. She told you to start walking, so you did. The people in Zounds are friendly enough. I saw you walking and gave you a lift." Micah's expression didn't change as he spoke. "Wolf hasn't seen this rental car, right?"

"Right," Ben agreed, scrambling to adjust gears fast enough to keep up with Micah's cool train of thought.

Micah whispered, and a chilling smile crossed his face. "Wolf Marley will never know he sat in his high-priced Cadillac and stared at the Mulligan Stew assassin."

"You're insane," Ben muttered, shaking his head and reaching for the door handle. Maybe his smartest move would be to wash his hands of everyone up here and return to L.A. right now.

"I'm sane," Micah told him, taking his comment seriously. "I didn't plan to run into Wolf. But here we are. If I don't stay alert and plan according to every possible scenario as it occurs, it will all be over. Do you see any flaws in telling Wolf you accepted a ride from a stranger?"

Ben opened the passenger door but looked over at Micah. He was right. This was his life. Micah had told Ben that he didn't wish this life on him. And it would be a life that sucked. Always having to watch your back. Looking over your shoulder with your every move. Never letting your guard down, and being ready to come up with a plan of action on a moment's notice, like right now. Ben didn't want that life. Who would?

Unfortunately, Ben couldn't help Micah with his current situation. Micah would be in hiding for the rest of his life.

"It sounds good. I'll make sure Wolf buys it."

"I know," Micah said, nodded once, and placed his hands on the steering wheel. "Good-bye, Ben."

Ben got out of the car, shut the door, and stood in the highway for only a moment as the Taurus drove off. As Wolf got out of his Escalade, Ben made himself switch gears just as fast as Micah had in the car. Ben wouldn't see Micah again. Maybe he would see Zoey. There wasn't time to dwell on either thought, both of which really upset him. Right now, he needed to pull off a convincing act so Wolf wouldn't give the man he'd seen driving that Taurus a moment's thought.

Angel stared out the window at the pale blue sky over the buildings downtown. It was the first time she'd had a breather all morning. News traveled fast in her town. Everyone had found an excuse to come in and buy a book just so they could learn firsthand what all the excitement had been about the night before. She had told each and every one of them the truth.

"Drama sure is good for business," she murmured, fingering the new, shiny lock Wolf had installed on her front door. The locks had been changed on the storage room door, too, for good measure.

Angel rubbed her lower back, knowing she'd be too sore

to move before the day was out. Wolf had also helped her put her store back together. She managed a smile remembering how he'd grunted when he had realized putting the mess Cortez had left for her back to order had entailed more than simply uprighting bookshelves and sticking books on them. She still had an inventory nightmare to sort through.

Turning her back on the cool, calm day outside, she stared at the stacks of destroyed books behind her counter. Maybe she should have a Cortez sale, in the man's honor, and sell the books that now had bent covers, or torn pages, or both at a serious discount. At least then her damaged books wouldn't be a complete loss.

Angel forced herself to keep working. Wolf had left an hour ago, telling her simply that he'd unraveled some new leads on his investigation and would be back soon. He had made sure there were bullets in her gun she now had by her register.

"And you better use it," he had told her, then had made her promise before kissing her senseless and leaving.

The gun made her nervous. It bothered her that she had to have it in her store. But she knew, even without Wolf making her promise before he left, that she would definitely use it before letting anyone lock her out of her bookstore again.

She didn't end up having much time to dwell on damaged books. Or where Wolf had disappeared to. Customers kept coming in, which made the day go by fast. Angel had made a list of everyone she knew who was being persecuted by Cortez in one way or another. If the people on her list didn't show up at her store, Angel called them. She was done being bullied. Zounds wasn't going to take Cortez's crap any longer. Not if she could help it.

"Detective Lassiter," Angel said, writing *San Francisco PD* on her notepad. "My name is Angel Matisse and I own a bookstore in Zounds, California. I want to know if you have any warrants for an Emilio Cortez. He has lived here in Zounds for the past ten years and has slowly managed to take over our bank, own our police department, and bully every

shop owner I know in my town into illegal leases and shares
of our profits. Honestly, I don't know how to stop him. So
I'm calling every city in California and surrounding states
and asking every law enforcement agency that will talk to
me if they have anything on this man. If you could call me
back, I'd really appreciate it." Angel repeated her name, left
her number, and hung up.

She smiled in delighted surprise when Maggie and Zoey
walked into her store.

"Come to get the scoop firsthand on the latest excitement?" Angel asked, feeling the caffeine rumble through
her system as she downed the last of her coffee in her mug.

"I'm not sure I want any excitement," Zoey said. There
was good color in the girl's face, but the solemn look in her
eyes was a dead giveaway.

Angel turned, noticed she'd managed to drink the entire
pot of coffee, and hurried to start a new pot. "What's wrong?"
she asked, taking in both women when they moved to the
end of her counter. "Now you both have me worried. Is it
because of my store? We managed to get it back together before I opened for business this morning, and I have all new
locks."

"What are you talking about?" Maggie asked, glancing
around her.

Angel felt a wave of pride that her friends couldn't tell
that her entire bookstore had looked as if an earthquake had
destroyed the place less than twelve hours ago.

"You changed the locks?" Zoey also looked around her,
her expression suddenly masked with fear. "Was it my father
or Wolf?" she demanded, snapping her attention back to
Angel.

"Wolf? God, no," Angel said, laughing. "You should have
seen him. He had me hiding on the floor of his SUV. I know
looking up was stupid and I could have been shot. I've already heard about it from Wolf, but ladies, he was my hero
last night. I swear I thought he was going to kill Brutus. And
I'm not ashamed to say I wish he had. But when he shot his
foot—" she said, and covered her mouth when uncontrollable

giggles threatened. It was adrenaline and exhaustion taking its toll.

"Okay, stop. You're scaring me." Zoey held up her hand. "I think you better start at the beginning. But first tell me that none of my father's men are on their way over."

"I seriously doubt it. Haven't seen a glimpse of them all day." Angel beamed and glanced at the time. "Let me close the store. Then we can go upstairs and get comfortable. I'll tell you the whole story."

"How about if the three of us go out to eat?" Maggie suggested. "My treat. It sounds as if we've all had some excitement in the past twenty-four hours. Let's go spoil ourselves a bit and catch up."

Less than an hour later, Angel sat facing Zoey and Maggie in a tall-backed dark-stained wooden booth. She stared over her plastic menu as the waitress brought their drinks.

"You had the strawberry margarita, no salt, right?" she asked, her smile friendly as she slid the large fishbowl-sized drink in front of Angel.

"Good grief," Angel commented, shaking her head at the drink, then at Zoey's and Maggie's frozen margs across the booth. "We drink these it won't matter if we have salt or not."

Maggie laughed easily. "We all deserve a night out. Everyone know what they want?" she asked on the waitress's behalf.

Several sips of her drink later and with orders of lobster and shrimp in with the cook, Angel finally agreed this might have been a good idea.

"I can't believe neither of you has heard about the store," she said, leaning back against the wooden back of her side of the booth and getting comfortable. "I swear I've had more business today than I've had all year," she continued, laughing and taking a long tug on her straw. Her drink was sweet and the tequila strong. It tasted really good. She took another drink.

"I've decided to give Zounds a break for a while." Zoey's sentence was loaded with emotion, but she also grinned.

When she sucked down more of her drink, then ran her finger along the salted edge and licked it off, her laugh was musical. "We should have done this a long time ago."

"I come up with amazing ideas from time to time." Maggie tossed her hair over her shoulder with a proud smile. "We discovered this place a while back. The food is amazing. Just wait."

"Tell me what's happened with you," Angel asked, shifting her attention from Maggie to Zoey and trying not to stare at her bruised face too much. Angel was proud of Zoey escaping her father and had to admit her two dear friends were smiling more than she'd seen either of them do in a long time. Maybe it was the alcohol, but so be it. Angel agreed with Zoey. They should have done this long before now. "What happened with you and Ben?"

"Oh no," Zoey said, wagging her finger in the air. "You don't tell us we've missed out on the best gossip in Zounds and then ask what's going on with me. Spill all, Angel. What happened? And don't spare us on any of the details."

Angel took that to mean Zoey didn't mind hearing about her father's latest criminal activity. So, not sparing any details, Angel told all. The food arrived. She continued her story between bites and all of them raving, and her and Zoey giving Maggie repeated kudos on how good the food was.

"I was supposed to be lying on the floor of Wolf's Escalade," Angel continued, waving a plump shrimp in the air between all of them while sitting back comfortably on her side of the booth. "But of course I looked up and peeked over the back of the seat. That's how I know Wolf shot the guns out of each of their hands without any of them noticing he'd pulled his gun yet. I didn't even see him pull it. That's how good of a shot my Wolf is," she purred, and reached for the straw in her drink and slurped the remaining contents down noisily. "I don't think these drinks are that strong. Do you think these drinks are strong?"

"We need another drink." Zoey pulled her straw from her empty glass, and remnants of her margarita dropped from the end of it onto the table. "Oops," she said, giggling.

"I'm starting to think both of you are sloshed," Maggie accused, but laughed with Zoey and plopped a napkin onto the spills.

"And you've appointed yourself designated driver," Angel noticed, and waved her shrimp at Maggie's over-half-full drink. "Which is a damn good thing. Because you're a damn good friend," she pointed out, grinning at Maggie and then Zoey.

Angel couldn't remember the last time she was drunk. And yes, she was sloshed. But it felt good. She felt relaxed. Zoey was glowing with her smiles. It was worth coming here just to see her so happy. Angel decided she wouldn't mention her efforts all day to find some law enforcement agency, somewhere, that wanted Cortez for any crime. Zoey might hate her father, but nonetheless, he was her father.

"So late last night we changed the locks. We spent all morning putting the store back together."

"I am so sorry you had to do all that work because of my father." Zoey leaned forward and reached across the large table. She took Angel's hand. "I want to shoot him dead myself. Do either of you have a gun?"

"The last thing you, or me for that matter, need right now is a gun." Angel laughed, giving her friend's hand a friendly squeeze before releasing it. "It would be just our luck one of us would miss, not kill him, then he'd live free while we rot in prison."

"I wouldn't get caught." Zoey's expression grew serious. "I've laid in bed more nights than I can count figuring out the perfect way to kill him and not get caught. I hate what he's done to you!" she wailed. "And I'm so lucky that the two of you even talk to me."

"Oh, Zoey!" Angel exclaimed before Maggie could say anything. "You have nothing to do with your father. Everyone in Zounds knows you're the biggest victim of all."

Angel hated the words the moment they were out of her mouth. Zoey stilled, her face going white, which only made her bruises stand out even more.

"Is that what everyone thinks?" she whispered.

"What Angel means to say—," Maggie began.

"What I mean is all of us have grown stronger because of your father." Angel grinned and reached across the table as Zoey had a moment before. She squeezed Zoey's small, delicate fingers. "Yes, your dad is an asshole. I'm sorry, but it's true."

"Yes, he is," Zoey agreed, her dark eyes large and not blinking.

"Sometimes I think because of the persecution, all of us are stronger women. We've been forced to stand up and fight for what we want. You're fighting for your freedom. I'm fighting for my store."

"And we'll get what we want," Zoey said, barely whispering.

Angel shook her head. "Enough of my store. What's going on with you and Ben?"

"Absolutely nothing." Zoey stuck out her lip and sliced her hand through the air. "I'm not seeing him anymore."

"But why?" Angel asked.

"Well, first of all because he wouldn't fuck me. And all because I'm a virgin!" Zoey wailed, gesturing madly with her hands.

Angel almost choked on the shrimp she'd just plopped into her mouth. Several people sitting nearby glanced over and smiled but quickly diverted their attention as if they hadn't just heard Zoey loudly exclaim she'd never had sex.

Maggie laughed easily. "You don't have to tell the world," she said, grinning.

"It doesn't matter. He's an ass."

Angel decided not to broach the no-sex issue. "He didn't hurt you, did he?"

"Not physically," Zoey said, lowering her voice so only her friends heard her. "But guess what. Ben is a bounty hunter. Yup," she snapped, and started nodding her head so that her long black hair fell around her face. "He came up here with your Wolf. They're working together. He never was planning on looking for work!" she wailed, once again forgetting to be quiet.

Angel's exasperation grew, but not for the same reasons Zoey's did. "Who the hell are they hunting for?" she demanded, looking at Maggie.

Maggie shook her head, looking as serious and frustrated as Angel felt. "I have no idea," she said under her breath. "But I think it's time for us to go."

Angel . . . injured her paw, but not for the same reason Zoey did. "Who the hell are they bantering?" she demanded, looking to Maggie.

Maggie shook her head, looking as serious and frustrated as Angel felt. "I have no idea," she said under her breath. "But I think it's time for us to go.

Chapter Fifteen

"Oh crap," Angel said as they pulled around the parked, dark Escalade and into the service alley alongside her bookstore. She giggled and couldn't remember when she'd last been so happy or so drunk. "I might be grounded."

"Are you going to be okay?" Zoey asked sleepily from the backseat.

Angel waved away Zoey's concern. "I'm absolutely perfect," she slurred. "Hugs. Give me hugs."

"I had fun tonight." Maggie wrapped her arms around Angel as Zoey leaned forward from the backseat and draped her arms around both of them. "I'm so lucky to have two such wonderful friends."

"I was just thinking the same thing." Zoey drew out her words in a slow drawl, then fell back against the backseat. "Except shame on you, Maggie, for getting me drunk."

Angel gave Maggie one last hug, picturing Wolf climbing out of his SUV and standing behind them, legs spread and his muscular arms crossed against that broad chest of his. Instantly she warmed inside, and it wasn't from alcohol.

"Yes, shame on you." She giggled and kissed her friend on the cheek. "The two of you can come in for coffee before you drive home," she offered.

Maggie hummed softly against the side of Angel's face before releasing her and smiling at her in the dark. "Not tonight. I wouldn't want to hear Wolf, umm, yell at you," she said, her smile revealing her thoughts.

Which were the same thoughts Angel was having. She grinned back. "I'll let him yell for a few."

"Got to stroke that male ego."

"You know it."

Angel stood in the alley and watched Maggie accelerate down the alley, before turning and disappearing down the narrow side street that ran behind the shops. She turned and walked to the back of her store. As she pictured, Wolf stood with his back to the building. His arms weren't crossed, but he looked sexy as hell nonetheless.

"Where in the hell have you been?" he barked the moment his face came into focus in the dark. With the streetlight glowing behind him, his muscular body was almost silhouetted and his facial features completely shadowed. The rumble of his deep voice was the final touch to the dangerous air about him.

Angel wasn't the least bit intimidated. "I was out with girlfriends." She walked around him to the back door to her store. "What have you been doing?" she asked, turning the conversation on him as she pulled her keys out of her pocket and searched for the keyhole in the dark.

"Sitting outside this store waiting on you," he said, sounding pissed.

"That is so sweet." She poked the key at the lock in the dark but couldn't find the keyhole. "Will you hold your phone up to the lock so I can see?" she asked sweetly.

Wolf's hands were rough when he took her keys from her and unlocked the door. Then holding the door, he waited as she punched her security code into her alarm system.

"This really is a lot of work to get into my store." Angel walked through the dark store straight to the stairs. "And this is a lot of work just to get to my apartment," she added, feeling the giggles come back on when she began climbing the steps.

Her world teetered halfway up the staircase, and she slapped her hands on the walls on either side of her. "Whoa,

Nelly," she ordered, closing her eyes as her world spun around her. "Have you ever wondered exactly who Nelly is?"

Wolf finished locking the door downstairs and resetting her security system before coming up the stairs behind her.

"You're drunk," he accused. "I suppose that is why you couldn't be bothered to answer your phone?"

"I am," she agreed. "And my phone?"

Wolf's strong hands gripped either side of her waist and almost lifted her up the remaining steps. He let go of her and turned on the nearest lamp. Angel looked down at her purse, then realized she didn't have it.

"Now I can't exactly answer my phone if it's not on me." Angel collapsed on her couch and once again closed her eyes. This world-spinning thing wasn't so bad after all. It might do nicely to lull her off to sleep.

"Where is your phone?" Wolf demanded.

She opened one eye and stared up at him. "More than likely in my purse."

"Where is your purse?"

Angel gave that some thought. It wasn't on her. That wasn't good. Damn, so much for lulling off to sleep. "Well, I remember leaving the tip. Zoey and I insisted when Maggie wouldn't let us pay the bill."

"Where were you?"

"Fisherman's Cove," Angel said, and tried pushing herself to a sitting position. Her arms suddenly seemed about as affective as two wet noodles. "It's the best little seafood restaurant in the entire state. I swear. You must try their lobster." She did her best to bring her fingers to her mouth and blow a kiss into them. "Best there is," she told him, and fell sideways as she kissed her fingers.

"Did you leave your purse at the restaurant?"

That's right. She didn't have her purse. "No," she said slowly. She was pretty sure she had walked out of the restaurant with her purse. "You're right." It proved easier to point at Wolf than it had been to kiss her fingers. "I bet I left it in Maggie's car."

"What was she driving?"

Angel blinked, then closed one eye to bring Wolf into focus. "Her car," she said, and the giggles returned.

Wolf scooped her off the couch with one fluid movement. Instead of rough fabric, hard-packed muscles were pressing against her body everywhere.

"Use my phone and call Maggie to find out if she has your purse." Wolf dropped Angel on her bed, which immediately began moving in slow circles.

Angel braced herself in the middle of it, mouthing the word, *Whoa,* as Wolf pulled his phone out and handed it to her.

"Can't," she told him, and kicked off her shoes.

Wolf sat next to her and Angel fell into him.

"Yes, you can. What's her number?" he asked, his voice gentler as one arm went around Angel while he held his phone in his palm in front of her.

"That's why I can't," Angel said, shaking her head. She immediately stopped when it quickly became apparent that she was too drunk for such a simple movement. "I don't know her number."

"Then what is Zoey's number?" he growled.

"Don't growl at me," Angel snapped, and pushed herself free from his wonderful hard-packed body. "Zoey got a new phone, remember? I entered it into my phone, but I didn't memorize it. And I've never had Maggie's number. She talks to me in the store."

Angel wondered at that as she dropped her head in her hands and forced her brain to work through all of the alcohol. "I shouldn't have drunk that entire margarita," she complained.

"I think you'll live." Wolf's tone was tender when he reached for her sweater and pulled it over her head. "Tomorrow we'll have Ben reach Zoey. If your purse isn't in Maggie's car, we'll go to the restaurant. If it is in her car, we can drive out to her place and get it."

"Okay," Angel agreed and let him undress her. "Wait a minute," she demanded when Wolf began removing her bra.

She slapped him away and scooted to the middle of the bed. "Ben is a bounty hunter," she accused, and found it easier to focus on Wolf when she glared at him. "Which of course you know already since the two of you came up here together to search for someone."

"Yes," Wolf said, and sat on the edge of the bed watching her.

Angel was sure his wary expression appeared guarded. Well, that guard was about to drop.

"I've been completely honest with you. You know everything about my life. But you're holding back from me and it stops right now or this—" She waved her hand in the air between them. "This isn't going to happen. I won't have a relationship of any kind with you if we aren't completely open with each other about everything."

"That really does sound like a relationship."

"What?" she whispered, curling up on her bed in her bra and underpants, less aware of how naked she was than what Wolf had just said. Suddenly the drunken vapors in her brain cleared and she felt depressingly sober. "What does that mean?" she asked, pulling her knees to her chest and wrapping her arms around them.

Wolf stared at her, not moving or saying anything. Streetlights from her window accentuated his features in her otherwise dark room. The lamp in the other room barely offered shadows. But Angel saw his face. She saw several different emotions slide over his face as she stared back at him.

"I'm not sure," he finally said.

"Well, I suggest you decide pretty damn quick what it means, mister," she snapped. "I'm done serving as a piece of ass while you're searching for whoever the hell it is you are searching for, because it's definitely not Cortez."

"At first, that was what was going on here."

Angel stiffened. Suddenly she was very sober. Watching him in the dark, she didn't dare speak. Instead she found herself searching her own mind, what emotions she was experiencing. And with outstanding clarity it dawned on her that at first a casual relationship, mutual pieces of ass, was what she had thought was going on here, too.

"And now?" she asked.

"And now," he repeated, then peeled off his T-shirt.

He wasn't playing fair. Angel hugged her legs against her chest. She stared at all that roped muscle flexing under his skin as his arms rose over his head and the T-shirt came off his body and fell to the floor. Wolf was easily the sexiest man she'd ever laid eyes on.

His gaze was haunted as he studied her once he was half-undressed. Maybe he drove her nuts with need, but Angel guessed those feelings were mutual. She wasn't concerned about their lust for each other. Those emotions she understood. After about a week, though, something else was tugging at her. Wolf had too many secrets for her tastes. He had to come clean, or she would have to end this.

Angel dealt with the tension that grew inside when she pushed the matter. "I don't want to end whatever is building between you and me."

"Good," he rumbled, and sat on the edge of her bed to take off his shoes.

"But I will," she pressed, feeling that tension tighten in her gut as she watched him pull one shoe off, then the other. "I can't keep doing this with secrets and lies. Wolf, who are you looking for? Why are you here?"

Wolf stood and undid his jeans. He shoved them down muscular thighs. The boxers came off, too. Then he was facing her, naked and hard. He crawled onto the bed, moving in on her so she had no choice to submit or retreat.

Angel's body sizzled with desire. When she darted to the side, her motor skills weren't as functional as she'd guessed. Maybe she wouldn't have slipped off the bed, but she wasn't going to find out.

Wolf grabbed her, sliding her back to the middle of the bed and pinning her underneath him. "You're not going anywhere."

There was no point in struggling when they both knew he

was a hell of a lot stronger than she was. That didn't mean Angel needed to admit defeat.

"I am if I don't get some answers right now," she whispered.

Their faces were close enough in the dark for her to see his inward battles. She had a right to know what they were.

"A week ago I might not have cared about your life," she told him, and when she breathed in deeply the tightly coiled hairs on his chest tortured her nipples to distraction through her lace bra.

Wolf took a harsh breath, and his body stiffened over hers. Good. Misery loved company. He could just suffer through this, too.

"And I will be the first to admit I want to fuck you hard and fast, right now," she murmured.

Wolf growled, his eyes widening as he locked gazes with her. "You're going to get fucked. Hard and fast, or any other way you want it, sweetheart. I promise you that much."

"Not with secrets and lies hanging between us."

Wolf grabbed her wrists. He moved like an animal, fierce and aggressive. Angel barely had time to think, let alone react, when suddenly he'd spread her legs, positioning himself between them as he pinned her wrists over her head.

"Let's put it like this," he rumbled, the growl in his throat making his words raspy. They scraped over her flesh as his eyes flared with something that bordered on anger. "I've never shared anything about my business with anyone. I'm not looking for a relationship, but I want you."

"I will not tolerate hearing anything about you from anyone else that I don't already know firsthand from you," she snarled at him, her teeth clenched as anger rose inside her. "Your terms, Wolf Marley, are not acceptable."

Wolf leapt off the bed, roaring as he did until he was in the middle of her bedroom. Then letting out another roar, he turned and hit her wall with his fist.

If losing her store had taught her anything, it was that she would never be bullied. No man, or any person for that matter, would ever coerce her into terms that didn't meet her full satisfaction. Angel leapt off the bed, too. Once again she was reminded of how much alcohol she'd had earlier when she almost spun around before managing to hold her bearings and prevent herself from falling to the floor.

As aggressive as his release had been a moment before, Wolf spun around, reaching for her with a touch gentle enough it singed her flesh clear through her body. The swelling between her legs exploded with so much energy, cream pooled between her legs. She steadied herself and didn't notice at first that she held on to both his arms while fighting to cool her desire and not succumb to it before seeing her terms out.

"There is a man known as the Mulligan Stew assassin," Wolf spoke in such a low whisper as he helped her straighten, then held her as they stood in the middle of her bedroom facing each other. "He has allegedly assassinated over fifty people. The assassin worked mostly in the U.S., accepting jobs and killing people already wanted for heinous crimes. His last known hit was a dirty CIA agent. Then just over a year ago, in Los Angeles, a man wanted for bouncing checks was shot with the same gun used to kill the CIA agent."

Angel stared at Wolf. His expression was intense. He was giving her exactly what she wanted. Her heart pounded so hard in her chest she could barely breathe. Even as they looked at each other and he shared the complete truth with her, she was hearing so much more than news about one of the most notorious criminals in American history. She and Wolf had just crossed over from casual sex. Whatever it was between them was evolving, and her heart hurt from the knowledge of it, as well as the weight of what it meant.

She blinked, forcing herself to focus on his words. Later she would dwell on the consequences of what his sharing them with her truly meant.

"The Mulligan Stew assassin?" she murmured. "The one they talked about on CNN for a good month, at least?"

"The one and only."

"And you think he is in Zounds?" Angel began shaking her head.

"Darling, I know he is in Zounds."

"You've been in my store during business hours. Everyone in town comes in and shares their business with me. I was born here, Wolf. My parents ran this store before me. This town trusts my actions, and they trust my decisions. If there is a problem, everyone who lives in Zounds knows I will do whatever it takes to fix it. I would know if anyone in Zounds was harboring a criminal." She let out a laugh, but it wasn't to mock Wolf. Angel simply couldn't accept that someone that well known, a man who had killed so many people and was wanted by the federal government, would be in her town.

"No one is harboring him."

Wolf stared down at Angel. He prayed he wasn't making the biggest mistake of his life. But at the same time, letting her know the truth of why he was here helped him see once and for all that Angel really didn't know anything about the Mulligan Stew assassin. At least not where he might be hiding.

There wasn't any ignoring the strong wave of protectiveness as Wolf held the woman who was staring up at him. He accepted that he probably would have told her the truth even if she hadn't made such fierce demands. Whether the alcohol had encouraged her actions or she'd been stewing on this for a while he wasn't sure. And it didn't matter. There was something growing between them. Something a lot stronger than lust. As much as he wanted to fight it, Wolf wanted Angel. He wanted her in bed. He wanted her in his life.

"Are you saying he is living here in my town, as one of us?" she asked, her eyes wide and sensual in the dark.

She was breathing hard. That lace bra of hers barely held her full, round breasts captive. They threatened to spill out of the thin fabric. Her nipples poked through the film of lace. Wolf's dick was so hard he doubted this conversation would last much longer. Angel had her terms, but so did he.

"He's been living here probably close to a year."

"Who is he?"

"I doubt you've seen him."

"Why do you say that?"

"I don't think he comes into town." Wolf wasn't going to mention Maggie. He wasn't sure what Angel would say, but already he knew her loyalty to her friends was as strong as it was to her town. He didn't quite understand that. He'd never felt anything for a community other than using it as a means to survive. "The assassin doesn't live alone."

Her mouth curved into a tight little circle. Wolf's dick danced with demands of its own between them. Angel glanced down, looking away from his face for the first time since he'd begun explaining the truth about why he was in Zounds. The moment she acknowledged his dick, the breath she sucked in spoke volumes. Her lashes were heavy over her incredibly dark blue eyes. Her brown curls were tousled around her pretty face. But when she finally raised her attention back up to his, the sensuality smoldering in her gaze released something primal inside Wolf.

"I'll do whatever you want to help you catch him," she said on a whisper of a breath.

Wolf swore that Angel saw what he felt erupting inside him. But he saw something in her. Submission. That primal side of him, so freshly released, roared with the urgent demand to possess and brand her as his own. There wasn't the slightest bit of argument in his brain telling him this wasn't what he wanted, or that he sucked at relationships, or that allowing another woman the chance to take all that was his and mock him while doing it would destroy him.

"You already are," he managed to mutter.

Wolf lifted Angel in his arms. He simply stepped forward, grasping her until her backside pressed against the wall. His brain didn't have time to focus on where the bed was. Angel had submitted to him. She agreed to help him no matter what it took. Wolf wouldn't need her help, but her support mattered more to him than he had thought it would.

"God, Wolf!" Angel cried out, and wrapped her arms around his neck as she let her head fall back and exposed her long, enticing neck to him.

"I gave you what you wanted," he snarled, his need for her so fierce it was eating him alive.

"I still want more."

"Greedy woman," he muttered, and pressed his lips over the throbbing pulse just above her collarbone.

"I am," she agreed, her voice thick with need. "I want all of it."

"Darling, you're going to get every inch."

He heard the words coming out of his mouth and was glad they made sense. Wolf didn't see any need for further conversation. Whatever it was that was locking the two of them together was too strong for him to acknowledge at the moment. Not when his cock ached to be buried deep inside her heat.

His woman.

That thought seemed to repeat itself with every pounding beat of his heart.

Wolf didn't dwell on it. Instead he shoved his body against hers, pressing her even harder against the wall. Angel responded by dragging her nails deep into his shoulders. A hum rose from her throat, and it raked over his flesh like waves of electricity. Already charged, he was like a madman, finally given what he'd craved for so long. And Angel was exactly what he needed. In the few moments that she'd suggested there would be nothing between them if he weren't honest, Wolf had known with outstanding clarity that he had to share everything with her. Losing her wasn't an option.

When she brought up her legs and wrapped them around him, then thrust her pelvis forward so that her soaked heat pressed against the tip of his cock, all coherent thought drained from his brain. Wolf needed to be inside her. He needed to bury himself in her heat and feel her wrapped around his cock. Just the thought of not having her tore at him with a pain he didn't know he was capable of feeling. When Rebecca walked out on him, it had stabbed at Wolf's pride. But just now, he'd known for the first time what a woman could do when she stabbed at his heart.

Angel had to have chosen the undies she wore more to torture him than for any other practical purpose. He thrust against the flimsy fabric and it held fast, refusing him entrance. She moaned and relaxed more against the wall, her arms draped over him and her head fallen to the side.

"Take them off," she murmured.

Wolf chuckled. "I'll rip them off."

Her head didn't straighten, but she opened her eyes. The look she gave him was more a challenge than one of cooperation. "I like this lingerie," she informed him.

"I don't," he growled, and pinned her hard with his arms as he prepared to do battle against a tiny piece of lace.

"I can take it off."

She didn't have a chance to move, not that he planned on letting her try.

Wolf thrust against the flimsy sheathing of her lace thong until his cock cried victory and he sunk deep into the fathoms of her pussy. Not once in his life had he known heat to be so incredibly intoxicating.

"Wolf, yes!" Angel cried out, grabbing his arms just below his shoulders and pressing her fingers into his flesh. "Oh my God! Fuck me . . . please."

Her plea faded into alluring moans that encouraged Wolf to dive deeper into her soaked pussy. He barely managed to register the thumping sound they made against the bedroom wall as he lost himself in pleasure so exquisite he wasn't sure how he had ever managed to live without it or her.

Chapter Sixteen

Zoey wandered outside, nursing her cup of coffee as her breath formed small clouds in front of her face. It was colder this morning than it had been the last few days she'd been there. As warm and cozy as it was inside Micah and Maggie's cabin, the icy chill of the morning woke Zoey faster than Maggie's incredible coffee did.

Winter was going to set in early. Zoey had lived in Zounds long enough to know what heavy gray mornings like this one meant. It was going to rain, and it would probably rain all day. Zoey didn't mind the cold weather; if anything, she loved it. There was nothing better than cuddling up to a warm fire and reading a good book on days like this. Except she didn't have any of her books.

The only Internet connection as well as all communications with the outside world, was all set up in a small room next to Maggie and Micah's. Zoey hadn't asked to go in there. Along with knowing her weather, she also knew when a room was off-limits. That one looked more off-limits than any she'd ever seen. There was a lot more than a computer in there, and Zoey wasn't sure she wanted to know what all of that equipment could do. She hadn't asked questions at her father's house, and she wasn't asking questions here.

No, not her father. She had made that decision the night she and Maggie and Angel had gone out together. Cortez had taken Zoey from her mother when she'd been a young child. She didn't doubt he was her father. A man like Cortez would know those things, and he sure as hell wouldn't have taken her into his home if she weren't his daughter. But Emilio Cortez hadn't loved her. There had never been a father/daughter bond of any kind. Zoey was simply another tool, a resource at his disposal that he would use when the mood hit him. Cortez had made it very clear how Zoey would be used in his never-ending plot to make more money and control more of the world around him. She wasn't going to have anything to do with him or his criminal activity ever again.

Zoey heard Maggie and Micah talking in the small shed behind their cabin. Maggie's happy laughter sang through the morning air. There wasn't any doubt in Zoey's mind that those two were the happiest couple she'd ever met. It was day three since she'd told Ben to leave. Zoey felt as if the rest of the world had disappeared along with Ben once Micah had taken him back to the cabin. Since then she'd taken walks with Maggie and Micah. Zoey had helped cook in the kitchen with both of them and cleaned up afterward. They had spent evenings talking. Never about anything important, just idle chatting among the three of them, or more like between the two of them. Micah usually reclined, listened, and commented occasionally. Zoey had told them about some of the famous people in history she admired, which had held both Maggie's and Micah's attention. Zoey couldn't say that she felt unwelcome, they were the perfect hosts. But she was bored.

Whenever Micah disappeared into his computer room, she and Maggie had been able to enjoy girl talk. Maggie had shown Zoey her books, which were stacked along the wall in her and Micah's bedroom, next to an incredibly large bed. They weren't the kind of books Zoey liked to read, though.

A mischievous wind picked up and whipped through the trees bordering the large yard surrounding the cabin. Zoey took too big of a sip of her coffee. It burned all the way down her esophagus just as the wind blew around her. She was damn near knocked off her feet. Just as she decided to hurry to the shed and join Micah and Maggie, Micah's booming laughter stopped Zoey in her tracks. She hadn't heard him laugh yet during her stay there.

Maggie insisted he was a quiet, cautious man but a completely different person when the two of them were alone. Zoey hoped so for Maggie's sake. The man Zoey had spent time with over the past three days was brooding, stared at her with dangerous-looking eyes, and hardly ever said a word.

She hunched down into the coat Maggie had let her borrow. It was warm and too large, which at the moment was a good thing, because she was able to wrap it around her hand with her coffee. She stared at the shed, with its door partially ajar, and almost hated joining them. Maggie hadn't complained once about Zoey being there. It had been quite the opposite. Maggie had informed Zoey enough times that there wasn't a safer place on the planet for her to be. Maggie had no problems bragging about Micah's abilities to protect Zoey, even though it was due to his skills as a murderer. And Zoey appreciated the two of them letting her stay with them. She was more than feeling like a third wheel, though. Now with bad weather threatening, God only knew when she'd be able to leave the cabin. Already she was seriously going stir-crazy.

She might have been stuck in that small cabin with Ben while it poured outside, she mused, stepping over uneven ground as she walked around the well-kept rustic cabin to the screened-in back porch. Opening and closing the screen door without letting it bang, she decided to let those two enjoy their time alone with each other. She relaxed on the porch swing and stared out at the breathtaking view behind the cabin.

Zoey wasn't in the mood for breathtaking views. Warmth flowed out of the partially open back door that led into the kitchen. The wood-burning stove probably would keep the entire cabin warm. Maggie and Micah were ready for winter. Those two would be able to live without the rest of the world in perfect happiness. Would Zoey ever get that same shot at being that happy?

"Are you really going to start feeling sorry for yourself

now?" she snapped, relaxing on the swing and letting the oversized coat fall open as she placed her coffee on the round table next to the swing. A nice crocheted cover gave the simple table a distinguished look.

Dishing her phone out of her pocket, she ran her fingers over the screen. Cortez had laughed when he'd seen the picture of Princess Diana on her phone. Zoey had loaded the picture as a reminder as to what happened to young women when they tried leaving families with enough power to prevent the women from embarrassing them.

Zoey studied the picture of Diana and her sad smile. At least that was how Zoey saw the picture. If someone were to take Zoey's picture right now, would she have a sad smile, too?

She saw the picture in new light now. All it had taken was the courage to walk away. Zoey wasn't in the hands of her father's hired thugs. She was being very careful and staying out of Cortez's radar. But was she free? Maggie and Micah weren't free. They were in hiding, continually checking their safety and always plotting their every move. They would never be able to have a picnic in a park, take lazy strolls downtown, or go shopping in a mall.

Clearing the screen saver, Zoey tapped the phone to make a call. Then placing the call before letting her nerves get the best of her, she held it to her ear and listened to it ring.

"Zoey," Ben said after it rang once. "Are you okay?"

He sounded worried. And incredibly sexy.

"I'm fine," she sighed.

"Are you sure?"

"Yes." Zoey made herself remember how she'd rehearsed this conversation when she'd first woken that morning. "I wanted to talk to you about the cabin and the rental car. The cabin is in my name and the car in your name."

"I'll drive up there right now and follow you back here," he suggested.

Zoey closed her eyes. Was he going to apologize? Offer some viable explanation as to why he'd lied to her and made her feel like a fool?

"I want you to stay in the cabin for the rest of the week since it's paid for," she continued, praying he'd say something so she could agree to come to him.

"I'll pay for the rental car for as long as it's needed." That wasn't exactly an apology or explanation. "And I'll head out the door right now. We'll have you back here before it starts pouring."

She took a deep breath. "Why would I want to come back there?" she prompted.

"Would you rather stay out there with Micah?"

"I thought he was your friend."

"He is my friend," Ben snapped. "There is no one who could protect you as well as he could. I've spent the past few days wondering if there is even a reason for me to stay here. Without you here," he said, then broke off without finishing the sentence. "I guess what I mean is, why don't you want to come back here? If it's about the virgin thing . . ."

"Oh my God!" she bit out, and hung up.

"I'm a fool!" she cried, hanging her head as a wave of sadness and overwhelming emptiness attacked her. "I'm a stupid fool. I read something into what was between Ben and me, and it simply wasn't there." Straightening, Zoey stared straight ahead and refused to let any tears fall. There was no point in repeating the short phone call in her head. She would only try to put meaning into his words. It was best to take it all at face value.

The truth of it was simply that Ben didn't have a problem lying to her. He didn't consider her someone he should have confided in. He was protecting her, and sex was natural between two consenting adults stuck alone with each other in an isolated cabin. Especially when there was a strong attraction.

And God, there had been such a strong attraction.

"Damn it," she moaned, letting her head fall into her hands. "Quit persecuting yourself," she ordered.

Just because he'd led her to believe he was a drifter searching for work, probably seasonal work as she'd believed at the time, when in truth he was a bounty hunter working a case wasn't cause for her to fall into a major pity party. She should be glad someone had found her who was actually capable of protecting her more than the average person. Her father—no, Cortez—hadn't found her yet.

When her hands started trembling, she couldn't make them stop. Ben didn't think he'd done anything wrong. In fact, he was considering leaving. He thought she was staying away from him because of her own issues. Well, maybe she was. Maybe she had an issue with men who lied to her. Once again the anger rose inside her. It welled up and consumed her, leaving no room for pity or regret.

"I'm not an idiot," she mumbled, and shoved her hair away from her face. "And I'm not reading something into what was happening between us. Ben just isn't the right man for me. Of course he wants me to come back there. He is on a case and why not have someone around you who knows the area, that he's attracted to, to spend time with and have sex."

But they didn't have sex. Ben didn't want a virgin. Okay, she would concede that point and maybe she shouldn't have hung up on him. Apparently, the virgin thing did bother her a bit, but only because he'd made such a big deal about it. Her being a virgin wasn't the issue as much as Ben not telling her the truth. He didn't see that as an issue. Therefore, they were incompatible. At least for having a relationship. They wouldn't have been incompatible sexually. What he had done to her!

"Oh my God," she wailed as her body was racked with sexual desire and frustration, knowing sex with Ben would never happen.

Slapping the phone down on the small table next to her, she hopped up and left the back porch. Marching around the side of the house, Zoey ignored the rain that had started to fall. She didn't care if she had to endure the perfectly happy couple being perfectly happy together. Anything would be better than sitting there fuming over Ben Mercy.

Maggie and Micah were speaking in contented conversation. The two of them were so in tune with each other that they finished each other's sentences every time they talked. Zoey found that as much amazing as she did irritating.

"Good morning," Maggie said cheerfully when Zoey appeared in the doorway to the small shed.

Tools of all sorts hung on the walls. Maggie and Micah seemed to have every creature comfort imaginable to man. Just like their cabin, which was rustic on the outside but modern and exquisite on the inside, the small shed wasn't anything to look at when approaching it. Once Zoey stepped inside the open door, it was a completely different story. The shed was insulated. She immediately felt the warmth. The walls were lined with cork, which made it easy to hang Micah's many tools. He had a worktable, and several benches made it easy to sit and talk to him while he was working.

Of course, as in Cortez's home, everything she saw around her had come from criminal activity. And, in this case, it was all blood money. Zoey simply escaped one prison to go to another. Granted, she was treated better here, but she still wasn't free. Maybe if she hit the road, relocated on her own somewhere far away from Zounds, she would finally be able to live her life the way she wanted.

In the year Zoey had known Maggie she never would have guessed in all that time that Maggie was married to a man possibly more of a criminal than Zoey's father. Although, hands down, Micah was definitely not as sinister. And he was a lot more famous. The Mulligan Stew assassin was definitely the most notorious criminal of this century, and he had been dubbed as possibly the man responsible for more murders than any man in the twentieth century. The media had claimed that if he remained at large, he would be the most famous assassin of all time. Zoey wasn't sure what he would be known as if he was ever caught. She forced a smile on her face. Micah and Maggie's life wasn't her problem. Her own life needed to be sorted out, and that was enough for her to deal with.

Micah looked at her when she stepped inside the shed, and his intense gaze didn't seem to miss a thing.

"Sleep any better?" he asked, although his face said he already knew the answer.

"Yeah," she lied, and wished she'd remembered her coffee, which was still on the back porch. "Figured I'd come find you two." There was no reason to share her conversation with Ben with either of them. It was sorted out, and she would move forward from here.

"Come sit here and dry off. Saints above, it's already pouring." Maggie patted the leather-cushioned bench where she sat. "Put your feet by the heater. It will keep you warm."

Zoey obeyed, joining Maggie on the bench. A small heater glowed with warmth and did instantly take the chill away.

"Micah is building me a bookcase," Maggie said, sounding delighted. "I finally can store all the books I keep buying at the bookstore."

"I need to get some books," Zoey said, staring at the wood shavings under Micah's workbench.

"Tell Maggie what you want and she'll go buy some books for you." Micah didn't look up when he made decisions for her but instead ran a pencil over wood with a straightedge.

She was done with men lying, and she was done with them trying to control her life. "I can go buy my own books," she said, looking at Maggie when she spoke. "I probably will go soon. This weather isn't going to get any better."

Micah sighed loudly but continued working. "Sweetheart, please explain to your friend that I can't protect her if she leaves."

Zoey was going to lose her temper. She gripped the edge of the leather-cushioned bench and met Maggie's gaze when she looked at her and opened her mouth to parrot her husband. Zoey spoke before Maggie could.

"I know how to drive myself to the bookstore." Zoey waved her hand at Micah. "He can continue playing protector once I return. As hard as it's raining it will be impossible to see me in the car, and I'm in a rental car, not my own car. Cortez doesn't know about the rental. It's in Ben's name. Please tell your husband that just because he is a mass murderer and stuck out here in the wilderness doesn't mean I am."

Micah dropped his straightedge and growled, "Tell her I'm not going to kill her in her goddamn sleep."

"Enough!" Maggie jumped up, shrieking her frustration as she threw her hands up in the air. "The two of you can fight this out. I'm not playing middleman for either one of you. I've had it!"

Before turning her attention to Micah, Zoey watched Maggie storm out of the shed and head to the cabin. The shed suddenly seemed smaller when he straightened, got off his stool, and slowly stalked to the doorway.

"Is that the first time she's raised her voice?" Zoey asked, feeling at least partially responsible for Maggie getting upset at both of them.

Micah kept his back to her and snorted. "Irish Maggie? Are you kidding? We're both damn lucky she didn't start throwing things. When that girl gets pissed, her aim is very likely better than mine."

"I've never seen her upset. If she's been that pissed at you in the past, you probably deserved it."

Micah turned and faced her. He ran his hand through his thick, long hair and stared absently at his worktable. "I'm no saint," he muttered.

"No, you aren't. You're the furthest possible thing from a saint."

"I don't deny who I am, Zoey," Micah said, sighing. He seemed distracted as he glanced over his shoulder at the cabin, then finally returned to where he'd been sitting and continued to work.

Zoey wasn't sure why she was glad he didn't leave her alone in the shed. It wasn't that she wanted to talk to Micah, but she admitted to herself, she wanted to talk to someone. Why not the man who had known Ben long before she had?

"Now see, that is the difference right there," she said, leaning back and getting comfortable. A part of her thought she would be smart to go inside and smooth out her friend's temper. But if Maggie did get as pissed as Micah suggested, maybe waiting just a bit and making a show of doing what Maggie said to do would look better. "You're a mass murderer, and you admit it," Zoey continued, shivering a bit as she stated the obvious about him. "Ben is a good, upstanding citizen, with an impressive job, and he lied about it. He made it out as if he were a drifter, coming into Zounds look-ing for work, when in fact that wasn't the case at all. I went on about how honest and full of integrity he was, and it was all a lie."

"He had his reasons for lying to you," Micah muttered, pressed his straightedge down on the wood, and ran a long line down the length of it. Then glancing at her with that un-nerving look he always used, he added, "And I was an assas-sin, not a mass murderer."

Zoey slapped the side of the leather-cushioned bench and stood, needing to pace. Which, although it wasn't the easiest task to pull off in the small shed, she managed as she walked to the open doorway. The moment she stood in it, she was blasted by the cold from outside. Turning, she stalked back, but only as far as the edge of Micah's worktable.

"What reasons are there to justify lying to someone if you're supposed to have feelings for them?" she demanded, but instantly wanted to take the question back when Micah leaned back and cocked one eyebrow at her. She diverted quickly, not wanting to hear any of Micah's logic as to how she had simply created feelings between her and Ben that just didn't exist, at least not on Ben's side. "And you killed so many people. You admit it." She waved a finger at him. "You're the Mulligan Stew assassin. Does it make you feel better about yourself by giving what you did a fancy title?"

"Ben was protecting you from an ugly and dangerous truth," Micah said, his voice uncharacteristically soft, al-most gentle. "Me," he added. "And I didn't choose the title Mulligan Stew assassin; I inherited it. My father and uncle brought skills to the table, skills they sold to the highest bid-der long before I ever picked up a gun. They taught me to hunt, and I loved it. Big-game hunting really appealed to me. But I was still a teenager when the thrill got old. I felt as if there was no game out there that would give me the chal-lenge, the adrenaline rush I had grown to crave."

Micah picked up a measuring tape, rotated it between his fingers, but Zoey didn't think he saw the tape. He sighed, put

282 *Lorie O'Clare*

it down on the wood, and kept speaking. She swore some of
the terrible demons he always kept at bay constricted in his
expression when he scowled and stared straight ahead.

"The first time my father and uncle approached me, it was
for a friend of theirs," he continued. "I honestly can't remember all the details now, but she was a battered wife and
the judge was taking her kids and giving them to the bastard
who kept beating her. That's right," he said, and snapped his
fingers. "Her husband had beat her and put her in the hospital several times. I remember we went and picked her up
once and I saw how bruised she was." Micah looked at Zoey.
"So much worse than the bruises you showed up here with.
But her husband was taking her girls and she was scared he
was already sexually abusing them."

"Oh God," Zoey murmured.

"I didn't hesitate when my father and uncle told me what
they had in mind. That was the first time," he informed her.
"And the only time I did it for free. Word traveled. No one
knew it was me. My uncle and father were very good at protecting me. When I took out that bastard of a wife beater
without a soul having a clue who had shot him, my uncle was
the one who came up with the idea of searching the country.
By then I was in my early twenties. The three of us often sat
at the kitchen table and discussed our day. After that, we sat
at the kitchen table and plotted the next kill. We became known
as Mulligan Stew. No one knew how many of us there were,
or if there was just one of us. Those who needed our services
didn't ask questions. Of course, finding lowlives isn't too hard
to do. My father and uncle set up all the jobs. I traveled to the
city, took a day or two to stake out how I wanted to do things.
There were crooked city officials and politicians, rapists, pedophiles, serial killers, every form of lowlife you could imagine. And each time someone wanted these lame excuses for
human beings to disappear, they were willing to pay dearly to
have it done. The stakes grew bigger and bigger. The cost to
do the job grew as well. And, if you ever watched CNN, you
probably know more about my last job than I do."

"So why don't you kill Cortez?"

The demons that had contorted Micah's face disappeared instantly. The look he gave her was cold, almost hateful. "Are you hiring me, Miss Cortez?" he asked in a tone that was chilling.

Zoey leapt to her feet, not remembering when she'd sat back down on the bench. "I can't. You're retired," she said sarcastically, and stormed out of the shed. She couldn't get out of there fast enough.

She prayed he didn't see her jump when he fired up the table saw and it roared to life.

It had been wrong to suggest he kill Cortez. She'd been joking, or at least for the most part she'd been joking. Zoey hated Cortez, despised and resented him with every fiber of her being. As long as he lived, she would never be free. But it wasn't in her to order any human being to their death. All she wanted to do was get him out of her life, not end his life.

But the look Micah had given her. Had he thought her serious?

"No," she told herself, the fight all the way drained out of her. "He was joking." Or more than likely picking on her. Which, she admitted, she deserved for making such a callous suggestion after he'd been so open and honest with her.

Zoey shivered, Micah's story pulling some deep, disturbing emotion out of her. And she had thought her family was messed up. What kind of father would encourage his son to kill, and for profit?

The vacuum was on inside the cabin when Zoey reached the front door. It was open, and over the hum of the machine Maggie was singing an Irish folk song. So much for her temper. Apparently, it didn't last long. Or maybe Maggie had thought leaving Zoey and Micah alone for a bit would help them defuse any ill will they had for each other and become friends. Zoey knew it would mean a lot to Maggie if she liked her husband. Maybe, for Maggie's sake, Zoey would try to forget that Micah had a past. At least Micah was being honest with her. Did he think his honesty would make up for his friend lying to her? Zoey shook her head. She would never understand men.

Zoey listened to Maggie sing, never having known how good a voice she had. Maggie even put a bit of the brogue into the words and her voice carried as loud as the vacuum ran. Glancing toward the shed, Zoey could still hear the saw. The rain had slowed to a drizzle. This might be her only chance. Zoey hated feeling as if she were a prisoner, forced to make a dash for it, no matter where she stayed. She was about to put an end to that. Maggie and Micah might feel they had Zoey's best interests at heart. But Zoey was done being controlled. It was time to start living her life on her own terms.

Zoey patted the keys to the Taurus as she hurried to it. She had made sure to keep them on her at all times, fearing if she left them sitting anywhere, either Micah or Maggie would pick them up and refuse to give them back to her. Sliding into the rental car, she shot one last look at the rustic cabin, then the small shed, turned the car on, and pulled it around. There was no looking back now. Zoey was headed toward freedom, and she would do it all by herself.

Ben scowled at the private number on his cell phone, knowing who it was before he answered.

"What's wrong?" he demanded instead of saying hello.

"It's Zoey," Micah said. "She's gone."

"What do you mean she's gone?" Ben immediately looked around the cabin, found his keys, and grabbed his jacket. "When did she leave? Where is she headed?"

"Slow down," Micah ordered, his voice cold and hard as he guessed Ben would be flying out the door. "Listen, man, and be smart. Hear me out."

"I'm listening, damn it. Talk!" Ben looked around the small cabin. Hurrying to the little kitchen, he grabbed the fork he'd been using to turn his steak and pulled the still-raw meat out of the frying pan. He tossed it on a plate.

"She was in the shed talking to me and not five minutes after she left I went to check on her and Maggie. The Taurus was gone."

"Only a five-minute lead and she got away?" Ben white-knuckled his phone as he pressed it to his ear. His beer was still on the counter. Ben stalked over to it and downed the rest of it.

Micah growled but didn't comment. There was a strain in his voice when he continued, though. "Maggie and I drove down the road, made it to the highway. It started raining so hard I doubted she could have driven so fast that we couldn't catch up with her."

Ben cursed. Zoey had been upset. He already knew that from when she hung up on him. There wasn't time to compare notes. He listened as Micah continued.

"By the time we reached the highway sheets of water were racing across the road. Coming down as hard as it is now. I thought we'd found her when we spotted her car parked along the highway. She was headed into Zounds by the look of it. But Zoey wasn't in her car."

"She took off walking?" Ben demanded, once again heading for the door.

"The hood to the Taurus was still warm. We were only minutes behind her. I don't think she took off walking, Ben. Are you listening to me?"

"I'm fucking listening to you!" Ben roared, and he didn't like a thing he was hearing. Why the hell hadn't he called Zoey back? His damn pride might have caused Zoey to do something stupid. She'd hung up on him, and it had pissed him off. Ever since then he'd been stewing about whether to stay in Zounds or just head back down to L.A. Something kept him from leaving, though, and it sure wasn't the creature comforts of this small cabin.

"We drove past the Taurus for several miles and then drove back. There aren't any roads cutting off the highway for the next few miles, and I don't think she would have headed into the woods, as nasty as the weather is. If she were running from someone, in the short amount of time from when she left and when we followed, we would have seen their car." Micah paused for only a moment. "Unless whoever forced her to stop caught her. If that is what happened, they were able to snatch her out of her car and leave within minutes."

"Goddamn it!"

"Ben." Micah's voice was annoying with its coolness. "What are you going to do?"

"I'm going to go fucking find her."

Ben stomped through puddles to his bike. With the tarp over it, his motorcycle would be dry. But in less than a minute, he was soaked.

"On your motorcycle?" It was as if Micah were standing right next to him and seeing, seconds before Ben did, how preposterous that plan of action would be.

Ben stomped back to the cabin door. "I've got to get out of here, Micah," he said, forcing himself to calm down and think. "I'll find her and I'll let you know as soon as I do."

"Keep your head on your shoulders," Micah advised. "I know you'll find her. I'll wait for your call."

Micah hung up, but he did so way too easily. Ben knew Micah, possibly better than anyone else other than Maggie, of course. He didn't just let go of a situation, especially one like Zoey disappearing into thin air. The odds of her father having found her were way too high. Micah wasn't the type of man to simply wait around for a phone call letting him know everything was okay.

Ben didn't have time to worry about Micah. He would do whatever he wanted and wouldn't share his plans with Ben even if he asked. But Micah had been right. Ben needed to focus. He stomped his boots one last time, left a puddle at the entrance of the cabin, and slammed the door closed. Then pacing the length of the suddenly too small living room, he brainstormed before placing his next call.

"Wolf," he said when the man answered. "I have a problem."

"I can't make it sunny and warm, my friend." Wolf sounded too damn cheerful.

"I don't fucking care about the goddamn sun. Zoey is gone!" he almost yelled into the phone, and stopped pacing, took a staggered breath, and rested his forehead against his free hand. Wolf would help him find Zoey. Ben didn't doubt that. But the man was quick and would see through a faulty story in a second. There wasn't time to repeat himself if Wolf didn't buy what he said the first time around.

"Gone? What do you mean, gone?" Wolf demanded, then repeated what Ben had just said when Angel asked questions in the background.

"We got in a fight on the phone," Ben confessed, using as much of the truth as he could without mentioning Micah. Ben's head was spinning. Time was wasting. But he had to focus, keep his damn head on straight. He'd already made one mistake by not calling Zoey back. He wasn't going to make another. He amended quickly, "I shouldn't have let her walk out this morning. I knew it was going to pour and I can't hunt for her on my bike."

"She was at the cabin?" Wolf sounded incredulous.

Ben worried a minute that Zoey might have said something to Angel about where she was staying. Angel wouldn't have thought anything of it to tell Wolf. But Wolf would snatch on to the slightest detail if he thought it would bring him closer to Micah. Ben was fighting to save two lives here, and both of them mattered to him.

"Yes," Ben confirmed, not hesitating. "Man, I can't search for her on my bike. Would you give me a lift? She's been gone too long."

"I'm already out the door," Wolf said. "Don't do anything stupid before I get there!"

Why the hell did everyone think he would do something stupid? Ben got off the phone and found his first soothing breath since Micah had called him. It didn't help calm his nerves or keep him from wanting to climb the walls as he waited for Wolf to show up.

Ben didn't like thinking about it, but he was pretty sure he knew what happened. Micah had said as much when he'd called. *She was snatched out of that car.*

Already Ben had been going nuts debating whether to stay in Zounds or head back to L.A. Even as he had weighed the pros and cons of whether to leave or not, he'd continued to stay in the cabin. Wolf had stopped by every day. The man was convinced Ben was getting closer to finding Micah, and his questioning had become nerve-racking. Especially when Ben's thoughts had only been on Zoey. Wolf had stopped by the previous morning but hadn't been by since. He wouldn't have known whether Zoey had been there or not. The story Ben fed Wolf would work.

Ben had his chance to find out thirty minutes later, although it had felt like hours as the small cabin closed in further as he continued pacing. The moment he heard the Escalade pull into the drive alongside the cabin, Ben flew out the door. Wolf didn't have time to get out before Ben was tugging on the passenger door for Wolf to unlock it.

"Now tell me everything," Wolf demanded, and put his SUV in park. He shifted to face Ben with an intense, focused look. Wolf had recently showered and smelled of something musky. His brown hair was damp and waved around the man's thick neck. "And don't leave out any details," he added.

"We were arguing," Ben told him, knowing Wolf wouldn't move until he was satisfied he'd heard everything. Ben had no problem talking fast. He'd had plenty of time to rehearse what he would say. "Trust me, it doesn't matter about what. What matters is that I hurt her feelings and was a stubborn ass and didn't say the right thing to prevent her from storming out the door."

"And you didn't follow her?" Wolf asked, narrowing his attention on Ben with those beady eyes of his. "You just let her take off and leave?"

"I didn't know she was going to get in the car and actually leave!" Ben bellowed, having already guessed how Wolf would take his story and ready to paint himself as a complete ass to get the man moving. "I went into the kitchen and grabbed a beer and threw a steak on the frying pan. It was sizzling pretty loud and I was preoccupied stewing about our argument. When I finally walked to the door and opened it, I realized the Taurus we rented was gone."

"How much time had passed?"

"Not long. Five minutes. But now it has been over half an hour and she isn't back. I can't go after her on my bike. She isn't safe driving around Zounds, especially when I'm sure she isn't thinking about where she is going, or who might see her driving."

"All right." Wolf finally put his Escalade in gear. "We'll find her."

Fortunately, Zounds was a small town. Wolf drove up and down the streets, and they didn't see the Taurus. Not that they would. But the two of them would have to find it together. There would be no viable explanation for Ben already knowing where the Taurus had been left.

"Cortez has her," Ben blurted when they'd scoured Zounds with no signs of her or the car. It was all he could do not to scream for Wolf to drive to the asshole's house.

"We don't know that yet." Wolf held his hand up, as if the gesture would calm Ben. "She might have driven to one of her friends' houses."

"Zoey doesn't have a lot of friends."

"Angel is on alert to call me if Zoey shows up there," Wolf said, and turned at the next intersection. He was headed to the highway that would take them to Micah's house.

Ben didn't ask what made Wolf decide to go this way. At the moment he didn't care. The Escalade's windshield wipers slapped across the windshield, but still, vision was limited.

"God, I hope she isn't out this way," Wolf grumbled, gripping the steering wheel at ten and two.

Ben didn't want to think about Zoey driving in any of this weather. He might not have much experience on roads like this, but he couldn't imagine anyone ever being an expert driving through torrents of rain when he could barely see the road ahead of him. And when he thought he saw something ahead on the side of the road, Ben wouldn't have guessed it was a car if he hadn't already known the Taurus was parked ahead.

"What's that?" Wolf yelled, his excitement apparent. He held on to the steering wheel with one hand and pointed but then gripped it again with both hands as he slowed to a stop. "That the rental car? It's a Taurus."

"Looks like it." Ben leaned toward Wolf when they drove by, looking out the driver's side windshield at the lonely-looking, dark car. "Turn around," Ben ordered when they passed it.

"I'm going to," Wolf snarled, glaring at Ben. "Give me a fucking moment."

Wolf maneuvered the large Escalade around in the middle of the road. Although the SUV was large and the road narrow, within a minute they were facing the other direction with no altercations.

Ben leapt out of the SUV and into a deep puddle. Water soaked his jeans up to his knees. He stared down at himself only for a moment before holding his hand flat over his brows. It did little good in shielding off the rain, and he cursed the day and the weather.

"Not used to weather, are you?" Wolf yelled over the large drops pounding against the highway.

"In L.A.?" he shot back. "Hardly. We have too much sense for such nasty weather."

He spoke as he rushed to the Taurus, wanting to see for himself what Micah had suggested. With water streaming across the highway, there was no way to confirm if another car had been there. Dark skid marks were behind the Taurus. From what Ben could guess, a mid-sized vehicle, possibly a sedan, left them. That wasn't a lot of help in narrowing down for sure where Zoey might be.

"Where the hell is she?" Wolf asked, confused as he stared up and down the deserted highway.

Ben yanked open the driver's side door. He could barely sit on the edge of the driver's seat without shoving the seat back. Zoey was just over five feet, shorter than anyone else Ben knew. She was so small that when she drove she sat with the seat pulled almost clear up to the steering wheel. At least he knew no one else had sat behind this wheel other than Zoey. She had been the last one to drive it.

"Ben!" Wolf called out from the front of the car.

"What?" he snarled, his grouchiness mixed with apprehension and frustration over letting this happen.

"Look." Wolf held up a damp, floppy piece of paper that looked like a ticket. "It's an order to have this car towed," Wolf supplied before Ben could push his way out of the car. "Most towns wait at least twenty-four hours, if not longer, before ticketing a car. And at that, usually they sticker the car as a warning first. Some states allow up to seven days."

Ben didn't need the traffic lesson. "Unless someone already knows the driver won't be returning to the car."

"Is this rental car in Zoey's name?"

Ben shook his head, scowling at the traffic violation, which from the rain was already hard to read, other than the letterhead indicating it had been issued by the county sheriff.

"I rented the car. But where was the ticket?" He hadn't seen it when he'd walked up to the car.

Wolf tapped the outside of the windshield, pointing, as water ran down his jacket and over his hand. "Right here," he indicated, tapping the bottom of the windshield just below the hood. "If the sheriff stuck the ticket under the windshield wiper, it must have slid from the rain so that it was almost under the hood."

"Good eye," Ben muttered, and supposed Micah might not have noticed the ticket.

"Why they pay me the big bucks." Wolf leaned over to see inside the car. "Anything in there give a clue why she took off without the car?"

"She didn't leave the car willingly. Cortez has her. I don't know how, or why she would have pulled off of the road. That part doesn't make sense. But I just know he does."

"My guess is that Cortez is padding the pockets of too many lawmen in Zounds, as well as possibly the entire county." Wolf seemed indifferent to the downpour as he looked up and down the highway. "I'm guessing she was pulled over, probably by the sheriff. That would make sense. He flashes his lights. She pulls over."

Ben didn't like the picture Wolf was painting. But now, with the facts more or less in front of him, an unsettling lump settled in Ben's stomach, making him feel sick. Outrage only ransacked his system further.

"The sheriff walks up to her car, takes her ID, and tells her to get in his car with him."

"Cortez might have put a price on her head," Wolf supplied, squinting at Ben. It almost looked as if there was compassion or maybe even sympathy in the man's tough exterior. "Once the sheriff confirmed from her ID that he had Cortez's daughter, he came up with a reason why Zoey would have to go with him, and he hightailed out of here."

"We've got to go get her, man," Ben said under his breath.

"Are you saying what I think you're saying?"

Wolf hadn't ever struck Ben as the type of man to leap into the belly of danger. He seemed more the type of man to plot and delegate. Ben didn't have time to do either.

"I'm going to go get her. You can help me, or not." Ben leaned back into the car and reached into the ashtray, which he'd noticed right away was barely open. He pulled out the keys to the Taurus. Zoey had left them there for him, probably knowing the moment she was pulled over of the sheriff's intention of taking her. Zoey knew Ben would come looking for her. Zoey didn't smoke. The ashtray wouldn't be open. She'd left the key for him to take the car. Ben wanted to scream his frustration.

He felt stiff when he stood and held the key up at face level for Wolf to see. "The car won't be here for anyone to impound. I'm not asking you to join me. The choice is yours. But after I move this thing I'm breaking into Cortez's house and pulling Zoey out of there."

Wolf followed Ben into Zounds, where he parked the rental car behind Angel's bookstore next to her car. Ben had to give it to Wolf for not taking time to let Angel know what they were doing. When she called him, all he told her was that he'd explain very soon but at the moment it was too dangerous for him to stay on the phone. Considering it didn't take long before they reached Cortez's Victorian mansion in the middle of town, he was definitely telling Angel the truth.

"Let's circle around the block." Ben pointed as he spoke. At the moment he was actually grateful for the rain. It cut down visibility if anyone happened to be staring out toward the street from Cortez's house. "I'm going inside alone," Ben continued, plotting how they would do things as they circled around the Gothic-looking huge old home. "Stay put. Keep the motor running."

Wolf had stopped behind the old home in an alley. The rain had finally slowed a bit, but there were large puddles everywhere. He rested his wrist on top of his steering wheel and surveyed their surroundings, as Ben did as well.

"Okay," Wolf said slowly. "I'll give you ten minutes, but then I'm coming in flashing badges, handcuffs, and guns," he added wryly.

Ben grunted and smiled for the first time. Adrenaline ripped through him as it always did when he was closing in on a hunt. It dawned on him that, for the first time, he was actually going to be the one to close in for the kill, in a matter of speaking. If he pulled this off, and he was going to do just that come hell or high water, he would definitely need to call his boss, Greg King, and give him every detail. The old man would be proud of him. Ben had no doubt.

He could hear King now. *Not surprised a bit that you pulled it off. Always knew you had it in you.* Just hearing his boss say that in his head was all the motivation Ben needed.

"It won't take me ten minutes," Ben promised, and hopped out of the Escalade and into the freezing and very wet world outside.

The old Victorian home might look Gothic or even romantic to the idle passerby. But Ben saw an entirely different picture. The house was as wired as Micah's small cabin had been. Which encouraged Ben to move even faster. He would bet his life that every square inch of the property surrounding the house, as well as the rooms inside, was monitored by sophisticated surveillance equipment. It was a bit harder to detect the monitoring cameras in the gloomy weather, but Ben spotted them. There were several cameras wired up in the trees, as well as along the outside of the house. He also noticed one just inside the back door facing the alley. Ben fought the urge to flip the camera off but decided muddy foot prints tracked into the expensive-looking home would be sufficient.

There wasn't anyone around and, to his surprise, the door was unlocked. He moved through one room, then another, searching for stairs. If Zoey was here, he guessed she would be locked in her bedroom. She had described it to Ben, and he knew it was on the second floor. Zoey hadn't told him how to get to the room, though.

The house was as quiet as a tomb. He didn't see anyone as he reached a hallway and finally found a staircase. There wasn't time to take in how magnificent the house was, how elaborately furnished, how impeccably clean each room was. Ben didn't care how magnificent the crime lord's lair happened to be. None of that mattered. Zoey was in here somewhere. He remained alert to any sound and continued searching each room, hallway, and staircase for devices that might deter or, worse yet, hurt him. So far he'd only seen surveillance equipment outside and at the entrance into the home. Cortez apparently didn't think anyone would dare enter his house.

Ben dared to do a lot more than that.

"Oh my God," a thin woman wearing a black maid's uniform gasped as she came around the corner from the other end of the hallway. Wisps of brown hair fell from a tight bun at the back of her head. Her eyes were large and terrified in her slender, gaunt face. "God, please," she sputtered.

Ben put his finger over his lips, praying the woman wouldn't start screaming. "Where is Zoey?" he whispered, banking on the fact that Cortez's servants probably hated his guts and wouldn't turn Ben over to him or prevent him from getting Zoey.

The woman's hands fluttered in front of her face as she remained frozen, looking terrified. For a moment it looked like she might either start screaming hysterically or drop dead in a hard faint. Ben wasn't sure which direction she was headed, but at the moment the woman was his primary focus. He couldn't have her doing either.

"Tell me where Zoey is," he said, keeping his voice gentle and holding his hands out to his sides, palms out, to show the women he wouldn't hurt her. "I'm going to get her out of here."

She continued fluttering her hands in front of her as if she might try flying away from him. When they settled on her cheeks, she simply stared at him a moment, frozen. Ben would give her a few seconds at the most to come out of her trance before leaving her standing where she was. He would find Zoey on his own if need be.

Fortunately for both of them, the woman finally moved and nodded to the stairs. "Third door on the left." She moved slowly, too slowly, when she lowered one hand and slipped it into a large pocket in her uniform.

Ben was fairly certain the servant wasn't armed. He watched as her thin hand disappeared into the large pocket. When she pulled out a ring with a key on it, she looked away from Ben for the first time.

"This will get me fired," she whispered, and sounded more as if she was accepting the fact than blaming him for the outcome of her action. "Her room is locked. No one is supposed to go to her."

"The worthless prick," Ben snarled.

He didn't move toward the servant to take the key but simply held his hand out. She took the steps necessary and placed the key in his hand.

"Where should I leave it?" he asked, already headed for the stairs.

"In the lock, I guess. Are you Ben Mercy?"

He stopped on the third step and looked over his shoulder at the woman. She was thin, weathered, possibly from the strain of this job, and definitely plain looking. She stared up at him with terror still lingering in her large dark eyes.

"Did Zoey ask for me?" A glint of hope swelled inside him.

"Cortez and his men are out looking for you."

That was just as good. "Nice to know," he said, and smiled at the woman. "And thank you."

Ben was up the flight of stairs in the next instant. In spite of the reassurance that the men who would eagerly kill him if they found him in this house weren't here, there was no telling when any of them might return. He almost slid to a stop in front of the third door and rammed the key into the lock.

Ben opened the bedroom door without making a sound but then let out a noise louder than the servant had when she'd first seen Ben. Although this sound wasn't a shriek of terror but more a roar of fury. Zoey lay crumpled in the middle of the large bedroom, on the floor. Her clothes were almost completely torn from her body. It looked as if she'd been whipped with a belt. There were bruises and cuts that had come from another object as well.

Her long, beautiful black hair was matted with dried blood. Zoey's face was bruised and cut almost beyond recognition. Ben was sick as he rushed into the room and slid to his knees.

"Don't worry, sweetheart. I'm going to get you out of here. I'm never leaving your side again, and if I have to kill the asshole myself, I swear to you that you'll never see Cortez again."

Zoey didn't say a word.

Chapter Seventeen

Angel knew Wolf wasn't telling her the whole story. She hung up the phone and stared at it for a moment. All Wolf had said was that he was taking Ben and Zoey to the hospital and he'd be back to the store soon. There had been stress in Wolf's voice when she'd talked to him on the phone after Ben parked his rental behind her store, an urgency in the way he spoke that had left Angel antsy. In his phone call just now he had sounded calm, too damn calm.

Walking around the rental car that Ben had parked behind her store, she hopped in her car and started the engine. It was still raining. Heavy downpours like the one earlier sent everyone home. Downtown became a ghost town. Angel hadn't seen the point in keeping the store open and had looked forward to spending the afternoon and evening with Wolf. Obviously, that hadn't worked out.

She pulled out of the alley and onto the road, not surprised that there wasn't a car around, in spite of it being late afternoon. Her automatic headlights came on when she accelerated. The thick, overcast sky would make it dark earlier than usual tonight. Angel forced herself not to dwell on how her evening could have been.

Zoey was hurt. Wolf didn't have to tell her for her to know. Angel didn't have to ask how or why. She would have liked to know, however, how badly. A few details would have been nice. Obviously, it was bad enough that Wolf was taking her to the hospital. Angel accelerated just over the speed limit, not wanting to give any of the cops in Zounds reason to pull her over. There were enough of them already on Cortez's payroll.

It would only take a few minutes to get to the small hospital. Angel worried about Zoey, but her thoughts were also distracted by Wolf. She thought about it as she sat at a red light, the small hospital in sight. She'd known Wolf just under two weeks now. In that short time their relationship had flown off the charts. All charts. Sexual and emotional. God, just thinking about the sex, the many places they had fucked in the past two weeks, took all chill out of the air. The emotional part, well, that wasn't quite as easy to figure out. It might have been better if she had kept it just sexual. But damn it, the man had crawled under her skin.

Angel really liked Wolf a lot. It was more than him being so handy around her store. They just worked well together, like a perfect fit. She and Wolf would talk to each other all day in between customers. If she got busy, the moment there was a lull in business, he'd pick up the conversation right where they'd left off. It was as if he really enjoyed her company and couldn't wait for the next opportunity to spend time alone with her. Should she focus on training Wolf to not run out the door when someone called?

"Ha!" Angel said out loud to the red light.

That would be like asking Wolf to trade in all he was just to be her boyfriend. She hated admitting it, but the adrenaline junkie in him turned her on.

Which brought on another question. Once she managed to nail Cortez to the cross and, once again, turn Zounds into the sleepy fishing community that it was before the bastard moved to town, would Wolf even like it here? Granted, he was here to catch someone who wasn't Cortez—the Mulligan Stew assassin. Once Wolf caught him, and Angel didn't have any doubts that he would, he was that driven, would Cortez keep Wolf here? Or would Wolf simply move on to the next job?

And the next lady in whatever town that sent him to?

That damn near had Angel seeing red.

The light changed. She headed to the hospital and parked in the visitor section. By the time she'd entered the ER doors, where Wolf had told her they were headed, she at least appeared calm.

"Oh my God," Angel said ten minutes later when Ben explained to her in whispers in the ER waiting room how he'd found Zoey.

No wonder Wolf had run out the door. He'd told Angel he couldn't talk on the phone because it was dangerous. He had meant it. He and Ben had been heading to Cortez's home.

She hung her head, fighting tears and hating herself for being so damn selfish. "Crap," she whispered under her breath, staring at the floor as she covered her face with her hands. She was a fool in the worst sense of the word. Lightening up over Wolf's behavior would be an understatement of commands she could give to herself. After all, wasn't he the perfect man when they were alone with each other? He fixed things around her shop without even a hint on her part that they needed to be fixed. When Wolf ran out the door, it was because someone's life depended on it, whether he was ridding the world of a criminal at large or saving her dear friend from a monster. A little leniency on Angel's part would go a long way.

Large hands pulled her up against a virile body. Then Angel did start crying, one because the man she had been giving thought as to whether it was worth her time to "train" or not was holding her close to him; and two because if Wolf hadn't been there, Zoey might not be alive right now.

"Thank you," she managed, pushing away just far enough to stare up at Wolf.

She extended a smile to Ben when she realized he was standing right next to Wolf, looking as miserable and unsure of what to do as Wolf.

"What for?" Wolf looked seriously confused.

Dear Lord. Could she be falling in love with this man?

"For being you." She slapped at her tears and managed to

keep smiling. "For not being afraid to run into dangerous situations in order to save someone's life. If it weren't for both of you, Zoey might not be alive if she'd been left in that house much longer."

Zoey was admitted. Since the nurse on the floor was one of the regulars in the bookstore, knew Angel really well, and understood there wouldn't be any immediate family coming in to sign for Zoey, she informed the doctor on staff as much. Although he made a show of reluctance—the young doctor wasn't from Zounds—he consented and informed Angel, Wolf, and Ben on Zoey's status. The head nurse further informed her staff that either Ben or Wolf would be in the room with Zoey at all times. If anyone, and the head nurse did mean anyone else, was to try to visit Zoey, Ben, Wolf, or Angel was to be notified immediately. Angel gave the nurse a meaningful hug and thanked her with more tears.

She really needed to quit with this crying thing. It wasn't her style.

"Her right wrist is broken. It appears from X-rays that it has been broken before, possibly when she was a child, from the amount of scar tissue. She'll have a cast for a while, and will need to schedule a follow-up with her regular doctor once she is released," the doctor had told the three of them outside Zoey's room later that night. "Otherwise, considering how she looked when she came in, she's got a cut on her lower lip that we put a few stitches in, but no other injuries. We've sedated her, but I've ordered some more tests in the morning once she is more alert."

Angel curled up on a chair next to the bed, shortly after midnight. The doctor's words kept replaying in her mind for some reason. Something told her that Zoey's *regular doctor* would be someone on Cortez's staff, which wouldn't do at all. Another thing that wouldn't do, Cortez couldn't live in this town any longer. Somehow, Angel needed to get the bastard to go, through the law or whatever means necessary. How did a person go about hiring the Mulligan Stew assassin, she wondered, then drifted off to sleep.

* * *

Wolf woke up disoriented at first, scrubbed his face with his hands, then dragged his fingers through his scalp, giving himself a little massage. Then sitting, he remembered how he'd decided to make use of the empty bed next to Zoey's. His hand brushed against hard metal, and he looked down at the tip of the gun he wasn't supposed to have in the hospital. He'd stuffed it under his pillow the night before.

Oxygen in use be damned. It wasn't in use in this room, and if Cortez or any of his bullies showed up, Wolf would be ready for them. He slipped the gun inside his coat pocket, which was still at the end of the bed. Angel was still asleep in the chair, curled up in an adorable ball. Her curls were tight around her face, which was so peaceful in sleep.

He'd noticed that before about Angel. When awake, she was on top of her act, running that store with tight efficiency. Not a soul walked through that door that Angel didn't know by name, other than the occasional straggling tourist. Angel knew everyone's likes and dislikes in books and always was around the corner of her counter, as if she had just been waiting for that particular person to enter her bookstore and had a recommendation for them.

But when Angel slept, all the focused determination on her pretty face faded. Although he knew her first name was really Angelina, she truly was an angel. Her face was so smooth and her expression one of peaceful sleep. Her small body was wrapped cozily into the chair, with her knees pulled up to her chest.

Wolf studied her body, the soft rise and fall of her chest as she breathed slowly, her narrow waist, and the soft curves of her ass and hips. God, he loved gripping those hips. There were so many things he could do with that sultry little body. Angel loved all of it. Wolf imagined what else he could do with her sexually. Would she go for anal sex? He hadn't asked, but just thinking about it woke up the rest of his body. He shifted uncomfortably in his jeans and glanced toward the door to the hallway. The morning shift of nurses would probably be parading in soon. Best to make use of the bathroom, then wake his sleeping beauty.

As he splashed water on his face and combed his hair with his fingers, images of Angel the night before came to mind. When she'd looked up at him with her tearstained face and thanked him, he knew right then he'd give her the world if she asked for it. With a grunt, as he glared at the mirror, Wolf decided right away it would be best never to let her know that. Angel was a smart woman, though. Would she be able to tell by looking at him how far he'd gone in falling for her?

Already he knew that he hadn't run out the door to help with Zoey because of Ben. Wolf's gut instincts had been right, too. Angel's tears had been more of a thank-you than her words. Wolf had helped with Zoey because she meant so much to Angel.

Walking back into the hospital room, Wolf pulled out his phone as he looked down at Angel. He shot Ben a quick text. *Need coffee. Come guard the room.* He looked over at Zoey, who looked so tiny in the hospital bed. Best he could tell, she hadn't moved since last might.

Her pretty face was so bruised. There was a cast around her petite hand and wrist, which lay over her stomach outside the covers. Her thick, long black hair was parted on either side and fell in long strands down her chest. He guessed he got what Ben saw in the girl. Zoey came with a hell of a lot of baggage, though. Even if she escaped her father's grip, she might never recover emotionally.

Which was why Angel was perfect for Wolf. He shifted his attention from one woman to the other. Angel had her act together. She didn't need Wolf; she wanted him. For him, that spoke volumes. When a lady was doing just fine on her own and still wanted him in her life, that was what love was all about.

"Love?" he snarled under his breath, then checked quickly to make sure he hadn't woken either woman.

Throughout the day, Wolf and Ben swapped off guarding the room. Zoey woke up that morning, and the doctor spoke with her. Angel sat by her bed, brushed Zoey's hair for her, and brought damp washcloths and took her time carefully cleaning Zoey's face and wiping down her arms. By the next day, Zoey was sitting, sipping juice through a straw, and was coherent. The doctor agreed to release her to Angel's care.

Which Wolf didn't care for one bit. Not because it would steal all time for him with Angel away, but because he would have to guard that store as if his life depended on it. It wasn't his life he was worried about, though. Angel would now be in as much danger as Zoey.

"There's nowhere else she can go," Angel pointed out to him as they walked slowly down the hall from the elevator to Zoey's room late that morning. "And think about it. She's actually really safe at the store. My bookstore is well armed with security now that would wake the dead if it went off."

He grinned inwardly remembering how they'd tested it after he'd installed it and Angel had damn near jumped out of her skin. Every dog in a mile radius had continued to howl their protest even after he'd shut it off.

"And I have an FBI agent coming into town this week." She grinned up at Wolf, that determined, energetic look planted well on her face. He loved how her eyes almost glowed lavender when she was enthusiastic about something, and getting Cortez out of town had become her lifeline. "He is very interested in investigating Emilio Cortez," she added, whispering.

"You'll get him." Wolf wrapped his arm around Angel, proud of her endeavors in making the law throughout California incredibly aware of what the bastard was doing to the little town.

Zoey's door was only slightly ajar. The wall where the bathroom was made it impossible to see into the rest of the room, though. Wolf reached for the door, ready to push it open, and paused.

"I'm telling you, man, you didn't slip on the job. She's going to be fine," Ben said inside the room.

Wolf put his finger to his lips as he stared down at Angel. Her eyes were wide as she stared up at him. She looked confused, but that was okay, as long as she remained quiet. Who was Ben assuring that they hadn't slipped up on a job?

"She's asleep right now. . . . Nope, out like a light." There was a noticeable sound of affection in Ben's voice. "And no, she didn't say a word to anyone. Yes. Quit worrying. I told you already. We found the car together and I didn't guide him there. Lord, have a little faith."

Wolf prickled. Ben had already known where the Taurus was? Was that what he was talking about? Wolf's ears burned, anxious to catch every word. Who didn't say a word to anyone, and about what? Was Ben talking about Zoey? If so, that meant she had been at Maggie's house the entire time she was away from Ben. Which would mean Zoey probably was leaving Maggie's in the Taurus when she had pulled over.

"Yes, she told me. It was Wolf who found the ticket pressed against the windshield almost under the hood. I had suspected the truth, but she was pulled over by the local sheriff, and yes, his balls were in Cortez's pocket," Ben snarled, his outrage justified by the fact. "Zoey didn't have a clue that was why he pulled her over. He told her there was a taillight out and asked her to sit in the backseat of his cruiser while he called in her information. The moment she was in the car, the fucking sheriff took off. Zoey had turned the car off before getting out and had slipped the keys in the ashtray, which apparently is where she normally keeps her own car keys." Ben, coming from a large city, had been as perturbed by this fact as Wolf had been when he'd learned about it.

"She told me Cortez had promised to disfigure her so badly that no man would ever want her again." There was silence only for a moment. "I told you, none of this is your fault. Zoey is a pro at slipping through fingers. She's spent her entire life sneaking around and knows how to watch her own back. I don't know that I could hold on to her if she didn't want it."

Wolf ached for more information. Would Ben at least say a name? If Wolf had that, he would have all he needed. He'd hold Ben at gunpoint if it meant taking him to the Mulligan Stew assassin. But Ben said good-bye and his tone changed when he started speaking in hushed tones to Zoey.

Wolf pushed open the door, giving Angel a quick shake of the head as her only warning not to say anything.

"Hey, man," Wolf said, entering the room.

Zoey looked at Angel and smiled, or what came close to one with her puffed mouth and thin line of stitches. Angel was immediately at her side. Ben stood from the bed, giving the women space.

"We're just waiting on the doctor. I hear she should be here any minute. I would really rather take Zoey back to the cabin."

Wolf would rather that, too. "Who were you just talking to on the phone?" he demanded, and enjoyed the moment of surprise when Ben wasn't ready for the question.

Ben was a pro, though. Wolf would give him that. The man masked all emotions in a heartbeat.

"When?" he asked.

"Just now." Wolf wasn't in the mood for crap. He had his fill of hospitals, especially one this small that didn't even have a decent cafeteria but instead just a snack shop. "I stood at the door and listened."

Wolf eyed him a minute, and the look Ben gave Wolf was one of complete challenge and aggravation. "A friend in L.A."

"Cut the bullshit, man," Wolf snarled.

"What's your problem?" Ben snapped right back at him. "You shouldn't eavesdrop on conversations. There are quite a few people in L.A. as worried about her as they are me," he insisted, thumbing toward Zoey as he did.

Less than an hour later, he and Angel led the way to the bookstore, with Zoey and Ben following.

"You know, I don't know about you, but I think Ben was lying to you back in the hospital room as to who he was talking to on the phone."

Wolf glanced over at Angel. "I know he was."

Angel stared out her store window at the light drizzle and gray day. There had been four customers so far that day, all her diehards. But it would get slow from now until the holiday season began; then everyone would brave the cold rain to hurry out and buy presents. Already she had orders in for special stock to accommodate.

Her mind wasn't focused on holiday customers or how dead it was today. She dwelt on Zoey, who had decided to take a nap, and her insistence that she was doing the right thing. Angel wasn't making a mistake by having Zoey stay with her above the bookstore. Of course it meant no wild sex with Wolf, who was leaning next to her on the counter, close enough she swore she felt his arm against hers even though they weren't touching. The sexual energy between them sizzled in the air. Angel would bet he was thinking the same thing she was. Where could they escape for a quickie? Although with Wolf, there was no quick sex. She enjoyed him way to much to rush sex with him.

"Penny for your thoughts," he grumbled.

Angel turned her head, looked into his eyes, and knew without a doubt he had been thinking the same thing she was. His smile was slow and predatory as she continued staring at him.

Since sex in the store during business hours wasn't an option, Angel came up with the next best thing to say. "Why would Ben have lied to you yesterday about who he was talking to on the phone?"

Wolf's expression immediately changed. He suddenly looked dangerous, if not pissed, and pulled his attention from her, looking toward the street. "I think he knows where the assassin is."

"What?" Angel gasped, but then shot a hurried look toward the staircase leading to her apartment before lowering her voice and returning her attention to Wolf. "Why the hell hasn't he arrested him, or captured him, or done whatever it is bounty hunters do?" It dawned on her that she wasn't completely sure what Wolf would do if he caught the assassin. That would be her next question.

Wolf pulled his gaze from the drizzly cold day outside and studied her for a moment. He didn't answer her right away. Angel would be damned if he brushed off her question with some ambiguous answer. Apparently, her expression said as much.

He blew out a long breath. "It's public knowledge that the assassin worked for KFA, the bounty hunters in L.A. where Ben worked, or still is employed to the best of my knowledge."

"No shit?" Angel whispered. "Ben knows the assassin?"

"Yup." Wolf's look was intense when he stared at her. "When I headed north, he followed me at first. On our way up here we called a truce and agreed to look for the assassin together."

Angel made a snorting sound. "And you bought that?"

He surprised her by placing a quick kiss on her lips. "What I like about you, kid. You're quick."

"Sharp as a tack," she informed him, then batted her lashes. "And sexy, too."

She'd never felt sexy before, but the way Wolf looked at her, as if he was ready to pounce, made her feel that way. This time she leaned into him and he kissed her again. It was a long, slow kiss, one that would send some of her customers running in shock if they were to enter her store. No one tried coming through the door, not that she was sure she would have heard the bell ring over the door if it had. When Wolf gripped her chin and impaled her mouth, everything around her faded away into an array of enticing shades of warm colors.

"I definitely want more," he growled against her mouth when he ended the kiss.

"Umm . . . me, too."

He grumbled under his breath, and Angel smiled, taking her time opening her eyes. It took time for the sexual fog to lift from her brain, and she didn't rush it. When she looked up, Wolf was staring at her.

"I love that look on you."

"What look is that?"

"Like you can't wait to have some of this gorgeous body."

Angel slapped his arm but couldn't help laughing. "Cocky bastard," she mumbled.

"Yup."

She needed distance and left him at the counter to wander among her shelves, looking for any misshelved books. With so few customers in so far, there wasn't much straightening to do. She made a show of doing so anyway.

"Ben said something about Zoey to whoever he was talking to," she said when a bit of silence had passed between the two of them.

Wolf hadn't moved and she had to return to the counter, remaining on the opposite side of it, to continue their interrupted conversation.

"Yeah, I noticed that." He fiddled with pens she had in a ceramic cup next to her register, then straightened several short stacks of business cards customers had left for others to see and pick up.

"Why did he say Zoey wouldn't say anything?" That had bugged Angel, but she hadn't had a chance to ask Wolf about it until now.

His hand remained on the business cards, but he looked up at her, once again that intense look hardening his gaze. "My guess is she knows the assassin."

"What?" Angel was instantly shaking her head. "Zoey doesn't know anyone. Wait—" She pointed a finger at Wolf. "The assassin isn't Cortez."

"No." Wolf laughed once, but it was almost a sad laugh as he shook his head. "For it to be that easy."

"Then how does she know him?"

"Because I think she knows his wife."

Angel stared at him. He stared back.

"Crap," she whispered. "Do I know her?"

Ben parked his bike behind Angel's bookstore later that evening. He had been texting Zoey most of the day. She was bored in Angel's apartment but wasn't going to go into the bookstore and scare customers. Ben doubted anyone who knew Zoey would be frightened by her appearance, more like pissed. The town needed to get pissed and quit being nice when it came to Cortez.

Zounds wasn't Ben's problem. All he cared about was Zoey. They needed to talk, which they hadn't really done since she'd started speaking to him again. He understood that there was attraction, but she hadn't explained to him why she'd been so mad at him. Ben hated feeling like the stupid man, clueless to the behavior of a woman or possibly to whatever he'd done or said. In past relationships if his girlfriend rolled her eyes and walked away from him in disgust, Ben shrugged and went on with his business. He accepted he didn't want to go back to L.A., and he also accepted there was now only one reason. Zoey. Micah had been warned. If he wasn't going to worry about Wolf being hot on his tail, well, he was a grown man.

Tapping on the storeroom door, Ben hunched in his coat against the cold. At least it wasn't raining anymore. He wasn't worried about Wolf giving him scathing looks or dropping crass remarks over what he thought he overheard when Ben had been on the phone. From the beginning, the man had suspected Ben knew more about Micah than he'd let on. Wolf still didn't know where Micah was, and that was what mattered. Ben couldn't babysit Micah any longer. It was time to get Zoey out of Zounds.

Wolf opened the storeroom door, looked at Ben, Ben's bike parked behind him, then into the darkness past Ben. Slowly Wolf opened the door farther and let Ben in. Ben spotted the gun Wolf had hidden in his other hand when he stepped back to allow Ben entrance. Wolf sheathed the gun inside a sleeveless down coat he was wearing.

"What's going on?" he grunted.

"Angel tell you I was coming to see Zoey?"

"Yeah."

Okay, so Wolf was pissed at him. He saw the tension, as much as felt it coming off the man. Ben didn't care. "Good," he grunted, and started past the man.

"Mercy."

"What?" Ben demanded, anxious to see Zoey. They had a lot to talk about, and the sooner he cleared the air with her the sooner he could convince her to leave town with him.

"You know where he is."

"I don't know shit."

He stormed into the bookstore and forced himself to relax at Angel's quizzical expression as she looked up from behind the counter. It looked like she was tallying receipts or something.

"Is it okay if I go upstairs and see her?" Ben had already spotted the stairs and had texted Zoey enough that day to have a good idea of the layout of Angel's home above her store.

Angel nodded at the stairs. "Make yourself at home."

Ben was grateful neither of them followed. He bounded up the stairs, took in the neat and cozy home, definitely influenced by a woman's touch. Lacy curtains hung over kitchen windows. The home was impeccably clean and looked like one of those homes where everything had a place and everything was in its place. There were large matching pillows on either end of a couch, which was in the middle of a large room and made for a divider between kitchen and living area. Angel had a large flat screen secured to her wall, a fifty-two-inch. He also spotted a stereo in the corner with a couple tall, narrow speakers on pedestals. Wires had been stapled to the wall. Surround sound. Nice.

"Hi," Zoey said.

Ben quit caring about Angel's home as his attention darted to a doorway toward the front of the home, or the part of it facing the street. Zoey stood in the doorway. He bounded toward her, feeling like a gangly oversized dog whose master was no longer pissed at him. With a quick swoop Ben wrapped her into his arms and lifted her off the ground as he straightened. Just the smell of her made him feel better.

"Oh shit," he said, immediately feeling selfish. He put her down carefully. "Did I hurt you?"

Zoey laughed. Her bruises weren't as bad as they'd been when she'd left the hospital, and the swelling was down in her lip. "Not at all."

She took him by the hand, her other hand with the cast

held protectively to her chest. She wore flared black pants that hugged her beautifully shaped ass. An oversized red sweatshirt almost covered it but not quite. Her black hair tumbled down her back. She guided him to the couch and sat down, motioning for him to sit next to her. Ben slipped out of his coat and tucked it behind him on the couch, wanting to be as close to Zoey as possible.

"I don't have a lot of dating experience." She was still smiling and her large dark eyes glowed, showing her sincere happiness. "But I do have a lot of experience being controlled, manipulated through lies—"

"Zoey, I—"

"Please," she stopped him. There was something so desperate in her eyes.

"Go ahead." He brushed his fingers down the side of her face, right at the hairline, not wanting to hurt her. "Tell me," he coaxed.

She smiled and he barely noticed the still slightly puffy indentation around the stitches at the edge of her lower lip and just below her mouth. Her entire face lit up. How could anyone lay a hand on this beautiful lady in anger?

"Oddly enough, it was Micah who helped me see." She kept her tone low and glanced at the stairwell when she spoke. But only for a moment; then those captivating large, dark eyes of hers returned to Ben's face. She searched it as she continued, as if needing to know his reaction without asking him to comment. "You lied to me. It pissed me off. I've had a lifetime of lies"—her hand fluttered to her face—"of abuse. But I see now that you didn't lie out of a need to control me. You simply needed to protect someone who means a lot to you."

"Yes."

"I get that now."

Ben wanted to yell at whoever came up the stairs to leave them alone but couldn't. This wasn't Zoey's home. It wasn't his, either. He turned, as did Zoey, when Wolf strolled up the stairs.

"Angel wants something to drink," he muttered, pointing toward the refrigerator as he walked toward it. "Glad everyone's decent."

Ben waited for Wolf to dig through the refrigerator. He seemed to be taking way too long to grab whatever it was Angel wanted to drink. The refrigerator light silhouetted the man's large frame. Otherwise, other than the lamps that were on either side of the couch the light was dim in the tidy home. Nonetheless, Ben saw Zoey watching him, instead of turning to see what Wolf was doing. She wanted this conversation as desperately as Ben did. As soon as Wolf was gone, Ben would ask Zoey to return to L.A. with him. There wasn't anything for either of them in Zounds.

Lighter footsteps hurried up the stairs. Ben groaned and Zoey hid a smile. He grabbed her hand, wanting alone time with her so much it made his insides hurt.

"I'm looking for the diet soda," Wolf said, straightening.

"There are cars outside," Angel said, breathless. She was pointing down the stairs. "I saw them pull up in front of the store, and they are going down the service alley." She looked, panicked, from Wolf to Ben. "I think it's Cortez," she whispered.

Ben flew over the top of the couch without thinking about how to do it. "Motherfucker is mine!" he yelled at all of them, pushing Angel out of the way and flying down the stairs.

He was through the bookstore and storage room without waiting for Wolf as backup or giving thought to the fact that his gun was in his coat, which he'd left upstairs. Ben shoved the storage room door open. Wolf grunted something behind him, but Ben didn't hear him.

Several men were getting out of a long, sleek-looking dark car. Ben didn't size them up. He didn't give any of them any of his attention, except one. A short man, a few inches shorter than Ben, dressed in very expensive-looking clothing, with sleek black hair, darker skin than Zoey's, similar dark eyes and shaped nose as hers, straightened his shirt as he sized up Ben.

"Ben Mercy, I assume," he said, as if he owned the whole damn world and Ben were a bug he planned to extinguish.

Ben had news for the asshole. This bug planned on living. "Cortez," he growled, then without a thought to any of the men closing in around him lunged forward and punched the lowlife waste of flesh square in the mouth.

"Kill him!" Cortez yelled as he fell backward—hard—against his open car door.

Ben had the incredible satisfaction of knowing his fist landed squarely in the man's face as blood exploded around his nose. At the same time the loud cry of pain the weasel let out when his back hit squarely against the open car door fed Ben's satisfaction immensely.

That's when Ben spotted the red dot on the thug standing closest to Ben. Ben turned, lunging into Wolf as he shoved him back into the storage room.

"Duck!" Ben yelled as four loud popping sounds reverberated through the air.

"What the fuck?" Wolf bellowed, not taking nicely to being pushed backward. Instinctively he pushed back.

Wolf was a big, muscular man and succeeded in sending Ben backward a step or two. But Ben's effort was successful. He turned, gaining his footing, and stared at four men, dead. They hadn't been shot through the heart; the aim would have been impossible. All four men had been shot in the head and lay, crumpled on top of one another, in the alley next to the still-running car.

"What?" Wolf leapt around Ben and the dead men. "Which direction?" he shouted, looking both ways down the alley.

Micah would be gone. Ben pointed, still stunned as he stared at Cortez's dead body, in the direction the shots would have come from.

Angel and Zoey ran into him from behind.

"Oh God!" Angel cried out.

"What?" Zoey said at the same time. "Oh God! Oh God!" she began repeating.

Ben turned, pushing both women back inside. "Stay in

here," he ordered. "Stay away from the windows. I don't know what's going on yet," he told them, it pretty much being the truth.

The next hour seemed to pass by within minutes. Ben acted on instinct, barely thinking but moving fast, without thought to any repercussions. Something told him there would be none.

"There's no driver," Wolf said, after searching as far as he could in the dark to satisfy himself that he wouldn't find the shooter.

"We've got to get them out of here," Ben said, staring down at the four dead men.

"Okay. How?"

Ben had surveyed the alley, the running car, his parked bike, which thankfully hadn't been hit. "We load them back into Cortez's car."

"Then what?" Wolf was already moving around to the other side of the corpses, which stunk from pools of blood each of them laid in.

The storage room door opened behind Ben. "I just called a friend." Angel stuck her head out of the door, intentionally not looking down at the dead bodies but instead shifting her focus from Wolf to Ben and back again. "Drive down to the beach. I have directions." She paused for a moment, still diverting her attention from the dead mean. "One of them is Cortez?" she whispered.

Ben finally felt the pain in his fist from breaking Cortez's nose. It was the best pain he'd ever felt. "Yup," he told her.

Wolf hurried to the door, pulling her into his arms and using his body to block sight of the bloody mess outside her door. "Stay inside. I'll be in there in a few minutes."

"Okay," she said, her voice wavering.

Then the two men worked fast, loading dead men, who were a lot heavier than they looked like they would be, into the trunk and onto the backseat of the spacious luxury car. Angel gave directions, and Ben drove, with Wolf riding shotgun. Angel and Zoey followed in Angel's car. Ben was surprised at the group of men waiting at the docks. Within minutes, the men moved methodically and the expensive car was set off to sea.

"Cortez is dead," Zoey whispered when Ben walked up to her.

He looked down at her, noticing the war of emotions on her face. "I know he was your father."

Zoey looked up at him. "That man was never my father."

A sea-weathered old man limped heavily, putting most of his weight on one foot, and stopped when he stood in between Zoey and Ben. He smelled of fish and the sea. Ben imagined he'd lived his whole life as a fisherman.

"You want my boat?" he asked, as if his question would make perfect sense to them.

"Your boat?" Ben asked.

The man's face was like leather, with thick creases and dark skin in spite of the time of year. "For your girl here. She will say good-bye to her father."

It seemed as if the world grew quiet. The old man wasn't speaking loudly. Everyone around them shifted, looking down as if this moment belonged exclusively to Zoey.

"Thank you," was all she said.

Ben didn't know a lot about boats. Fortunately, the old man walked them over to a small speedboat, the *Christina*, as it said on its side in red cursive letters. Ben helped Zoey in, then cranked on the motor. It took off over the water as if she needed no driver. In spite of the chill in the night, water splashed up the sides of the boat to the point where Ben stripped out of his jacket and sweater, just so he'd have dry clothes when they returned to shore.

"The car went down over there," Zoey pointed.

Ben circled around the area over the descending car and finally cut the motor. He slipped back into his jacket and let the boat drift. Zoey sat next to him, cuddling into his arms. He wasn't sure how long they sat there. But the thick blanket of stars on an incredibly black sky and the dark inky water lapping at the side of the boat shrouded the two of them.

Zoey didn't say anything. She didn't cry. She never tried moving from his arms. Ben knew her past would haunt her

for quite a while, possibly even years. He prayed she was
able to let go of a little of it as she relaxed against him. He'd
say this much. That old sailor had offered Zoey a wonderful
gift. When she finally looked up at him, and nodded it was
time to return to shore, the demons he'd seen on her face
earlier were gone.

Chapter Eighteen

Ben pulled into the narrow drive, one hand covering Zoey's two smaller hands, which were wrapped around his waist. It would be a cold ride for a while, but they were headed to a warmer climate. He couldn't wait to get home. There was one thing the two of them had to do before leaving Zounds.

Micah walked out of his shed at the sound of Ben's Harley.

"Nice bike," Micah said, grinning as the two of them climbed off the bike.

Maggie was out of the cabin almost at the same time Micah appeared. Zoey ran to her, and the two women hugged.

"We came to say good-bye," Ben said.

"She agreed to go home with you?"

"We're going to give it a shot. I, personally, think Zoey would be perfect running the shop at KFA, if I can convince Greg and Haley to give her a chance."

Micah was still smiling and rocked up on his heels. "I heard those two were slowing down a bit, going to enjoy the golden years."

Ben shook his head. "They are way too young for golden years."

"You might be right, but you never know. We're enjoying them."

Ben shook his head. Micah was a strange man, but then

given his background and history there was no denying why. "What are you two going to do?"

Micah shrugged and looked over his shoulder at the cabin. Zoey and Maggie were standing not too far away. The women looked at the men when they noticed they were being watched.

"What?" Maggie demanded, her eyes sparkling.

"Just enjoying the view," Micah said, using his dark, ornery tone that could mean so much and told so little.

"That's no lie," Ben agreed.

For a change, the sun shone down brightly against a deep blue sky. Both ladies were so beautiful in such very different ways.

"How is Zoey doing?" Micah asked, keeping his voice low so the women didn't hear as he studied Ben.

"Pretty good," Ben said, not sure if he wanted Micah to know that she had actually mourned the man who had destroyed the first half of her life and at the same time rejoiced at his death. It had been a hodgepodge of emotions Ben hadn't been sure how to handle, other than holding her and letting her have time for the emotions to come out. "The doctor at the hospital gave her a clean bill of health when he removed her cast." It had been a long couple of weeks, and Ben was glad they were behind them.

Ben didn't know whether Zoey heard them or not, but she started across the yard, Maggie in tow. With the bright yellow bandana wrapped around Zoey's head and pulling her black hair back, along with the matching yellow sweater and her tight-fitting jeans, Zoey had informed Ben she was going for the "biker chick" look. Ben would never tell her that she'd failed badly. Zoey looked way too adorable.

He held his arm out to Zoey, but instead of walking into his embrace, she walked straight up to Micah and wrapped her arms around him. The surprised look on Micah's face was comical. Almost as funny as petite Zoey hugging the tall and muscular Micah.

"Thank you," Zoey whispered into his chest.

"For what?" Micah seemed hesitant in putting his arms

around her but looked down at her head as he slowly placed his hands on her back.

"For giving me my life back," she said, and pushed away to look up at him. "I can't even mourn the loss of my only parent. I tried. I think I thought I was supposed to, but I couldn't. He was mean to me from the moment he took custody of me. Now it's over. Thank you."

"Oh." Micah looked incredibly uncomfortable as he stared over Zoey's head.

He stared into the woods behind Ben, and his expression changed. Ben heard the popping of gravel, of someone approaching, a moment later. Micah pushed Zoey away from him, and she let out a start as Micah pulled his gun from his waist where it had been holstered.

It was too late. Ben turned as Wolf walked into the clearing from the woods. Wolf had waited for the exact perfect moment when Micah's guard would be down, and he'd found it.

"Wolf!" Ben yelled, staring at the man and the rather large gun he held, aimed directly at Micah.

"You know it's just him I want," Wolf said, not looking at Ben. "But then you knew that from the moment I entered KFA. You followed me up here only to warn him. Now get the fuck out of my way, Mercy!"

"Wolf," Ben said again. His gun was on his bike. For Zoey's sake, he hadn't worn it figuring she'd been around enough violence for a while. Ben didn't doubt for a moment that if he moved, Wolf would shoot him.

A car pulled into the drive. Both men barely gave the car a glance as they continued aiming at each other.

"Oh my God! Wolf!" Angel yelled as she leapt out of the car, but then, spotting Micah, came to a frozen halt. "Maggie? Zoey? Ben?" she said, her voice having gone up a notch.

"Angel, just stay there." It was Maggie who spoke. She held up her hand in warning.

"You're the assassin," Angel continued, her attention still transfixed on Micah. "Wolf, you found him," she whispered, sounding in awe.

"He's my husband!" Maggie yelled.

"You're the one that I knew," Angel responded, still speaking in awe.

"Get back in the car!" Wolf yelled.

Ben had no idea how Angel knew they were all there. At the moment, he didn't want to see anyone shot. Later he'd worry about how this little party came together. "Both of you lower your guns. No one needs to die today."

"Die?" Angel wailed.

Micah fired! All the women screamed, making the scene even more insane. There wasn't a silencer on the gun. Wolf roared and it was all Ben could do to hold on to both women. He didn't have ahold of Angel, though. When she screamed, she rushed into Wolf.

"Goddamn it!" Wolf yelled, managing to brace himself against Angel's charging into him and shaking his hand that a moment ago had held his gun.

Micah had just shot Wolf's gun out of his hand. The weapon skidded across the grassy area next to him into the brush. Wolf looked in that direction slowly, then returned his attention to Micah.

"You son of a bitch!" Wolf roared.

"Don't you dare kill him!" Angel shouted at Micah. "Maggie, if he's your husband tell him to put that thing down," she continued, saying both sentences so fast she almost spoke them over each other.

"One way or another, I'm taking you in," Wolf swore.

"I'm not going anywhere with you," Micah said, his tone cold. "And you aren't hurt," he pointed out.

"No one is going to get hurt." Ben pushed Zoey and Maggie behind him and stepped toward Micah.

"Stay back," was all Micah said. He straightened his arm, aiming at Wolf.

"Oh God," Angel whimpered.

"Angel, go to Maggie," Micah instructed.

"Go," Wolf encouraged, but kept his attention aimed on Micah.

"Please, don't," Angel begged, and hurried over to Maggie and Zoey. "Maggie, God. He did such a good thing. Don't let this happen."

"What do you mean that he did a good thing?" Maggie demanded.

The whole lot of them grew incredibly quiet. Ben kept his focus on Micah. The man was focused, yet his face looked relaxed. Had he killed so many times that he'd become immune to it? Ben couldn't see it that way. And he wasn't blind to Micah's nature because the man had bailed him out and allowed him to get his life moving forward. Nor did he feel he only knew one side to the man. Right now, Ben would swear Micah was more worried that Angel, who was definitely the core to all town gossip in that bookstore, might have picked up on something from Wolf. The two of them were getting mighty cozy together. And if she had, all of Zounds would be talking about having their very own personal assassin who cared enough about them to rid them of the monster who had been sucking the life out of many of Zounds's citizens. That kind of gossip would cost Micah his life.

Ben imagined Micah would do just about anything, except kill to protect himself. He would kill for Maggie, though. Micah had fallen hard for her almost the moment he'd slapped handcuffs on her over a year and a half ago. From that point forward, he'd fought to save her from the men who'd been framing her. Ben couldn't swear to exactly when Micah had told Maggie who he really was. She'd joined Micah out of love, knowing and believing he'd retired from a terrible past. Micah had spent a lifetime helping people out from under monsters and evil that was indescribable in some cases. Granted, his means had been extreme and he'd been paid well for his services, not to mention what he had done had been against the law. But he'd killed rapists, pedophiles, serial killers, and men like Cortez. Ben couldn't see Micah killing Wolf.

"Oh. Well, I was guessing really," Angel blurted, breaking the silence.

Ben glanced away from the men to find Zoey. She stood next to Maggie, who stood next to Angel. Both women were looking at Angel. She shot furtive glances at Wolf and Micah, then at Ben. He didn't take time to notice the incredible breathtaking backdrop behind the women. Nor did he care that even the chattering of birds in the woods surrounding them had stopped. All he could focus on right now was how to end this very bad scene. Wolf had obviously followed Ben and Zoey to Micah's, which made this his fault. He should have thought through that Wolf might have guessed Ben would seek Micah out before leaving town. Ben and Zoey had stopped at the bookstore before coming here so Zoey could say good-bye to Angel. As excited as he'd been to share with Greg and Haley about pulling Zoey out of Cortez's home, Ben would be embarrassed and ashamed to tell them about this situation. It was simply proof of how much he still needed to learn about paying attention to his surroundings. Although for the life of him, he had never noticed Wolf following them here.

Ben focused on Angel when she continued talking. Micah wouldn't chance studying her as she spoke. But Ben had that liberty. He would like to think he'd be able to tell by her body language, if not how she spoke, whether she was lying to them or not.

"It's just that I saw those four men in the alley outside my store," she reminded them, looking at Ben as she spoke. When she looked toward Wolf and the gun aimed at him, her voice cracked as she continued. "You raced outside," she said, nodding at Ben. "You didn't grab your coat. I saw your gun in it." She looked again at Wolf, her voice quivering. "Wolf went outside but was behind Ben. Neither of them could have shot those men," she finished, her voice trailing off to a whisper as she stared past Ben to Micah.

"Who else knows this?" Micah demanded without looking away from Wolf.

Angel started crying. "God. *Please* put that gun down."

"Who?" Micah yelled.

"Don't bully her, motherfucker," Wolf snarled, and started toward Micah.

Micah raised his other arm, holding the gun now with two hands. "Move another inch," he hissed, "and I'll end this fiasco."

"Answer the question," Maggie insisted, begging more than demanding. "Angel, answer the question," she repeated. "Who else knows?"

"All of you, I guess!" Angel wailed.

"Who in Zounds?" Micah clarified.

"No one!" Angel yelled. "I guessed, okay? Now put that goddamn gun down now!" she yelled.

"You're right," Wolf said, his voice calm. He held out his hands in surrender. "End this fiasco. Shoot me or put it down. Everyone has had enough."

"I'm not going with you," Micah said under his breath.

"I'm not going without you." Wolf continued standing with his hands extended. "I've spent too much time searching for you. There is a million-dollar bounty, and I'm going to collect it."

"That's what all of this is about, isn't it?" Micah asked. "A million dollars. It doesn't matter who I am, or what you think I might have done."

"Good one," Wolf snarled.

"I'm right, aren't I?" Micah pushed. "This fiasco all of us are enduring at this moment is because you want a million dollars."

"Don't think for a moment that I'm the bad guy here." Wolf shook his head and pointed one of his extended hands at Micah. He shook his finger at Micah. "You're the one with the bounty on your head. I'm the bounty hunter, the law-abiding citizen."

"And at least five people in Zounds know you assisted in sending four men to their watery grave."

"Because you killed them!" Wolf roared.

Micah didn't say anything for a moment. The silence once again grew. Micah was contemplating something. Ben watched him. His expression never changed. The day was brisk, seen with the sun shining high above all of them. Ben could feel himself sweating under his coat but swore there wasn't a gleam of sweat anywhere on Micah. He looked very cool and collected.

"Maggie, sweetheart, come here," Micah said finally.

Ben stepped to the side when Maggie darted to her husband. Micah kept his gun trained on Wolf but put one arm around Maggie and whispered in her ear.

"What's this all about?" Wolf demanded. "I don't have all day and—"

"Yes, you do," Micah interrupted him, then continued whispering to his wife.

Maggie looked up at him, nodded, and ran to the cabin.

"She will only be a few minutes," Micah informed Wolf once the door to the cabin closed behind Maggie. "I'm going to give you your million dollars."

"You aren't going to *give* me a dime," Wolf snarled. "I earn my keep. And I'll earn my million dollars when I turn you over to the officials. I do believe that Angel, rather conveniently, has the FBI arriving in Zounds sometime today. They might find it odd that her store is closed when they arrive."

"Something she should have thought of before coming up here," Micah said with an indifferent shrug.

"I put a note on the door saying I'd be back in an hour." Angel looked at Wolf apologetically. "I guess I'm a bit too possessive for my own good, but I think I'm falling in love with you," she admitted, and her cheeks blazed instantly a deep rose color that made her eyes an even more brilliant blue. "You have taken off so many times since we've met without a word of explanation, and a few times without even saying good-bye. Right after Ben and Zoey left, you disappeared out the storeroom door, and this time I was going to go right after you. Serves me right for following you, huh," she finished with a nervous chuckle. "But Micah," she continued with barely a breath, "if you are indeed the Mulligan Stew assassin, as far as I'm concerned you're more a martyr than a criminal, because, if Wikipedia is correct, all of your alleged murders were people as bad as Cortez, if not worse. Wolf isn't a bad man. I understand that you don't want to go with him, but shooting him isn't your style. If you do kill him, it will make you as bad as those you've killed—allegedly."

"I'm not going to kill him," Micah told her, his voice softening as he took a moment to look at her for the first time.

Wolf took that same moment and tried lunging in the direction of his gun. Micah fired again. Zoey screamed and rushed into Ben. Although he wasn't as prepared as Wolf had been when Angel had run into him, Ben managed to keep Zoey from moving any closer to Micah. He pulled Zoey into his arms and held her close to him as she trembled. Angel let out a terrible wail and Ben wasn't able to grab her before she ran toward Wolf, who had slid to the ground and now held both his hands in the air over his head.

"I hope your boyfriend doesn't make any more stupid moves," Micah said, and for the first time lowered his gun.

Maggie raced out of the cabin. "What happened?" she shouted.

"Just keeping everyone on their toes," Micah told her, and even took time to glance over his shoulder at her. "How's it going?"

"Just another minute." She ran back inside.

"I'm good enough to shoot off the tip of your finger without the bullet grazing any other part of your body."

Wolf lowered his hands. Angel had slid to the ground and knelt next to him, her face tearstained. "Wolf, oh crap," she whispered. "What are we going to do?"

"What the two of you are going to do," Micah began before Wolf could say anything, "is get up and come here."

Wolf leapt to his feet and pushed Angel behind him. "She isn't coming anywhere near you, or that gun."

"I already told you I'm not going to kill anyone. Do you want your bounty, or not?"

"Put down the gun."

Micah lowered it, cocked his head, and smiled. "I could put it in my back pocket and still shoot you before you found your gun."

Wolf started toward Micah but pushed Angel at Ben. "What's your game, Mulligan?"

Micah stepped toward Ben as well and handed him the gun. Ben frowned, reaching for it slowly, and gave Micah a questioning look. The gun was warm from Micah having held it all this time. Wolf paused, equally confused, but Ben barely spared him a glance. Wolf might not be thinking it through, but he had more than Micah against him. Ben wasn't going to let Wolf take Micah anywhere, and Ben didn't want to think what Maggie would do to protect Micah. Although Ben was fairly certain at the moment she was packing the two of them up to leave.

"I'm going to need you to cover my back, if you don't mind," Micah told Ben.

"You're committing a felony." Wolf pointed at Ben.

"Shut up," Ben snapped, and took the gun.

Micah gestured toward the cabin, and Wolf started walking. Angel rushed to his side, leaving Ben's.

"What are you going to do?" she demanded, slipping her arm around Wolf's but looking worried when she glanced over her shoulder at Micah.

"Don't bother asking questions," Wolf told her, but stopped when they reached the door to the cabin, blocking it so Micah would have to push him out of the way to open it. Instead he faced Angel and pulled her into his arms. "I love you, too," he whispered, and kissed her on the forehead.

"Oh, Wolf," she gasped, and another rush of tears streamed down her face.

Maggie saved Micah from having to break up the moment. She opened the door on her end and stepped to the side. "Come inside," she invited, making it sound as if she'd just had guests show up for a party.

"Ben, keep the ladies in here." Micah pointed to the living room but pushed Wolf toward his kitchen.

Zoey put her arm around Angel and gave her a fierce hug. Ben didn't have to worry about either of them. They held each other in the middle of the living room. For good measure, in case Angel did try to do something stupid, he closed the cabin door and locked it. Then keeping the gun aimed at the floor, he glanced around the corner into the kitchen.

A kitchen chair had been pulled away from the table and placed in the middle of the room. Ben looked at Micah and Wolf in time to see Micah push on Wolf's shoulder, with a bit of force, and pick up a pair of handcuffs that were on the table.

"Run all you want, but I'll find you," Wolf swore.

Micah pulled Wolf's arms behind the chair and hand-cuffed him. "That won't be necessary." Before Wolf could say anything else, Micah picked up a folded bandana, shook it out, then gagged Wolf.

Maggie came to the door carrying two suitcases. She placed them by the door and handed Ben a piece of paper. Without any explanation, she then turned to Zoey and Angel.

"I'm going to miss both of you," she told them, and tried for a group hug.

Angel took a step backward, hugging herself. "What did you do with him?" she asked, her eyes puffy and bloodshot as she nodded toward the kitchen. It was incredibly quiet from that end of the house.

Maggie gave Zoey a fierce hug but then released her and dropped her hands to her sides. "Angel, my husband is a very good person, better than most men, and I'm the luckiest woman in the world to have him. He already told you, and he doesn't lie, he isn't going to hurt Wolf." She then turned to Zoey and with the same loving touch as a mother might administer stroked the side of her head. "You're going to love L.A." Maggie gave her a piece of paper similar to what she had just given Ben. "When you have time, look up my parents for me. Let them know I'm happy, head over heels in love, and miss them."

Zoey simply nodded, smiled, and dabbed at her face with her fingers when a tear fell. "Take care of yourself," she whispered.

"Most definitely."

They all jumped when there was a knock on the door. Maggie laughed and unlocked it. Micah stepped inside the doorway and picked up the suitcases. "Until next time," he told Ben, grinned, then held the door for Maggie to come outside. "I'm sorry I don't have keys to those handcuffs," he added, then let the screen door close and headed across the yard to their car.

Angel skidded out of the living room into the kitchen and yanked off Wolf's gag, which allowed him to immediately let out a spew of profanities. Zoey remained in the doorway, staring outside as Micah and Maggie disappeared down the driveway.

"Think they will make it?" she whispered, glancing over her shoulder at Ben.

He had no doubts. "Most definitely."

Chapter Nineteen

Ben had friendlier conversations on the phone with Greg and Haley, but he understood their apprehension. In spite of what Greg had told him when they talked, Ben knew they were coming home because they were curious about Zoey. Not that he would tell Zoey that.

"Is that them?" Zoey peered around his shoulder when Ben opened the door to his apartment and stared down at the nice rig the Kings had, with Greg's Harley on a three-wheeler being towed from behind.

"Yup. Come on," Ben said without ceremony, taking Zoey's hand and pulling her outside into the warm early-evening sunshine. "Let's go see how their trip was."

"Okay," she said slowly.

In the week since they'd been back in L.A. her face was finally bruise-free. A few walks on the beach, something Ben had seldom done before, had brought the luster back to Zoey's naturally tan skin. He'd taken her to his doctor, the doctor Haley had insisted all her employees went to for annual physicals, and Zoey was given a clean bill of health. Ben had given Zoey his room, had been crashing on the couch, and was taking a lot of cold showers.

At the moment, though, he dragged her down the stairs. "You two sure know how to take a long vacation!" he yelled the moment they reached the parking lot.

"It's always one of my boys," Haley said, sounding as if she were complaining but with a huge grin on her face. "I have to be close to take care of you."

She closed the passenger door to their motor home and held her arms out. Haley was tan, her hair windblown, and had never looked better. Ben didn't know if he'd ever tell her that she meant more to him than his own mother, whom he'd never told that he'd left L.A., let alone was now home. He let go of Zoey's hand to give Haley a big hug.

"Did you save the world while I was gone?" Greg asked in his booming baritone. At six and a half feet, he looked down at Ben, shook his hand with a mean grip, but then let go and tilted his head.

Zoey had disappeared behind Ben. He didn't let her stay there but took her hand and pulled her to his side. "Greg, Haley, this is Zoey Cortez. Zoey, these are my bosses."

"Bosses?" Haley was still grinning. "Lord, make it sound so impersonal." She stepped forward, took Zoey from Ben, and gave her a hug. "I'm Haley. You'll call me that. This is Greg. Don't let his size intimidate you. He's a pussycat."

"Roar," Greg grumbled, glaring at his wife. "I'm not a pussycat." He extended his hand and shook Zoey's as soon as Haley let go of her. "Good to meet you, Zoey. We're glad you're here."

"Yes, we are." Haley put her arm around Zoey and started away from the men. "Let these two do their guy-talk thing. They get boring when they start trying to outdo each other with their stories of saving the world." She made a face at her husband. "We'll go have girl talk. That is so much more fun. Ben, I really hope your apartment is clean."

Ben watched Zoey walk away next to Haley, knowing Haley would learn every detail about what had happened in Zounds, and how Zoey felt about being here in L.A. before either man was welcome in Ben's apartment.

"Pretty girl," Greg told him as the women climbed the stairs.

"She's gorgeous."

"Oh yeah. Zoey is pretty, too."

Ben laughed and Greg slapped him on the back. "So you two are living together now?"

Ben shrugged, turned, and walked up to Greg's rig. "I'm not rushing her into anything. You know you two didn't need to come back on my account."

"You know the minute you called Haley and told her you were home with a young lady that we were coming right back home so she could check her out," Greg said, although he didn't sound too put out. "How did things go up there?"

Ben understood the question. Greg wanted to know about Micah. Greg led the way to the side of the good-sized motor home, opened the door, and climbed inside, ducking his head until he sat at a spacious table with a large window that allowed them to see the closed door to Ben's apartment. Both men looked out the window, and Ben was sure Greg was as curious about what the two women were talking about as he was.

"How's Micah?" Greg asked before Ben could answer his first question or slide in across from him at the table.

Ben did so, looking out the window and hoping Haley wouldn't go too rough on Zoey. Even with her loving, motherly ways, she might not realize how fragile Zoey was right now.

"Your girlfriend is fine," Greg informed him. "Probably a lot tougher than you're giving her credit for. By the looks of it, she's made it through hell and it's all smooth sailing now."

"Sure hope you're right. And Micah is good. Too good. Cocky as ever."

"And once again has disappeared," Greg said, nodding already without waiting for Ben to confirm it. "Who was abusing your girlfriend?"

Ben and Zoey hadn't put a label on their relationship, and having Greg refer to her as his girlfriend threw him off. He wouldn't correct Greg. He just went with it.

"Her father, who is now dead."

"Sounds like a good story."

The door to Ben's apartment opened, and both men turned to look out the window.

"It is," he said, watching the two women descend the stairs.

In spite of Greg insisting Zoey was stronger than Ben gave her credit for, he still studied her face as the women approached. He knew how strong Zoey was. For a petite, adorable woman she was larger than life in so many ways. He knew both Greg and Haley would love her. But also knew he was head over heels in love with her. Zoey was strong, stronger than most. She'd been through so much, though, and he didn't see anything wrong with wanting to protect her and make sure her world was perfect from this point forward.

"We've decided," Haley began as she came through the door into the motor home. "The four of us are heading over to the house. You two are grilling and we might be persuaded to fix a salad."

"A salad?" Greg raised one eyebrow.

"Is very good for you," Haley informed him.

Ben was used to their bantering. He searched Zoey's face and was thrilled to see her smile.

It was a perfect evening. After filling Greg and Haley in on all events that had transpired while Ben had been up in Zounds, beginning with how he'd first spotted Zoey walking down the street the first night he'd arrived and known at that moment she was the most beautiful woman in the world, and ending with the two of them leaving Zounds on his bike, Ben drank his beer as the four of them lounged on Greg and Haley's back porch. He smiled over the rim of the bottle and winked at Zoey. She blushed and made a face at him.

"Yes," she said, waving her hand at Ben across the table as a breeze off the ocean blew strands of her hair across her face. She brushed them away and kept talking. "I saw this bad boy on a motorcycle and knew I should run for the hills."

She'd relaxed considerably during dinner. Greg and Haley were the perfect couple to pull anyone out of their shell. Zoey was laughing and eagerly chiming in to speak her share of any story as the evening progressed.

Haley had sat comfortably at an angle in her chair facing

Zoey, who sat next to her, but was still able to shoot her husband or Ben appropriate looks when she approved or disapproved of anything they said. She ruled her roost comfortably from her wicker chair.

"Sweetheart, we both should have run for the hills."

The women laughed, and Ben could only smile, sure he had to be glowing with pride. The evening was perfect. He was sitting with two of his favorite people, and the sexiest, most alluring woman he'd ever known kept flashing flirtatious smiles at him. The soft yellow sleeveless dress she wore showed off her dark skin, and her black hair glowed in long silky strands over her bare shoulders. The cut of the dress showed off her perfectly shaped breasts. Every now and then he stretched his legs under the table and brushed his foot against hers. She flashed her long, thick lashes at him when he brushed his shoe against her sandaled foot. Her dark eyes glowed against the setting sunlight filtering in from the beach behind them. Ben fought to keep his dick from getting hard.

He shifted the conversation to what happened their last day in Zounds up at Micah and Maggie's cabin. The seriousness of the events Ben and Zoey explained to Greg and Haley helped him keep his mind off what he dreamed of doing with Zoey once they returned to the apartment later that evening.

"You should have seen how furious red Wolf's face was while he had to wait for us to break into Micah's shed to find a saw to cut him out of that chair and handcuffs," Zoey offered, filling Greg and Haley in on details that Ben hadn't witnessed while he'd been breaking into Micah's shed, which had been conveniently locked. Not that Ben had rushed, but the time it took to free Wolf had been plenty of time for Micah and Maggie to disappear. "I honestly thought Angel was going to smack him at one point. He was throwing a fit and bouncing all over that kitchen while handcuffed to that chair."

"Sometimes we need to smack them around," Haley told Zoey, winking and then smiling lovingly at her husband.

"Uh-huh." Greg stretched. "I'm getting another beer.

Anyone else?" he asked. "Don't tell any good stuff while I'm gone."

"How can it get better than what they've already told us?" Haley called after Greg when he disappeared into the kitchen. "This story is amazing."

"Oh, it gets better." Ben smiled and nodded to Zoey when Greg returned, passed out ice-cold bottles of beer, removed the empties, and sprawled comfortably in his chair. It matched the other four chairs around the table, except he fit perfectly in his while both women looked very small in the oversized King wicker chairs.

"How could this get better?" Greg asked, and narrowed his gaze at both Ben and Zoey, although his expression was very relaxed and amused. "Are the two of you going to turn this into a tall tale?"

"No way we could make up what happened next." Ben pulled out his wallet from his back pocket and removed the first of two neatly folded letters. He would destroy both of them. There would be no memorabilia this time. But he'd wanted to show them to Greg and Haley first. Leaving one letter neatly tucked in his wallet, Ben pulled free the other one, the one Maggie had given Zoey. Handing it to her, he nodded to Zoey. "You should do the honors."

Zoey had been sipping her beer and nodded, placed her bottle in front of her, and wiped her mouth very unceremoniously with her hand. "Before she left, Maggie handed me a note. In all the confusion, I didn't look at it until Ben was back in the kitchen. He had found a lock pick set in the shed outside of the cabin and picked the lock on the handcuffs. I'd been holding the paper Maggie had given me the entire time but at that moment decided to read it—"

"And she shrieked," Ben interrupted.

"I wasn't going to add that part." She pouted and glared at him.

Ben relaxed against the high-backed chair and grinned at her. There must have been something in his look that gave away the fantasies he was having of getting her naked later, because Zoey cleared her throat and looked away first. When

Greg gave him a speculative look, Ben simply smiled and returned his attention to Zoey.

"What does it say?" Haley demanded, nodding to the neatly folded piece of paper in Zoey's hand.

Zoey unfolded the paper. She still had some pain when using her right hand, which the doctor had told them was normal since the bone was still healing. But being right-handed, she unfolded it slowly and carefully straightened the typing paper until everyone saw the large-font message typed on it.

She angled it toward one of the candles burning on the middle of the table, and Greg slid it closer to her. Zoey glanced up and smiled, the glow of the candle making her caramel-colored skin glow in the light.

Zoey read:

"'A dead man meeting the description of the Mulligan Stew assassin has been found behind the cabin. He's been shot in the head, although facial features match physical descriptions offered during interviews after his last known appearance in Los Angeles. After a thorough search of the cabin and surrounding property, the conclusion is clear this is where the assassin has been living for a number of months. There is no indication of the woman, Maggie O'Malley, believed to have left Los Angeles with him.'"

"Are you serious?" Haley let out a hoot. "That's hilarious. And Micah wrote this?"

"We aren't sure if he wrote it, or if Maggie did." Ben accepted the creased piece of paper when Zoey handed it to him.

Greg reached for it, and Ben handed it over, noting the man's hard features and deep frown as he reread the typed note. "Who is the dead man?" he asked in a low, serious tone.

Ben shook his head. "No idea. But we found him. From the angle he was shot, it looked like the guy had taken his own life."

"And now will go down in history as the Mulligan Stew assassin?"

"Last we knew, Wolf would have nothing to do with the short bio typed out for his benefit. After I got him out of the handcuffs, he stormed around outside of the cabin. We all followed. Wolf was hopping mad, but there wasn't much he could do. Micah was gone."

"So this dead man will go down in history as the assassin?" Haley repeated the question and nodded to the letter.

"Last we knew. Zoey and I left shortly after that."

"Angel told me on the phone yesterday that the FBI agent she'd spoken to on the phone showed up at her store a day late," Zoey said.

"The owner of the bookstore had contacted the FBI about Micah?" Haley asked, glancing from Ben to Zoey.

"No. No," Ben told her, raising his hand. "Angel, the bookstore owner, was focusing on Cortez."

"My father," Zoey offered. Her expression remained relaxed, at peace, as she continued explaining. "Although he wasn't much of a dad. Cortez never cared for me other than how I might benefit in helping him make more money."

"I'm sorry to hear that," Haley said softly, the pain she guessed Zoey must have endured showing in her eyes.

Zoey smiled at her, a comforting smile that made her words all the more sincere. "I'm happier now than I've ever been in my life." She shifted her attention to Ben, although only for a moment. "Angel told me she and Wolf decided they would go with telling the FBI agent everything Cortez was doing to the town and let the agent tell them he was dead after investigating."

"Good thinking." Ben reached for her and stroked her arm. Her skin was so smooth. He was ready to get out of there and take Zoey home. "And it worked?"

When Zoey smiled, her entire face glowed, showing the happiness she professed to have. He liked thinking her contentment in life had a bit to do with him.

"Apparently," she told him. "Wolf met with the FBI and they combed over the property around the cabin and dissected every inch of it inside."

"Shame, too. The place was beautiful," Ben added, although didn't feel too much remorse. Micah would rebuild, and possibly this time as a truly free man. The hunt was over. Whether Wolf liked it or not, Micah hadn't left him a lot of options. There were no clues for Wolf to follow this time. Micah had vanished.

"I suppose he'll get his bounty," Greg mused, holding his beer bottle in his hand and staring at it as he spoke. His mind was a thousand miles away.

Ben wouldn't speculate on where Greg's thoughts had headed. It could be anywhere, including despising Wolf for hunting down a man who had worked under Greg and whom he'd respected as a bounty hunter. Micah had been good, but then all the necessary skills had already been in place. Micah had been a hunter prior to working for KFA. He'd hunted to kill instead of to capture. It had simply been a matter of fine-tuning already existing habits to comply with his new line of work.

Or Greg might have been reminiscing on hunts of the past. Ben knew of a few at least that could have been compared with this one as time-consuming and dangerous. Micah might have been right. Greg and Haley might be nowhere near their golden years.

"I'm sure we'll hear if he does," Ben said, and looked toward Zoey when she stifled a yawn. "I think we're going to call it a night."

The Kings walked Ben and Zoey out to the front of their home and Ben's bike. Haley hugged each of them and rubbed Ben's back as he helped Zoey fasten her helmet.

"Are you coming back to work?" Haley asked.

"I thought you two were slowing things down," he said. "Hitting the road and traveling for pleasure instead of for the hunt."

"There's a difference?" Greg asked as he stood toward the front of Ben's Harley, his arms crossed. It was dark, but it was easy to see his eyes light with amusement. At the same time, Greg was serious.

Ben understood the passion and love for the hunt. It was in his blood as it was in Greg's and Haley's. "None that I know of," he told Greg, but caught it when Haley rolled her eyes at Zoey. "And don't let her fool you," Ben told Zoey, wagging his finger at Haley. "This woman loves the hunt as much as her husband—"

"If not more," Greg interrupted. "We're heading back on the road in a few days. We're going to Colorado to see the boys. Marc, our oldest, and his wife, London, are expecting their first baby. London's due date is next month, and Grandma here doesn't want to miss it."

" 'Grandma,' " Haley said blissfully. "I like the sound of that."

"Congratulations." Ben climbed onto his bike after helping Zoey onto the seat behind him. "That will be one spoiled grandchild."

"Grandson," Greg said, beaming. "We already know. You should see all the baby stuff packed in the back of the motor home," he said, nodding in the direction of their R.V. parked at the end of the circular drive.

"Congrats again," Ben said, beaming at the proud grandparents-to-be. "But why are you asking me to come back to work if you aren't going to be here?"

"Haley is answering the office phone on the road," Greg explained. "We've got three bounty hunters on call and Haley contacts them with their assignments every day. I get to consult while driving if needed."

Although that sounded like a killjoy for their vacationing, Ben had a feeling both of them ate up any opportunity to talk shop or brainstorm with their employees. He could easily see the two of them sitting next to each other in that big rig while discussing a hunt via speakerphone.

"Well, if you need another man, I'm more than willing to come back to work." He'd rather work for KFA than have to find work elsewhere, which would probably mean doing security work until he found something better.

"Never thought you left," Haley said, smiling and leaning against Greg's large, thick chest as he wrapped his arm around her. She looked so small next to her giant husband but was larger than life in her own right. Haley was going to be the best-looking, youngest grandmother Ben had ever known. She shifted her attention to Zoey. "Once you're up to it, let me know. There is a lot of office work I can't handle from the road. That is, if you're interested in working."

"Am I?"

Ben didn't have to see Zoey to know her entire face lit up. Oddly enough, Cortez had left Zoey as his sole beneficiary. She wasn't thrilled about receiving so much dirty money, but Zoey wouldn't have to work for the rest of her life if she so chose.

"I can start whenever you like," Zoey said, sounding delighted.

Ben took his time driving home. Zoey was relaxed, her cheek resting on the back of his shoulder. Her small hands were tucked under one of his hands at his waist, and her breasts tortured his back. It was a perfect fall evening, and he almost considered a long drive out to the coast. There was so much of L.A. to show Zoey. With such a huge city, there was a lot they could do. In the short time since they'd been home, she'd gotten to know his neighborhood and the beach. She'd pointed out to him that she could imagine living in a small town since they always went to the same grocery store, same gas station, or same other place to shop. Granted his grocery store was also a discount center and surrounded by a strip mall. Anything they could possibly want they could find in a ten-mile-square radius, which was still just a fraction of Los Angeles. He loved how she laughed and commented frequently that she'd never seen so many people walking, or in stores, or driving on the street. She had been ten when she'd moved to Zounds, and although she had lived in and visited larger cities, Zoey had reluctantly admitted that over the years she had become a small-town girl.

"I had fun tonight," she said once they were inside his apartment. "You were right; those two are an amazing couple."

Zoey's cell phone rang and Ben groaned.

"Don't answer it." There wasn't anyone he could think of they needed to talk to right now, except each other. And he had a lot more than talking in mind.

"It's the bookstore," Zoey said after fishing out her cell. She smiled at Ben. "It's Angel."

She answered the phone and moved to Ben's bed. "Of course it's not a bad time," she said, her grin broadening as she let her gaze travel up Ben's body. "We just got back from having dinner with Greg and Haley King, Ben's bosses."

Ben leaned in the doorway, willing the phone call to be short. Zoey looked amazing in her snug-fitting yellow dress. He couldn't wait to get it off of her.

"What? Really? Oh, Angel, that is such good news."

Angel said something and Zoey looked down. Was she blushing?

"Can I get back to you on that one?" she asked, lowering her voice to a sultry breath of a whisper.

But when she shot Ben a quick glance, he had a feeling he knew what Angel had just asked.

"Yes. I love it here. I'll call you tomorrow, okay?"

He gave silent thanks when she hung up the phone.

"Wolf is moving to Zounds," she said without ceremony, her bright smile as intoxicating as the rest of her. "He and Angel are going to live together." She closed her cell, stood, placed it on his dresser, and picked up her brush. "And it appears he has quite a bit of money that he thought would be well invested in Angel's bookstore."

"I wonder where he got that." Ben didn't really wonder. At the moment he didn't care either.

It was closure for Micah. That was all that mattered. Not that he didn't wish Wolf and Angel the best, especially since Angel and Zoey were so close. Wolf would have hauled Micah in if he'd had the chance, though. Ben was grateful as hell that Micah would possibly now have the chance to live life without hiding and looking over his shoulder every second. The life he had painted for Ben while they'd been together in Zounds hadn't been a life Ben would have wished on anyone. Possibly with the bounty paid, Micah and Maggie would now have a shot at living a normal life.

"I hope they'll be happy." Zoey returned to brushing her

hair. "Kind of like Greg and Haley. That's the type of relationship I want."

"They're best friends." Ben watched when she began brushing the tangles out of her hair. "Something you don't see enough of today."

"It just takes hard work and dedication." She smiled at him but then made a face when her brush caught in a tangle.

Ben came up behind her and took her brush, then, pulling her backward, sat on the edge of his bed and planted her between his legs. Then brushing her hair, he took his time, working the windblown tangles out of her long straight black hair.

"I've never had a problem with hard work and dedication." She turned her head to look at him, not flinching when the brush caught in her hair again. "Are you suggesting we give it a shot?"

"I was already planning on it," he informed her, putting the brush down and turning her farther for a deep kiss.

All evening he'd imagined what he might do with Zoey once they got home. Since they'd first arrived in L.A., there had been a lot of foreplay, but he wasn't sure he could wait any longer. Zoey hadn't discouraged him from having sex with her. But he'd needed to know she wasn't haunted by too many ghosts when he entered her. Maybe he was a selfish bastard, but he wanted to be the only man on her mind when they made love.

Her head fell back and she sighed as he cradled her and found the zipper to her dress, which was underneath her arm of all places.

"Are you going to tell me no again tonight?" she murmured, her long, thick lashes shuttering her dark eyes.

"Do you want me to?"

"No," she said on a breath, and opened her eyes to look at him. "I don't ever want you to stop."

"Then I won't."

He barely managed to get her zipper down to her waist causing her snug yellow dress to hang on her when she leaned forward. Zoey adjusted herself on his lap and began tugging his T-shirt up his torso. She had lost weight since he'd pulled her out of her father's house but in just the past few days seemed to be recovering faster than those two weeks in Zounds after Cortez had been given a burial at sea. Her color was good, her appetite restored, and her energy level back to normal. The bruises were gone. And she smiled all the time. Zoey was a different person from the hesitant young lady he'd first met outside a bed-and-breakfast in Zounds.

The moment Zoey pulled his shirt over his head, Ben pounced on her. His breath caught in his throat when he managed to get her dress to her waist and spotted the tiny yellow thong that barely covered her freshly shaved pussy.

"Oh crap," he managed, and stared down between them.

Then slowly raising himself off her, Ben lifted his gaze to her face and began pulling her dress up the rest of her body. A tiny lace bra, matching yellow—and it was tiny—barely covered her hard brown nipples.

"Zoey." He could barely choke out her name.

Her smile was seductive. "Yes?" she whispered.

Even her voice enticed and made his blood boil. "It's a damn good thing you don't want me to stop."

"I never did," she reminded him.

Ben knew that but also knew she would enjoy herself a lot more now that she was free of the torture of her father and demons of a life now behind her.

"Where did you get—" He didn't finish his question but instead freed her of her dress, dropped it to the floor, and ran his finger along the lacy edge of her bra. His dick swelled painfully in his jeans when her nipple hardened even further. "Damn. You're so incredibly sexy."

"I found it the other day when you were buying beer."

Ben remembered when they'd gone to the store. He had thought he'd left her to pick out fresh vegetables while he'd gone to the other side of the store for beer. He had taken so long trying to choose a nice bottle of wine for her.

"And wine," he reminded her, and pulled her off the bed into his arms. Burying his face between her breasts, he died and was in heaven as he breathed in her scent and felt her soft flesh against his face.

"Wine does sound good."

God, he wasn't sure he could move enough to get out of his jeans, let alone walk into the kitchen. All he wanted was to dive deep into her heat, feel Zoey's tight pussy squeeze the life out of him. When his thoughts were teetering dangerously close to making him lose all self-control, Zoey leapt off the bed. She was nimble enough to escape his grasp and laughed as she trotted out of the bedroom.

Ben collapsed with a loud groan where she'd been lying. "You aren't supposed to kill me, woman," he complained.

Her laughter from the other room only succeeded in getting him even harder. A feat he hadn't known himself capable of until that moment. Rolling to his back, he managed to pull off his shoes and jeans just as Zoey returned with a chilled bottle of wine and corkscrew in one hand and two wineglasses clinking in the other.

"If you're trying to get me drunk, I'm here to tell you, I'm a sure thing."

Her big smile lit up her eyes. "Better safe than sorry. You haven't been putting out much lately."

Ben took the bottle and corkscrew that she had in one hand. Zoey held up the glasses. He twisted the screw into the cork, glancing up several times at her breasts that were almost spilling out of her bra. When he caught her staring at the rather large tent in his boxers, he hid a smile and focused on his task. In spite of himself, his cock did an eager dance for her, and Zoey hissed in a breath.

"I'm really wet," she whispered.

Ben pulled too hard on the cork, and it came flying out of the bottle. It was good wine, but he still almost dropped the bottle and managed to spill some on him and Zoey. She jumped backward, laughing.

"Now I'm really, really wet." She giggled and turned toward the bathroom.

"Oh no, you don't." Ben lunged for her, but his hands were full. "You aren't leaving this room again."

"What are you going to do, lick the wine off me?"

Ben grabbed her, put the wine on top of his dresser, and took both glasses from her hand and set them down.

"But I might be thirsty," she complained, laughing when he tossed her to the bed.

Ben came down on top of her but braced himself so that he wasn't smashing her. "And I might want to lick the wine off of you."

He gripped her arms at her elbows and ran his tongue down from the bottom of her bra to her belly button. Zoey giggled and squirmed under his grasp.

"Zoey," Ben said. "Look at me."

She was smiling broadly when she raised her head and looked at him. Zoey sobered as she stared at him.

"Keep watching," he instructed, and ran his tongue farther down her body, from her belly button to the edge of her thong.

Zoey moaned and her head fell back. Ben stared at her full, round breasts and the lacy yellow material that barely covered them. He let go of her arms and she reached for the edges of his bed. For the past week he'd teased her and been teased out of his mind. They had flirted, cuddled, spent time talking and time making out. But he'd held back, wanting all of her.

"Zoey," he whispered, and dragged his tongue along the length of her thong as it disappeared between her legs.

"God. Yes," she panted, and lifted her head again.

That was the look he wanted. Tortured, passionate, full of craving and pleasure. There were no more tormented clouds haunting her pretty eyes. Her expression was relaxed instead of pinched with distracting thoughts. Ben knew it would take a lot longer before her past was simply that. She might never be able to forgive her father for his crimes. But as long as she didn't think she was to blame for how Cortez had abused the citizens of Zounds, she and Ben were making progress.

Ben slipped her thong to the side. He eased his finger down the length of her slit.

"You were right." He could barely think straight. But he

wanted all of Zoey's attention. He wanted to know she was enjoying every minute of their passion. She deserved the best first time, and he would see that she had it.

"Right?" she breathed.

Her eyes were glazed over, but it was from desire, lust, a craving for the pressure that was building inside her to break. Ben saw it not only in her eyes but also in her expression. Her entire body was tense. He couldn't wait to see her bask in her orgasm.

"You are soaked."

Her eyes cleared and she studied him, a slow smile appeared on her face, Ben grabbed the thin straps that curved over her hips and yanked them down her thighs.

"Oh God!" she cried out, and managed to lift her ass off the bed.

Ben pulled, moving to a kneeling position, and dragged the gauzy thong down her legs. It was tossed to the side of his bed along with the rest of her clothes.

"Should I take off my bra?"

"It's fine." He would get to it in due time if she left it on.

At the moment he was high off of her incredible pussy. Her scent, so rich and fresh, and the knowledge that he would be her first, and her only if he had anything to say about it, were so intoxicating. He moved between her legs and nestled himself so he could taste her.

Ben had died and gone to heaven. She soaked his face. Her cream was thick, pungent, and tasted so good he might have feasted on her all night.

"Ben!" she cried, gripping the bedspread with both hands. Even her right hand was grasping the blanket as tightly as her left hand. "Oh my God! Wait! I can't . . ." She trailed off.

"Yes, you can," he told her, and continued licking, sucking, and devouring her wonderful smooth, wet pussy.

Zoey came off the bed, moving to a full sitting position as she grabbed his head. She was pushing him away and trying to move his face closer at the same time. One hand was shoving while the other held on. Ben wouldn't have moved if his life depended on it. He drank from her, positive this orgasm was better than the first orgasm he'd given her in the cabin in Zounds. He got so damn hard with that knowledge he was barely able to breathe.

Before she'd come down from her climax, he came over her. Easing her up his bed, he basked in the flushed look on her face. Ben managed to reach for the small box of condoms he'd placed in his bedside drawer and ripped the box open. He tore the condom from its package and fumbled far too long putting it on.

In truth it probably took seconds. They were seconds he didn't want stolen away from her. Soon he would discuss birth control with her, but for tonight, possibly their first few times, condoms would work fine. He just needed to learn how to put them on without looking away from her. There had never been a woman before who affected him the way Zoey did. Ben didn't want to lose a moment of time with her. It didn't matter that he planned on keeping her by his side forever. He wanted to enjoy every single minute of the rest of their lives with her.

As he began easing into her, Zoey's soaked heat tightened around him. Ben moved slowly. It would kill him. When he realized his eyes were closed and opened them, Zoey stared up with an erotic fascination on her face.

"I don't want to hurt you," he murmured, lowering his mouth to hers.

"Deeper," she urged.

God! He was only a man. Zoey was young. It was her first time. And damn it, he wanted this to be perfect for her. But when she ground her nails into his shoulders, urging him forward, he plunged deep inside her.

"Oh!" she cried.

He stopped. It killed him. Blood boiled in his veins. His heart pounded too hard in his chest. His vision blurred.

"Ben," she begged.

He wasn't sure if it was from pleasure or pain. Ben had never had a virgin before, and he never would again. This needed to be perfect for both of them.

"Does it hurt?" he asked.

Zoey shook her head. "Make love to me."

"I love you," he told her, the words coming so easily as he began moving inside her.

"I love you, too."

Chapter Twenty

"Who was that?" Ben asked as he dropped his gear from his truck—his bulletproof vest and harness—on the couch inside the KFA office.

"Maggie O'Malley's brother." Zoey walked past Ben and flipped the CLOSED sign around on the door to the office, then pulled the Bluetooth from her ear.

"Maggie's brother?" Ben peered out of the window at the small red Kia pulling out of the circular drive.

"Yeah," Zoey said from behind him, not elaborating.

In the past six months, neither of them had talked much of their first meeting in Zounds or of Micah and Maggie. Ben had thought about Micah from time to time. He figured he always would. The way he saw it, no news was good news.

"What did he want?" He couldn't imagine her brother seeking out a bounty hunter. Or if he did need such services, the last place he would come to was KFA.

"Well," Zoey said, and walked behind her desk. "He dropped off this."

Ben walked over to the desk and noticed the pile of paperwork that had been there when he'd left earlier that day was gone. Haley had been more than impressed with how efficiently Zoey ran the office. And Zoey had taken over the place as if it had always been her business. She was a natural at organizing and loved the job. Ben loved seeing her while he was working. Win-win all the way round.

"What's this?" he asked, wrapping his arms around Zoey's waist and resting his head on her shoulder as he looked at what she had in her hand. "A brochure for a bounty-hunting school?"

"Not just any bounty-hunting school," she explained, and held up the front of the brochure. "It is the Maggie O'Malley School of Bounty Hunting."

"Are you serious?"

Ben took the glossy brochure from Zoey and held it up, staring at the cabin-like structure set back on a large, grassy lot in the picture. Underneath the name of the school it said; *Let no man or woman go missing.*

"Catchy." Ben flipped open the brochure and glanced at the courses offered. "Greg King is teaching a class?" he asked, shocked.

Zoey inched closer to Ben. "I hadn't had a chance to look at it yet. But that's amazing. Of course they would want Greg to teach. He's the best there is."

Ben looked down at her and smiled. In the time they'd been together, Zoey had worked to learn everything about bounty hunting there was to know. She had no desire at all to get a private investigator's license, in spite of Haley's gentle teasing. But Zoey was a wiz in the office and wanted to understand every aspect of what they did at KFA.

"Are you up to taking a ride?"

"Sure. Where?"

Ben tapped the brochure. "Let's do a drive-by. The O'Malleys obviously put up some money for this school. I know her family is distraught over her being a missing person, and are even more sick that they believe she's dead."

"You said that's how it has to be," Zoey said under her breath, staring at the brochure.

"Yes, it is." He hugged her close. "I'm impressed they want to start a school to help men and women be the best bounty hunters they can be. Greg is an amazing teacher."

"He made you a great bounty hunter."

Ben could get real used to the look of adoration Zoey gave him. "I have a lot to learn. And if you'll remember, I didn't find Micah. He found me."

It was mid-March and a beautiful night. Had they been in Zounds, it would have been freezing. But as they drove up the coast, it was perfect weather for a ride. Zoey was tucked in behind him, wearing her leather jacket, which was a miniature version of his. She fit on his bike as if the motorcycle had been built for both of them. His day had been long, grueling, and he was glad to be off work. As much as he loved his job, spending time with Zoey off work made his life complete.

And she loved his neck of the woods, so to speak. Zoey loved shopping in the mall. She loved walking barefoot on the beach. She loved making their townhome into a cozy home for two. Ben loved everything about Zoey, absolutely everything.

Zoey tapped Ben's shoulder, and he nodded. Part of her job description was answering the phones for KFA, which was a 24/7 job. The phone was ringing, and she wouldn't be able to hear or talk very well on the back of his bike. Ben pulled over and put the kickstand down.

"KFA," Zoey said in her businesslike tone, which was soft and sultry. Whether someone needed a bounty hunter for good or bad reasons—there were all kinds out there—they always wanted KFA in their corner after hearing Zoey's gentle, friendly voice on the phone. "Haley, hi," Zoey said, the enthusiasm in her voice picking up as she spoke. "We've left the office. Actually, we're driving out to this new Maggie O'Malley school. . . . You are? . . . That's great! We're almost there, I think."

Ben nodded to confirm.

"Sounds great. We'll see you there."

She hung up the phone by tapping her earpiece as Ben turned in his seat to see her better. "Greg and Haley are heading to the school, too?"

"They are already there."

Ben and Zoey pulled to a stop a bit later in front of a very large, rather old-looking home that looked as if recently it had been completely remodeled. Its Spanish architecture wasn't uncommon. There were new red tiles on the roof and a wide, large porch that wrapped around the front of the stone-structured home. The two of them climbed off the bike behind the Kings' black Avalanche. Ben searched the area, not sure where Greg and Haley were.

"Want me to call them again?"

"Let's walk around a bit," Ben suggested, taking Zoey's hand and leading the way to the large home. He glanced up at a sign above the front porch that said: School of Maggie O'Malley Bounty Hunting.

"Someone put some money into this place," Zoey commented once she and Ben had walked up onto the front porch.

"What I was thinking."

Ben took in the new windows and noticed the porch had been freshly painted.

Along the side of the house were stairs leading off the porch. The two of them strolled to the rear of the house. Greg and Haley were standing behind the house talking and looked up at the same time as Ben and Zoey came into view.

"Pretty impressive, huh," Greg said when the two joined them.

"Very," Ben said, and sensed the apprehension in Greg's tone but more on his face when they faced each other. "When does it open its doors?"

"They are offering a couple summer classes, then full-time this fall," Haley offered.

Long shadows stretched off the backside of the house. Haley looked among all of them up at the large renovated home.

"We were just discussing the conversation we had with the O'Malleys earlier today," Greg said. "I was surprised they approached me to teach a class when the man they blame for the abduction of their daughter and sister worked for me."

"If they are going to do this, it doesn't surprise me they want to do it right," Ben said.

"That's just it," Haley began explaining. "This wasn't their idea. An anonymous donation was sent to them. Maggie's brother contacted us a couple weeks ago, but at that time he wasn't too friendly, and almost a bit more accusatory about having received the letter and money."

"Money?" Ben questioned. "As in a check?"

"No," Greg said slowly. "It was a money order. In fact, there were quite a few money orders, enough to total several hundred thousand dollars."

"And," Haley continued, picking up when her husband took a breath, "this house had already been purchased, with cash, again by an anonymous buyer. Everything had already been set up for the school to open."

"Let me guess, this anonymous buyer and whoever provided the donations also had the name of the school picked out."

"The boy's quick," Greg said, looking at Haley as he thumbed in Ben's direction.

"Did I get the call from Maggie's brother?" Zoey asked, her brow narrowed as she frowned at the ground between all of them. She looked up as she asked her next question. "You said he first contacted you a couple weeks ago?"

"Yup," Greg confirmed.

Shadows descended around all of them, but none of them noticed. Ben already knew Micah was behind the donations and buying this huge old home. Greg and Haley knew it was him as well.

"Did he believe Micah had sent the money and bought the house?" Ben asked.

Greg and Haley both looked at him at the same time. When Haley started walking toward the house, Greg took her hand and walked with her. Ben and Zoey followed. It seemed sunset moved faster that night than usual. It was almost dark as the four of them started around the house.

"They were positive the money and home were because of Micah," Haley said. She didn't look over her shoulder as she spoke but at the quiet surroundings, with its variety of trees from sycamores to palm trees and sage scrub beyond the immediate grounds. "That's why it took so long for Maggie's brother to come to us."

"How long did he have the money and know about this place?" Ben asked. He glanced up at the tall house as they walked alongside it. Numerous windows indicated it had at least four or five bedrooms, if not parlors and dens or other rooms not officially deemed bedrooms.

"Her brother was curt, to say the least, when he first called." Haley laughed.

"But we insisted we meet in person," Greg said, taking over the conversation. "We came out here with him yesterday, but he didn't have a key."

"We can't get inside the place?" Ben asked.

"Wait a minute, when were the brochures printed? It says you're one of the instructors."

Greg glanced over his shoulder and grinned at Zoey when she pointed out what she and Ben had seen on the brochure. "I agreed to do that two weeks ago, before Maggie's brother even wanted to open the doors to this place."

"We knew the school would open," Haley added, smiling up at her husband. "The O'Malleys just had to come to terms with the fact that this was what their daughter wanted. It's Maggie's way of showing her parents that she is still alive."

"Or they could take it as Micah's way of showing them that Maggie is dead," Ben pointed out, taking the devil's advocate role.

"Ben," Zoey scolded.

They came around the front of the house toward Greg and Haley's Avalanche and Ben's bike.

"So we can't go inside?" Ben asked.

"Ben!" Zoey demanded, tugging his arm and pointing toward the house. "Look. What's that?"

"The front door is open," Haley announced, excited as she let go of Greg's hand and ran to the door.

Everyone was right behind her.

"But this." Zoey kept pointing. "Oh my God, look!"

The two women raced up the front-porch stairs at the same time. It was Zoey who scooped up the baby rattle that was on the front porch, a light blue rattle.

"This wasn't here before. I swear it wasn't here," Zoey announced, her voice shrill with excitement.

Haley was already pushing her way through the front door and running through the large parlor, although she stopped at the large doorway that led into a very spacious living-room area. She was looking around frantically, her eyes wide when she stared at her husband in the dark.

Greg pulled out his phone and turned on the flashlight that he had on it. Ben did the same, and soon the women followed. Beams of lights chased one another around the interior of the front of the house, which didn't make it any easier to see.

"I don't see a light switch," Ben announced.

"Here. By the front door," Zoey told him. "The power isn't on," she added after flipping the switch and staring up at the small chandelier hanging inside the front door.

"He isn't here," Greg said, his tone solemn when he wrapped his arm around his wife. "Remember, Micah Jones, as well as Micah Mulligan, is dead. Bounty collected, end of story."

"What about this?" Zoey held up the small baby rattle.

The four of them stood in the large empty living room and stared out the window that faced the front of the house.

"Micah is sending a message," Haley said, nodding to the rattle that Zoey still held up for all of them to see. "And it appears, it's a boy."

"Going to be a boy," Zoey decided, grinning at the rattle. "We just saw Maggie six months ago. Maybe she was pregnant, but I think she hasn't yet given birth."

"Another Mulligan," Greg mused.

Haley hugged him and cuddled in next to Greg. "Micah is dead. But you never know who might show up to learn from you at this school. Everything happens for a reason."

No one said anything. All four of them continued staring at the darkness outside. Tomorrow would be another day, and all of them were far from their golden years. The pursuit would keep the four of them looking forward to the next day; make that the six of them.

Don't miss these acclaimed novels by
Lorie O'Clare

THE BOUNTY HUNTERS

PLAY DIRTY
GET LUCKY
STAY HUNGRY
RUN WILD
SLOW HEAT

THE FBI SERIES

TALL, DARK AND DEADLY
LONG, LEAN AND LETHAL
STRONG, SLEEK AND SINFUL

ANTHOLOGIES

THE BODYGUARD
MEN OF DANGER

Available from St. Martin's Paperbacks